Of Love and Discord

a novel

Weidan Sima

Second Printing, 2020

ISBN-13: 978-0692103319
ISBN-10: 0692103317

Dedicated to Tina, the first friend who finished my novel entirely and gave me genuine encouragement and feedback.

Part 1: Love

-Chapter 1-

It is not fair to say that this tale of lovers and lovemakers was a myth created by soothsayers. Nor is it fair to just call it a story of immortal and mortal beings that have lived in our world of technological advances ever since the dawn of time. It is however, right to call this a chance encounter arisen from the power of attraction, and a deep emotion for someone that will possess the limits of mortality. If love is everlasting, then its origin begins here. By an unheard voice silent to mortality, but present in the chaos and discord she will bring to this day in Spring.

As cars waited in traffic on the morning of this city called Liberty, people raced by on the sidewalk rushing to work, oblivious to each other's existences other than a mere background. The tall buildings that house day-to-day work, covered the denseness of fumes coming from garbage and the combustion of automobiles. There were horns and trolley tings, followed by yelling that filled each street block. It was here that on one of the buildings on high lay a little Scottish Terrier dog that watched mortal life go by. As he waited with his master, he noticed a police officer walking down the street in a proud but tight uniform swinging his baton casually near a butcher shop.

"What have we here?" said his master, "go Mayhem, let's have some fun with our usual today."

Immediately, the little dog descended and followed the officer from a distance on his patrol. The officer was a heavyset fellow who took pride in his job in keeping order in this district that was not far from Park Central, Liberty City's finest and grandest park. Nodding to the people who passed by him in his menacing tight blue uniform, he puffed his chest and caressed his "Teddy Roosevelt," mustache, all the while swinging his baton authoritatively. When he came by the florist at her shop, he looked at her as she prepared her flowers for a special customer that was coming in today.

While the florist continued arranging the flowers, the officer continued to eye her with a glare as if he was waiting for her to acknowledge him. When she looked out from her window, she finally noticed him and was silent until he uttered a sound.

"Ahem," the officer coughed, with his mustache wiggling. His hand then went up to his badge, slowly stroking it.

"Why hello, Officer Frank," the florist said, realizing that she had forgotten how much this bumbling cop often wanted some form of acknowledgment. Officer Frank then nodded, accepting her supplication as he continued along his patrol. Making his way up the street, he saw the butcher laughing loudly as he escorted one of his customers out.

"Alright my friend, enjoy the lamb. I'll get more tomorrow so please stop by again," the butcher said in a foreign accent, gesturing his farewell to his customer. Officer Frank came by the corner of the block and stopped close to the butcher. He looked at the sky idly with his narrow eyes twitching beneath the sun's glare, waiting for another acknowledgement.

"Oh, good morning, officer," the butcher muttered.

"Fine day isn't it?" Officer Frank declared.

"Yes, every day is a fine day. Especially when you, officer, are around," the butcher replied, trying his best to please him.

"Yes, precisely," Officer Frank concurred. He then continued his patrol back the other way. This time, however, the Scottish Terrier stopped following him, and was now eyeing the meat he had smelled a block away, inside the butcher's shop.

"Shoo shoo, you mutt! Get away from my meat!" the butcher yelled when he spotted the dog inside his shop sniffing at some sausages hanging from the table. The butcher quickly approached the dog with his broom just as he took a bite from a sausage. Startled, the dog scurried away through the meat shop, prompting the butcher to chase after him around the splattered floor over table legs and crannies. At a moment's haste, the dog made for cover after he leaped to the top of a table that had pounds of stacked meat and a severed pig's head. Squeezing between them, he had knocked it all down.

"You son of the devil! I'm going to chop you up just like what we used to do in the old country," the butcher reacted with rage.

Quickly evading repeated broom attacks, the dog found an opening in the butcher's assault and dashed out from the shop. This was not before knocking more meat onto the floor.

"Good riddance," the butcher yelled angrily as he scrambled out to guard his shop. After what seemed to be a triumphed farewell, an unheard female voice in the background lamented after seeing her dog's close encounter:

"Aww, poor puppy. Don't worry, mommy will clean this up."

When the butcher proceeded back into his shop, his next step suddenly staggered, losing balance from a piece of smashed meat on the ground. He fell backward, knocking his head onto the floor. It was an impact that made a small quake. Although the butcher remained conscious, he saw stars all around his ceiling. Soon after, the dog returned to lick a piece of meat that landed on top of the butcher's head. The background immediately echoed with unheard giggles.

When a trolley had stopped near the florist's shop, an older lady got off. Dressing quite over the top for a woman her age with a fur coat and a hat with exotic feathers, the dog saw another candidate that his master found interesting to play with. When the lady stopped by the florist shop to pick up her special arranged flowers, she paused to admire some flowers displayed outside, basking in their smell.

"How lovely," she commented before walking inside.

"I prefer them black and grayed," said the unheard voice. Quickly, the flowers shriveled.

"Good morning," the florist said, welcoming her special customer who had ordered a bouquet that was very specific.

"And did you make sure it was the right genus, color, and cut like the way I wanted?" the lady demanded.

"Yes ma'am, evened throughout with not an odd number of leaves on each side. If you change your mind, a few are outside if you want more," the florist said nervously.

"No," the lady said immediately, "these will do. Good, I don't want anything that was picked yesterday. I am normally allergic to another species of these, but not these."

The florist smiled, helping her wrap up her purchase and handing the bouquet to the lady.

"You don't say…" said the unheard voice, quickly changing the type of flowers.

As the lady smelled the flowers, it was already too late.

"Thank you," the lady said to the florist. But just as she was prepared to leave, the little dog came by, smelling the lady's feet. This startled the lady, prompting her to react with hostility.

"Get away from me, dog!" the lady demanded. The florist tried to help but was too late as the dog scampered under and through the lady's dress on his way out. This caused the lady to bawl with rage as she tried to kick the dog out.

"How dare you!" she scolded before the florist tried to calm her after the dog exited. Suddenly, the florist had a look of surprise when she looked at the lady's face again.

"What? What is it, dear?" the lady demanded.

Seeing the lady's face bloated with red bumps, the florist could barely tell her what had happened to her face. But when the lady began scratching the bumps, she began to scream in panic.

"I swear," the florist pleaded with her, "those were the flowers you wanted." This was left with discord while the unheard voice laughed in the background.

Meanwhile, Officer Frank was writing a ticket for a bunch of construction workers that had placed their equipment in a public area for a few minutes when they went on their lunch break. Of course, he could not let this go unpunished. When they had returned, they were burdened to see that the officer was writing separate tickets for each of them.

"What's the deal, mac? Can't you let us go this one time?" complained one worker.

"That's officer to you. I don't take kindly to lawbreakers in my neighborhood," he replied.

"Jesus Christ, what am I going to tell my wife about this ticket?" said another.

"Don't ye take the Lord's name in vain boyo," pestered Frank as he tapped the worker's hat with his baton.

While this was taking place, the little dog ran through them, knocking some of their equipment down and quickly snatching the tickets with his mouth.

"Hey!" remarked the officer, quickly blowing his whistle, thinking it would stop the dog.

As officer Frank ran after him, the dog went through the intersection, dodging the oncoming traffic. Immediately, many cars had brake controllably just in time when they saw the officer, stunning him as he stood there disillusioned. Unfortunately, one car was not so lucky as one driver rammed his car into a sports car parked on the side Officer Frank had been on. When the man went out to inspect the damage, the owner of the other car had just so happened to be in the area just after the car had rammed it.

"Hey four eyes, you going to explain to me what happened?" the owner yelled. As the driver tried to explain, an argument was sparked when the dog passed them just as Officer Frank got back to the sidewalk.

"Hey officer," the owner of the crashed car demanded, "make sure this man pays for every damage he inflicted on my roadster."

"You're insane!" the driver dismissed.

As Officer Frank listened to the rowdy argument, he saw the terrier waiting on the corner, panting. Immediately, Frank stopped what he was doing and blew his whistle as he chased after the dog again amongst the rush of crowds coming outside during the lunch hour. With the officer gone, the rowdy argument soon became a fist fight.

Running after the little dog under scaffolding nearby, his hefty body tried its best to fit through tight spaces the dog hid himself in. At what looked like a moment of triumph, Officer Frank found himself cornering the little terrier inside a cranny just below some wooden planks. The dog whimpered in terror as the officer laughed victoriously. When Officer Frank tried to grab the dog, he was immediately bitten, propelling his arm to raise his baton in the air to strike the dog. This failed as Officer Frank had instead knocked a wooden plank above him, causing a worker above to trip and catapult a plank that contained a bucket of paint to descend, ultimately falling on top of Officer Frank. Having a wide head, it made a perfect helmet that stuck onto him. The little dog took this opportunity and escaped his blinded, desperate grasps. Yelling and desperately trying to get the helmet off, he missed the dog several times before slipping on the paint and falling facedown, knocking him out. With a look of relief, the dog walked over him and disappeared into an alley.

A great laughter was unleashed after these acts of chaos and discord were performed by the powers of one small canine and his master's help. When it subsided, the unheard female voice finally yawned, relishing her recent entertainment.

"That was absolutely wonderful. These mortals always have something interesting to prey on," remarked Eris, stretching herself on a balcony railing on the thirteenth floor.

As she lay on the railing, comfortably putting her arms behind her long, wavy dark hair and resting her diabolical head, the mischievous dog came up beside her.

"There you are darling, what a good boy," she smiled while petting him. Here was the Goddess of Chaos and Discord in the flesh, laying there sunbathing and watching the mortals below fall upon her tricks and mischievous acts.

There was no true color to describe her smooth skin other than it was like the color of the ocean upon a setting sun—blue yet not too light nor too dark. She wore a black tunic dress that seemed a little too large and loose for her heart-shaped shoulders. So much so that she had to often adjust it. And from the bottom of her torso, her tunic ran tightly, wrapping just a little down over her wide hips. Her pose and posture made her look like a nymph among rocks in a river, with both her bare legs and feet left wild and untamed by the civilization of men. After caressing her little sidekick, she sat back up, cradled her legs and smiled. It was a smile that beamed off her pair of alluring, scheming eyes.

"Okay, I'm ready for more," she said out loud as she stood up. And then immediately, she jumped thirteen stories below her. In what seemed to be a leap succumbed by gravity, she had instead merely landed gracefully on the pavement. Within the impact of the landing, however, the street had been affected by her chaotic powers. The fire hydrant next to her exploded and the road erupted with little cracks. With her faithful and immortal dog coming down to her, she strolled along the street toward Park Central. And as she walked, her impressive height made her long legs look as if she was a ballerina, hips moving like that of a dance, step by step, gracefully crossing traffic. And although mortals could not see her, traffic yielded for her while every car fell victim to pavement cracks, engine problems, and sudden brake stops. Of course, angry arguments caused by her persuasive manipulative lips were her favorite mischiefs upon pedestrians.

After entering the park, she saw that it was a beautiful day to ruin some picnics or evoke greed for a robbery. Perhaps even a carriage ride gone wrong if the moment called for it. The sun was near its zenith and the air of coming spring blew across the park.

"Go on darling, go play and unleash havoc upon our dear friends," she told her dog, seeing him happily run off through the park after her command. And at that moment, looking ahead, there lay a perfect opportunity for Eris. A young man and woman were over by the bridge quarrelling about something as it appeared. "Let's listen in," she thought, and proceeded to the lakeside. Gently, she dipped her toes into the water. As her body went deeper through the cold and calm waters, her legs grew frailer and shorter. Her body grew feathers as her neck grew longer, slowly transforming her entire self into a swan with black feathers. Why she did this was peculiar for a goddess who appeared invisible to mortals. But becoming part of her victims' surroundings, either as a person or physical object, was essential to how she worked her powers of discord onto the world. It was important that she became active on this stage she would create for her unfortunate characters. She was the director and the lead actress. And because of this, she felt she had an invisible audience to entertain by creating works of tragedy. As she swam under this vista beneath the bridge, she quietly came closer, listening to woes.

"I don't know, George, my parents…what would they think of me marrying you and heading far outside the city?" the young woman burst out emotionally. Eris gazed high upon a young fetching, innocent girl of at least nineteen. She had been looking out into the defrosted lake and to her surprise, suddenly noticed a black swan that seemed to be out of place and randomly present by chance, and almost looking straight at her.

"I'm telling you, Mary, my brother already has a place for us. His boss is going to give me a job once I get there," said a young man who came behind her, trying to comfort her. The young man was rugged but was a handsome fellow beneath the hat he wore that covered part of his face.

"And do you know what you are going to do there? Don't you think that he might just swindle the both of you?" She looked at him with a slight tear coming down her eyes.

"I know my brother, he's got marbles. He's been working there for over a month now. And he's living with Betty. They found a pleasant place to raise their kids," he tried to assure her.

"I'm sure outside a mining area is a fine place to live," she rebuked, unconvinced.

"Come on now, Mary, I'll talk to your parents and I'll show them the money my brother has been sending me as proof," he looked at her warmly.

"And what would you say to them?" she replied.

"I'll say…Mr. and Mrs. Wagner," he coughed playfully but seriously. "There's a lucrative job out there waiting for me and I'm taking your daughter with me because I love her. I promise I will do everything I can to make her happy so that we can grow old together," the young man expressed confidently. After hearing him, the young woman looked into his eyes with her big beautiful pupils and embraced him.

"How sweet! The boy sure knows how to move a lady. We shall see what he thinks of this," the goddess chuckled. In the near trees where the man was facing as he embraced his lover were a trio of young beautiful ladies playing and giggling as they passed by. They caught the gaze of the young man. For that second, he was enchanted by their beauty, femininity, and playful nature. And they winked at him just as the young lady turned her head, immediately seeing what he was looking at. She forcefully let go of his embrace and stared at him fiercely, turning her head with a whish of her hair, then walking away from him with her head held high and eyes seemingly closed.

"It's not what you think! I…I just saw them. They were looking at me!" he protested as he rushed back to her side. At this moment, the goddess went ashore back to her goddess form, smiling as she followed them in the distance.

"Mary, please. I love you," the young man continued, following her. Then suddenly, the goddess noticed something strange with the boy after he paused for a second from following her. He then did something unexpected.

"Mary, if you're not going with me. I'm not going to go then. I'm going to go over that hill and jump into that pond," he declared as she continued walking away from him. There was doubt for his proposed actions as she knew he could not swim and the water was still freezing. There was sincerity and seriousness in his voice as the goddess listened clearly.

"I can't live without you," he said as he rushed up the hill. Curious to see this pathetic attempt by this boy, the young lady glanced and saw her lover running to the top of the hill, so determined.

"Stop!" she yelled back. The young boy had heard her, but was determined to risk his life to prove he loved her. Immediately, the goddess rushed back to the bridge to get a better view of the hillside.

"Come on, lover boy, let's see a tragic ending," Eris excitedly yelled. As soon as the young man reached the top, he made for the pond as planned, diving head-first into the waters as he leaped.

"ARGUHH!" the boy yelled, suddenly realizing how stupid he was as fear took its hold on him.

"George!" the young lady yelled as she rushed up the hill and then down to find him. Thankfully, what she found was more humorous than tragic. There was no splash but the cracking of twigs and a loud thud. The young man lay face down, recovering from a nasty fall. A tree branch snagged his coat just before he jumped, falling halfway from the icy water. She rushed to him while his coat was still up on the branch, dangling in the wind.

"Mary?" he groaned softly, slowly getting up just as she came to hold and caress him in her arms.

"Why did you do that, silly boy?" she asked, tearing up a little.

"I told you already. I love you and I'll do anything to prove it," he smiled. After he said this, the ring that he bought yesterday fell below from his coat onto the ground near them. The young lady noticed it and picked it up, surprised. There was an inscription on it that read:

Not even discord can separate us, yours always

At this, the young man took her close, and she embraced him. They kissed as all lovers would.

Eris was not pleased by what just happened. She sat down on the bridge rail and grumbled.

"By the gods, that was almost too perfect," she puffed. Suddenly, she heard laughter from the tree that had broken the young man's fall.

"All it takes is a little shot of love to make a man do anything," sang a voice. From above, the massive tree unraveled its cluttered branches and out came a handsome radiant man.

"Ah, Eros. I should have known it was you to spoil a girl's fun," said Eris as she got up, crossed her arms, and turned her body away from him. The god of love smiled, showing his shiny white teeth. He adjusted his golden curly hair, gelling it to the back of his head with his palms. Unlike what mortals think of the young god with wings and arrows, for the last thousand years, he had matured into a handsome gentleman, with his suit and bow tie, he had kept up with the latest mortal fashions. With his playful eyes, he focused on Eris and approached her.

"On the contrary, my dear, I instill excitement and joy upon the hearts of all women," he replied.

"Whatever, just take your excitement somewhere else, away from me," she dismissed before turning in the other direction to walk away.

"Even such a beauty as divine as yourself," the god of desire remarked as he suddenly appeared before her again.

"No thanks, I have better things to do," she uttered, pushing him away.

Without a moment of notice, Eris fell over on her backside after tripping. She was then quickly caught by Eros, grabbing her waist just in time, positioning her as if they were dancing the tango. With his body bent over her, the god of desire stared into the violet colored eyes of the goddess.

"Then let us do better things together," he said smoothly, gazing at her romantically.

"Why of course, let's make love at the Elysian Fields and drink merrily, for time stops when our lips touch," she answered sarcastically with a smirk on her face. The god of love grinned. Believing in what she said, he closed his blue playful eyes, puckering his lips as he moved down to kiss her. In that moment, she had had enough of his antics and blew a flame from her fair lips that burned him. With his head on fire, Eros panicked, quickly letting go of her as he jumped into the pond to extinguish the flame.

The goddess smiled as she got up and walked away from the bridge, leaving her passionate dance partner. After the god of desire stepped out of the lake and dried himself off, he took out his compact mirror and began checking himself, re-gelling his boyish hair. His face, still flawless and pearly, gave out a glowing yellow light around him as he smiled at it. Alone, Eris continued walking the pedestrian road path, busy looking for other victims to conjure.

By the time Eros found Eris again, she had just finished scaring a bunch of school children that were playing ball nearby in the field, causing their ball to go off angularly, making it hit a bunch of pigeons. This caused the pigeons to go crazy, bombarding feces on them. It was chaotic, for these pigeons were relentless and quite evil, as a matter of fact. While laughing, she continued to stroll along until Eros confronted her again.

"I don't know how you find pleasure in such trivial pursuits," commented Eros, returning to her side.

"Trivial? I'll have you know, sir, that I am not as wild and lucky as I was more than a decade ago," she said, referring back to her encounter years ago while vacationing in Serbia.

"Such a masterpiece, yes, one of my bests I would say," she said, smiling. "One little archduke killed, and a great pandemonium among the world. I couldn't ask for more."

It was indeed the goddess of chaos who helped shoot the first bullet that erupted the Great War. Disguised as a military officer attached to the guard protecting Franz Ferdinand the night before the assassination, she listened in to a young, zealous, and nationalistic Bosnian Serb's aggravations about the Archduke's visit. And while drinking in a pub one faithful night, she had so discreetly convinced him to kill the Archduke with her help. At the time of the assassination, it was her who directed the traffic towards him and then disappeared during his capture.

"Well, a girl has to go through many to find the right man," she sighed eyeing her polished hands in satisfaction.

"Such a shame, if only I had been there to find him a wonderful woman that would have persuaded him to pursue other things. Things more intrinsic and worthy of the soul," replied Eros, with his face pressing in front of her.

"What? Romance? Love? Desires of the flesh?" the goddess smirked, "don't bother me with another one of your past antics Eros. I have no desire for sexual games and mortal thirsts for companionship. My true love is sweet destruction," she said, crossing her arms.

"Love is utterly a passionate game of seduction and attractions. An overrated enterprise that people participate to do Mother Nature's bidding," she concluded.

"A game? Coitus you say? No, No! You are mistaken, my fair goddess. Love is indeed more than just attaining companionship. Please allow me to explain," Eros joyfully lectured.

"Please do go ahead. Explain to me your philosophy and discourse on love. For I, Eris, the goddess of discord doth not know of Helen and Paris," she replied sarcastically, rolling her violet eyes.

"Very well, I shall enlighten you so!" he continued.

As he began, the dark-haired goddess sat herself on a park bench, crossing her bare long legs together. Facing forward, her eyes scanned for potential victims to conjure while the god of desire sat next to her, facing her up close and personal.

"Of course, not even my own mother, Aphrodite, could resist the temptation of your apple of discord that you dropped for the fairest among goddesses. Athena and Hera still despise you to this day."

Upon hearing her past achievement, the goddess of discord smiled as she gently touched her apple of discord, now a pendant between her breasts. It was the source of all her powers, now contained beside her dark heart.

"Vanity, the only love I can appreciate," she said, thinking about her sweet revenge on the gods that led to the first masterpiece of hers among the mortal realm.

"Ah, you just made an excellent point there," replied Eros. "Indeed, it is vanity, the love for oneself that brings about love for others. For you see, it is the soul of all things whether they are mortal or immortal to seek beauty of some kind. Beauty of not just physical tangible things like objects that entice our senses, but also the complementary mind of another selfish individual."

Eris looked at him, puzzled at such a cynical yet feasible statement. It is true that human beings and immortals like herself desire beauty of some kind. She continued to listen to his speech.

"Yes, the love for oneself is so strong that we want to share it with a person or persons. At such a moment when we find someone we admire, we are stricken to have them become part of our lives. It is here, that our love of oneself is transformed to a love for another."

The intricate face of Eros livened up as his dimples bloomed, exposing his high cheek bones and the radiance of his skin.

"When you dropped your apple detailing that it 'shall go to the fairest,' each goddess erupted with vanity thinking that this apple was placed here for the fairest. And that someone is me, so each one thought. When Paris of Troy was given the decision of granting the apple, each goddess sought to persuade him for the title of 'the fairest of all goddesses.' For Hera, she offered power and riches to him. And Athena, it was victory in battle and of course, wisdom. But it was my mother, Aphrodite who offered him love. And thus, he sailed with Helen, the most beautiful woman on earth to Troy. And the rest…we all know what happened. The point being made here my dear, is that love was pursued over the rest offered to him. Why you may ask? Because it is the highest calling. It is the one thing that riches, power, and wisdom cannot offer: To possess the kindred-soul of another."

Eris was lovingly playing with her long wavy hair, carefully twisting the silky threads as she barely listened. Appreciating her love of vanity however, she indulged in Eros' account of her work, but was uninterested in the morals he was trying to make. She merely daydreamed her greatness in the story.

"And in terms of romance, which I specialize in, people are enchanted as they helplessly fall for the soul's other half. To know that you are complete in this cruel, yet beautiful short life is one true value of 'to love.' And that is the miracle of mortality. Oh my! I sounded like a mortal, didn't I? Well, I did love one," Eros chuckled.

As Eros began his love story of Psyche, Eris stared into the blue skies and then across the field. Her right hand nested her head as her other hand adjusted her shoulder strap. She leaned on the bench trying to show to the god of love that she was not interested. Such a pity that even gods cannot read what a woman conveys indirectly. Something caught her attention as she looked away. There were a bunch of boys riding their bikes across the field. They were about ten to twelve years old by the looks of them. As they raced and called each other, one boy was falling behind, drawing Eris' attention to him. He peddled helplessly to catch up with the other boys that had zipped across the bridge. After crossing this bridge, this long-eared boy ran into some trouble. A rock she accidently loosened caught on the boy's tire, propelling him off. She acted on her impulse to prey on the weak. It brought some pleasure as she listened to the painful background of Eros detailing the accounts of his lovemaking.

There was something about that boy that made Eris feel different after he had fallen. It was a feeling of dislike and charm brought on by the boy's suffering. The other boys were too frantic about winning the race to even notice him. His knee began bleeding and he began to tear up a bit. Suddenly, a petite young lady nearby came by after witnessing the fall. She had crossed the bridge and went to the boy to help. Eris could not see what she looked like entirely. The young lady wore a long coat and a hat that had cloaked most of her appearance. Something about her was delicate in the way she presented herself elegantly and gracefully. She helped him up and used a handkerchief she took out from her purse to clean the wound. Surely any person there would feel joyous and warm for this kind act bestowed by that young lady. But for the goddess of chaos, her feelings of fun were crushed.

"And that is how I must say that your judgment on love is rather shallow. Surely if you gave love a chance you would see it to be worth pursuing over destruction," said Eros at last, catching her interest for a moment again as she turned her soft face back to him.

"Perhaps someday you will. Anyways, it was a pleasure chatting with you, but I have an appointment later today for someone special," continued Eros as he took out a small envelope from his breast pocket.

"Ah, another one of your victims, I suppose," joked Eris.

"Victim is a bit negative, not to mention grim, my dear. I like to call them patients. After all, we are all sick when love is missing from our lives."

The god of desire took out his red pocket watch with his other hand and he glanced at what looked like a beating mechanical heart that showed him not the time but letters that Eris could hardly make out.

"Well, what is it this time?" she asked. Eros opened the envelope, the seal already broken, and sneaked a peak at the card inside.

"A concert pianist. And a delightful lad too. He's in a show performing tonight."

Upon hearing "concert" and "show," she turned her body towards him.

"Yes, in a concert hall for only distinguished guests. Many university compatriots will be there also," Eros assured.

"Let me see!" Eris playfully beamed, moving closer to him.

"I don't think so, Madame. It's meant for the eyes of the god of love. Yes, business you don't have to concern yourself with." Eros laughed playfully as he slid back the card inside the envelope.

"Ta Ta." He smiled, patting her head gently. Before Eros had a chance to get up, Eris suddenly rushed to grab it as she leaned over the bench. He was quicker and held it away from her.

"Come on! Please? I just want to know where it is." Her violet eyes were glazed with interest. She saw a chance to steal the show. She continued desperately, trying to snatch the envelope away from his hands.

"So, shall we continue where we left off on the bridge, chère?" he said, smiling. Looking at his face, Eris finally noticed that her hand was mistakenly placed on top of his lap. In that moment, embarrassed and by impulse, she slapped his face lightly and rushed away, blushing a little.

Eros smiled as he polished his cheek, amused by what just happened.

"Alright, tell you what. Be my date for tonight's event and you can come along. Do we have a deal? I promise it'll be quite a performance," he told her.

She paused and thought about it for a second before answering, "Fine! Just stay away from the fun I will have tonight, alright?" she told him, looking away and crossing her arms and legs.

"Splendid. We shall have a wonderful time. Why, I can't wait to pick my mortal disguise for tonight. I'm thinking I shall be a European this time. Perhaps from Spain, Yes! I shall be called Alfonzo...Salazar Romero! A motion picture producer and writer. While you can be my exotic wife of the orient, Uhhm...Roxanne, yes! That's the name of Alexander the Great's wife."

Eris looked at him with amusement, but with a change of heart, thinking that it might actually be fun playing a part in tonight's event, even if it meant pretending to be his date. With all his excitement, Eros took her hands and dragged her out of the park.

"Hey! Wait a minute, where are we going? It's not till tonight," protested Eris as she reluctantly followed him. He began muttering on about the show and how he wanted her to come see the outfits he had prepared for tonight.

Leaving the entrance of the park, Eris looked back and noticed that the boy was now with his friends, and they began teasing him about his little accident and his new crush for the mysterious lady that helped him. As she returned her gaze back to Eros, they had passed the same young lady as they staggered out. She was boarding a taxi in front of them. It was in that instant that Eris finally saw a glimpse of her face for a quick second as she got into the car, slightly turning her head as she looked once more out to the park. All that could be made out was her pink lips smiling lightly and her dainty nose. It was an interesting yet strange encounter when their faces met; because despite being invisible to mortals, Eris saw an almost mutual transparency between each other with this girl. It was like she could see her plainly as she saw her.

Meanwhile inside the park, a dog wandered around, wondering where his master had gone off to after another chaotic event he had performed that involved a nearby hotdog stand.

-Chapter 2-

It was about an hour before sundown when the maintenance staff of Carnegie Theater began climbing on top of the façade to put the letters on the sign for tonight's event. Traffic began dispersing as day turned into night. A day in the concrete jungle had ended for some, while the nocturnal life of entertainment, speakeasies, and crime had just begun. And it was here that the gods came to join in for some mortal fun too.

Coming up the street just to the corner of the theater intersection was a woman dressed stylishly for an event. Eris, wearing a dark blue fishtail evening gown, her heels clacking as she walked, came to a halt across from the theater façade in her mortal disguise for tonight. She adjusted her long hair that was tied back as her fingers gently combed her bangs away from her eyes that ran down her cheeks. She had come early for the show to plot a perfect situation that would lead to a perfect show. A stage lighting error that would kill a bunch of people? Or a show that ended up being a comedic discourse for tomorrow's paper perhaps? Pondering so, she stretched her arm out to view the theater in her compact mirror from behind her. She adjusted her eyeliner while she schemed as the line of her eyes became darker. As she was doing this, the director for tonight's performance came out from the front entrance to inspect the sign. He began calling loudly to the workers up on the sign:

"No! You have it crooked now! Adjust it to the left. No wait! Adjust it just a little to the right. Yes! My God gentlemen, you spaced it too close now," the director said as evidence of what was shown:

Carnegie Theater Events
PRESENTS AN EVENING OF THE ROMANTICS
BY THE UNIVERSITY OF PARIS SYMPHONY
ORCHESTRA
TONIGHT ONLY!
GUEST PERFORMANCE BY STAR PUPIL OF
PROFESSOR FRANK VALENTINI
HENRYL__EON

"Never mind gentlemen. Just hurry back in. They need you inside now," he remarked after glancing at his watch. Just then, a taxi stopped in front of the theatre with a young man and an elderly woman stepping out.

"Henry! The star of the show. I'm glad you made it on time," said the director, touching the young man's shoulders.

"Professor, I'm so sorry. You said 5:30 but it's already 5:45. I was practicing at home after work and lost track of time... Oh, here are my new compositions I'm going to play," said Henry urgently, pulling his portfolio from under his arms.

"Yes, Yes. We shall be glad to hear them tonight, my boy," the director smiled, then turned his attention to the elderly lady who was adjusting the young man's tie.

"Hold still dear, you can't perform looking like you just got into a fight," she said, looking attentively at it.

"Oh no! Do I really look that bad?" The young man started buttoning his cuffs and then dusted off lint and a piece of string from his messy brown hair. He adjusted his tuxedo tail that had slipped inside his pants pocket.

"Ah, Mrs. Leon, I presume. It is an honor to meet you at last. Henry always mentions his darling mother." The director kissed her hand and smiled.

"The pleasure is mine, Professor Valentini," she replied kindly.

"Is it a full house tonight, professor?" Henry asked, looking nervously as he flipped through his portfolio to make sure that everything was there. His glasses glared at it while his slouched posture gave evidence of his nervousness.

"Yes, everyone is just dying to hear my pupil's debut. But don't worry, boy, you'll be fine. Just play as you would at my office." The director then patted Henry's shoulders.

"This night is the night," Henry commented nervously while mumbling some other words as he inspected his own work.

"Henry, please forgive me; they spaced your name too closely. I swear I can't get good help these days," the director pointed, laughing. They looked up.

"We will get it fixed before the show starts. But hurry inside to the back. You can rehearse a little bit. I shall escort your lovely mother inside." He held out his arm as Henry's mother smiled at him and took it.

"Break a leg, dear," she said lovingly as she walked inside with the director. Henry then rushed around back. Just as he did however, he unknowingly dropped pieces of his papers on the sidewalk.

While in the alleyway across from the front of the entrance, Eris smiled with glee after seeing Henry, this so-called star pianist of the show. She could recall from Eros that the name of the pianist was Henry, and he had been described as a rather awkward boy, too. She turned and was about to leave when suddenly a man pressed her to the wall and held a knife to her neck. The man was a large fellow who was nothing less than a stupid thug, to Eris' surprise.

"Do as I say lady, and you'll walk away to see another day," he said in a deep boorish voice. Eris contained her amusement as she thought about how stupid this man was. Here stood a common disgusting man who wanted to rob her and perhaps take advantage of her, a goddess, of all victims.

"Don't make me laugh," she wanted to say. To humor him, she decided to play along and did as he asked, also acting frantic for the part. She took her necklace off slowly and was told that she had to put it inside her bag.

"That's right, put it there and then give me your purse," he demanded. Eris opened her bag and was slowly conjuring out a blunt object from beneath it as she carefully slipped the necklace in. While this was taking place, Henry came out looking for his missing papers and had found them on the ground. As he picked them up, his eyes were horrified to see what was happening before him across the alleyway. He sneaked across the isolated street and was behind the thug by the time Eris had her club ready.

"Hey! Hurry up, will you lady," the thug retorted as Eris paused to see Henry behind him. Henry jumped on the man and successfully knocked his knife away to the ground, surprising Eris.

"Run!" Henry yelled as the thug nervously tried to fight him off. Seeing this boy come to her rescue, she was caught off guard until she made the effort to beat the thug with her purse. Shielding himself from the beatings from Eris, the thug desperately tried to push Henry off his back. When he succeeded, he pushed his back onto the wall, dropping the boy. The thug then ran away, frightened of the beatings and the sight of people gathering about. Henry tried to regain his composure after hitting the ground. He was alright, nothing but minor bruises. Such an act, although brave, was something he never imagined himself doing until now. A small crowd gathered briefly, asking if they were alright. "Good teamwork!" one fellow commented. "Shall we alert the authorities?" a woman asked.

"We are fine, thank you for the concern, everyone," Eris replied, embarrassed. They soon dispersed, with Henry and Eris now alone.

"Are you alright, Miss?" Henry asked as he searched for his glasses that had fallen off and dusted himself off. Looking at this strange hero coming to her rescue, the goddess of chaos was amused by what had just occurred. Out of fun, she thought this would be a chance to seduce him.

"I am now, thanks to you, hero," she said sweetly and innocently. She found his glasses and carefully put them on him. She suddenly came very close to him and touched him briefly on the cheek. She felt his warmth in doing so.

"He didn't hurt you, did he?" she asked. Henry grew red as he nervously became uncomfortable when Eris came closer, cornering him by the wall.

"Well, that's good to hear, Miss," he uttered, slowly pulling himself away from her, "have a good day," he stifled.

Quickly, he rushed back to the theatre just before a car suddenly braked in front of him. Stunned that he was almost hit, the driver yelled at him, but nevertheless he kept on moving, not looking back.

Eris was left confused. "He didn't even bother to look at me twice." She huffed, putting her hands on her hips. Suddenly, clapping noises came from down the street and Eris turned to see Eros walking up to her.

"What a show! What a show! I see you met Mister Leon. Charming young lad, isn't he?" he said. The god of love was dressed elegantly tonight too. Not only did he get an amazing tan, he also had a matching cape with his tuxedo. He even fancied a nicely trimmed mustache that curved lightly. He was really having fun with his mortal disguise.

"This is the boy you plan to poison, Mister Romero?" She came up to him, "He can't even handle a woman," she persisted playfully.

Laughing, Eros held out his arm for her to hold.

"No, because you are not a woman, but a masked siren," he joked.

She looked at him disdainfully, but took his arm.

"That may be true," she smiled. "But mystery is essential to keeping them interested."

"Perhaps, but you were not mysterious as I could witness. I believe we still have much to discuss about love. Come, people are lining up for the show already."

Eros was enjoying himself in line as he partook in conversation with a group of university students in the line. There were three females and one male in this group. Being such a flirt that he is, Eros did not mind the conversation with mortals, for he enjoyed the company of these young bloods.

Eris, still holding his arm, looked blankly as she was uninterested in the things they were chatting about. She was not into small talk and had no desire to conjure something deviously fun before the show; for she was bewildered with her feelings for something else. It was Henry's awkwardness that fascinated her demoralized ego. She was still irritated he had rejected her in the alleyway.

Since the dawn of time, Eris could always charm a man whether it was through lust, power, greed, or the whole lot of men who desired it. She was in no way afraid of Aphrodite's monopoly on desire. Perhaps she just lost touch of what it meant to please a man in the last hundred years, or maybe Eros had interfered somehow. Regardless, she was now extra excited for the show.

"He was amusing, but he's about to see his dreams of being a concert pianist go down in laughter and embarrassment. I will crush his heart before Eros has a chance to shoot it," she assured in a conniving thought. As she thought out her scheme, which involved a possibly horrible freeze inside the theatre or instrumental failure, she snickered, and appeared wacky to Eros' entourage.

"Are you alright? Was it something amusing I said?" remarked the male university student, looking confused. Everyone was looking straight at her. This came at a bad time because he was just enlightening everyone here on the architectural interior schemes of the theatre.

"Nothing at all, fly boy! Your knowledge is just fascinating, that's all," she replied with moxie. "I'm sorry, I can't contain my excitement for fun facts from smart cookies like yourself," she recovered.

Tonight's performance was close to a full house and it looked to serve Eris' plan well. She looked around the immense crowds that were being shown to their seats. The ceiling's elegant renaissance style dome created a perfect setting for sabotaging music, all to kill its beauty.

"Name, sir?" asked a bald attendant.

"Yes, I am Alfonzo Salazar Romero! Motion picture screen writer and literary critic. I'm sure you've heard of me," Eros replied delightfully, emphasizing his accent. The attendant did not pay attention to his statement other than a tired "ah ha," as he checked his papers. Eros turned to Eris and smiled.

"And this delightful creature is my wi…" Before Eros had a chance to say wife, Eris interrupted him.

"Roxanne," she uttered, smiling. The attendant glanced up at her and he smiled lightly.

"I'm sorry sir, I don't see a Romero," the attendant said, looking back to Eros.

"What? Impossible!" Eros interjected. Before they had come in, Eris wanted to play a little trick on Eros by changing the name the seats were under.

"Try Smith," she asked confidently.

"Smith, yes, here you are Miss Smith. You and your date, please come this way."

Eris had then abandoned Eros' arm, following the attendant on her own, swaying playfully and leaving Eros looking like he was some sort of idiot. As to why Eris picked the last name "Smith," it was a random surname she thought of from somewhere.

"Here you are ma'am," the attendant gestured as Eris and Eros were shown to their seats in the balcony. Scooting down to her seat, she gave a "thank you" to the attendant.

"Such wonderful seats, darling," Eris complimented for the part, looking at her so-called- husband. The god of love sat down and brushed his thin mustache with his fingers. Eris turned to him, resting both her elbows on his armrest, her chin on her knuckles as she gazed at him with curiosity.

"So tell me Eros, what are you intending to do with my tall naïve hero tonight? Shoot him when you catch him glancing at an unexpected beauty? Or better yet, enflame his playing with passion so that no lady here can escape his charms?"

Eros giggled, hearing those statements.

"I need not to. If you had heard his playing before you would know he does not need my help at all. Such a talented boy really. But yes, he is not my only target. After all, it takes two to love."

"You're going to shoot some other forsaken soul tonight, eh? Sheesh, lucky girl," Eris said, widening her eyes.

"Love takes time, my dear. Simply making him fall in love at first glance tonight is too simple. It will be a distraction for him in the most part," he continued. There will be many other distractions than that, she thought.

"In any case, tonight shall be a memorable one. When the time is right, you'll see," Eros gestured sweetly.

"Gosh, you can't give me any hints, can you? You men, always with the secrecy and the logical rigidness of things," she said as she drooped in her chair, head backwards.

"And you women, always longing for immediate excitement, and those expectations," he replied, doing the same. She puffed her lips and looked at the ceiling dome until the lighting dimmed. The show had begun.

Clapping commenced as the director of the ceremony walked to the podium. After the director finished his speech, his shoes caught on his laces and he tripped off the stairs coming down. There were minor laughs.

"I'm alright!" he called out, embarrassed, while a few people helped him up. After the conductor finished his quick speech, he stepped onto the platform. The orchestra then began with Franz Liszt's *Hungarian Rhapsody No.2*. Eros turned his gaze at the goddess, looking at her with a face of no surprise. She looked calm and uninterested at the little accident, but he may have had a sense that she was a little pleased inside.

Though no matter how the music was provocative to everyone else, it was of no interest to Eris. Eros was enjoying it, but then, he usually enjoyed anything that provokes passion of some kind. Being the odd one among these avid listeners, Eris flipped through the event program and searched for Henry's name. He was the last act, after intermission. Bored, she began looking around the theater, trying to find interesting people to interrupt.

Already ten minutes into the performance, the door entrance slowly opened, and an attendant stepped in. He held the door for a young lady that was late. Eris noticed her as she came down the aisles discreetly and gracefully, following the attendant to her seat. At first glance, there was something about this young lady that made Eris attracted to her. Perhaps it was her outfit that complemented her petite body. Eris admired her white smock that had a Peter Pan collar and its long bow. Being shown to a seat that was a column across from the right of Eris, she entered the row and smiled at the attendant as she sat down, adjusting her long blue skirt.

Eros turned his head and glanced at the young lady for a quick second. "Ah, not a moment too late," he commented, then continued watching the orchestra. Upon hearing his comment, Eris was now curious. She continued eyeing the lady, concluding that this was Eros' other star of the show tonight. The young lady took off her cloche hat and unveiled her short bouncy flaxen hair. At that instant, Eris knew why she had been so drawn to her.

"That goody-good girl from the park today," she said to herself. Despite the darkness of the theater and seeing only a part of her face, Eris was certain it was her. Without her coat, it was her poised movements and that innocent smile that was distinctive enough to identify her. Eris looked forward onto the stage and thought to herself that she might want to have a little fun with her when Eros was not looking. Eros eyed the goddess of discord with a face that read, "this is going to be a delightful night. What devious plan is she concocting?" The immortals smiled separately, both going unnoticed by the other.

Intermission out in the foyer was a relief for the audience after reliving the coldness of winter during the performance. Throughout the performance, Eris had been hesitant to play tricks on the orchestra in part because they were too solemn to pick on, making her less creative. It was also because she did not want the crowd to depart before she had a chance to ruin Henry's chance of performing horribly among the orchestra. She did, however, created a harsh atmosphere for the musicians, by making the theatre hellishly cold.

With her right arm out holding a cigarette attached to a holder held in her lotus-like fingers, and her other arm on her hip, she blew out puffs of smoke with her head held high, eyes devilishly searching for the girl on the crowded marbled stairway. Eris was in Eros' crowd, still unimpressed by their comments on the compositions that had been played. In the light, she could see the girl with ease now. She was talking to the director, her gray eyes widened with warmness as she smiled and listened to what he had to say. Everything about her made Eris feel she was one of those pure girls. She had soft facial features. Her skin was white as snow, yet her face was not perfect like hers, for she had a few freckles under her eyes. But her complexion was radiant, comparable to a sunflower. She had a plum face with cheeks that dimpled and seemed to blush even though there were no instances that would provoke her to. Her makeup was gentle, but nothing too provocative, like most flappers. And of course, her petite frame completed this image of her charming youth.

"You sure know how to pick them, Mister Romero," Eris interrupted Eros.

"Yes, I am quite a connoisseur when it comes to the classics," he replied.

"No, dear, I mean our little friend over there," she nodded her head in the girl's direction.

Eros looked and smiled. "Ah, so you've spotted her. Just what are you planning to do, Discordia?" he whispered to her, his mouth close to her ears.

"As you said, love takes time. We are merely here to study and examine our patients," she whispered back to him.

"I'm so glad you've finally taken interest in it. Ah, time to go back. Shall we?" said Eros.

Back in their seats, Eris noticed that the young lady did not come back to her seat by the time the theater darkened and the clapping commenced when the curtain opened. In fact, she reappeared on the floor seats just a few rows away from the front. "How did that happen?" she thought. Eros suddenly grabbed Eris' hand and kissed it. She looked at him as he smiled. "Why you little…" she wanted to say, but she simply smiled back. She asked the attendant when he passed by how the girl was able to change seats.

By some chance, she learned the young lady's change of seating had come because the director was the one who recommended her to sit there after she had commented how hard it was to listen in her section, and that he had a vacant seat behind him where she could feel more comfortable. But was it Eros who had prompted a missing person that initiated this change? Eris knew it to be so. Whatever it was to her, the show was about to start again with the director's last lines at the podium.

While claps opened Henry's entrance toward the piano, both Eris' and Eros' eyes widened with mutual interests. The young man appeared clean now since being dirtied in Eris' daring rescue. He adjusted his gelled brown hair backward revealing his rather noticeable long ears and swished the tail of his jacket sitting down. His face was blank, but concentrated. He showed a bit of nervousness as he adjusted his tie lightly. The conductor initiated the orchestra to play Chopin's *Piano Concerto No. 1 Op.11*. When it was Henry's turn to begin his accompaniment, Eris had planned to strike him with a technical error on his piano. However, just before acting, she paused. Slowly she was drawn into the music and for some reason she couldn't explain, did not act, and instead decided to let him play a little more. Turning to look at the young lady down below, Eris thought it would be better to be closer to them both. She discreetly got out of her seat and made her way down the aisles.

Eris sat on the row behind the young lady after deliberately forcing her way through the seated rows that had one empty seat in the middle. She looked on at Henry, still so concentrated in his playing. When the first movement of the piece had ended, she knew it was time to act. He was indeed very talented, she thought, but her task must be done regardless of this magically attained respect for him. But what shall she do? As she gazed at the piano, she was ready to manipulate the strings inside. Before she was about to, however, something calmed her down by the time the second movement of the piece came into play. Her eyes shifted to Henry's face and his flowing motion. His hands played softly, every articulation in the mechanics of his fingers had feeling and passion in them. Eris continued to listen and stare attentively. It was like no experience before for her. What was it that compelled her to stop and listen? Was it this new melody? No, even after hearing him playing in the beginning, she seemed drawn to his playing throughout it. It came to her then that interrupting him would have to wait. Watching his face reflected on the polished surface of the piano, created a mood of tranquility for her. He did not have his glasses on this time, perhaps forgetting them when he had come on stage. Although he was not the most handsome fella around, his posture and dedicated composure made him look memorable, at least. He had a thin face that had sharp features that made him look noble. Like most pianists who perform a Chopin piece, they were immersed into a dreamlike state Chopin had created for them. It was a charming sound, so delicate, yet so passionately sharp. Eris continued to listen, and at times, closed her eyes, not because of fatigue or boredom, but captivation.

Unknowingly to her, she had forgotten her plans to ruin the orchestra and Henry's performance. Applause filled the theatre after the third movement finished. Henry took a bow, and the director came back on stage.

"Now, ladies and gentlemen, Mister Leon is pleased to showcase some of his compositions to end the night. Henry…" the director said, nodding to him.

After putting his papers in front of him, he began. The crowd was surprised and amused as the music shifted to a jazz performance. Yet it still had a classic atmosphere, however. His compositions not only provoked a new sense of shift; it took to a complementing light to where his Chopin performance ended. Indeed, the audience could feel that maybe the great George Gershwin wrote his composition. The theater felt like a place for dinner with smuggled wine and romantic chatter. Eris looked on, being part of the audience.

When the show ended, following the crowds out, Eris had forgotten she came with Eros. She stood outside the theatre waiting on the sidewalk as people passed her. While waiting for her taxi, Eros had found her and came beside her.

"Quite a performance, wasn't it? I said you would have fun," he said, smiling with that devious mouth of his. She yawned uncontrollably and tried to cover it with her hands.

"Fun I cannot say, it was compelling however. Thanks for tonight. I'm going to hit the hay," Eris yawned, having been snapped out of that trance, and wanting to go home.

"Why goddess, the night is still young! Let's dance the night away. I know many places we can go for some drinks and of course, many new people to meet."

Eris was truly tired for the first time. Chaos and fun at parties across this city would be enjoyable, yet she had had enough for tonight for some odd reason.

"Another time, lover boy. I'm heading home to catch up on my beauty sleep." Eris waved for the taxi as it pulled up.

"Then let us slumber together," he replied to her. Eris merely giggled, not looking at him as she entered the car and closed the door in his face before Eros had a chance to go in with her.

"Ta ta," she mouthed, waving in the window as the car drove off through the flickering lights.

In a still lively street, the moon shined in the starry night. Eros, amused by her rejection, walked away. He pulled a pencil and that envelope he had this morning out from his front coat pocket. He then scribbled something on it. Soon, the god of love quietly disappeared through an alley as easily as he had come.

-Chapter 3-

The Lexington building on Smith Street was an old apartment complex that had always remained a historical and infamous cauldron of stories. What remained of its prevailing beauty was the presence of gilded angels on the corners of its upper façade, alluding to a certain bourgeois taste long past due. Such stories of fires and tragic demises of families long before had now become legends to those who live across from and beside it. This was where Eris had found her home in this city.

About mid-morning, when the sunlight shined through the faded balcony glass doors, the scotty dog had finished sniffing around the balcony and had quietly and slowly poked his nose to the side surface. Pushing the door in, he let himself inside the room. When he entered, there was a bed with a young woman still sleeping, a cabinet table with a pair of heels and a cigarette holder on top, and a beautiful mahogany dresser that had an oval mirror, damaged with cracks zigzagged across its surface. The room was rather gloomy and plain except for this inconsistent image of that young woman sprawled face down on the bed. She had slept diagonally, her arms spread, one on each side, and her legs dangled near the end of the bed. With her face on the pillow and her long wavy hair covering the remainder of her face, Eris continued to sleep. The dog, seeing her move slowly, turned to a prostrated angle as he went up to her, licking her palms. Sounds of the wind through the city crept into the room as Eris lifted her head up, her eyes suddenly opened as she gazed at her little minion.

"Hmm…morning already. My little Mayhem, did you miss me last night?" she smiled, slowly sitting up. After doing so, the dog pounced onto the bed and came close to her, wiggling his tail. Taking him in her arms, she embraced him. After a yawn, she reached for her comb on the table. She sat cross-legged in the middle of the bed in front of the dresser across from her. Looking at herself, the distorted image on the cracked mirror was in no way a disturbance or hindrance to her daily ritual. She combed her hair gently as any woman would at a lucid polished mirror for royalty. As she did so, every stroke made was like a violin bow playing downward delicately, the sound evoking a mellow and gothic tune, as she gazed at herself blankly. Her curved eyes looked onto her sculpted face, her hair draping on the shoulder straps of her silky nightgown, the necklace of the apple still dangling on her chest. She was humming a childish melody as she continued. The dog began digging through her bedsheets as she continued, wondering to himself whether his mistress had brought anything for him the other night. After finding nothing, a noise outside provoked him to take interest in the pigeons on the balcony. He left her side with a swish of his tail, scurrying upon the wooden surface. Eris then got up and went into the washroom, closing the door behind her.

When that door reopened, heat and water vapor escaped out to the living room to where Eris had slept. After her shower, Eris dressed in her short black tunic dress again with her hair in a knotted updo, ready for another day of chaos.

"Mayhem! Here boy!" She called her dog who was barking outside. Outside, the barking ceased as she looked down on Mayhem playing with a pigeon he had caught with his paws. She leaned on the balcony railing with her elbows out, her chin pressed on her palms, and she looked at him with a smile, admiring his cute devilish curiosity. She then turned to look at the streets below, seeing people going by with their usual business: the food stand man serving his famous cappuccino, the paper boy on the corner of the other side of the street advertising today's post, and the daily automobiles driving by. It was then that Eris noticed an armored car amongst them going down her street, turning around the corner. It appeared to be one of those bank vehicles that had loads of money inside, she thought. She suddenly became interested. Seeing an opportunity for chaos, she jumped down and followed the direction it went.

Turning right from Smith Street, Eris found the armored car pulling up next to the American Union Bank. Soon the security guards began to help unload cases and bags of what could be cash or gold bars inside. One guard that Eris noticed was quite armed and had a look that showed his nervousness while he stood on guard. It was then by chance that a couple of coated men loitering across from the bank happened to be nearby, looking in his direction. Eris saw this opportunity for some fun with these gentlemen. Coming towards the officer disguised as a paper boy, Eris began yelling out the current headline for today's news.

"Paper, Sir?" she asked the standing guard. The rest of the guards had just finished unloading some cases and were wheeling it inside the bank when Eris arrived. Feeling assured that it was just a paper boy and protected by his rifle, the officer agreed to the paper boy's paper. While digging into his pocket for some money, Eris created a nasty gust of wind around them, blowing the newspapers around, some hitting his face. Those idle men across from them took advantage of this situation and quickly rushed to snatch a bag of cash behind the opened car door, running away immediately after.

Reacting late, the guard quickly went after them, shooting off a round in the air from his rifle, creating panic in the vicinity. They ran, taking off with great speed as they disappeared into an alleyway just before he could aim. The officer dashed after them in desperation. Alone with the vehicle, Eris quickly took one glance at the bank doors, closing them shut with her powers just in time as the other security guards returned to help from inside. As the guards tried desperately to open the door, she climbed onto the back of the car, quickly stuffing wrapped bills into her newspaper bag. One by one, she stuffed them with pleasure and greed. She then jumped out, landing like a child smiling at what just happened. It was an early celebration for she gasped at the sight of the arrival of the security guards barging out from the bank's back entrance.

While carrying all that money inside these bags, Eris moved through crowds in her little boy form. With the security guards tailing her, she searched through the alleyways for a way back around Smith Street, where the real paper boy had been stationed. Stepping in one alleyway, she stopped momentarily as she was cornered by police officers who had appeared on the other side, with security guards on the other end.

"Uh oh, what to do?" she thought.

"End of the line, kid," they remarked.

Eris quickly ran toward the police guard, who tried to seize her as she came towards him. With great speed and a bag worth almost ten pounds of cash, she ducked his grab and instinctively smashed the bag right into the officer's abdomen, taking him down. She then quickly swirled around him continuing to run as she dodged traffic to cross to the other alleyway before the police were able to capture her.

This little adventure caused a commotion throughout the area, while Eris was having the time of her life. Disguising as a mortal always meant that she shared the thrill of mortal danger, compared with her invisible goddess self whose divine powers often made things too easy and unfair.

It was by some dumb chance that Eris had turned the corner when her tiny head bumped into the chest of somebody. She almost fell for a second but regained her composure as she looked straight up at a young man's face. To her surprise, it was Henry's. Looking at him, he appeared rather modest compared to that other night.

"Are you alright?" he asked softly, looking down on her through his glasses. She paused for a second, surprised by this encounter.

"Ah...Yes," she replied.

"I'll take one. Here," he said, handing her three cents. Eris hesitated at first but looked through the bag for a newspaper. She took one out that was curled beneath the wads of bills.

"Thanks, have a good day," he said, taking it from her and passing her soon after.

"So Hero Boy is going to leave me with all this dough is he?" she thought, amused with this encounter. Now she knew what to do with this bag of money. She came up with a devious idea of placing the bag with him, all to frame him when the police caught up to them. Carefully, she followed him amongst the crowd.

It was peculiar, as Henry was oblivious while Eris followed him for the last three blocks. Soon, Henry reached his destination, stopping under the sign that read, "Walden's Bookstore."

"A bookstore?" she commented, "what a bookworm. No wonder he's shy around women, being around books all the time," she thought. She looked inside the glass window out front upon seeing him talk to a man who may be the owner. She listened in, trying to find a juicy situation to make her next disguise.

"I tell yah, those places are damn full of liquor. If I had more sales in, I would be going to them to get some more. But hey, kids these days rather listen to radio and go dancing then read a good book…I don't blame them when there's a drink and a gal to enjoy it with," commented Jack Walden as he counted the money at the register.

"Henry, there's some new volumes that just came in, in that box over there. Put them in front, will you?"

Henry got busy piling and re-shelving some books as he heard this command from his boss, who was now smoking a cigar as he closed up the register.

"Dammit, I just wish I didn't have a nagging wife to go with. I'm telling you, she's like one of those flappers who won't pipe down about how jealous they are about the other couple, and just starts complaining about her own fella. It's always, 'why don't you ever take me there?' Or 'she and Charlie went to Hawaii for their honeymoon.' I drove you to Niagara Falls," he complained, having carefully mocking his wife's voice.

"How's today's business?" asked Henry as he went through a list of books that needed to be checked.

"Crap, that's what. But hey, I'm not going to let that stop me from this place I heard from Mason yesterday." Walden puffed some smokes before grabbing a tray from the counter for the ashes.

"Well anyways, I'm going to get going. I'll be back soon. Hey, is that today's paper?" Walden pointed.

"Yeah, you can read it first if you want," Henry replied, handing it to him.

"Thanks," Walden said.

The ringing bell from the door opening evoked Eris to turn towards Mister Walden as he came out. She looked at him with a youthful smile, still dirty and roughed up from the bank chase. He glanced at her, and then walked away not caring, heading down the street. Now Eris had something new in mind. It certainly would be an unfortunate accident if Henry or she herself did something that would cost him his job. As she thought about it for a minute, a hand grabbed her shoulders from the back.

"Hey, why are you following me, kid? Are you spying on me or something?" Eris turned around and saw Henry's face in front of her. His eyes looked menacing, staring down at her with his dark pupils.

"Nothing, I was just passing by and saw an excellent place for a headline," she quickly replied in her childish tone.

"Oh really? Well, I suppose outside a bookstore would be ideal," he said, suddenly smiling. It was just then that Officer Frank, who was watching this boy the whole time out of suspicion, noticed the commotion and came about to inquire what was happening.

"Is everything alright, sir? Trouble with this paper boy?" he asked, glaring at Eris.

"Yes, officer. I was inquiring why he's outside loitering," Henry replied.

"Why is that a fact? Tell me boyo, why are you following this gentleman?" said the officer, who wiggled his Roosevelt mustache. Before Eris had a chance to answer, Henry interrupted.

"Not to worry officer, I know this boy. He's just playing a trick on me for fun's sake. Yes, everything is fine." Eris noticed that something was odd with how Henry phrased that statement, also adding a unique hand gesture in doing so.

"If you please, I shall give him a lecture behind my store," Henry said, smiling to the officer.

"Very well, move along then," Officer Frank nodded, walking away with his stick swinging again. Henry held the boy by the shoulder and escorted him to the back of the store.

"So? What's the reason you've been following me?" Henry asked again.

This time, Eris gazed into his pupils and saw a transparency of color unnatural to her. It was then she figured out what was going on.

"I wasn't following you. I was following that book clerk inside," Eris replied calmly.

"Book clerk? I am that book clerk. What kind of game are you playing?" he demanded.

"Cut it Eros, I know it's you. I can see it in your eyes," she asserted. It was then that Henry smiled reluctantly, and his eyes became blue as his face soon emerged sculpted with smoothness.

"Ah darn it, I was about to have some fun too. How did you guess?" cried Eros, back to his boyish handsome self, crossing his arms as Eris also transformed back to her goddess self.

"Details love, your disguises need a bit more work to fool me. But then anyhow, I suppose mine needed work too if you could see through me. And you know, it is utterly impossible for immortals to not smell the scent of each other," Eris commented.

Eros laughed, "Yes, Yes. I just wanted to see what would happen, that's all. I happened to be passing by and saw you follow him to his workplace."

"It's none of your business," Eris snickered, walking the other way, going back to her business.

"What are you planning to do with Mister Leon today? Up to no good as always, I presume?" guessed Eros, watching her sway away before turning her head back, blowing her glossy lips as she mocked him.

"Come now, don't keep me guessing. I was the one who introduced him to you. Let me at least help you," he continued, placing his arms around her shoulders. Eris was still silent, but the childish nagging of Eros had got to her as he begged her.

"You? Help me? I'm not trying to make him fall in love with me, nor do I need any help from you to do it anyhow," Eris dismissed, her palm pushing Eros' chest away. "I'm going to cast a plague of destruction and bad luck upon him, starting with this bag of money and his job."

"Ah ha, I suppose no matter how much I try you will never see the power of attraction and the heart," he concluded, laughing with amusement.

Eris was suddenly offended by this kind of statement as she stared at him with contempt. Was it a challenge? Sure, both immortals saw love differently but that use of "never" seemed condescending.

"Eros, you are about to eat those words because I am going to prove you wrong. You just wait, I'll have him begging to take me out. Before long, he will love me. He shall see his mortal life be dedicated to me," she proclaimed, with her index finger pointing up to his face.

"Yes, let's see it, old girl. And I shall obediently sit back and watch," Eros expressed with his playfulness and delight, bowing and tipping off his boater hat to her amusement.

Eris prepared herself before she went into the bookstore. She now had a plan to get Henry's attention. Eros promised to be part of the audience, standing outside the window and viewing her as she entered the store. She disguised herself yet again, this time as a young and "interesting" woman.

The ring of the door shook as it slowly opened. On the countertop, Henry was writing a musical composition on one side of the table and reading a novel on the other. His head gently glanced up to see a figure emerge from a glare of light that formed around it, sparkling, as Eris came in.

"Hiya stranger," Eris said confidently, her voice as lively as her posture and pose. "I'm looking for a certain book. Maybe you can help me?" she said with a sly smile, protruding her rose-red lips that were nicely done to match her fine dark eyeliner. Eris had transformed herself to become a highly fashionable lady of the times, with a white patterned silk ascot that tied around her neck to one side making her look like a racer or a pilot. She fashioned a bobbed cut, wearing a headband that draped downward near her cheeks and her hair.

She had one gloved hand on one hip and the other in the pocket of her sateen burgundy coat that she wore buttoned up. Below her slender figure, her bare shins angled like a V making her feet poised as she stood tall on covered laced heels. She was something of a showgirl and an adventuring quaintrelle combined. Upon her presence, Henry paused for a moment, entranced by her before replying.

"Uhm, what is the title of the book you're looking for?" said Henry as his voice stuttered.

"I can't remember. My memory is a little foggy. Be a hero and help me, if you will."

"Perhaps the author? A famous one? And how about the genre?" Henry knelt to pick up a catalog for a list of books accounted in the store. He cleared the front of papers and put the volume catalog on top, and then began flipping pages.

"All I know is that the story involves a young woman and a young man who are constantly thwarted by the cruelties of war and the notions of society," Eris made up in the back of her head, all the while flapping her eyelashes. She then turned her back to him and walked the other way to a bookcase, carefully ungloving her hands and striding with those hips of hers while doing so.

"Gosh, well that shouldn't be too hard. Romance, I think. Let's see here. Do you remember what time or where it's set? I might have read it," he asked seriously.

Eris looked backed and smiled. "Yes, I believe it is set…" she thought to herself before speaking, "It is a tale set in a time before our grand age of technology and science. In a quaint little world amongst the bloody chaos soon to roam within it. There were towns…no, a city perhaps, where talented men and beautiful women scheme throughout the story."

Hearing this, Henry suppressed a smile and scribbled some things on a piece of paper before closing the catalog.

"Well, I think I have a few ideas about what book you are looking for. Let's pick some out and you can read through them. Maybe that would spark a memory," he said enthusiastically. He walked over to her with a list in his hand and began searching through the bookcases for her book. He went straight in search for Jane Austen first, taking out *Pride and Prejudice* from the shelf and handed it to Eris. Then he went off to another shelf. Surprised by his gesture of concentration and effort in this search, Eris looked at his dull head that was covered with his messy hair and a pencil he left on one ear. She had a humorous puzzlement on her face because of how he had just acted.

As the search continued, the accumulated books began piling up. The search was disappointing for Eris as Henry was more determined to complete the list rather than pay attention to this beauty in the store. A good 15 minutes had gone by, and soon enough, he began searching for more books above them from his ladder. When she could not hold them anymore, Eris placed the stack of books onto a nearby chair. Tired and warm from this search, she unbuttoned her coat, revealing her blouse that had not been buttoned fully. It was during this time that Henry was just above her.

"Ah, and here we have something set thousands of years ago by Homer. A true classic," Henry said to her, still concentrated on the shelves as he took *The Odyssey* out. He handed the book to her without looking back at her. However, this time, he had found it not received by her hands. Curious, he turned his head to glance to check if she was alright. Her gaze had been on the books on the shelves, her fingers running down the spines of the volumes, admiring the leather bounded texture with engraved words which she read quietly to herself. Eris, although immortal, and having lived through a millennium, had never read a book nor taken any interest in them before until now. She was mystified at how mortals found pleasure in them and was deciphering it so

Baffled by this young woman's curiosity in the books, Henry hardly noticed her wardrobe modification until she turned her body back toward him. Catching her at the right time, his gaze from on top was perfectly positioned by the trajectory of the way she was angled, settling on her V-neck blouse revealing a dark tunnel made by her porcelain chest—cleavage no mortal man could ignore. He quickly glanced away, embarrassed, and blushed a little as soon as she looked back up at him. Unfortunately for him, however, she noticed.

I have you now, piano boy, she thought.

"Alright, we'll just see whether you can recall anything from these books here," he grinned, dismissing his embarrassment. Trying to forget what had happened, Henry slid down the ladder and placed Homer on top of the other books she had placed on the chair. He lifted them, trying with all his might to not drop them, carrying them over to a study area.

"Over here, if you would, miss. Miss? Miss…?" he turned his head, waiting for a reply.

"Roxanne. Uhmm Smith," she said as she came over, taking small feminine steps.

"Alright Miss Smith, call me when you remember or need another list to check out. And I'm Henry." He offered his hand and she shook it, only to realize how quick and awkward the handshake was. It was a weak handshake, one where someone could sense uncertainty in the person. Despite it, Henry's hand was smooth and soft, provoking a sudden thought of that night at the concert for Eris when she had gazed his hands in motion.

"I shall be at the front." Henry laughed, slightly embarrassed by their introduction. The laugh itself was also quite strangely expressed.

"Trying to escape?" Eris perceived.

"Wait!" she called to him. Henry slowly turned around and looked at her once more.

"These books are filthy. Just look at them." She pointed to the books that were now crawling with worms and tiny insects. Seeing them crawl on top of an opened one, Henry quickly came over to the table and wiped them off, stepping on some that had landed on the ground.

"My apologies. This is strange. I didn't see any when I was taking them out. Let me get them cleaned for you." Henry went to the back to get some brushes and dusting materials. As he rushed on to clean the mess, Eris took off her coat and placed it on the table.

"Now the fun begins," she thought deviously.

"I'll have you know Miss Smith that Walden's bookstore is a clean establishment. I will certainly have these books inspected and cleaned thoroughly for every purchase. Let's see." Henry sat down on the chair next to the books and brought out the equipment, flipping through the pages and inspecting them one by one.

"Quite alright, let me also have a read too. I mind as well start recalling what I remember of that story. Maybe I can after these volumes." Eris smiled as she sat on top of the table next to their stack, adjusting her flared peplum skirt. When

Henry noticed this, he had wanted to offer her a chair but hesitated because of her commanding and assured presence. She took a book from the stack, held it high, and began reading it to herself. Briefly and together, they both flipped pages and concentrated on their individual tasks. No matter how Henry tried to stay focused on the job at hand, however, he was taken aback by her strange behavior.

Eris crossed over her legs slowly, carefully bringing those ballerina devils into view when she stretched them away from the stack. Her motion revealed her smooth bare skin and her womanly features, sliding off the table as they sprouted from her skirt. Her violet eyes glanced from on top of the book she was pretending to read, dilating and searching for a reaction. To her surprise, Henry was fixated upon the books being inspected. Carefully, he recorded details as he searched for molds behind a magnifying glass. Undaunted, she was not going to be ignored for a pile of old books. She closed her book gently and proceeded to another move.

"All this reading is making my eyes dry," she said, yawning. She then slowly leaned on the table towards him, her elbows near his hands. He instantly leaned backwards on his chair.

"Sorry, is it the lighting?" Henry burst nervously. In a rush of movements and tenseness to find the switch for the lamps, Henry knocked over some books and papers.

"Ah, excuse me, let me get them," he said, rushing to the ground to retrieve them. Eris got down from the table and proceeded to help him.

"Yes, thank you," he said, taking them from her hands, looking up into her eyes as he did.

"No, thank you for helping me search and clean these books up, you're a real hero," she said, looking deep into his innocent hazel eyes behind those giant glasses of his.

There was no sudden pause of seduction as Eris had hoped would happen. Instead, Henry merely smiled with jitteriness and had quickly regained his composure as he restacked them. It was just then that the bell on the door dangled and rung for another visitor. This time there was no glow of light but a loud bang as the door closed.

At the entrance of Walden's Books stood a girl, a girl that Henry noticed but bashfully hesitated to come out for. She stood there looking around the bookstore, waiting, while eyeing some book that interested her on the shelf. Henry moved from his spot, slightly hiding next to a bookcase as he stared at her from afar.

"Hello? Is anyone there? I've come to return my books," she said in a high-pitched voice that emitted a tone of innocence and friendliness, like an octave above middle C. Eris also noticed that she had a foreign accent of some kind.

"Hello?" she called out a second time. It was then that Henry suddenly snapped out of this trance.

"Excuse me," Henry said to Eris as he came out of the section where he had been with Eris, proceeding to the counter. Eris stood behind the bookcase, quite astonished that she was being ignored again.

"Good afternoo—oh hello, is Mr. Walden here? I've come to return these books to him," the girl asked Henry, while noticing something quite familiar about his face. When Henry came, he made himself look busy as he searched the counter for paper and a pen. His eyes avoiding eye contact, his interior frozen with nervousness as she began talking to him.

"No, he isn't. I'll take them," he replied quietly, mumbling his words as he did so. The girl handed Henry the books, and as she did so, she smiled with those cheeks of hers dimpling a little. She had wanted to say something as she focused on Henry's face but hesitated as Henry took them to the side counter and inspected them immediately. As he was busying himself, the girl looked around and walked to the book cases that Henry and Eris had gone through. She went about inspecting every new book that was placed on the shelf Henry had been working on. Checking the condition of each book she had borrowed, Henry seemed amazed at how many books she read in the span of one week. He took a glance at her every time he could. While she browsed, she seemed to be thrown into a world of her own while reading.

"Rats! Foiled again by Miss Tardy two-shoes," Eris cursed. Eris identified her. The very same one from his concert that Eros was supposedly to match Henry with. Was it Eros' doing to put this girl here to mock and thwart the goddess? It must be, she surmised, for Eros had sabotaged her that night too. The girl turned around just about the same time that Henry glanced at her for the third or fourth time. She was surprised by his innocent yet warm look. Embarrassed, she smiled at him, one that a girl gives to a boy that stuns his interior, making him feel like he just won the jackpot. The girl then gestured a goodbye to him.

"Thank you," she said sweetly, just as she proceeded out. When the door closed, Henry felt the heaviness on him as he sat down on his seat, sighing soon after. He covered his head with the palms of his hands, utterly embarrassed by his lack of courage. Amused by what had happened, Eris finally understood Henry's condition.

"No wonder! The boy lacks a backbone when it comes to the female presence. How amusing," Eris said to herself. It was then that Eris thought of a brilliant scheme, one that would be more fun than a mere seduction of Henry's heart. She grabbed her coat and swung it on.

"What was your name again?" she asked Henry as she stood before him. Quickly alerted by her presence, Henry stood up straight; she had forgotten how tall he was.

"Oh, sorry for abandoning your little project, Miss Smith. It's Henry. Henry Leon," he replied.

"Quite alright, Mr. Leon. Tell me, who's that girl? You two are certainly friendly to each other," Eris grinned.

"Oh, uhm, no one. It was nothing," he said, blushing red as he turned the other way and pretended to do "things." Eris went to his front counter like a girl staring at a pearl necklace on a glass counter as she looked down on Henry, who had just dropped some papers on the floor. Henry, surprised by her sudden appearance when he rose, seemed reluctant to confess the truth of this encounter.

"Really? Nothing, Hero Boy? It seems to me this girl knows you from somewhere," she asked again with her hands upon her pampered face. "I can tell when a girl notices a boy. So, what's your story?"

"She's just a regular. An acquaintance of Mr. Walden's. That's all I know," Henry replied reluctantly. "That's right. I have to get back to inspecting your books."

"Trying to change the subject? That's fine. I'll get it from you later. I haven't found what I was looking for. Maybe next time we'll try again. Thanks for all your help, till another time, Mr. Leon," Eris maintained her coolness.

"Are you sure?" he called out as she was about to make her way out.

"Yes, I'll see you again real soon my book hero," she smiled deviously. She slowly turned and walked toward the door. It opened for her as Henry's boss returned.

Outside, Eris still in her human form, walked alone to an alleyway until she was greeted with pleasing giggles.

"Good show! It was a good try my dear. Perhaps another time you'll get him. Come along, let's have a date," Eros proclaimed as he came in front of her looking excitedly satisfied.

She gave a look of seriousness to him and then smirked.

"It's just the beginning. I don't know why you are so excited over a first act. Everything will fall into place soon," she said as she continued walking.

"Come now, please pray tell," he said as he continued after her.

"That girl you've sent inside. You were trying to make my task more difficult, weren't you?" Eris snickered.

"What? No, no! I did no such thing. As honest as I can be, I was but a mere audience. I stood there watching the whole time, I swear," he said, crossing his fingers on both hands to show to her.

"Whatever, I'll have you know, Eros, that it doesn't matter that you chose them to be together. They will be pawns in my game of destruction. Please stay out of it from now on."

Eris stopped at the corner of an intersection and faced the god of desire as she said that. Eros looked at her with a face of elation and confusion.

"By the power of Zeus, I did no such thing, sweetie. As you've heard from Henry, she is a regular. It is by chance that she would come along. But right, please explain to me what you are going to do. I am dying from anticipation."

Eris stretched her hands and her knuckles cracked, showing her collected serenity.

"No doubt the boy likes her. A girl can tell. So, why not play matchmaker first? Then in time, I'll steal his little heart, or better yet, cause an unfortunate accident for these two love birds. Of course, breaking both hearts is better than one," she explained.

Eros replied with a laugh.

"Hey, stop laughing. I mean it. You think you're the only one that can get people to love and be together?" she asked.

"Oh goody! Then why not make a wager with me?" said Eros after his last giggle.

"A wager? What sort of wager? And whatever can you give me?" she asked.

"A wager to prove your ability to do my job. Make them fall in love with each other. And I think this would interest you." Eros took out the heart-shaped pocket watch from his suit pocket.

"A trinket!" she said, dismissing it.

"To the untrained eye," he replied, holding it up to her and unlocking the front cover. After he opened it, Eris saw a device with gears that pumped blood throughout the numbers, tubes like arteries that circulated the time and lifework of any individual that can be seen within its center face, all laid out in a nicely finished mirror.

"If you succeed with bringing Mr. Leon into your little game of love, this device can be yours," Eros commented.

"To track time is of no importance to me," she replied.

"Why, this is no ordinary watch. It is my assistant, my portal or telescope, if you will, to the darkest reach of the minds of men and women alike. Here, you see, is a gadget that does not just measure time but measures the rate of emotions before, during, and after love according to the fabric of time. Every movement of time matters in love and I am its keeper. With it, I very much hold the very heart of every fickle-minded soul. May I offer you the possession of the *Ticking Heart?* What do you say?" Eros grinned as the chain dangled in his hands in front of her.

The Ticking Heart, a watch that can measure the mind's wants and the heart's desires, just like a heartbeat that measures life. With it, one can know whether a person is really in love or not. Such a device, thought Eris, would bring her immense power, and with it, enhanced joy.

"And if I don't succeed? What would you gain out of this?" Eris asked, knowing it was an easy task to complete but knew that Eros was lusting for a greater profit if he was willing to risk such a powerful tool.

"Ah…if I win. I shall be content with your acknowledgement that I was right. Believe me, my dear, there is no greater pleasure, except for love, than to know that one was right all along," he said confidently.

"Right? About what?" asked Eris.

"About everything we had discussed about love, of course! I'm telling you this. Leave it to someone who understands what romantic love is. Let me be frank, I cannot say for sure your little game of it will succeed," said Eros.

"We shall see. Very well, then you must promise to *not* interfere," she demanded, looking at him directly in the eye.

"But of course, Discordia. I had always done so. No tricks under these sleeves," said Eros, showing his two sleeves to her, "I promise. Make these two mortals fall in love with each other and do what you will with them to make it all happen, for *true love*. Give me a show to remember," he declared, then held out his hand for her to shake. "And of course, be prepared to admit you were wrong about love all along," he added.

She agreed to this proposal and shook it, his grip so warm and tight. Then after a brief pause after letting go of his hand, she took out a cigarette from her coat pocket. Like a gentleman, Eros lit it for her as she leaned into the lighter. She blew a few puffs, then she looked up toward the sky and thought to herself. And with that, she turned away from him.

"Just have the payment ready when the show is over, Mr. Romero," she reassured.

-Chapter 4-

Eris quickly went to work to set up Henry and the girl that he liked to win the wager. Not only had she been stalking and learning about this girl, she kept a professional business relationship with Henry and his duties as a book clerk. While requesting the services from Henry to find her the story of the book she had come to search for, Eris now had made some progress in fostering a closer acquaintance with him at last. And in all the times she saw him, she slowly began to learn more about him personally and about his subtle interest in this girl. It was not until one day that she decided that her research now needed a final catalyst for them to come together. Quite precisely, "the girl" herself.

"Really? Why isn't that so? I must say, Henry, it will be an immense pleasure to come to see one of your concerts some time," remarked Eris enthusiastically after hearing his aspirations to be a concert pianist. Eris looked at Henry's face as she waited for a reaction. Henry, although grateful of her compliments, was busy fixing the tea Mr. Walden had suggested he serve to her since she was his regular customer.

Henry murmured a "hmm, yes," in response to her praise, carefully pouring the tea. In these few book assistances with Henry, Eris often thought that he was a tough nut to crack open. There was very little excitement to be found in his social

61

and emotional life. He was often stoic and too formal on topics she wanted him to open up about. For Henry, it was strange for him to hear her curiously ask such topics. However, Henry didn't mind her questioning. He was amused by her presence and enjoyed her company. After all, this was the first time any female had given him any attention at all.

In a moment of silence after his reply, Henry sat back across from her and continued his hygienic inspection of the books he had picked out for her to read. Throughout her time here, Eris was uninterested in the books laid out for her. A couple of sentences here and there, and maybe she would flip through a few chapters, but she could not stand to be in these silent environments. As for Henry, he sat there unbothered and concentrated. Among the many books, tripled this time on their table, Eris, slouched on them, forcing herself to read before flipping through some more pages. She tried to think of something clever to start another conversation. Though nothing came to mind, she took it upon herself to release her intentions and get straight to the point. She looked up back at Henry, smiled and broke the silence as he carefully held the warm teacup, his lips taking a sip of the hot blend of spices in it.

"What part of a woman fascinates you the most?" she asked confidently. As one may guess, at that instant, Henry choked on his tea, almost catapulting it out from his mouth.

"Pardon me, come again?" he replied, embarrassed and blushing a little.

"Just an honest question if you will, Henry, it's to help me with my research. How do you feel about romance? There's got to be something about females that fascinates you men and I want to know what you think," she continued.

After regaining his composure, Henry calmly tried to understand what she was talking about, covering his reaction.

"Well, Miss Smith, I can say the least that every story has romantic qualities. For example, tales of chivalrous knights fighting for honor and for their lady is a common heroic element found throughout the framework of literature. It is something I too admire most. I can't say for sure what provokes men to possess such passions for acts of bravery, but it's a reoccurring theme in all romantic tales. Maybe that's why we are having a tough time finding that book for you," he said, laughing a little at his own response.

"No, no… I didn't mean that research, I meant…" before Eris finished her sentence, she noticed that her question was a bit vague and sexually provoking, remembering that appealing to Henry's man-brain never worked. As Henry looked on with confusion of what other possible research she was doing, Eris changed the subject and asked a series of business-related questions about the bookstore and his schedule.

"And do you still see that girl? That girl that I asked you about the day we met?" she interrupted him as soon as he mentioned the customers.

"Ah, this question again. I haven't seen her here lately. I don't know. Perhaps her visits here are finished, and she found business elsewhere," Henry dismissed sadly.

"Well, I wouldn't say that. Perhaps she is just feeling a little *under the weather* or simply busy," replied Eris. She carefully held the teacup and then took a sip. She thought to herself, knowing that the girl was indeed absent because of some unfortunate events bestowed upon her by a clever goddess.

"I'm sure you yourself, Mr. Leon, do miss her presence. Oops! Why, that was rude of me. I didn't mean to insist that you have a possible attraction for her."

Henry smiled a little at this bluntness. "No, not at all. I guess it's obvious that I did show interest last time she was here, didn't I?"

Eris smiled and sipped some tea, carefully crossing her legs as she listened to Henry finally opening up to her.

"Well, it doesn't matter. She probably has better things to do," he said, closing one of the books on his side.

"And what makes you think that? A girl has her own life, but it doesn't mean she won't be back to the place she often visits. In fact, the place she often visits are part of her life," she replied.

Eris finished her tea and placed it back on the table while glancing around the bookstore unnoticeably.

"She read many of the books here. Some I haven't even read yet. I kept track of what she read. But for records of course!" he caught himself saying, "But anyhow, she must be getting her books from the school library instead."

"Ahh, so she attends university?" remarked Eris.

"Yes, I believe so."

"Do you see her often?"

"Why no, like I said, I haven't seen her here lately."

"I know. You said so earlier. I mean have you seen her in class?" Eris leaned closer and her eyes were focused on Henry's.

"No, Franny is often at the library," Henry replied, accidently revealing that he knew more than he presented.

"So! You do *know* her! Go on, tell this old girl everything. This book search can wait."

Embarrassed, Henry had no choice but to reveal what he knew. There was something about this bold flapper sitting in front of him that showed that she would not leave if he avoided this subject any longer.

Are all women like this, always with the gossip and details? he thought. Soon after, he reluctantly told Eris of the life of Henry Leon no one knew about. That really, Henry was like most school boys his age, often noticing the attractive girl who comes to a particular spot on campus, and in his case, the library's old book collection section that was restricted from lending. In the past weeks, he noticed her by chance from the second story deck balcony, hiding himself among the walled carrel desks as he glanced at her every moment he could while she read the book she had un-shelved. He assured Eris that he did not follow her or learn why she was there. He tried but failed to convince her otherwise.

"In fact, I didn't even find out she attended my university till weeks later. I hope you do not think me strange for this coincidence. It's childish, I know. She is a stranger that I happened to know during that time I was inside studying. I had to look," he defended.

As for knowing her name, Henry learned this on the accord of Mr. Walden's conversations with her. They were always friendly to each other and he assumed that Jack Walden would not appreciate him ruining their personal business relationship.

From listening to Henry, Eris felt an amusing satisfaction deep inside her mind as she found out what she needed to know just in time. The clock mounted on the wall turned its long hand onto six, 10:30.

"I'm thirsty, can I have some more?" Eris changed the subject and handed him the tea cup and china pot.

"Yes, of course, let me make some more," answered Henry.

"I don't feel much for tea this time. Let's have some coffee," Eris said, leaning back on her chair as she stretched herself. As she did so, Henry smiled and obeyed, setting forth to the back with the pot for the coffee. In his absence, Eris looked out the window and saw that her special guest had arrived just in time.

When the door rung after opening, Mr. Walden was in the middle of smoking his pipe and reading the daily journal while the record player was playing a collection of famous composers. He glanced up and saw a familiar face that had been missing for a while.

"Franny, you've been gone for quite a while. How are you feeling?" remarked Mr. Walden.

"Good morning Jack, I've been much better. I caught something awful that time you saw me. But I'm feeling wonderfully well now. What have I missed?" she said happily.

"Why, a lot! But don't you worry. I've saved a whole list for you to look through," said Mr. Walden, who began searching for it under his counter cabinet. She began looking around the store as she waited, humming to herself softly to a smooth Beethoven sonata playing in the background. Mr. Walden searched desperately for the list, and at the same time, took short pauses as he stopped and smoked.

"You like that stuff?" he asked her, hearing her hum.

"Pardon?" she responded, smiling.

"The music. You know it?"

"Yes, Beethoven sonata No. 15 in D major," she responded in her delicate voice.

"Huh…yeah I can never really get into it. Henry puts this music on all the time. That boy never stops playing, even in here. Oh yeah, maybe he knows where I put it, Henry!" He called him, but there was no answer from him. Instead, a substitute appeared alongside the book case.

"He's a little occupied, Jack. Why isn't it my darling girl, Francine," Eris commented, leaning a hand on the shelves, as she made her way toward them.

"Miss Roxanne?" said Francine joyfully. They hugged each other lightly, with both looking surprised to see each other.

"I'm so glad to see you again. How are you?" beamed Francine sweetly.

"Wonderful, as are you, I hope? Oh Franny, I've heard you were in bed for weeks after," Eris said, smiling at her as she sat herself down near the counter.

"I've been much better. I didn't know you come here too. Do you come often?" she replied.

"Miss Smith here has been visiting us quite frequently. Henry is helping her find some book she forgot the name of," interrupted Mr. Walden.

"Really? I'll be glad to recommend you some," she replied.

"Always the little scholar as I can see," Eris laughed lightly, "darling, my hero inside is doing that for me. And's he's quite good," she continued, winking a little to Mr. Walden, thanking him for Henry's help.

"Henry! Get your musical butt over here. So how long have you two gals known each other?" Mr. Walden called out before inquiring.

Francine giggled a little at his command that went unanswered the second time.

"Why, not long ago actually. Miss Roxanne…" said Francine before Eris interrupted her.

"It has been long dear! I worried about you all night long after you had gone home. I knew something was brewing when you were sneezing up a bit on your front porch."

"You saw me?" Francine asked innocently.

"Yes, dear. You see Jack, Franny was soaking wet when I first met her. She had been waiting in front of the university library amongst a crowd of students. Beasts devouring the latest spaces on the steps that still had cover above them. Poor girl here, barely had any cover from the storm." Eris took out a cigarette from her pocket case and held it towards her mouth, prompting Mr. Walden to light it for her. She then smiled as a sign of thanks.

"That's dreadful. Why didn't you make for cover inside the library?" Mr. Walden asked, pushing out a chair nearby for Francine to sit.

"I was going to, but I couldn't get through the crowds. And I was already trying to get a taxi, but I had no luck getting one," Francine answered eagerly.

"By the time I got to my ride, I'd seen Franny being shoved and passed on by other students getting into their rides. And you know what she was doing? Still utterly hugging those big books of hers like she was protecting her own infant," added Eris.

Mr. Walden grinned, amazed to see her dedication, and as well, Francine laughed along, surprised and embarrassed to see how foolish she acted till now.

"Then you came along then to rescue this damsel in distress?" Mr. Walden asked.

"Yes, certainly. I already had enough, seeing three-four cars passed her, splashing their filth all over her. She was like a stray kitten, poor thing. I came over and picked her up. She was quite polite to not jump in of course, but I assured her that I was heading in her direction and that I was quite fine about sharing a cab. That reminds me, did you finish that soup I gave you that day?" Eris looked back to Francine attentively.

"Why yes, I did. Thank you again so much for giving me some," said Francine.

"That's good. Nothing beats warm soup after a rainy day," Eris commented, smiling her radiant lips, knowing what she had done to it to make Francine sick in the first place.

"Henry! Come here, boy!" yelled Mr. Walden. Henry had just come out from the back counter after finishing a fresh brew of coffee. He came over to the front and greeted the guest in front of him with a smile, hoping that this girl he had only gazed at from afar did not notice the complexion of his face turning mildly red. At this long-awaited moment, she returned a smile at him, her eyes as radiant as they were warm.

"Dammit boy, are you already taking after Beethoven already? I called you three times. But now that you are here, take this list and get the books from those shelves for..." said Mr. Walden, handing him the list right before Francine interrupted him.

"That's alright, Jack, I can find them on the shelves on my own, I also don't want to burden Henry, pardon me, I mean Mister...?"

"You mean you two haven't met yet after all this time you've been here reading my books for free?" joked Mr. Walden.

Eris, puffing her cigarette, looked at them curiously.

"Introductions are in order," she declared with a grin.

"I'm Henry. Henry Leon at your service, miss," said Henry, offering his hand.

"I'm Francine. Francine Daye. Pleased to finally make your acquaintance, Mr. Leon," she replied, her small hands gently shaking his smooth long fingers.

Though it was quick, Henry felt at long last what should have been done a while ago. An introduction that made all the difference in the world.

"Well, now that we all are acquainted, get on it with that list, Henry, can't keep a lady waiting," insisted Mr. Walden who held his hand up, gesturing to Francine to sit tight and that it would be Henry's pleasure to get it for her.

"Oh, and bring those cookies my wife baked earlier this morning over here," he called to him. These words, having passed through Henry's ears, did not move him from his trance despite his boss commanding him to. He was still looking at Francine and summoned what courage he had to make the most of the moment.

"Where are you from, Miss Daye?" he inquired.

Francine, surprised that he ignored Jack but was nevertheless intrigued by his curiosity, replied warmly, "London, England."

"England! Well, that explains the accent," Henry remarked gleefully, wanting to know more. Mr. Walden interrupted when Henry saw his infamous glare, the same one when he wanted him to do something.

"Oh sorry," he replied, embarrassed. After looking around dazed, Henry had forgotten that he left them in the back while talking to Eris earlier. Quickly, he rushed to the back, bringing the cookies over.

"Move along with those books," Mr. Walden commanded, giving him a stern look as he cleaned his pipe, then turned back to Francine. "London, you don't say? I was there last year, a beautiful city."

Eris finished her cigarette and placed it on the ash tray. "Franny, how are your studies? That reminds me…you go to Empire State University, right?" she asked.

"Yes, I do. It's been quite busy, but being sick hasn't gotten me down," replied Francine, taking a cookie from the tray, slowly biting into it. As she ate the cookie, Eris asked her school related questions, then it led to her telling her funny stories about her little experiences visiting her school.

Henry noticed from above on his ladder that they were having fun chatting without him. Indeed, the laughter of young flappers, the aroma of caramel tea, and gingerbread seemed most pleasant to be part in. And here was Henry, amongst the books, no matter how focused he was searching them, the echoes of chatter whispered toward him like a bass getting gradually louder that climbed on the other side of that mysterious melody. She sat there, focused, her eyes concentrated on the person speaking but for a second, then stopped and glanced back to the pianist once again.

The conversation eventually shifted to something most intriguing.

"No, it's not that Jack. Sometimes the authorities are just plain oblivious to these events. Not everyone is corrupt, just those who think the law is corrupt," commented Eris.

Mr. Walden nodded to this statement, then got up from his chair to tend to a catalog at the front shelf. As he did so, while complaining about the last "events" he had attended, Eris looked back at Francine.

"My dear," she called.

"Yes?" Francine replied politely.

"I have a favor to ask you. Do you happen to know where Luna Island is?"

"Why of course, it's on the east side of campus. It's a quaint town along the coast, many people visit the beach. It's lovely to walk along the boardwalk there. It's been a while since I've been there. No time at all."

"Perfect. I was recently invited to a little event mentioned to be on that boardwalk. I don't know if you've heard of a 'new carnival' that's going on Friday night?" said Eris. It was then that Mr. Walden's eyes brightened with interest, recalling a speakeasy that was going to be secretly held near there.

"I might have heard something from some classmates, but I'll be more than happy to direct you there," replied Francine.

"Nonsense, what are you doing Friday night?"

"Studying, most likely."

"Baloney, let's go out and have some fun!" Eris expressed eagerly.

"What sort of carnival are we talking about? Student-run?" asked Mr. Walden.

"Hosted by the Zimmerman's Circus. There will be students…and anybody that is anybody I hear will be there," Eris answered instantly.

"Will there be games?" inquired Francine, innocently.

"Why yes, darling, many," Eris answered, smiling.

Mr. Walden leaned closer to Eris, setting his arms on the table before whispering to her, "we are talking about empty bottles…and imported ones, right?"

"Yes indeed, the finest juice straight from port," replied Eris, winking.

"I don't know. I don't feel comfortable at night parties. Perhaps I'll check my schedule for another time. I…" Before Francine could say anymore, Eris interrupted her. It was then that these three grew softer with every sentence, but more it appeared to Henry that their conversation was becoming more secretive.

When Henry had finished finding all the books for Francine, he brought them over to the counter neatly packed. He wanted to join their conversation but was surprised to see them suddenly now agreeing and laughing as he arrived. What were they talking about? Only a mere five minutes ago did he cease to hear their conversation while he was tying the books with a ribbon into a bow in the back.

"Finally, here it is," said Mr. Walden, seeing Henry with the books. Francine walked over to Henry and slowly and carefully received the books from his hands.

"Thank you ever so much, Mr. Leon," she said, smiling lightly. As she did so, he looked at her but was disappointed to see her eyes not looking up to him but down to the books. As she held them, she took out her purse wallet and was prepared to pay Walden.

"It's fine, I'll collect the tab next month. As always, if you finish them early, return them, and you'll owe nothing," he said.

"Thanks Jack, I'll try my best. Have a good day everyone, farewell," she said while waving goodbye, heading toward the door.

"And Franny, don't forget Friday night, 7 p.m. sharp. I'll meet you on campus!" Eris called to her. Francine nodded, and her sunshine presence left the building.

"Darn it, that reminds me. I got to run too. I have to go pick up my nagging she-wolf of a wife now. Henry, do your job," said Mr. Walden as he cleared the counter. He then took his coat from the rack and quickly dashed out. Henry smiled and looked at Eris who was eating her cookie very loudly and playfully like a child. She twirled from her stool to face Henry, then gave him a mischievous look.

"You three sounded wonderfully chatty. Going somewhere Friday?" he asked. Eris finished her cookie and handed him the tray.

"Why yes, but nothing that would concern you, I'm sure," she told him.

"Oh, alright then," Henry said sadly as he took the tray of tea and walked back to the table where all their books laid. Eris gave a confused smile and then followed him. As he sat down with his eyes working on the book he had been reading, Eris stood beside the table, adjusting her makeup as she called back to him.

"Cheer up, Henry, I was only joking," she said while taking out her lipstick and mirror. "Of course you are more than welcome to join us. I know you will be happy to get to know her more."

She saw her violet eyes in her mirror as she began to slowly rub deadly venomous dark red on her lips. Henry did not know what to say to her and stopped to ponder. Deep down, he wanted to be with Francine.

"I can help. Perhaps, get you two to go together," she finally commented.

"You will? How?" blurted Henry who instantly looked interested.

Eris finished applying her lipstick and smiled again at her reflection.

"You said you see her often around your university, right?"
Henry nodded, "yes, but I can't just go up to her and talk to her like that."

"Why not? You two are acquainted now. Just go up to her and start a conversation. Easy as apple pie," said Eris.

"But what will I say? I barely know her. She may think I'm strange or something."

"Well, are you so?" questioned Eris who was thinking the same thing.

"At times, I'm not a great conversationalist by any stretch," dismissed Henry.

"Hmmm...so," she continued, getting closer to him. She hunched down to him and his book, with one hand on the table and the other on her hips, she looked down onto him. "Then we'll have to work on your confidence first. A man will always appear awkwardly strange to a woman if he lacks assurance in his words, no matter how pleasant they may sound. Well Mr. Leon, do you or do you not want to enjoy the company of Miss Francine Daye Friday night?"

"Yes, I do," he replied seriously.

"Then, we shall make it so," she said confidently.

"But how? I don't want to be a burden to you, Miss Smith."

"No, not at all and no need to be so polite and formal, Henry. Consider this an act of friendship. Address me as friends would," She said walking to her chair for her purse.

From her purse, she took out a card and handed it to him.

"Come see me at my place, Monday afternoon," she concluded, handing it to him. "I will be delighted to have you over for tea and discuss this with you even more."

Before Henry got a chance to glance at what it said, Eris took her belongings and went out to the front door.

"Goodbye, Hero Boy. Be there or else!" called Eris loudly before stepping out. Henry glanced over the card that read:

Madame Roxanne Smith
A New Matchmaker for the 20th Century
010 Smith Street Unit 601

With the many books laid out before the table they were previously selecting, he noticed that she had forgotten to take them.

"Wait!" he cried running out. By the time he was outside, however, she was already gone. As he stood outside, Henry was smitten by the thought of seeing Francine soon.

-Chapter 5-

On the day of his scheduled visit, Henry was anxious to see Madame Roxanne. Since meeting Francine, he had never stopped thinking about her. Putting his trust in his new friend, this unheard-of matchmaker, seemed to be the miracle he was looking for. Henry glanced at the card again that was given him to make sure he was at the correct address. He looked up at the historic building which lay heavenly above him. Even so majestic as it looked, however, Henry found it hard to believe that Miss Roxanne lived here, in a neighborhood not so different from his own. Indeed, the intersection between Barnes and Smith was a not so charming area. It was dirty and congested with the city's wretched, poor immigrant families, holding to that constant romantic atmosphere of pursuing after that American dream. Surely, Miss Roxanne was a woman who traveled and dressed well, but also must have the means to live quite comfortably, too, he questioned. Henry proceeded through the door and came into a shabby lobby. It had furniture and coffee tables that were covered with cloths, collecting dust along with the closed shutters. It was dark, and only the grand staircase remained lit. After passing the front desk, Henry was about to go upstairs when he heard voices above him. An elderly man and woman were arguing and yelling in a different language. There were also children playing and crying in the background as he went up.

"Hey!" called out a deep imposing voice behind him, prompting Henry to turn around.

"Who do you think you are?" asked the man who suddenly appeared before him behind the front desk. He was a round, heavy-built man who had a glorious thick moustache.

"Well? Are you going to answer me or wait till I bake you a cake?" the man asked sarcastically.

"I am looking for Madame Roxanne, Sir," Henry finally answered. "I believe she is on the sixth floor?"

"You mean that new wild harpy that moved upstairs weeks ago? You a friend of hers or here for another delivery?" asked the man.

"Yes, friend," answered Henry.

"She had a lot of things moved up lately, hiring all these people and having deliveries every day. She makes a bunch of noises and thinks I run some hotel or something. Alright, hold on, I'll make her come down to get you. I might as well collect her rent while I am at it too."

"Oh, it's perfectly alright. I think I can find her door," Henry protested.

"Nonsense, you stay... It's about time I give her a talking to," the man interrupted as he escorted Henry to an old sofa. The man then moved for the mounted phone on the wall, picked up the receiver and dialed while smiling at him.

By the time the call was received, the man's face lit up with joy upon hearing Eris' voice.

"Morning Princess! I have another one of your guests here. Why don't you come down and bring…," the man said before the other end interrupted him with a quick commanding utterance, then there was silence before he could retort her. A rage came over him as he grumbled to himself, hanging up the receiver forcefully.

"So that's how she wants it? Alright, let's go. She wants me to escort you up," he remarked, irritated. As Henry got up and started toward the stairway, the man touched him on the shoulder and told him to use the newly renovated elevator with him.

"It was a deathtrap until your rude friend had it renovated," the man said, closing the gate in front of them and pulling the lever. As the ascension began, the gears ticked and clanked as the slow sound of old metal rubbed against each other like a factory.

"She came knocking on my door one day and wanted me to personally fix it. And when I said this thing was broken, she demanded that I find a mechanic. And when I told her that it's never been attempted, she handed me money telling me to call the one in the paper she'd found instead. I thought it was a joke until she personally brought him over, and in two days, this thing was running again in tip-top shape."

Henry nodded and agreed that Roxanne Smith was indeed a demanding woman. The bell dinged as they arrived on the sixth floor just after the man started to complain about her excessive water use.

"Sir, pardon me, but we're here," interrupted Henry.

"So we are," he replied excitedly. As they exited, Henry could smell newly painted plaster on the walls down the hallway that led up to her suite door. The man led the way with Henry closely behind him, striding down until he reached her gilded door that was carved with reliefs of flowers and loose leaves. The man knocked as loudly as he could and at the same time inspected the delicate craftsmanship with his stubby fingers. He had a face that spoke, "How can she do this without me knowing and even less get the time and money to do it?!"

There was a moment of silence before the doors of her suite began to unlock slowly. When she opened those doors, the two gentlemen were thrown off guard at the presence of a lady who had her hair and body wrapped in towels, leaving her shoulders and legs exposed.

"Henry!" said Eris cheerfully. She gave a smile at the boy who looked surprised as always.

"Is this where all my water is going to? To your showers!" retorted the man. Eris then gave a look that said, "and why are you still here?"

"Thank you, Carl, I was pre-occupied at the moment," she told him and then turned to Henry. "Please Henry, come inside and sit yourself down."

"Hold on, I need to talk to you about my money," Carl intruded. Eris showed Henry in and paid no attention to her landlord until she faced him before he tried to come in.

"So you have business with me?" she inquired.

"Yeah, it's about you here," he continued. While an argument started to fester, Henry tried his best to not get involved as he walked through her house to find a seat. The gradual sound of Carl's shouting began to fade in his mind as he tuned them out. While doing so, he saw a magnificent home. Besides the frescos painted in her walls and the art-deco furniture around him, he saw antiquities displayed on her cabinets and the fabulous silk curtains on her balcony windows. What he noticed right away when he first came in was a rug in the center of the room that had many Greco-art depicting sexual acts. The rug ran around the living room and led to the answer that Carl was wondering about. There was a small black granite fountain just before entering her study that sprouted water. He sat on the sofa and turned his gaze back to the door. To his surprise this time, Carl was not as agitated as he was before. In fact, he was smiling quite authentically, and such a display was actually amusing for Henry to see as his moustache wiggled with laughter against Roxanne, who was whispering to him in a softer tone.

"Yes, well I'll see what I can do about that. Sorry to keep you from your meeting like this Miss Smith," Henry heard Carl say.

"No, no, not at all, please do see me again later tomorrow perhaps," she replied.

"I will, I will. Have a splendid day," he finally said. Eris closed the door softly and returned to Henry.

"Sorry, I'll be right with you. Help yourself to some coffee and pastries on the table," she said as she stood before him in that brief moment, still undressed and her skin still wet. Henry looked away blushing and mumbled "not at all," as she hurried away to get dressed.

Henry walked over to get the tray of china and pastries from the kitchen counter and noticed how wonderfully it was done. The smell of coffee was fresh and hot, while the pastries were lavished with cream and chocolates. Each plate and teacup was exquisite and decorated with ornaments from the orient. As he carefully carried them to the living room table, he noticed a tapping sound outside the balcony. After placing the tray, Henry went to the door to see what was making this sound. Looking outside through the glass, he saw nothing. But in that instant, he heard something come in through the open window onto the floor. He turned around and was shocked to see a small hairy dog staring at him. There was a sudden pause as they looked at each other, both puzzled at each other's presence. Henry slowly moved away from the door but when he did so, the dog suddenly barked at him loudly. Henry jumped back with fear as he made for a chair close to him, going behind it positioned like a lion tamer. The dog continued to bark at him.

"Mayhem! There you are! Where have you been?" cried Eris, dressed this time. The dog continued to bark louder.

"Quiet! That's not a pleasant welcome for Mr. Leon."

At the presence of his mistress, Mayhem stopped barking and quickly scampered to her, jumping forward into her arms as she cuddled him.

"You didn't tell me you had a dog," Henry said, recovering from his sudden panic.

"And you didn't tell me you had a fear for canines either," remarked Eris, smiling and carefully sitting herself down on her lounge chair.

"Please take a seat, Henry." At that moment Henry suddenly felt an uncontrollable weight on his legs that was pushing him down on a chair behind him. In that moment, he thought it must be his lightheadedness that had been telling him to sit after this surprising encounter with her dog.

"Forgive me, Madame, I get startled easily. It's why I'm shy," he replied. Eris laughed lightly at this comment while Mayhem excitedly turned his head and panted, responding to her reaction.

"Then we shall certainly make sure that you won't get startled by Francine," joked Eris as she looked into Mayhem's eyes, playfully opening her dog's mouth to reveal his canine teeth. Henry laughed along and took his cup, carefully sipping away his embarrassment. Eris placed Mayhem on the other end of her seat for a moment as she sat up straight, carefully focusing on Henry. Her eyes were so relaxed yet impossible to decipher. Henry was compelled to think that she was inspecting him, and that he could not hide anything from her.

"Now, about you and Franny, as I have promised," she said.

"Yes, how will you ask her to agree to go with me?" inquired Henry immediately. Eris giggled at this question while Henry gave her a look of confusion.

"No silly, I'm not going to ask her, you are the one that will," she replied cheerfully.

"Me? I can't possibly. I...we barely know each other. And she will surely refuse such a strange request."

"Utter nonsense! Get to know her, book boy! I may be an expert when it comes to seeing a love match, but I can't make the girl do everything, you see. It's also not how we girls work."

"I don't understand. How do girls work?" Henry asked, looking at her attentively, waiting for the answer to that universal question. Eris knew she would have a tough job ahead of her as she looked at him with amusement. He was adorable with that serious face of his, and his long ears that made him appear even more childlike. Eris leaned in while Mayhem jumped off the chair and onto the floor, scurrying around wondering what was on the table.

"Perhaps I tell her to go with you, and she may agree. But you see that is not the approach she wants. A girl needs a man that not only can show how special the invitation is by his directness and confidence, but also wants to see his sincerity and appreciation for who she is, face-to-face."

Henry nodded to this statement but was still baffled at how he would ask her to the carnival.

"Me? But I have a feeling she won't agree to it," commented Henry, then sighing after.

"Let me give you a few secrets on women. Such powerful secrets that will guarantee you success. In other words, I'm going to tell you how to do it," replied Eris, guessing what Henry was looking for.

"How?" he asked eagerly.

Eris closed her eyes for a moment and held her head high before speaking: "First, let me ask you this: How far are you willing to go to get her, Hero Boy? An honest reply if you will."

"Very far! I assure you. These past days since meeting her I've been thinking about her nonstop. And even before that, my heart aches because I never had the courage to talk to her," Henry confessed.

"Ah! That is precisely what I wanted to hear from you. I believe you are closer to finding out one of the secrets than you think," she pointed out.

"Really? Should I tell this to her? Is this how I can get her to agree?" said Henry, sitting up straight, his shoulders erect.

"No!" Eris laughed, "but in due time, you could. What I mean is that you are beginning to understand something that women love, 'Self-assurance.' Like I have said once, confidence in your words and especially actions are the sword and shield that make you look gallant." Eris then pointed out something crucial as she gestured with her index finger. "But remember and heed this dire warning: Do not confuse self-assurance with vanity and pride. Believe in yourself but do not brag." At this realization, Henry nodded, understanding what she told him and keeping it to heart.

There was a short pause as Henry remained silent and thoughtful.

"I can't believe it, you seem to understand my problem really well. I would give anything to overcome this," he finally commented. "But…"

"No butts. When you talk to her, do not let your fear of failure and uncertainties dictate your actions. Just do it. And here is what you shall do."

Eris turned away from Henry to find Mayhem. "Mayhem, darling! Bring my supplies to Henry," she called sweetly to him. Soon after, Mayhem reappeared before them with a notebook in his mouth. He dragged it over to Henry and he gently picked it up, smiling with a new feeling of comfort for the dog now. As Henry flipped through the book, he noticed it was all blank. Eris winked at him as she nodded to Mayhem, returning with a pen in his mouth.

"Thank you," Henry said to the dog, taking the pen out from his damp jaws. Her little assistant climbed back up by her side as Eris sat comfortably.

"Alright, let's start with the approach," she began.

Eris began her discussion of the courtship of dating, and her lecture filled Henry with confidence and wisdom throughout the next hour. And in the moments afterward just before Henry left her suite, Eris requested a condition for her services. Happily agreeing to it, a promise was made by Henry pledging to always listen and do everything she said from now on, unquestioned. Henry was to be Madame Roxanne's pupil on love.

-Chapter 6-

The church bells tolled loudly a few blocks down from Henry's music theory classroom. The soothing sound calmed him as his mind tried to clear all the thoughts that were racing through him earlier. As he listened, he imagined the clapper swinging from side to side hitting the shiny bronze bell creating the smooth vibrations that were entrancing the melody. The big hand on the classroom clock had just reached five minutes before 2 pm. Henry had glanced at it, irritated by the fact that his theory professor only referred to his wall clock for the ending of his class. Most people would set their time a few minutes ahead rather than vice-versa. He was in no way concentrating on the lecture overhead on chord progressions. He looked out the window as his mind wondered how he was going to ask Francine to the carnival now, for he had not seen her in the store or the library in the past few days. But on a brighter note, he was not disappointed, for he was dreading it all along and was glad that he did not have to face her and then tell Roxanne about how terribly it went. Instead, Henry tried to relax and daydreamed for the next few minutes about his next concert perhaps being in Europe just before his class ended.

As he waited for the trolley's arrival to the station, Henry looked forward to getting home and practicing his music. Hearing the horn, Henry gathered his stuff and waited in line to get on board. By the time the trolley started off, a sizable number of people from town and the university filled in right after him. Henry had gotten a seat near the window with a pleasant view of the creek, his route he took every day. And it was today that he noticed a large dark bird in the water overhead. With its crescent long neck, he thought it was rather strange to see one completely alone as it swam looking toward the approaching vehicle. Henry adjusted his glasses and focused on the bird as it carefully turned its head to look straight at him. When the vehicle made a stop at a busy station, people moved and budged as they tried to get out. Henry looked away during this moment to see what the attendant was yelling about in the front. As the trolley began to empty, Henry turned once more to see this bird and saw its dark winged figure flying over them suddenly as soon as he searched for it.

A new crowd of passengers entered the trolley slowly as he looked up front. There were a few young boys who brought their rowdiness on board, two elderly ladies that were dressed very colorfully, and three businessmen with briefcases talking amongst themselves. Then, there was also a peculiar man who had boarded last. Henry noticed this man as soon as he made conversation with the conductor on how one pays. He was a round old man who stood like a giant with his hefty coat and tight belly. He had gray grizzly hair and fashioned a full beard. As the old man paid for a validated ticket, Henry looked over him and wondered how much that man reminded him of Santa Claus, as the old man had rosy cheeks after smiling a thanks to the conductor. If it were not for that smile of which Henry had seen, his natural face, which always appeared like a frown, would have terrified everyone on board. When he slowly came forward through the aisle, people naturally moved out of his way, intimidated by his massive stature. Henry could not help stare until the man grinned at him politely. Henry noticed that he was missing a few teeth. The old man then turned to the row behind Henry's and asked a young man sitting there if he could move down. He had a deep stern voice. Instead of moving down, the young man got out of his seat and gave the whole row to the old man. He thanked him politely and sat down just behind Henry. As the vehicle continued to move, Henry lost his attention at the old man and instead took out a textbook from his bag to read.

While reading through the next few stops, Henry could not shake the feeling that the old man behind him was staring at him. Perhaps he was curious to see what he was reading for homework tonight. Henry tried his best to not mind it but repeatedly glanced up from his textbook, disturbed a little. As he looked out the window, he noticed that it had begun drizzling. The rain drops slowly crept through the open window and onto his arm.

"Ah shucks, forgot to bring an umbrella," he mumbled to himself. The trolley then made a turn to the inner-city station, stopping for more passengers. Glancing above his textbook once more to see the sign on the platform clock, he noticed his ride was running behind schedule. It was then that new passengers boarded.

As the vehicle started off after receiving the last passenger, he noticed that among the crowds there was a familiar presence. It did not occur to him what it was until he spotted her. Standing just a few feet away from him in the front was the girl he dreaded to see.

Francine did not notice him at first, for she was facing the opposite side and was looking out the window. There she stood, a small creature standing among the crowd of giants, her expression was so calm and angelic that her face seemed to have a joyous thought even though it was blank. At the sight of her, Henry's heart began to beat fast.

"It can't be! Why now of all places?" he thought. As she stood there in her long magenta coat and purse on her side, her eyes looked around trying to find space or a seat. Henry looked away from her, trying to blend in with the passengers, carefully grasping his book tightly as he pretended to read, whispering to himself the words that had no meaning other than the sounds his lips made. Henry felt a pressure on his heart, the same one he always got from seeing her. This time it worsened, for he knew he had to ask Francine out. As he pretended to busy himself, Henry's heart hoped that Francine had not noticed him and that this trolley would soon come to his stop. It was pathetic, and a part of Henry's mind knew he was being a coward. In time, his conscience wants were battling his heart for control.

"Do it," his mind told him, "go to her and say hi. Stop being a little boy and be the man Madame Roxanne told you to be."

Suddenly, Henry heard the old man behind him snort loudly and cough.

"Confidence, Henry! If you could perform in front of large crowds what makes this any different?" said Henry's mind again.

"That is different. This girl is not like any piece of music I've played before, and not just any person I had known before. I am unworthy of her," replied his weak heart.

"Remember one conversation starter Roxanne gave, just greet her and talk about the books she checked out."

"Yes, of course," his heart remembered. Henry closed his book and placed it back into his bag. "But…it might be silly if I go up to her now. It's crowded and what would people think?"

"Here you are little lady, why don't you take my seat. I'm getting off on the next stop," said one man who sat in front of her. Henry glanced up to see what was happening, his eyes focused.

"Are you sure? Thank you, sir. Have a good day," she replied, smiling. As she sat down, Francine carefully placed her purse onto her lap. She then took another glance toward Henry's direction but was too late to spot Henry as he quickly turned his head toward the window. Leaning on the window shield, Henry turned to glance back at Francine. She was digging through her purse and took out a book, beginning to read as Henry had earlier. Henry searched for the words on the cover: *The Great Gatsby* by F. Scott Fitzgerald. A light bulb went on inside his head. Henry was familiar with Fitzgerald's works and had read some of his short stories before. He knew that he could use this to start a conversation just as Roxanne told him to find physical clues about Francine's likes and dislikes. Henry smiled to himself. He was now determined to move as he gathered his things. However, this proved difficult as the passenger who sat on his right was now looking up at him. Something in this man's eyes told Henry that he did not want to move.

"Maybe I should wait," his heart was telling him. He stopped moving and took another glance back at Francine but was shocked this time, for his glance caught her eyes. Francine noticed him and put down her book for a moment to wave at him. She whispered a "hi" to him as she smiled. Henry waved back, barely containing himself as he smiled, uncontrollably jubilant that she noticed him.

"It's now or never," his mind was saying.

"No, I'll look desperate now if I come over to her," his heart replied.

After a minute of debating with himself, Henry felt a kick on the back of his seat. Henry looked behind him and saw the old man from before, snoring as he moved around on the bench. Henry almost forgot about him after Francine had boarded.

"If only I was as relaxed as Santa Claus here," he thought, "alright, I'll just scoot over and go to her. I'll ask her about the book and that will help me get acquainted with her. But wait, that would be silly to her if I just showed up in front of her asking about what she was reading."

Henry relaxed a bit to ponder it a little more until he felt another kick behind his seat. Henry turned around and saw the old man, relatively unchanged and asleep. It was as if he was telling me to do it, Henry joked to himself. The trolley made a stop at Parker Avenue, a high-end business district. A lot of passengers got off, including Francine as she quickly put her book back. She then waved a quick goodbye to him before exiting. She alighted the steps onto the sidewalk, not even looking back at him along her way. His perfect moment was gone as she started to rush toward cover from the rain that was now beginning to pour. In a moment of hurry, Henry scooted out of his seat and made for the doors but was too late as the door flaps closed on him and the vehicle soon began ascending the sloped avenue. With just two steps away from his exit, Henry saw his girl getting away.

Henry was stricken with guilt as he tried to sit himself in defeat. Stunned by his failure, he pondered whether he would ever see her again. Henry's hands covered his face in shame, dreading to tell Roxanne the sad news. After a minute of feeling sorry for himself, something soon sparked inside him.

"I can't give up, she must not be that far away," he thought, "yes… I got to try. I got to!" And with all the courage he could muster up Henry demanded the driver to stop. His eagerness and impatience unleashed as he grasped the steel bar handle tightly to the front. When the doors had finally opened on a stop, he ran down the hill like a maniac in search for the girl of his dreams through the chilly rain, knowing that she may be blocks away from where he last saw her by now. But he did not care, for he knew his chance of asking her to the carnival was slipping away.

Running through the inner city was harder now than ever. The rain had hindered the traffic and people without umbrellas were scrambling for cover under roofs and tarps. As Henry dashed from each road and intersection, he had to avoid many automobiles that were stuck in line, all the while trying his best to not step in puddles. He would look like an idiot if she saw him covered in mud.

Henry squeezed himself through crowds and kept his focus on the main avenue while he descended back to the stop where she had gotten off. Ten minutes had passed since he last saw her and perhaps there was still a chance to see her around the vicinity, he hoped. But what if she was long gone? What if she already went home? These thoughts went through his head as he entered the square that she alighted from. As he looked around, he noticed that the street lights were on and that there were many people crowded inside a department store patio in front of him. The yellow glow mixed with the mist pulled him there, as he hoped that she might be there. Amongst the dozens of people nested there waiting for the rain to die out, he searched through them hoping to see her, and to his surprise his fatigue from his run was well worth it.

Francine looked up to the hazy dark cloudy sky while rain continued to pour. Seeing these crystal droplets descending from the heavens shimmering with the city lights reflecting on them, inspired a thought of the beauty of existence in her. There she stood, mesmerized by the tranquility and peace the rain brought. Although she was trapped in it alone, she felt a sense of joy as she gently closed her eyes to listen and feel the rain. After a moment, she reopened them and turned her head, expecting to look inside the store with its bright lights that had pulled her there. This time however, it shined upon a boy soaking wet, smiling in front of her.

"Henry?" said Francine, covering her mouth as she gasped.

"Hello…" replied Henry, still catching his breath.

"What are you doing here? Did you miss your stop?" her delicate voice asked him.
Henry's mind was blank as he inhaled and exhaled looking down from her gaze. He did not plan this far and thought that what Francine said was true; he had indeed missed his stop. As his eyes looked directly into hers, he smiled and spoke:

"I wanted to ask you something but couldn't earlier."

"What was it? Has something happened? Are you alright?"

There was a sudden pause as he tried to regain his composure. "I wanted to ask you…if…"

"Yes?" she smiled.

"If you liked that book you were reading on board earlier."

"Ahh, you mean *The Great Gatsby*?" asked Francine, her face so astonished and wide. She took the book out and flipped through it quickly.

Henry nodded as he gently combed his damp hair with his hands. His heart was pounding.

"I suppose I do, though I haven't finished it yet. I just finished chapter five on the trolley. How come? Have you read it?" she said, laughing as she looked at him closely, her eyes bright and gleeful.

"No, I haven't, but I am familiar with Fitzgerald's work. I've read some of his short stories before," Henry replied confidently.

"Really? That's great! This is one of his latest novels. I just began reading him, to be honest." Francine noticed how tall he was as she continued to look over him. He was like a wet dog, though an amusing and lovable one.

"Did you run all the way here just to ask me my opinion of it? My, what a passionate book critic you are," she joked.

Realizing this awkward introduction, he quickly remembered last time's meeting.

"It's not that really, I just wanted to know how you were doing," justified Henry.

"How I was doing? I'm doing fine. Why is that? And…how are you doing?"

"I'm good too, thanks. I asked because I heard…from Jack…that you were sick before and wondered if you were doing better."

"Why yes. Of course, I'm doing very well now. Thank you for your concern," she replied, astonished. Henry noticed that her cheeks were rosy and dimpled.

"I just hope I don't catch it again. That's why I'm here evading the rain. Do you live nearby, Henry?"

"No, I do not. I... I just live a mile further down this avenue." Henry laughed as he noticed how stupid that must have sounded. "Did you just end class?" he asked her.

"No, I don't have class today. I just had some errands to take care of. But I am dreading my project that's due in two weeks. Studies have been very stressful lately. How about you?" Francine asked him.

"Yes, I did, hopefully this Friday's carnival will be a stress reliever," he commented. At that instant Henry suddenly remembered the carnival.

"You're going too? I'm glad. I'll see a familiar face there. Did Miss Roxanne invite you to go with her too?"

"Yes, she did ask me. I was wondering... Do you want to go together?" And at that precise moment, Henry's words came right out directly to Francine whose face looked astonished.

"Of course, I meant let's meet her there together," he reassured.

Without thinking at all, he had said what he wanted to say at last. He exhaled after saying it, the pressure finally released.

"That sounds great," Francine replied warmly. "Shall we meet on the campus entrance then?"

Henry could not believe what he had just heard. With utter joyfulness he smiled greatly and nodded. Francine smiled too and the two agreed on an exact meeting spot and time.

Henry was not a moment too late this time as the rain began to clear.

"Well… I really must be going. It was fortunate to see you again, Henry. See you on Friday." Francine turned around and walked down the steps from the patio. She took one more glance at him and waved goodbye. Henry was awed, admiration and fulfillment was all he felt as he kept on looking until she disappeared amongst the concrete jungle. In a moment of elation, Henry started for home, proud and standing tall, still not minding that he was still wet all over. After walking a block from the square from where he asked Francine, he realized that he still had a great deal of walking to do until he reached home.

"How stupid of me not asking her earlier on the trolley," he thought. But in a moment of gratefulness, he knew he was lucky today. It was as if she waited there for him because fate had determined it. As Henry walked up the road, he noticed from afar that the old man from the trolley ride was walking in his direction. His obvious giant physique did not go unnoticed as he marched, frowning with his magnificent beard. As soon as Henry yielded a side of the sidewalk to him, he walked on and smiled, showing the old man what a wonderful day it had been. Henry nodded to him and the old man replied one in return. As they went their separate ways, Henry walked on, feeling an angel was on his side.

As the old man continued walking down the road, he whispered something to himself: "That a boy. I knew you could do it, Hero Boy."

-Chapter 7-

It was Friday morning when Henry came over to Eris' suite to tell her the good news. When Eris had just awoken an hour before and had breakfast. She yawned as she came out onto her balcony from her bed. There was a parade down below her beginning to form as today was the beginning of Easter. Eris looked on wondering if she could have a little fun before her possible guest arrives. The steam from the teapot boiling called to her back inside to make tea and pancakes. With a movement of her wrists, the batter poured inside one pan as the other one received three eggs levitated from midair, cracking itself one by one and landing on the pan, sizzling as the fire ascended from the stove. As the table set itself slowly, Eris took her tea and the daily paper to her lounge chair. She reclined and cooled her tea, breathing in and out the aroma as she began reading the news.

"How absolutely boring! No fires, robberies, or untimely deaths…just the rich getting richer and politics. Why Eris, you have been slacking on your game lately. Get it together old girl, this city needs your help," she commented.

Eris thought about how the concept of romance took time. She wondered how Eros could be so patient about it when chaos can easily be gratified in a moment's notice.

"As soon as I win this wager, I will be certainly glad to show him a thing or two about indulging in people's misery," she thought out loud.

There was a loud knock on the door when Henry arrived.

"Well, who could that be at an hour like this?" Eris reacted sarcastically. Henry kept on knocking as he called out loud behind the door:

"Madame Roxanne! I have great news."

Eris smiled as she got up to the door. After carefully unlocking it, she gave a look of surprise as she saw Henry smiling at her.

"Henry? What a surprise, what brings you here so early?" she joked.

"My apologies for dropping in so early," remarked Henry sincerely as he entered her suite. "But I have done it. I've asked Francine to the carnival and she agreed!"

Henry relayed to her everything that had happened in detail and could not help but blush at parts he found very embarrassing. And the whole time, Eris sat there listening and smiling, taking small bites from her eggs.

"I need your guidance. Please advise me again. I don't think my confidence is enough for a whole night." Henry had a look of excitement but uneasiness in his appearance after finishing their meal.

"I'm sure that's all you really need," replied Eris, "just be yourself and talk to her with interest and flair."

"Be myself? Are you sure? That has never worked well with me before," said Henry, chuckling. Eris had a look of disproval as she sat up from her chair and started to pace around the living room.

"Why Henry, it seems you are losing that confidence I repeatedly told you about," she scolded. There was a moment of silence as Henry realized his poor self-esteem creeping back at him.

"Sorry, I forgot that it was me that had convinced her to go," Henry said out loud as he contemplated his stress. Eris nodded back at him.

"Exactly, you need to loosen up. As for my help, hmm…" Eris pondered, wondering about the best approach to teach Henry about her next principle as she kept on pacing. As she did this, Henry looked on confused and eager to learn as he took out a notebook from his bag; it was the same one he received from Eris. Eris naturally stepped out of the living room for a moment as she heard commotion from outside. The parade had livened up as she heard the drums and the people shouting. It was then at last that Eris thought of something perfect. She stepped back in when she saw Henry approaching her again. She suddenly paused and asked him, "Say Henry, are you someone who likes surprises and excitement?"

"Yes of course."

"Good."

"But doesn't everybody?"

"Yes. That is precisely what you will be learning this morning."

Henry had a look of confusion as he watched her enter her bedroom without a word.

"What do you mean by that?" he called out to her. When Eris finally stepped out of her room after a minute she had her belongings with her and a red scarf on.

"Are we going somewhere?" he asked.

Eris looked at him with approval and asked him about his book bag. "Are your piano compositions in there?" she pointed.

"Yes, but why does that matter? I thought you had advice for me," he continued. "Tonight's the night that I…"

"In due time, Piano Boy. Gather your things and follow me," Eris interrupted. While Henry followed her outside her door, she quickly locked it with her big key. She then grabbed his arm dragging him down the hallway to the elevator.

"Where are we going? What's going on?" Henry protested. There was urgency in his voice. As Eris called for the elevator, she quickly began a condensed lecture on how girls are interested in someone who can share and provide an experience of some kind. And as well, discover a deep intellectual understanding about each other. She then went into detail about how mystery and playfulness has always given out a scent of attraction.

When the elevator had arrived, Henry tried his best to listen to her speedy explanation as they entered. Henry was unprepared for her metaphors and tried to ask questions, but she lectured on as if she was giving orders to him. Eris finally paused her explanation after closing the elevator doors. She looked at him and gave a face that asked him if he understood what she had just explained.

"Not a problem, you'll get what I mean later. Now let's go, shall we?" Eris pushed the switch for the slow descent but soon felt awkward by the silence she brought to Henry a moment after.

"Let me show you something my mechanic installed for me," she said as she pressed a switch at the bottom near the circuit board. After pressing it, they heard a smooth jazz melody being played in the background. Henry and Eris smiled at such a sound. Henry had no idea that such things were possible but what he had learned was that Madame Roxanne was always making the unbelievable happen.

"It's a new invention. Don't tell Carl about it. I like to hear music as I make my way," Eris joked, "speaking of music, can I see your compositions?"

Henry handed her his large portfolio notebook carefully from his bag and wondered to himself how the subject of Francine had switched to his music. As she held it in her hands, she inspected it tenderly. After they reached the ground floor, Eris stepped out of the elevator with Henry's portfolio in her hands opened flat on her palms. As she glanced at this book that looked like a foreign language, she smiled to herself. She continued inspecting it as she walked toward the entrance. As Henry followed her sudden rush to the door, he felt the sense of urgency rising again.

"Hey, what's going on? Could you please continue what you were telling me earlier? I'm still not ready yet," he called to her. While both Eris and Henry stepped out of the building entrance, confetti sprinkled on their heads as the streets near them were crowded with people celebrating and watching the parade on the streets.

"Is this what you had in mind for fun?" Henry commented, looking overhead. There were giant balloons and automobiles lined up for the occasion. The stands were decorated and people were hurrying in every direction seeing the event. He now had an idea of what she was up to.

"Not exactly," said Eris. She had a smirk on her face as she held the portfolio tightly on her side. "Alright Piano Boy,

I'll tell you the rest of what you should do tonight if you can catch me."

Henry turned to her with confusion. "What?" he cried, and in a second, Eris parted from him, vanishing into the crowds with only her red scarf showing him the way amongst the tightly packed bodies he would have to go through.

Henry ran after her quickly, carefully evading the clumps of people as best as he could while trying to grab her. Eris laughed childishly as she escaped his narrow grasp of his hand.

"Hey! Watch it!" cried a man Henry had bumped into.

"Sorry!" said Henry as he continued tailing the red scarf.

"Watch where you're going young man," cried an old woman as Henry tried to squeeze through a crowd that was watching street performers dancing. As he tailed her, he apologized to those he shoved, and to those whose views his height had blocked; he awkwardly hunched as he passed discreetly.

"Better catch up if you ever want to see your music again," Eris called out from somewhere. Music played in the parade, including a small ensemble of violinists and a cellist from New Orleans. There were drums beating, just as the chase staggered on in this midst of excitement. Everyone in the crowds except for Henry were dazzled with the approaching floats and country servicemen. They came down the road one by one as the sun shined on the giant balloons floating above them. One balloon was a giant bunny that had humongous eyes looking down at them. All that concerned Henry as of now was to catch Roxanne and get back his compositions. Being lost, Henry called out again amidst the gradually louder volume of chatter and music. Naturally, there were some people who turned around as he called out. Their look of curiosity and irritation had embarrassed Henry as they were disturbed by a mere false voice calling out to them in an arbitrary manner. As Henry looked on, searching through the streets of oceans, it appeared that he lost track of her after crossing three blocks. After a good 15 minutes of searching, Henry kept his cool physically, but was troubled as his adrenaline rushed throughout his body. It was impossible to find her now. But as soon as he turned around, thinking of giving up, Eris suddenly appeared before him with his music held out towards him.

"Aww…Don't tell me you've given up already. You almost had me. How will you ever catch Francine?" teased Eris as she grinned. Henry took back his compositions and looked relieved to see her.

"I haven't given up. I believe I just caught you," replied Henry as he gently and briefly touched Eris' shoulder. "Now, please fill me in about tonight's plans." While Henry laughed at his comment, Eris gave a wry glance at him, sympathetic to his efforts.

"Hold your horses, Hero Boy. I will tell you after we finished the parade." She then suddenly grabbed his wrist and told him to follow her. Eris then dragged Henry to the front of the parade as he pleaded helplessly about how he was tired and uninterested in parades.

"Nonsense! Who doesn't love parades? You'll love this one," she called back to him. Eris pushed ahead, almost marching her way through the crowds, all without caring about the unsuspecting people she passed over. Making a zigzag path through the thick crowds, Henry apologized to many of them. As they made their way up front, they stopped and watched

incoming automobiles, latest models filled with affluent
playboys and their girls throwing flowers all around. The sound
of engines and the smell of scented flowers mixed with exhaust
filled the streets with clamor. As they passed along, Henry and
Eris clapped happily with the appeased crowds as they all
looked over the second wave of giant balloons coming into
view overhead. With a glance at the balloons, Eris received an
idea. Seeing that the parade was going down the slope, Eris
wanted to have a little more fun with Henry and perhaps also
fulfill her need to spread chaos again.

"Come on," cried Eris as she took his arm, dragging
him forward in the direction where the giant balloons were
coming from.

"Where are we going now?" Henry cried back. After
three more blocks, they found the area that erected those giant
behemoths.

"With the use of those pumps and human labor they've
managed to make monsters," commented Henry as he admired
a slowly growing wide-eyed rabbit erected by shirtless laborers.
Eris looked around the enclosed lot that they were in and
noticed an open stairway to a building that was positioned
perfectly near the balloons. As Henry watched the balloon
being heaved up, the sight of Roxanne caught his glance as she
slowly walked up the stairway.

"Hey!" Henry said as he followed her up the stairs. "I
don't think we are allowed up here," Henry called again at her
while he blindly ascended higher.

After reaching the peak of the stairway, Eris paused and
calculated to herself the right time, wind direction, and position
of that giant bunny balloon that was now getting bigger as its
eyes descended upon them.

"Please, I think we should get going," commented Henry as he breathed heavily. Eris turned around and looked at him.

"Henry, do as I say, alright? Do as I tell you and never let go until I say so, is that clear?" commanded Eris.

"What?" answered Henry with a look of confusion when Eris suddenly held both his hands tightly and gave a serious look.

"Is she afraid of heights?" Henry thought. Thinking this to be true, he nodded and grasped tightly. Eris smiled at him, with that same look from her scheming eyes.

"It's time to loosen up," Eris said lastly before suddenly leaping over the ledge with Henry.

Henry's eyes were terrified as she insanely and impossibly pushed him, dragging him towards the ground. The feeling of freefall and panic had unleashed inside Henry's heart right before he fell. With everything perfectly executed, however, they soon found themselves landing on top of this giant latex creature. Henry shrieked with immensity while bouncing lightly on the surface of the balloon that was now gradually moving with them on it. Henry continued his frenzy, gasping for life until their bouncing slowly depleted and they landed softly on their chests. Lying there after noticing that they were not dead or in pain, Henry felt the rubber surface and reopened his eyes to see her in front of him. Eris had not let go of him and was assuring him that all was fine.

"Are you insane!" Henry cried out loud, "we could have died!" Henry went about scolding her as she nodded sympathetically and apologized for what she had done. Indeed, his life was almost threatened but his anger was quickly cooled as he found himself feeling a new emotion as he looked around. Aboard the giant bunny and still being alive, he felt a sense of euphoria within him as he looked over the unsuspecting crowd up ahead. Despite being still scared, he felt something that had died within him when he had jumped. He did not let go of Eris' hands and was silent as he looked down. He was more than a hundred feet above ground and did not know what to think. His palms were moist and his heart continued to beat uncontrollably.

"You can let go now," said Eris.

"Absolutely not!" Henry instantly replied. Eris giggled and assured him,

"I've done this before when I was vacationing in Europe. Only, it was on zeppelins. Trust me and do as I do. You'll be safe while you're with me. You promised me you'll always listen to me, remember?"

Henry did not want to let go but the thought that he was grasping her hands too tightly and awkwardly made him feel otherwise. He gradually released his sweaty fingers. When he had released them, Eris then took his hands and placed them on the rubber surface. He could feel the elastic surface and the concentrated air under his palms. This texture was soft. For some reason after holding on to the surface of the bunny's head, Henry felt secured and could feel his body being able to grasp the tension of the balloon as he laid there like a spider on a wall. As he watched the parade below him, he was in awe. He looked back at Eris and realized that he was experiencing a moment like no other. Henry suddenly turned away from her smile and thought to himself. He was having fun—fun he had not had in quite a while.

"Is something wrong?" asked Eris who looked concerned. At first, Eris thought Henry was having a seizure or a breakdown but was surprised to hear laughter on his side of the balloon. She smiled again as he turned back to her gaze, all the while laughing madly, embracing this thrill. Together they laughed wildly as their Easter bunny descended upon the parade, above the crowds that were thinking how awfully jolly that giant bunny was to them, with all the realistic sound effects.

"Never done anything like this before, have you, Piano Boy?" called out Eris as the balloon made its way down the slope. The sound of the crowds and the music were getting heavier as confetti rained from the rooftops overhead.

"Heavens, no. It's like flying on a cloud," replied Henry, "but what was the point of almost killing me? I don't think Francine would appreciate me threatening her life if that's what you were trying to show me," continued Henry.

"Of course not. I wanted you to experience what I call an adventure. If I had simply just told you that a girl likes fun and daring boys I would give you the wrong ideas of being someone you're not," said Eris.

"There is a fine point between adventure and doing crazy and dangerous, not to mention immature, actions," he rebuked. Eris nodded her head in agreement and replied sarcastically, and then seriously.

"Bad me, I'm sorry for being an immature girl, Mr. Leon. I merely wanted you to let loose your rigid self for tonight. But just as I promised, I will now tell you my advice for Francine."

Although her methods were extreme and mad, Henry agreed that he never felt looser than he was now. He listened with enthusiasm.

"When you are together with her, always listen well. Pay attention to the details of what she talks about. Have an opinion and express it when you think appropriate. In any case, be understanding and mindful, and then find irony in it, all to make her laugh. Make her smile. Take the initiative to make her feel alive. Be comfortable with yourself as you are now, girls don't like stiffly men. And as always, be caring and don't be vain," Eris earnestly told him.

Henry listened well to her words and nodded. After more emphasis on her advice, Eris turned away with approval as Henry waved to crowds; she looked below them to see the laborers carrying the ropes that hoisted the balloon as they participated in the parade. As they tugged and went forth along the road with the balloon, the crowds were oblivious that two people were drifting above them.

"Now it's time for an unforeseen accident," Eris thought.

As Henry enjoyed the ride waving, amongst the surprised crowd, Eris pointed to a spot with her nail on the bottom of their balloon and drew a little imaginary circle. She then pointed her index finger to its center, bursting that invisible circle she drawn, creating a tiny ripple on the latex surface throughout. And in that moment, air suddenly escaped from this newly created hole. The sound of this whistling air soon alerted two balloon carriers, noticing it when they saw that their balloon had gotten out of control.

"Hang on tight, Henry, this ride is about to end," said Eris. Henry had a look of concern as Eris forced his head down. It was then that the carriers lost control of the ropes and were then flung around until they had no choice but to let go of the balloon. It accelerated down the intersection with great speed as it gradually deflated. Amongst this disaster, there was widespread panic as crowds dispersed upon the sight of the creature's rapid confusing movements. The balloon descended further down the block as Eris and Henry hung on while it rushed to the ground. The air escaping was all that Henry could hear and feel as he closed his eyes for the approaching impact. Thankfully, this was all he heard as Eris laughed merrily at this spectacle she had created.

When the giant bunny balloon was about to reach its landing, they were already near Park Central. And in this time, Officer Frank was busy writing a ticket for an unsuspecting vehicle on the side of the street that was parked crookedly.

"Another troublemaker! My, what a day I'm having," he said as he shook his head in disproval. Some people ran past him on the road as he took a second glance at the car. When he noticed them in a hurry, he called after them, commanding them to stop. This proved futile as he realized a moment later that they were running away from a giant balloon coming rapidly towards him. Quickly, Officer Frank blew his whistle for its attention but finally ran when he realized it was out of control. He hurried inside the park for cover as it followed him, his uniform squeezing his belly as he sprinted. This large cloud covered the sky as its dark shadow shaded him. Slowly getting closer, he breathed heavily and looked back frantically as it crept just a few feet off his head. Fortunately, Officer Frank dived and splashed into a nearby pond just before the behemoth had a chance to envelop him. Soon after, his whole head and moustache emerged from the surface seeing if it was safe to come out after.

The balloon soon landed softly on the grass as its supply of fuel depleted. This huge white tarp that covered the field finally flattened as the two people on it began to rise slowly from beneath it. Eris was the first to emerge as she stood up slowly, carefully fixing her hair. When she turned to look for Henry, she gazed at a humorous sight. Henry was across from her and had suddenly lost his balance on this slippery tarp when he got up and instinctively tried to prevent himself from falling over, sliding both his feet forward and backward in a dazzling motion. His hands had also wavered wildly in the air, while he desperately balanced himself. Eris grinned surprisingly and clapped joyously at his spontaneous but flawless Charleston.

"Spectacular moves, Henry," she commented as he finally regained his balance.

"Uh, thanks," replied Henry, embarrassed.

Walking out from the exit of the park after a joyous laugh, Eris had a few words of extra advice for Henry while reminding him to dress radiant tonight.

"Try to be the best of yourself and be confident," she concluded while adjusting his tie. When she finished, she walked a few paces backwards away from him.

"Now it's time for me to get ready for my date. See you tonight, Hero Boy."

Henry waved goodbye to her then parted in opposite directions. But as soon they went their separate paths, Henry heard her calling him again and faced her as she approached him.

"I almost forgot. Franny is an artist. She likes to paint. That is her study, I suppose," she told him, "something that may help you figure her out."

"I'll keep that in mind, see you tonight…and thank you, Roxanne," Henry replied confidently.

And with a sudden warmness and appreciation in that last gratitude, Eris suddenly realized why mortals cherished the pursuit of love so much. It was becoming more fun for her as well.

-Chapter 8-

Henry had planned to come early to campus to meet Francine so that he would have more time to talk to her before Roxanne came to pick them up. However, this proved to be difficult as his excitement to finally be alone with her was thwarted by the addition of Francine's friends.

Henry froze with uneasiness as he saw Francine waiting there with three other female acquaintances, laughing and chatting with her as they stood all dressed up in their party dresses. Henry was across from them near the corner, debating whether that young woman on the end who had also dressed flouncy was truly Francine Daye, the girl who had usually dressed quite modestly. Henry took a deep breath and exhaled as he stood behind the wall. He adjusted his bow tie as he glanced again at the ladies who were now putting some last touches to their faces before walking over.

Francine followed along with her friends' conversation with a patient look as she stood there listening to their latest gossips about people coming to the party tonight.

"Well, it's the absolute truth. Men just go nuts after they had a taste of her. Don't ask me why, I just know Julia doesn't settle for just one fella for long. Isn't that right, Margret?" said one girl who was multitasking, putting eyeliner on another girl who had tilted for her as she held her chin, and at the same time, turned her head to seek support from her other friend.

"That's right! And now boys like Peter and Scott are planning to avoid her this evening," replied the other friend as she looked playfully at her feet that were moving swiftly up and down, itching for the dance floor.

"It shouldn't be too hard, they'll have us to focus on," commented the girl having her makeup done. Francine giggled along with them as they felt the excitement for tonight.

"And there, all finished! After tonight, he'll be asking you to the end of the semester ball," one girl beamed.

Approaching them, Henry was smitten to see a few eyes turning up to him as he slowly stopped by Francine's side.

"Hello Francine," he called, diverting his gaze at her as soon as she quickly turned around.

"Henry," she responded with a smile, surprised to see him so soon. "You're here."

Henry felt the spotlight shine on him as her friends continued eyeing him with curiosity. What should he say? How should he act, now that her friends had made a surprising entry to his plans of impressing her tonight? Francine turned to her friends and introduced Henry to them one by one:

"Henry, this is Bernice," she pointed to the one who had her eyeliner done.

"Hey," Bernice replied, uninterested.

She continued, "Ruby."

"A pleasure," replied a tall young woman with dark lipstick on.

"And Margret," concluded Francine as she presented him to a girl who grinned silently.

"Friends of mine," remarked Francine.

"Best friends," corrected Ruby. Francine nodded joyfully as she agreed to her blurt of bluntness.

"A pleasure to meet you all," Henry said softly as he gestured a small bow to them. The girls contained their giggles as they were amused by his stiff rather formal gesture.

"Are you ladies ready for some fun tonight?" he instinctively asked.

The girls continued their playful nature as they responded with enthusiasm.

"We sure are," answered Bernice, who took out a mirror to double check her face.

"I just can't wait to get my hands on the good stuff they said just came from port. The last place I've been to, they were almost dry by the time the party started," uttered Ruby as she bent down a little to glance at the mirror with Bernice.

"So how long have you two known each other?" she continued, gesturing to Francine.

Francine was surprised by her comment as she did not know how to respond right away.

"Wait, you look familiar," commented Margret, pointing to him. "Let me guess, aren't you one of those creepy artist boys who eye her out every class?"

Before Henry could respond with a no, Francine interrupted him:

"Definitely not, Henry is a music major," she blurted.

Suddenly, Henry had a look of surprise as he wondered how she knew that when he knew he had not mentioned it to her before.

"A music major? Are you in George's Jazz band by any chance?" inquired Ruby.

"Unfortunately not, but jazz has certainly influenced my writing and playing," replied Henry, embarrassed.

"But then you must know George Stanford. He and his band have been playing at every club in town. I've had the pleasure to meet him twice," continued Ruby.

Margret clapped her hands as she looked at Henry playfully, suddenly recognizing his face.

"I've got it! You're that romantic pianist I've seen on all those posters near the music rooms."

The girls then cheered with astonishment as they recognized him. Upon hearing this new gained fame, Henry could not help smiling as he remembered that Professor Valentini had pinned the posters at every corner at school.

"A romantic pianist! How divine, a girl can always appreciate a good love song," she teased, leaning on and glancing at Francine who suddenly looked pressured.

"A romantic pianist doesn't mean he writes love songs, Margret," retorted Ruby. "It's a musical style."

Henry nodded his head in approval to Ruby who looked at him with her questionable stare.

"Oh," uttered Margret who reacted bubbly at her mistake.

"Yoo-hoo! Fellas! We're over here," yelled Bernice suddenly, waving to a car that had passed around a corner. When the car finally stopped after, two heads stuck out the window to check behind them.

"Those boys must be blind or something to miss us out in the open like that," commented Ruby.

Bernice yelled again to the two men inside the car, until the car had finally reversed swiftly going toward them. Its engine growled as the sound of friction between the tires and the dirt road rolled.

"Come on, let's go! The doors are opening soon!" yelled a handsome young man inside the automobile as he honked for them to come.

"Hold your horses! We're coming. I swear, boys, no patience at all," Ruby remarked, "thanks again for the update on today's class, Franny. We'll see you two later at the show." Ruby gave Francine a light and quick embrace before boarding the car.

"See yah, Franny!" yelled Margret as she popped out half of her body out the window to wave to her. "You too, romantic pianist!" she yelled again, while winking at Francine.

They drove off quickly as the smoke and dust lifted from the ground. Henry was now finally alone, waiting with Francine among a cloud of dust slowly waning.

There was a moment of silence after Francine's friends left. Henry's heart started to beat fast again as he glanced at Francine, who had also glanced back, slightly smiling. She was a little embarrassed after her friend's remark and was now a little shy at restarting the conversation. After glancing at her, Henry noticed her appearance. Her beauty made it more difficult for him to talk to with her flowing dress, her hair pins and her lightly made-up face; bewitching as they stood alone. Remembering what Roxanne said, he took the initiative and slowly and softly uttered a question. "They're not coming with us?" was all he could respond with.

"Not with us. I've told them I already had plans to go with you and Miss Roxanne," she replied, "sorry, I hope they didn't embarrass you."

"No, no. They seem like friendly people," said Henry. He rocked himself gently and playfully on his feet before sliding his hands into his pockets.

"How do you know them?"

"Let's see, Ruby is a classmate, and Bernice and Margret were past roommates of mine. They so happened to know each other very well. They originally asked me to go to the carnival with them, but I was sick that time to consider it. Speaking of which, how are you doing now? I hope you didn't catch a cold last time we met."

"I'm actually quite well, thank you," said Henry delightedly. There was such sincerity in his heart to hear that she remembered he had been soaked when he himself had forgotten all about his cold shower.

"That's good," she replied. There was another pause between them after they heard a few stray cats in the area meowing. The sun's orange rays splattered like paint on the canvas sky as it began to set above them.

"Have you finished reading *The Great Gatsby*?" Henry asked. He looked at her with a friendly face.

"Why yes, I have. The ending was heartbreaking," replied Francine with a frown.

"So, I'm guessing you didn't like it?"

"No, I enjoyed it very much. I can relate to the characters. Are you reading it now?"

"Why yes, I am, I…" responded Henry before Francine interrupted him.

"Then, I better keep my mouth shut, I don't want to spoil the ending for you," she gasped.

Henry smiled, seeing her serious look of astonishment.

"Not at all, I often like to hear a reader's opinion. That's why I work at a bookstore," he said proudly. "How are you liking that list of books you picked up last time, from Jack?"

"I am enjoying it. There's a lot I still haven't read yet. Walden's always has the latest titles on its shelves. Thanks again for getting them for me," said Francine enthusiastically.

"No problem. You know if you like, we have a great selection on art. I know some great books about contemporary artists you may like to read," said Henry, "you paint right?"

Upon hearing from Henry that he knew she painted, Francine gave a look of wonderment as she remembered she had never mentioned it to him before nor checked out any books related to art at Walden's but had done so only at the school library.

"That would be perfect, thank you," she told him as she nodded questionably. Before she could ask him how he knew, Henry already asked her about something that was puzzling him since her friends had left. "Pardon me, but how did you know I was a music major?"

Francine was surprised by his sudden inquiry.

"Why, the posters all around campus, of course, silly!" she uttered.

"Yes, that's right! It was my professor's idea, to be honest," dismissed Henry who started laughing by how embarrassed he felt for asking. Francine had indeed seen those posters, but honestly, she had seen them only after his concert. In her defense, she was hoping that he would not ask her about whether she went or not. She had enjoyed it and was too embarrassed to acknowledge him about it. She did not want him to know her admiration for his skills on the piano.

"What do you like to paint?" Henry asked.

Francine smiled at this sudden question pointed back at her studies and at his curiosity as she tried to contain her blushing amusement.

"That's a secret," she replied mischievously. A look of confusion on his face, Henry was mystified by her answer. He hoped he did not offend her.

"Hey, how'd you know I was an art major?" she asked boldly.

"Well…" was all Henry could reply with until honking from an automobile interrupted his train of thought. He had a feeling she was getting suspicious of him and the spotlight of being investigated had turned on. The honking continued as Henry was saved by the arrival of Madame Roxanne who had waved to them from the seat of a convertible driven by Jack Walden.

"Hello darlings! Sorry for being a tad late. We had a little problem," Eris expressed. She was well-dressed with her feathered headband and long strands of pearls dangling over her neck adorned with a fluffy boa scarf to boot. Her black sleeveless dress glittered with beads and lace that revealed her crazy dancer side.

"A flat tire after we'd crossed a perfectly paved bridge. Can you believe that?" muttered Mr. Walden.

"Miss Roxanne, I'm so happy to see you again! Glad you could come, Jack," cried Francine as she went up to the car.

"Me too, kitty cat," replied Eris as she looked at her, joyfully bending forward to unlock the door.

"Henry," greeted Mr. Walden as they shook hands. Henry was silent as he followed Francine into the backseat.

Closing the door, the engine roared and they were off. Eris turned around from her seat and gazed at them.

"If we get lost, make a noise, alright, Franny?" said Eris. She nodded and Eris' curious eyes then turned to Henry. "Have you two wait long?" she asked.

"No, not at all," Henry and Francine both responded instantly. They looked at each other with embarrassment at their coincidental response. Eris smiled as she turned back around, her eyes glowed with interest and pleasure as she glanced over the front mirror reflection that showed the two love birds resisting each other's heat.

Throughout the car ride, Henry and Francine remained silent, merely looking at opposite directions as both tried to search for words to say to each other. They both now knew that the other knew more about them than expected.

It was sundown by the time they arrived at Luna Island and not as late as they had thought. The field that was just perpendicular to the boardwalk, which ultimately led to the coast, was lined up with automobiles all around. As they drove in to find parking, rowdiness filled the air as rows of cars burst by, delivering a mass of people plagued by a festive fever of cheers and name calling. It was as if the party had already started.

"Looks like a full house tonight," commented Mr. Walden. Eris nodded and suddenly smiled at the crowds that were waving to them while they passed by.

"Well if it isn't Miss Roxanne Smith!" cried some of the men who were with their dates, joyous to see her familiar face.

"Glad you could make it dear! It's not a party without ya," yelled a couple of ladies in another crowd.

"You seem awfully popular, come here often?" commented Mr. Walden who looked intrigued.

"Why no, I've just been around, and all these people are just regulars from town. They're always excited to see a familiar face. You just wait, Jack, after a few more places you will know everything about them; where they work, and who they're cheating with."

They both chuckled just as Mr. Walden found a space for the car. As Eris led the way with Mr. Walden next to her, Henry followed innocently just behind Francine toward the pier. Luna Island was a famous spot for students and town folk to visit for its beach carnivals and county fairs, and it was where city people came to swim and relax on its beaches. But tonight was going to be different. People were not coming for the usual carnival games. In fact, "carnival" was a secret coined term used by all who were invited to partake in a special event tonight that was hosted by a circus owned by the ringmaster Alfred Zimmerman whose objective was more than just a circus show tonight. The Ferris wheel lay at the end of the boardwalk unmoved, and still unlit as the sun sank beneath the horizon, oozing lower like a drop of honey. Passing it, Henry thought this was strange as he gazed at the various booths that were still unopened. It was indeed odd as he noticed shadowy figures, men who were loitering about along the boardwalk rather than the incoming crowds of young souls and city people who were all walking toward the beachside.

"Why haven't the games opened yet?" puzzled Francine.

"Right, the whole boardwalk looks deserted. Not to mention the lights haven't turned on yet," agreed Henry.

Eris turned around to answer after enjoying herself with Mr. Walden's jokes about his wife.

"Why, tonight there won't be any of your traditional carnival games. Sorry to disappoint you, my dears," she told them.

"No carnival games? Well, that doesn't seem like a carnival," replied Francine.

"Don't worry, Franny, I assure you there will be other types of games and excitement tonight. Types you don't see in jolly good England I'm sure. Isn't that right, Roxanne?" commented Mr. Walden playfully as he gestured to Eris.

Eris nodded and smiled at him before taking Francine by the arm, locking them with hers.

"Well alright, I can't wait then," Francine dismissed as they walked sisterly together. Henry was disappointed as he could relate to Francine. He had looked forward to playing some carnival games with the hope that he could win Francine a prize for this evening. Perhaps that would have impressed her. He looked over at the Ferris wheel one more time and thought that a ride with her would make their night together unforgettable. As they came upon the beachside, their eyes glowed upon the reflection of a large mountainous-shaped tent lit up in front of them just as they arrived. It laid there on the beach like a sand dune gobbling the excited groups entering through its glowing flaps. This "carnival" and Luna Island itself was a disguise, an elaborate hoax for a circus like no other.

It was dim as they entered the arena. The line that they were following led them to a gigantic man that stood like a redwood tree, whose frown and gaze looked upon the guests like a gatekeeper as he directed them to the seating above the stands.

"Oh my, he's enormous!" said some of the ladies in the crowds discreetly. Indeed, they were all awed by his stature and protruding emotionless face as they followed his command. Coming to just a few people ahead from this giant long-legged man who wore a frock coat, Francine was stunned in wonder. Eris joked with her as she suggested to Francine that she should ask him where he got his clothes made. They giggled as Henry and Mr. Walden followed up close to them.

"H-o-w ma-ny?" the tree-man said slowly in a deep baritone voice, his face emotionless and stern.

"Four," Eris replied eagerly. Just after the tree-man pointed to a row, Eris interrupted his gesture.

"Please excuse us, but my friend here wants to ask you a question." Eris then pulled Francine out in front of her and held her on her shoulder as she smiled joyfully at her waiting for her to do her dare. Francine, embarrassed and surprised by Eris' mischievousness, reluctantly cleared her throat and politely asked him.

"I was wondering…Sir…Where do you get your clothes?"

The tree-man looked at her after a pause as if he was trying to understand her question. With his eyes wooden and hardly blinking, he gave a blank impression.

"I'm so sorry, I didn't mean to offend you," Francine finally said just as Eris reached for her hand to escort her up the stands.

"Fro-m the sa-me place you did," replied the tree-man finally, as he slowly grinned a warm smile. Francine then smiled back as she and Eris giggled at his surprising comeback. Mr. Walden and Henry joined in their fun as they followed them up to their seats.

"Why, I didn't know you two shared the same tailor," joked Mr. Walden, "you two ought to exchange outfits."

Francine responded to him with a playful glare as they sat down. Francine sat in the middle between Eris and Mr. Walden. For some reason, Henry had lost his cue given by Madame Roxanne, who gave an eye gesture when he was the one who went in to the row last so that he could sit next to Francine. There was a bit of regret as now an intimate conversation would be impossible. Chatter grew louder as more people filled the rows.

"He seems like a warmhearted humorous gentleman," Francine commented. "I like that about people. I bet he has a charming personality."

"Why, it seems Franny has a little crush on that tree-like man," joked Eris.

"Yeah, it looks like it," agreed Mr. Walden.

"No, I don't. I was just commenting how friendly he was, that's all," she protested, "people are just like books as they say, one can never tell who they are by just the cover alone."

They continued to chuckle until Henry found himself interrupting boldly.

"It takes time to read and digest them like one also. People are a never-ending story."

Franny turned to him and gave him a smile, one that continued their secret unspoken conversation. "That's right," she whispered.

With the popping of the spotlights and the sudden occurrence of fog and silence in the arena, the show had begun. From the darkness came forth an elderly man with whiskers wearing an oriental robe that covered the floor. Though he was partially hooded it was obvious he was bald as his head had patterned lines tattooed all around. He mesmerized the crowd with his mystical presence. As he stood in the middle on top of a platform with the spotlight shined on him, he spoke with a mystic voice:

Ladies and Gentlemen! My esteemed members of commerce and civil society. Tonight, I welcome you to an evening of dazzling wonder as we are about to embark on a journey through a mystical fantasy land of pleasure. But before that, I, Zimmerman the Magnificent, want to warmly welcome you all to my circus of beings that all defy conventional reality. I am speaking of giants, dwarves, wizards, and supermen! Take with you your mind of curiosity as you are soon to be delighted with a fine show tonight. We ask you to follow us to our circus and become part of our strange family.

When the announcer finished those words, the man then burst out from his hood, unleashing white sparks of light from his hands while his whole body glowed bronze. Immediately, sparks shot out through the air from random space as acrobats flew past the jubilant crowds. As they flew by, sparks of fire in the arena suddenly appeared as Zimmerman slowly seemed to teleport away from his platform, disappearing back into the darkness with only his long claw-like nails gesturing to the crowd to come hither. While this was happening, little men entered the arena from the side, lighting the way to Zimmerman with torches. An arched opening in the middle of the arena below came into view. This captivated the audience as these little men dressed in an unusual garb showed them the way down a tunnel of mystery.

"Follow the crowd and see what kind of show they have prepared for tonight," commented Mr. Walden who began following the crowd. Everyone made their way down the stand and followed the tree-man who led them through the two rows made by these little men, who were now breathing out fire for their coronation. Excitement from the crowds made itself clear as they all began chatting away with anticipation. As they followed the mass entering the tunnel, Eris held onto Mr. Walden's arm as she dragged him forward further ahead away from Henry and Francine.

"Follow along kiddies! Last one there is a rotten egg!" she called back to them. There was pushing and shoving as the audience came closer together densely into the tunnel. There was a sudden instance of surprise on their faces as they were left behind together.

"Miss Roxanne! Jack! Wait up," they both called, but it was no use as they continued forward.

"Come on, let's go after them," said Henry as he walked with her closely through the tunnel that was now lit, sparkling ahead as they noticed the appearance of reflections in the hundreds. She followed him and together they went through it. They entered a labyrinth of mirrors. With Francine beside him, and just as mystified as he was, Henry's mood livened up as they both embarked through the hundreds of worlds reflected around them. Mirrors that distorted body sizes created laughs among the onlookers and surprised Henry as he saw a giant elongated girl beside him in the mirror.

"Dear lord, the tree-man must have mistaken you for this tall lady here," remarked Henry as he pointed to the reflection of Francine.

Francine covered her mouth with her hands, containing her giggle at his remark and amused by his playfulness. She returned him a playful glare. Henry's glee faded to a blank, thinking he may have offended her again.

"You two 'tall gentlemen' must have similar interest in tall ladies then," she rebuked as she continued forward by herself, all the while proud of her witty reply.

"Wait! Hold on Francine. I was only kidding," he called after her. He followed her until they stopped at the back of crowds who had come to a standstill. The beat of drums and the rhythmic sounds of horns at the end of the tunnel led the crowd out to an exuberant world. Out they came to a warehouse decorated with greenery, forests like those in Eden, and a steel piped waterfall flowing to a pool, all thanks to a large pumping generator, hand-cranked by two giant musclemen in leotards; And above them, a stage box containing a Jazz band wearing masks from African tribes. With the music playing jubilantly, the party began.

-Chapter 9-

Amazed by what he was seeing, Henry's expectation of Roxanne's idea of a "carnival" was not what he had in mind as he stood there with Francine motionless and bedazzled.

"Yoo-hoo! We're here," called Eris from above the steps. The two had found a table and seats on the walkway above them and were already shooting out bottles of champagne with their neighboring table friends. Francine walked up the steps, hurrying over to the fun as Henry followed along, watching the circus begin its party games. There were roulette tables and all other game tables with dealers who wore painted white faces much like playing cards. The acrobats from earlier swung overhead above Henry as he gazed throughout this whirlwind of fun. In due time, the little men had returned, this time joining in with the crowds.

"Come on, Henry, over here. Come join the fun!" called Eris again as she held out her glass; it was already her second drink. Henry came to her table and found her with four other guests already talking amongst themselves, drinking merely.

"Everyone, this is Henry Leon, the pianist I've been telling you all about," Eris introduced excitedly, touching his shoulder and sitting him down next to Francine just as Mr. Walden poured him a glass.

"Well that's a surprise, you got his stiff bones to come out," remarked a familiar face that Henry immediately recognized. It was his school's orchestra first-chair cellist and friend, Maxwell Stevens. He smiled at Henry with a calm attractive composure as he sat there lounging on his chair with a martini in his hand alongside his beautiful date for tonight, Mary Ann Warren.

"Hey, Max, you're here too? With Mary Ann?" gasped Henry.

"More than half of the music department is here. I've been telling you to go out more. Fancy seeing you here tonight," expressed Maxwell.

"Great, you two already know each other," Eris interrupted as she had her third glass poured by Walden. Henry did not know the other two guests on the other end. Eris introduced them to be acquaintances of hers who were from the Midwest and had come here for the excitement of city life. They were a young married couple who Henry believed struck it rich from the new business. The music combined with laughter and cheers drowned out below them as they all began conversing on the latest news in town and in the world. Henry sat there innocently as he listened patiently and semi-interested. From time to time, he would glance at Francine, who always seemed like she was enjoying the conversations. Henry noticed that she handled her drinks well while he was taking little sips of it to cover his lack of strength. It was to portray that he was masterful in the art of conversation and alcohol consumption.

"Come on, another one before the next dance, Piano Boy," Eris called out loud, "you've only had one glass. We need to get those legs moving with some energy so we can all see those dance moves of yours."

"Yes, I want to see that. Always at the keyboard stretching those finger of yours but now let's see Valentini's pupil play one on the dance floor," agreed Maxwell who patted his friend's shoulder.

"No, I'll make a fool of myself," said Henry as he laughed, embarrassed, waving his hands as he reluctantly received another refill.

In place of a shipment of elephants and lions, crates of rum and whiskey stuffed its cages. And above these cages on display were women clad in nothing but feathers whose seductive dances made them look like harpies suspended from above. But, they were mere decorations as the true hostesses of the party were the mermaids clad in seashells near the pool. Their flirtatious natures raised the mood of the various gentlemen playing cards near them. Despite the Zimmerman Circus not bringing their showcase of animals for entertainment tonight, the audience would serve to become animals themselves. Wildly, they stampeded onto the dance floor when the band began playing "The Charleston."

Immediately, the horns called people to join in, with the beat also propelling Maxwell's girlfriend to embrace his arm with anticipation.

"Maxi, it's started! Let's go join in the fun."

Maxwell nodded his head with eagerness and informed Henry he would see him later when his feet and hands were aching and shriveled like a corpse after dancing with his girl. Naturally, the whole table followed them including Eris as she cheered and was led away with a quite frenetic Jack Walden. Henry however, stayed behind as he did not know how to dance and wanted to wait for Francine who had gone to the restroom. While the attendants, who were on unicycles, continued to empty their trays and clear out his almost windblown table, Henry felt a little lightheaded and tried to regain his composure before Francine returned.

The way the energy that Walden and Eris emanated while they danced with their legs changing weights in quick movements distracted Eris from what was going on above her. She was too busy being led and swung side to side closely by her partner to think of what lay behind the scene. As they danced and chortled for the next minute until the song ended, Eris felt a familiar presence in the crowds scrutinizing her after Mr. Walden caught her in a finishing end. As the dancers cheered, some began dissolving for replacements or refreshments. It was then a handsome man appeared in view, clapping happily for them as they caught their breaths.

"Bravo! If I might say to you sir, you are quite the dancer and you my dear, I had never known you could look so amazingly radiant and skilled all at once," he complimented. Eris smiled immediately, seeing Eros before them.

"Why thank you," replied Mr. Walden who was half drunk and dizzied from the bursts of energy he had unleashed.

"Mr. Romero, so nice to see you here tonight, came to crash the party? Oh Jack, may I present to you Mr. Alfonso Romero. He is a colleague of mine," Eris said as she looked at Eros with a watchful eye.

"A pleasure sir, and I am here not on business," said Eros winking as he held out his hand.

"A colleague, eh? Well, good to meet you," mumbled Walden as they shook hands. The next song began playing and this time it was a slower beat as people began embracing each other for the second dance.

"I'm sorry to ask, but may I have the pleasure of cutting in?"

Eris nodded as she gave a glance of approval at Eros' request.

"Sure, of course," said Mr. Walden as he took a step back and then left them as he made his way to visit the mermaids that were performing tricks nearby. Eros took her hands and led her as they continued. As they danced, Eros began whispering in her ear about how he heard there was a "mad bunny" terrifying the city today.

"I was just having a little fun with Henry and showing him a thing or two about attraction," replied Eris, giggling inside.

"You have an odd way of showing it. Don't tell me you are planning to corrupt him with your so-called 'chaotic pleasures.' The poor boy hadn't even eloped with her yet. And by the way, how is that going along?"

"Very smoothly, thank you, 'Mr. Love.' Henry has made contact with her and they seem to be getting along smoothly. It's just a matter of time until he asks her to go study and who knows…marriage! He is a wonderful student and he'll learn from the very best."

"That's stupendous. My compliments my dear, but what's this? They don't seem to be fond of each other as I can see," said Eros as he smiled gesturing to Henry's table as he rotated their position around for her to face them.

Henry and Francine were alone together at the table. Although sitting next to each other, they were not engaging in conversation as Eris had hoped but were instead staring into opposite spaces as they oddly waited for each other to say something.

"He's just shy. Just you wait, he'll make a move on her and get her to dance any minute now. As you may know, love takes time," assured Eris.

"Yes…but this wait is killing me. Please, may I step in just this once to elevate this situation? I—"

"No! That's not part of the agreement. They are mine to do as I wish so I'll be the one who's going to call action when it's needed. Now put more emotion into your knees or I'll get Jack back here to dance with me," she joked.

Eros laughed.

"Yes, yes. But these jittery moments of young romance are just too scrumptious to resist."

When Francine returned from the restroom, Henry was happy to see her in high spirits as her gaze noticed his lonely awaiting presence.

"Where have they gone?" she asked him timidly and politely.

"On the dance floor. There they are, well, somewhere among the crowds, I believe," answered Henry who smiled as she sat down. Now that Henry was finally alone with her again, there was a bit of pressure for him to act as he was planning to ask her to dance as soon he could find the initiative to. Francine spoke first as she admired and searched widely around the dance floor for them.

"They sure are in high spirits, aren't they? I can't believe how many glasses they drank while I could barely hold my own."

Henry nodded approvingly and could only muster up an agreement.

"How come you're not dancing? You don't like to dance?" Francine looked at him with that look of hers that utterly froze his complexion, and indeed, Francine had also wanted to inquire on whether he refrained from it because it was to wait for her but thought this was too impolite to say. However, this unsaid revelation did not stop her face from showing it.

"No, I just…can't dance," answered Henry as he unknowingly blurted out his secret only to realize how stupid and jeopardizing his response was. But in a moment's haste, he covered it up with a chuckle and then instantly took a glass from the table to sip as he tried to imitate Maxwell's usual gestures of tranquility, something his friend had always incorporated debonairly when he rested from speaking.

"Well, that's absurd. You don't need to know how to dance to dance. In fact, I'm not a skilled or great dancer myself but I still have fun making a fool of myself," Francine proclaimed.

Was that an invitation? Henry's eyes instantly glowed with confidence as he sat up and turned his body and headed toward her. "Then may I have the pleasure to…" he uttered just as his head collapsed forward suddenly onto the table with a sudden dizziness.

"Are you alright?" Francine exclaimed, placing her hands on his shoulder and standing next to him as he tried to regain his composure. Henry's face was red from the last drink he had and was looking at her with a confused, embarrassed look.

"I'm okay. That last one was a strong one," he tried to say.

Francine helped him up as he leaned back.

"I think that's enough for you tonight, mister. I'll go get you some water. Just try to relax and lounge on the chair for a bit, okay?" she said. She then hurried to one of the attendants and received a pitcher of water that she poured for him.

"Here, drink and don't get up until you're all better."

Henry drank it and thanked her continuously. He then tilted his head away from her as he felt so embarrassed and dizzy that he could not talk to her when that moment was brewing. Francine sat back down on her chair next to him and looked in the other direction, covering her reaction. Francine was a little worried, but at the same time was humorously amused by Henry's lightweight drinking and his childlike irresponsibility. There was a minute of silence as she thought about what to say to him to make him feel better.

When Mr. Walden came back upstairs, Francine waved to him.

"How was the dance, Jack?"

Mr. Walden had looked a little distracted while he came up to the table.

"Not bad, a little crowded but we managed to get some applauses," he boasted as he sat down across from them and lit his cigarette.

"Really? Are you two that spectacular? Wait, where's Miss Roxanne?" Francine looked around.

"With another friend of hers dancing together. What's with Henry?"

"I believe I had too much to drink," interrupted Henry who shook himself out of that quick trance he was in between self-pity and light-headedness.

Mister Walden took the glass bottle that was near Henry and inspected it.

"Well you sure did, this has about 40 percent alcohol. Just be glad you didn't drink the whole glass," Mr. Walden chuckled.

It was just then that the warehouse suddenly dimmed, and the spotlight was aimed toward the band. The dancing then stopped. There was a quick introduction of the circus's own special musical duet as they welcomed a young petite woman dressed like an acrobat and the tree-man from earlier on stage. The acrobat-girl began to prepare herself to play the piano. But she was to do it while on top of the grand piano, while bending down her spine completely backward with her hands on the keys. The crowds were awed immensely by her flexibility and wondered how long she could sustain it, let alone play the piano backwards. The tree-man stood behind the microphone. And as soon as the band played the beat, the tree-man unleashed his baritone voice for the first time. There was no hesitation in his song as he sang fluidly, pleasing and exciting the crowd.

"That's incredible. See what I eluded to earlier?" Francine whispered joyfully, admiring the hidden talent of the tree-man. When the time had come, the acrobat-girl joined in with her accompaniment, smoothly playing each key with perfect balance all the while in her position.

"Isn't she remarkable?" Francine told him as she tapped him on the arm lightly.

"Yes," Henry acknowledged, relieved by the show's distraction from his condition. The mood of the song began to change, and the giant and the elastic girl shifted to a slower beat. Soon, the duet welcomed everyone to dance along with their new song.

"Franny, care to dance?" asked Mr. Walden who offered his hand. Henry's eyes were surprised by this intrusion and looked at her reaction.

"Sure, that sounds fun," she answered, surprised yet willing. "Will you be okay here by yourself until we finish?"

Her eyes were genuine as she looked at Henry, seemingly searching for approval.

"Yes, I'll be fine Francine. Go on ahead and show Jack your skills," said Henry winking.

"Okay, no more drinking tonight," she commanded, smiling at him before being led away with Mr. Walden to the dance floor below them. Henry was by himself again. As she danced, Henry saw how radiant she appeared as she turned and moved about so fluidly. It seemed to Henry that she was merely humbling herself about how she could not dance well. She had a lot of energy and as Mr. Walden guided her throughout, every glance at them was hard for him to bear.

"Beautiful. She is a sight to behold, isn't she, old boy? A fairylike princess," said a voice coming from a well-polished gentleman spectating beside the railing that was near Henry's table. Henry had thought this man was talking to him as it interrupted his thoughts but dismissed it at first. He turned around and looked at Henry with a glass in one hand smiling at the boy with his charming figure.

"Yes, I'm talking to you," he confirmed while Henry had a confused look. Eros walked over to him and sat down next to him.

"Sorry to interrupt your admiration for that young lady but I was curious of how concentrated you were at her," said Eros who took the liberty of placing his drink on the table. At the sight of this gentleman, Henry hesitated to speak and felt a sense of guilt.

"May I help you, Mr...?" mumbled Henry as he looked upon this man's friendly doting eyes.

"Ah, Mr. Romero is the name," Eros said, "And may I ask if I can partake here along with you? I assure you I am just a spectator who has lost his own party, unfortunately." Henry agreed and nodded with suspicion of this stranger.

"Thank you," he continued as he took a pitcher with one hand and filled a glass slowly and gracefully. "So, tell me, what brings you here all alone?"

"I'm not alone, all my friends are dancing and I'm just having a drink," Henry replied.

"Yes, I can see that. What a shame you couldn't dance with your girl tonight."

"She's not my girl," Henry protested.

"But you two must be. I can see such eyes of affection coming from both of you. Please pardon my intrusions, but you must act quicker to keep her affections for you." Eros sipped his glass and crossed his legs as he stayed attentive to Henry who was stricken by that comment.

"What are you talking about?" said Henry who was suddenly engaged in what he had to say.

"I mean to say that you should be more direct and sincere. Do not hesitate if you want to ask her to dance."

"I did! I mean, I tried at the least. But I couldn't get over what to do," interrupted Henry, "I just can't dance."

Eros gave a chuckle. "Can't dance? Why, is that all? Not to worry, the night is not over yet. Please permit me to give you a lesson on talking with debutantes like that."

"Alright, but I don't get what you mean. I believe she and I are becoming friends."

"That right? Well that's not entirely good. You must not act too friendly."

"What? That doesn't make sense." Henry sat up as he was now completely recovered from his lightheadedness.

"Trust me, old boy, don't make these conversations you've been having with her so dry with topics like university or books. Indeed, she might be interested in them as much as you are, but it is no fun if there is no play."

"Play?"

"Yes, make it a game of acquiring information and withholding secrets. Tease her a little and find a moment to excite her with sudden childlike endeavors of play. You see, information and dialogue are like a magic show. There's no fun when all the tricks are revealed, don't you agree? To show that you like her, release that tension and anxiety inside you and just be blissful with your intentions."

"What do you mean by that? Be blissful with your intentions?"

Eros leaned closer to him and grinned. "Be direct by being indirect," he said. Henry gave a look of confusion at this answer, and Eros knew that this statement was ambiguous as much as it was contradictory.

"Keep her guessing. Show by some physical action and words of flattery that you 'may' want her."

"But I do like her," Henry protested.

"Yes, I know, but do it in small increments. At least until the time is right for you to confess your love. And when that happens, don't be afraid to express it sincerely and verbally."

Upon hearing the assumption of loving Francine, Henry blushed.

As Eros continued detailing him on the aspects of humorous conversation, Eris came by with her arms crossed and amused by what she was seeing.

"Ahem!" she interrupted just as they ceased their whispers and turned to be startled by her presence and that of Mr. Walden behind them.

"I see you two are already acquainted. This is where you wander off to when I specifically asked you to bring me a glass of water," she said as she glared at Eros. Eros' eyes suddenly lifted as his face turned into a joy of embarrassment.

"My goodness gracious, my apologies. I was talking to this interesting young lad here on some matters and forgotten my whole purpose of parting from you in the first place. Please, pardon my long absence, here we are," said Eros as he reached for the pitcher of water and poured a glass for her. Eris knew that Eros meant to leave her in the first place for more than a glass of water and had been suspicious when he offered this kind gesture after the dance.

"Henry, how are you feeling?" asked Eris as she faced Henry once again, "I heard from Jack that you weren't feeling so good."

"I'm much better, thank you," he said as he stood up, "where is Francine?"

"We've been trying to find her. She told me she needed a break and flew off somewhere," answered Mr. Walden nonchalantly.

"Yes, we were hoping she returned, but it seems she wandered off," said Eris, "why don't you go look for her? I'm sure you would have better luck."

Eris gave a discreet wink at him that only Eros caught.

"Sure, I'll look around," said Henry who looked eager.

"Try the terrace on the third floor, we haven't looked there," informed Eris.

"Alright, well it was great chatting with you, mister," Henry said to Eros.

"A pleasure! Remember, *Direct by being indirect.* Best of luck to you."

After shaking hands, Henry soon disappeared amongst the constant bustling crowd. Soon, Eros, Eris, and Walden began a card game at their table. Eris glared at Eros, all the while he smiled intently at her.

Henry squeezed through a crowd that was conversing near the doors to the terrace. Looking around, Henry noticed that there were only a young couple together drinking and conversing together sweetly at the end of the corner on the railing, and just next to him were also two young gentlemen sitting down chatting on the matter of finance and the market. He walked off by himself, away from the people and found a spot on the terrace to relax. He gazed over at the dark ocean in front of him. Hearing the waves coming onto shore, he saw the luminous glow coming from behind the circus tent over on the beach from where they all had been earlier. Henry surmised that the circus tunnel that led them here was not as far as he thought. This warehouse that hosted their event was just over on the cliff side where the town lighthouse was. Henry noticed a stairway on the corner of the terrace that led below to the beach. Gazing out, he saw the lighted boardwalk over on the so-called "carnival" he thought they were originally going to.

The Ferris wheel slowly moved. There were people over there. Not many, but he could see figures and the silhouettes that moved about through the red and yellow lights. During this moment, he turned his head only slightly, suddenly catching the sight of a ghostly figure in front of him over by the railing, a few steps away from him. And it appeared that she was also admiring the glowing lights. Seeing that it was Francine, Henry noticed she had a serene but melancholic look on her face as she gazed out like a lost child waiting to be found.

"It's beautiful, isn't it?" interrupted Henry after approaching her.
Francine suddenly turned to him and he noticed her inviting gray eyes of hers return.

"Yes, it is," she said surprised by his company, "how are you feeling?"

"Better," Henry replied as he leaned on the railing next to her. "All thanks to you."

She smiled. "You're welcome," she replied.

"You know they've sent me to come find you."

"Oh dear, really? Sorry, I was feeling a little lightheaded from the dance and wanted to get some fresh air. They were busy talking so I didn't want to interrupt them. I didn't know I was that hard to find," Francine remarked.

"Of course not, after all that fun you had dancing brilliantly on the floor I knew for sure I would find you off and about somewhere tranquil," he proudly said, trying to apply what he had learned of her.

She was amused by his sudden compliment.

"Hmm? How are you so sure of that?" She had that same ludic tone she used when she was suspicious of him hours ago. "Were you searching for me from above?"

Her bold inquisition temporarily stunned him, but he soon realized that she was playing with him, testing whether he had feelings for her just as Mr. Romero had mentioned. This time Henry knew just the right response to her witty discourse of play.

"I do believe that searching for you from above the second floor would still be difficult for a girl so special a stature," Henry said, chuckling.

"Always ridiculing my size, Mr. Leon?" she said unamused by his reply. She shifted away from him, walking to the other side.

"Sorry," Henry dismissed as he followed her, "but the first part is true though. I just had a feeling that a book person like me may enjoy a moment of silence. I was honest though, that from above you truly dance beautifully. Do you have such wondrous lights like these in London?" Henry asked, changing the subject. He looked out to the boardwalk hoping for a sign. Francine's composure began to lighten. Feeling his words ripple through her mind, she recollected some bits of her childhood memories on the banks of the River Thames before she answered him.

"Yes, there were lights like these when I was growing up, colorful and mysterious. I used to often look out over my bedside window at night before bed and they were always twinkling out there. The street lamps were always lit dimly though. But nothing as bright as this."

"I agree," said Henry who continued looking outward with her, "I can't imagine seeing them so bright and magically more than ten years ago when I was in grammar school. Technology has really brought us far, hasn't it? Time sure flies."

"Time does indeed," she murmured, "I often look out at those flickering lamps and I dream of what lies over there. They are like stars that have finally come down. But have actually, become even farther than the actual ones in the sky.

Henry smiled at how poetic she sounded. "What do you mean by that?"

"People search for them, looking for answers in their lives wherever they go. Like the stars in the sky they guide them to somewhere, but unlike real stars they never seem to show you the right way. A star is always a dream while a lamp fades out when you're on the other side of your dream. And then…you seem to be chasing them again only to find yourself going after something created by someone else."

"What a metaphor you have created," acknowledged Henry warmly. Francine turned to him and smiled lightly, waiting for his response. After hearing her speak these mystifying words, Henry felt her words resonating in a deep black hole somewhere hidden in that friendly appearance of hers. It had touched him so.

"Francine?" he called to her as he turned to her, suddenly catching her facing him. His eyes widened with surprise upon gazing at her attentiveness.

"Yes?" she answered sweetly.

"You should paint this," he said gesturing to the tent on the beach, the whole boardwalk with the lights and the Ferris wheel. "I would love to see what you have described to me through art."

Honored by this compliment, Francine carefully controlled his surprising request and was instantly reminded of how he knew she was an art student.

"You know, you never finished telling me how you knew I was an art student," she asserted.

"A guess," Henry blurted.

"A guess? Truly? How did you manage to guess that?"

There was a short pause, but Henry had remembered all the times he had seen her before, recalling a vivid memory of her one fine afternoon at the school library. He did not want to tell her the truth of how he found out. Of how he would wait to see where she went for class. Of course, he did not tell her this.

"Your dresses always had a little paint splatted on them," he said instead.

"A keen observation," she encouraged, "well after all, I suppose you should be a keen observer since you are a famous concert pianist."

Henry was flattered by her compliment and shook his head.

"Perhaps someday," he said nonchalantly.

Unconvinced by his peculiar change of tone, Francine's eyes glowed with confidence as she replied, "I'm sure you will be. Maybe someday I can see you perform your latest concerts all over America."

"Not after I see your grand masterpieces displayed at all the museums in Europe," he replied warmly back. "What about you, what do you want to do with your life, Francine?"

Francine looked at him with a glance too embarrassed to reply.

"What's the matter? Too big of a dream?" he said.

"No," she finally replied after a quick deep contemplation. "I just thought it'll be too silly to you if you heard it."

"No, never! If anything, my dreams are silly," Henry countered.

"What do you mean? You've already performed in concerts and you're the star of the music department. I'm sure it is a matter of time until an agent signs you," she said.

"It's not that easy," he replied sadly. "Even if they do, it's not all I want to do. I don't want to just practice, practice, practice, and perform my whole life."

"And?" she asked curiously.

"I want to perform my original work. Just like I did one concert ago," Henry said while looking out to the boardwalk once more. He held out his hand to feel the wind blowing. Francine remembered that concert's conclusion. Although it was brief compared to the whole concert, she was impressed by how charming his music sounded. It had cemented her greatest respect for his talents.

"Do you want to be an artist?" he said, steering the conversation back to his question.

"I do," she said, letting out her breath. "I've come here to paint. That's all I know. Pardon me, I can't give you an answer on what I want to do with my life."

Henry smiled, "I'll take that."

He felt the same about it. Everything in his life now felt like a white canvas. Although he had dreams, he felt as if they were the only people who could see life as bright as the stars, but they were too far away.

"There's no better place than Liberty City. Hey, I hope to see you paint this backdrop for me," he pointed to the lights in the pier. "Perhaps something like *San Giorgio Maggiore*."

"I'm impressed, I see you know Monet," she answered and then pointed her index finger at Henry playfully, "but I'm not going to paint it if you're asking for a commission."

"What? Why not?" Henry said. "Then... How about I play you something on the piano in exchange?"

"Perhaps," she thought amusingly.

"How about I show you the music room next week? Will that change your mind? Maybe you'll show me your art studio after?"

"That would be too easy for you. And why do you want to see my work?" said Francine grinning, "and I don't know about that, I only let close friends inside my studio."

Henry laughed at this comment and leaned closer to her.

"Can I be your close friend then?" he asked.

"I don't know," she said, teasing, "I might consider it if you can play Chopin for me."

"Chopin? Ha, that's my nickname. I'll see to it!"

They both faced each other now. Francine's eyes were fixed on him as he looked at her with his determined and curious face. Henry noticed her gaze and was immediately drawn into her eyes, deeper than ever. And by impulse he began leaning even closer to her. Francine, out of embarrassment, suddenly turned away from his gaze, and instead, took a few steps behind her to sit on a stone bench near the wall. Henry although naturally self-conscious about his impolite stare, followed her to the bench. She continued to smile at him discreetly, letting him know he was welcome to sit next to her. While she started distracting herself by fixing her hairpin and curling her flaxen hair, his heart was pounding with excitement. What should he say to her now? He wondered. He had thought that it was a perfect time to move in and kiss her, but it seemed to him that he had made another mistake. Perhaps, the best course, he thought, was to refrain from it and get to know her some more.

"What are you doing this Sunday?" he asked.

"Some errands and a stop by the school studio," she said looking back at him carefully. "Why?" She had to ask.

"There's an art exhibit on campus and I was wondering if you had plans."

"Yes, that's precisely why I'm going back to the studio, to help my department out with some work."

"That's great! Oh, I mean, I guess I'll be seeing you there too then. I was thinking about learning more on the histories of artworks. And I had planned to visit the department to see the latest exhibits."

Francine's face was content with his answer and she nodded her head.

"You don't have to say anymore silly, I'll be there if you need a tour guide," she answered with glee. And it was then that Henry's heart was instantly pleased to hear her say that.

"And...would you like to join me afterward? For tea or coffee?" he continued.

Francine, surprised by his boldness for more, was silent.

"I mean you don't have to. I was just curious if you wanted to talk afterward," Henry dismissed.

"That would be," Francine had a short pause before speaking, "delightful."

"Delightful." That word filled Henry with happiness. They looked at one another with a shy yet powerful gaze soon after. In a short silence, they looked over the boardwalk and the lights one more time together before they were suddenly interrupted by a loud "bang" of a door.

Unknown to these blossoming companions, the authorities had already entered the scene of the party and were beginning to clear the warehouse from the huge ruckus that presented itself up on this hill. Many were drunk and not bothered by the police until many of the guests started dashing away with what they could carry from the imported liquor carts through the back doors.

"Stop! Hold it right there!" the officers yelled while some of them blew their whistles. It was then that Eris, and Mr. Walden, who was now completely drunk from the glasses he had gambled in his game with the immortals, showed up on the terrace entrance looking for them.

"There you kiddies are, time to blow this joint," said Eris who was holding up Walden along her shoulders.

"Miss Roxanne! Is everything alright? What happened to Jack?" cried Francine.

"He had a little bit too much to drink with all the luck he was having," she replied urgently, "no time to explain, let's go before the coppers come. There! Down those stairs."

Henry hurried to help Eris as he carried Walden on his shoulders, who was half-awake and mumbling a tune while they went down the stairway toward the beach.

"Hey there, honey," Walden commented as he looked up to Henry, dazed. When they had finally gotten to the beach, they continued to walk swiftly, following after Eris who rushed with jitteriness up the sandy hill. Henry noticed flashlights coming from on top of the warehouse and other party guests escaping from the law. He could also see how relaxed Francine was as she stood by his side. When at last they approached the parked cars, Henry tiredly forced Mr. Walden to the backseat, placing him inside.

"Shall I drive?" Henry turned to Eris.

"No, it's fine, Henry. I can take the wheel. Just keep Walden busy in the back," she replied. And in less than five seconds, as soon as Henry sat down in his seat to glimpse one last look at Francine's sudden messy hair and assuring smile once more, the engine went off. Eris drove like the wind, dodging cop car lights racing through the rest of their evening of thrills.

By the time Eris had pulled into the section of the street where Francine's home was, Henry and Walden were recovering from the woozy ride that had befallen them. Everyone took notice as Walden suddenly got off the car without a word to vomit as they made their first stop.

"Opps, sorry for my piloting!" exclaimed Eris, "at least we lost them." She had a look like a child that acted innocent and joyfully sorry.

Francine wore a look of worry as she got out of the car and watched him behind a trashcan, bent forward and gasping for life. Henry also got out of the car and was glancing around the neighborhood as his balance of gravity was slowly regained.

"Quite a ride wasn't it?" Francine commented. Henry nodded and was astonished that she was perfectly well and not feeling nauseated as he had been.

"This is where you live?" he asked, "it's quite dark here."

"I live on the corner at the end of this street. They haven't installed street lights yet," replied Francine.

"Well, this isn't a place for a charming and beautiful girl like you, darling," said Eris as she got out of the car after fixing her hair.

"Henry, why don't you walk her to her house?" Upon hearing that command, the couple was suddenly stricken with embarrassment at this response.

Being polite as always, Francine tried to decline the offer, but Eris insisted as she pulled them together and smiled at their mutually shy smiles.

"Now run along, I'm going to check on Jack. Hopefully, he hasn't fainted on me again," she said as she left them, her heels clacking along the way.

They walked together down the street side by side and silent as they were alone yet again. Henry was pleased to be her escort and so was she. One need not speak to convey the warm words two people have left off in their past conversations. Their footsteps came to a stop by an iron gateway as Francine looked up to her home within—an enclosed courtyard complex that had a flight of stairs in the center of the lawn. It was a lovely home, especially for such a blithe girl.

"Here it is," Francine stopped. "Thank you for escorting me." She had that same irresistible smile that Henry loved, the exact look she gave to him when he first saw her at the bookstore.

"You're welcome," he managed to say, "I hope you had fun tonight."

"Yes, it was most enjoyable, minus the police," she said, trying to unlock the gate while she was still locked onto his face. "And did you have fun?"

"I had fun too. Well," he tried to say, "I hope you have the rest of a pleasant evening."

Henry did not know how to conclude this evening more romantically. He wanted to try to kiss her again but negated this because he thought a safer approach would be more appropriate.

"See you Sunday at the art exhibit," he continued, giving an opened palm. He tried to offer her a handshake but Francine ignored this response. And instead, she suddenly pushed closer to him until she was just a pencil away from him, clasping her arms around his torso without warning. She could hear his heart beat despite her ears barely reaching his chest. It was an embrace Henry had never felt before. He wanted to kiss her now even more. With his arms slowly touching her back, he lowered his head to kiss her. After letting go, Francine's hair flowed away from Henry's contact before he had a chance to even touch her cheek.

Foiled again, Francine pulled away from him and glanced up with a sly smile. He watched her turn away from him quickly, making her way inside the gate and through the grassy lawn. Dumbfounded, he called to her just before she made for the steps.

"Remember to show me your artwork! I want to see your masterpieces someday."
Francine's hair swayed back as she turned to smile back at him.

"Not until you play for me, Mr. Chopin."

"I will!" he called back, waving a goodbye. And then he turned away right before Francine parted one last glance from him. He raced back to the car, barely containing his joy.

-Chapter 10-

On the day of the art exhibition, Henry paced nervously outside the campus library, which lay just across from the other side of the art department lawn where the exhibit had begun. There were crowds of people enjoying the galleries on display this sunny day. Canvases and tables showed student projects and vendors selling anything from student originals to knockoffs of famous paintings. Henry had been intimidated by the thought that many of these male artists or connoisseurs would know more about art and were just as talented enough to impress Francine on a day like this. He stood behind a corner as he pondered how to act on a day alone with her.

"The paintings are just as beautiful as the artist," Henry practiced, thinking about what he could say to her. He cleared his throat as he began to calmly repeat it to himself. He thought it was a good opener, but it needed to be wittier than lavishing.

He smiled and uttered another possible opener:

"Francine, how pleasant to finally see you in your habitat."

"Did you meet her in a zoo, Piano Boy?" interrupted Eris, who was above him and laughing at his lines.

Henry gave a look of puzzlement as he thought about what he had just said.

She climbed off and landed in front of Henry.

"Charming words, but those lines need a bit of work. What happened to my little lecture on being yourself?" she continued.

"I am," he protested, "but I have to make a good entrance. Things have to be smooth and enticing for a polished intro. Sort of like an etude before playing something more serious."

Eris playfully indulged him, "the concert musician knows all about romance, does he? Very impressive. So, what's the plan today?"

Henry pondered as he stood there looking at Roxanne who was gazing at him with an amused smile.

"I'm going to get to know her better and enjoy every moment I can with her, I suppose. At least until she finds my demeanor repulsive." He laughed before clearing his throat.

"Of course, that's impossible because I am playing the notes of her heart with my uttermost feeling," Henry saved himself, making a playful face. His confidence, although hesitant in front of Eris, spilled some boldness in his bones. Eris knew Henry had improved. He was ready to woo Francine, but he just needed a bit of help along the way.

Eris nodded her head. "Not bad, smarty pants. Try not to strike out the third time or you're out."

"Promise me you won't come in to save me?" he joked.

Surprised, Eris' face twitched after hearing this statement.

"Why Henry, I have the uttermost confidence in you to do this alone," Eris replied as she touched him on his shoulder. "Make me proud."

Eris motioned her hands, waving a half-farewell as he left. She smiled, thinking about another arrangement to guarantee his success. As he made his way toward the art on the lawn, Eris followed closely, carefully disguised, of course.

The beginning of Henry's so-called meeting with Francine was not as he pictured it in his mind. He was not to be guided like a distinguished guest through the art gallery as she said she would do. Instead, Francine welcomed Henry like another friend and reintroduced him to Ruby, the other art student from that other night. Throughout their time, Ruby had recounted to him how disappointing the other night's circus party went because of the crazy crowds and the police crashing the party in the end. Contrary to what she felt, she seemed to have had some sort of fun for she was jumping up on tables that night as Henry recalled from memory.

As much as he enjoyed being in the company of Francine's friend, he felt Francine was isolating herself from him a little as she was either chatting with Ruby or concentrating on the art. They barely talked to one another. However, the chance finally opened when they were alone in one gallery inside one of the university rooms when Ruby excused herself to go to the restroom. When most of the crowds shifted to another exhibit, Henry seized the opportunity, making comments and asking about her opinions on some interesting artwork.

"Mr. Leon, you are absolutely dangerous," she teased.

"Dangerous? I'm just being honest," Henry declared as he looked surprised yet pleased by his last comments on the artwork.

"A dangerous counterrevolutionary to the future of art, that is," she continued after his last witty comment that communicated how the paintings were most likely painted by drunk men on grounds of its downright simplicity.

Henry laughed. "Well, if that is how he paints, I'm sure you can paint something better than this."

Francine's eyes focused on Henry's after that statement.

"What are you trying to imply sir? They are my peers, it is the latest rage in art," she continued with a tone that was neither good nor bad. A tone that waited upon your next reply to really determine it.

"Nothing. Just trying to get you to tell me your taste in paintings. Or better yet, why don't you show me yours?" he refuted playfully.

"You are bold, sir," said Francine, awed by his demand.

"Like the bold lines of that painting," Henry gestured.

"But I do believe I have refused that offer," she replied.

"And I do believe you said you'd show me when you and I are friends. Well? Am I compelling enough to be your friend now?" asked Henry.

She made a disgusted but playful face.

"Not compelling at all, Mr. Leon. You are quite conventional, however. For a concert pianist who plays the classics, you fancy yourself in composing quite a rhapsody of jazz, I do believe," she continued, looking up at him face to face.

"How do you know that?" he marveled with a sudden thirst to know.

"I will tell you later, perhaps," she motioned her fingers aside her secret pink lips. "Pardon me, I have to go check on Ruby," Francine interrupted him before excusing herself.

"Do tell me after, Miss Daye," he called out just before she left him in the room alone, her eyes dilated with secrets as she peered out from the wall opening after leaving his side.

"Not compelling at all," she said as she shook her head before exiting. Henry merely smiled back.

After she was gone, Henry began to calm himself as his heart raced with utter delight. It was so much fun to talk to her. He did not know why he could not do this before.

While Henry waited, a shrouded woman followed Francine inside. Entering the restroom, Francine saw Ruby waiting for her on a chair with a look of intrigue. Eris slipped through their presence barely noticed, going into one compartment. She peered out and heard them speak.

"About time!" complained Ruby, "I was done ages ago."

"Sorry, I was talking to Henry," replied Francine as she began to check her face and hair.

"I'm kidding, I was wondering when you were going to excuse yourself," Ruby razzed.

Francine contained her composure as she looked back from the mirror.

"Well Ruby?" Francine asked, "What do you think?"

"A bit of a flat tire," she exclaimed, "too stiff for me. If I wanted that I would go find a choir boy." She then had a sudden revelation of her own comment. "Actually, on second thought, that's quite scandalous and naughty! Yup, I'll take the choir boy any day," she concluded.

"Really? I do find him quite interesting," Francine commented.

"Well, well! What's this? Franny isn't fixing me up with some jazz hound after all, is she?" Ruby remarked.

Francine froze a little as she turned her head in reply.

"I'm just saying," she said. "I just wanted to know what you thought about him."

"Franny dear, there's no need to hide," Ruby replied, "your face always glows pink when you talk about him."

Ruby was right, her face suddenly began to flush a little.

"You've never stopped mentioning him since that concert," Ruby chuckled. "I know you like him and Mama Ruby thinks he's a pleasant, intelligent fella. You have my permission, darling."

"Not at all," Francine dismissed. "I don't like him like that. I just find him to be a compelling subject that's all."

"You are so cute when you play hard to get," Ruby smiled, "we'd better hurry, I think your interesting friend has waited long enough."

"Ruby, I'm trying to be serious," Francine reproached.

"Yes, you are," Ruby equivocated as she placed her arm around her friend, leading them out.

"He's probably gone by now. You scared him away," Francine concluded.

By the time the girls left the restroom, Eris stepped out of the compartment with a grin.

"Yes! The *Ticking Heart* is as good as mine, Eros!" she cheered openly, her hands motioned. "Not that I ever need it after all, as you can see," she said with an evil laugh. It was then the restroom door opened once again, and Eris was quickly startled to see Ruby reentering.

"Must have been that soda pop. It won't be long dear, you go ahead. Let me actually use the john this time," she called out. Eris quickly hid behind the compartment again just as Ruby entered the one next to hers. Eris stood up from the toilet and gazed upon this girl. She thought about how this girl reminded her of herself. There was a gasp as the compartment shook about. Ruby had finished her business but walked out a different woman.

Henry had been seated on a bench listening to a small lecture going on with some students and a leading tour docent when they returned. When Ruby and Francine finally spotted him in another gallery, they walked toward him, unnoticed.

"I told you," Ruby said, "he's in love with you." She winked before pushing Francine to go first.

"Oh hush," Francine protested as she looked back at her.

"Enjoying the history lesson?" Francine whispered to him.

Henry turned his head from the lecture, surprised to see her radiant face again.

"Francine," said Henry, clearing his throat. His mind quickly began to be filled with delight again. Ruby sat next to Francine at the end and smiled back to Henry as they sat down.

"Sorry," Francine continued, "thanks for waiting."

"It's quite alright," he said while his heart began beating a little faster. The proximity of their legs possibly touching could be as much as two inches apart. Their shoulders and her head brushed his side just a little before the lecture on a Van Gogh painting concluded and the tour began moving again. The three of them sat there while Henry felt a stiffness in his body. He wanted to turn and break the silence until Ruby made a comment.

"Darn it, we only had ten seconds of it. Guess I'm glad I ate that bad muffin an hour ago or else I'd have to sit here and listen to more big wigs thinking they know art," she said.

"Ruby! That's rude. Sorry, she's quite ill in the head," Francine atoned.

Henry chuckled as they all stood up to exit the gallery.

"Probably ill from talking to me, I suppose. Pardon the lack of alcohol in my head. Someone has to be sober at a professional event," Henry teased, finally making a joke that impressed Ruby for once.

"Wow, piano hands can bark after all," Ruby replied, "be careful, Franny, he may *bite*," her arm gestured. Francine looked at her with an embarrassed glare before Henry took notice of her changing attitude and expression. Francine, it seemed, was different in some odd way. "Was she hiding something?" he thought.

"So how about a snack? Shall we try that food stand on the corner of the lawn?" Henry then suggested.

"Absolutely," concurred Francine.

"Absolutely not," protested Ruby.

"Why not?" they both commented.

"Henry, you don't want to try that place. It's quite boring and not to mention grotesque," she continued, "I know a coffee shop not far from campus."

"What? But when you and I go there you always praise their coffee," interrupted Francine before Ruby covered her mouth with her hands. "Hush," she whispered.

"Is that right? Lead the way," agreed Henry, who loved the idea of adventuring farther with Francine.

"Of course, but first let me get my rain coat," Ruby replied.

"But it's so sunny today," said Henry.

"Yes, but you never know. I also have some things to get from my locker. I have some, some art supplies to take home after," Ruby hesitated to say.

"I'll come with you," Francine suggested.

"No," Ruby insisted immediately. There was a surprised look from her objection.

"I mean, my dear, I can manage it. Stay here with Henry. It's just upstairs," she motioned.

"You mean downstairs," Francine corrected.

"Oh right. Yes, downstairs is my locker, Henry. I have a beautiful locker by the way. It is spacious and perfect for a girl like myself. Franny, let's see if you remember which number it is," Ruby said.

Francine had a look of confusion before answering. "*2102?*"

"Exactly! Alright I'll see you two outside the building in a jiffy," she announced as she raced way across the hallway while they watched her.

It was quite some time until Henry and Francine realized that Ruby had taken too long. Henry followed Francine to the lockers of the art department classrooms that were downstairs in the basement. As they descended, both noticed that it was quite empty and that the building itself was quite dead.

"That's strange," Francine said, having peered through the hallway, "she's not in any of the classrooms either."

"Looks like she also left her rain coat on top of this chair next to her locker. Look, there's a note here," Henry pointed:

Franny and Music Boy,
I'm afraid I must cancel that luncheon outside the campus. I just remembered I
must meet an old friend for some art business. Have fun you two.
–Ruby

"How strange, we didn't bump into her before she left the building," he commented.

"Right, she couldn't tell us so herself before she had to say goodbye?" Francine pouted.

"Well, Francine," Henry cleared his throat. "Do you still want to have that meal with me?"

Francine broke out of her trance of disappointment over Ruby's sudden disappearance to look up to his question.

"Why of course," she replied bashfully, "shall we go to that grotesque snack stand?"

"Sure, grotesque sounds lovely," he cheered, "it can't be that bad. Let's go."

As they embarked together, Francine had told Henry to grab Ruby's coat just in case they ran into her if she did return.

Unknowingly to the two, Eris had made sure that Ruby, who was incapacitated after she was knocked out, was sent to the university infirmary by the time Eris had finished disguising as her. Her excuse for the nurse was that her friend had eaten something bad and had fainted when she found her. Naturally the nurse accepted this, and Eris was assured that Ruby would be out cold until the end of the day.

After Eris had gotten out of the medical building, she quickly went to find Eros while Henry and Francine were busy having a snack and time alone. She arrived at the university garden entrance after hearing rumors that couples often meet and partake in the act of sacred displays of affections here. And it was just her luck that she heard something only immortals could hear. There was a loud rippling in the wind, followed by a crackle sound that let out a shot of incredible speed in the air. In the distance, Eris saw the signs of love being transformed into an art form, after seeing a young man and woman caressing each other near a fountain that had a little statue of cupid blowing water into the pool. As she looked ahead from where that sound originated, she found a figure on a building rooftop about a block away. By the golden curls of his hair, Eros was spotted.

Eris came up the rooftop steps urgently, forcing open the penthouse doors and seeing Eros viewing the area with his binoculars kneeling behind the ledge, calmly unbothered by her presence behind him.

"Eros! I need a favor from you," she demanded.

"Why hello *Roxanne*," he commented nonchalantly, "a pleasure as well."
She walked over to him and looked over his shoulders as he concentrated.

"Eros, I need you to petition a request to boss man," she continued.

Eros sighed as he lowered his binoculars to his chest. "One moment," he motioned.
Eros took the rifle from his side and aimed down the sight as he prepared for a shot.

"There's a woman," he began, "a staff worker at this school. She has been eyeing this instructor for days now. I have always missed the perfect opportunity for her and this gentleman to be out and about like this on such a coincidental encounter."

His concentration was steady as he pointed the barrel toward the direction of two people near a picnic table in the distance. As Eris could see, the girl was waiting (hoping) for him to approach her as he started walking past her table obliviously.

While waiting for the shot, Eros pulled out the *Ticking Heart*, the pocket watch that could measure the feelings of love. He held it close and waited as it ticked. And when the time was golden, he fired the shot. The loud bang and recoil had caused Eris to jump a little. She quickly gazed out to see the results of his marksmanship. It was perfect. The man was suddenly hit with a new sense of affection for the woman. They then began flirting.

"You make it seem so easy," she commented.

Eros laughed, "you see my dear goddess, such power lies in the beauty of one who loves love."

"You are so pleased with yourself, aren't you?" she scoffed.

"I try," he smiled, "now what's it you come here for? Needing advice to make Henry and Francine fall in love, are we?"

"No," Eris said. "I just need a change of scenery. Tell him to throw more of those thunder bolts of his and make it rain."

"But it's so beautiful today. Must you ruin it with more of your darkness?" he said.

"It's for a worthy cause, trust me," she replied.

"Why must I do this?" he protested, "isn't that what Hermes is there for?"

"He's on vacation."

"Oh, that's right. Then how about you go yourself?"

"You know damn well why I can't go up there anymore to freely show my face," Eris beamed.

Eros giggled, "Well it seems your past works of chaos hasn't paid off its debts yet, has it? I don't know, what's in it for me?"

"What? Are you serious?" said Eris irritated.

"Must our relationship be so one-sided?" Eros pleated dramatically. He then began batting his eyelashes.

Tired of Eros and wasting time, Eris gave in. "Alright," she grunted. She came closer to Eros and whispered to him in the ears what he wanted to know. Upon hearing this delicious ultimatum, his shiny lips began to grin, hearing that he had been invited to see Henry and Francine alone together.

Clouds had begun to form by the time Francine and Henry had finished their meals. They were taking a stroll around campus as they chatted. When they had reached the entrance of the library steps, Henry had a sudden burst of energy in his bones as it carried him to the top of the library's lion statue. Laughing, he lowered his head under the jaws of the beast and made a playful grunting face.

"Now, paint this and let me know what your professors say about expressing too much humor in your works," Henry cried before dropping Ruby's coat that he was carrying.

"Henry!" Francine chuckled.

She continued to laugh as she watched him climb up to do more outrageous performances to ridicule her professors' criticism of her works.

"It's true Francine, perhaps they are right. Perhaps your work needs to be more plain and melancholic like this," said Henry as he laid down beneath the bottom of the lion's tail and played dead.

Francine came up to him, having recovered from laughing uncontrollably. She knelt in front of him behind the statue.

"Then I suppose that would be the day the art community would take you seriously, and you would go back to London renowned and rich," Henry whispered as he slowly opened his eyes and sat up. Francine now felt a change in her face. In an instant, her smile became a frown upon hearing his last comment.

"Wouldn't it?" Henry hesitantly asked.

"I don't know," she finally spoke in solemn manner, "I don't want to be known."

She then stood up and walked to the library's portico. She was serious, as Henry could see.

Henry stood up and went over to her as she began to read the postings that were on the wall.

"Are you feeling alright?" Henry said, touching her shoulder.

"Are you going to compose for the symphony one day?" she turned, back to her bubbly self.

"Compose?" remarked Henry, "Valentini keeps telling me my stuff isn't good enough and that I should just keep with what I know."

"That's not true," she said, "in fact, your performances were always spectacular."

It was then that Henry noticed her comment finally revealed the truth of all her evasions.

Amongst Henry and Francine's conversation, Eris and Eros were near them in the bushes watching. Eris looked patiently as she held Mayhem in her arms. The Scottish terrier panted as he watched alongside Eros who was in front of him looking so gleefully at them.

"Marvelous, marvelous," he commented.

"Don't get too excited lover boy. The best part is yet to come," remarked Eris. "Now you've done what I asked right?"

"Of course. Estimated time of the payload shall commence in 5, 4, 3, 2..."

Henry stood side by side with her as she looked to a darkened sky. It was then that a shower of rain began to pour in the area.

"And I thought this morning was going to be a beautiful day," Francine commented.

"It's okay, we have your dear friend Ruby's raincoat," he said, smiling as he placed it above his head.

"Care to get under my wonderfully crafted umbrella?" he joked.

"It's not enough for the both of us," she declared. It was then that Henry remembered something else that he was holding.

"My bag!" Henry cried as he rushed back to the lion where his book bag lay. He quickly grabbed it and rushed back for cover. After pointlessly wiping away the soaked rainwater, he took out his portfolio that held some of his music sheets. He then sat down to look at them.

"They're not damaged, are they?" said Francine, noticing the dampened papers.

"It's not too bad," he said distressfully. He began laying them out page by page on the dry marble floor until a strong gust of wind blew his stake of papers around them. He grunted a little as he went after them.

"Here, let me help you," she said, breaking the silence. She began to stack the pages and looked at them meticulously.

"Henry, did you compose this?" she commented.

"Yes," he replied, taking his eyes off them for a second to see her gazing at the work around him.

It was then that her eyes saw a familiar gaze in the damp hair of Henry, much like that other day he came back from the trolley specifically to see her again. Only now, it was not the same awkward boy who had humored her with his intention to see her again. He was like Beethoven. A genius with wild hair and a deep passion for what he loved. She blushed as he looked at her for a few seconds.

"Here you are," she said as she handed him the rest of the pages.

"Thank you," he smiled before putting them back in his bag.

The droplets began to diminish a little by the time Mayhem took his role in Eris' plot. He raced toward the rear entrance and up the steps until he found Henry's bag on the side. Remembering what his Mistress had just commanded, *remember darling, don't harm his bag of music, keep it dry*, he quickly snatched the bag before Henry had a second to respond.

"Hey!" he cried. "Come back here."

Henry immediately chased after the dog.

"Wait! Henry!" Francine cried before following him as he ran down the steps. She quickly took Ruby's raincoat and placed it above their heads like a tarp. "Get under here," she said.

He took the coat and smiled as he held it high to cover them. They huddled together and went after the dog through the rain.

The chase was not long as Mayhem had led them just two buildings away from the library. Soon, unexpectedly to them, they had stumbled upon the music department courtyard. Mayhem entered the colonnade entrance of the department and dropped the bag near the stairs to the practice rooms. He quickly disappeared in the rain, which began to pick up again as soon as the two caught up to him.

"There he is," Henry called as he gave the coat to Francine and rushed toward the abandoned bag.

"Strange that a puppy would want your papers. Did you have food in there?" Francine said.

"No, I'm clueless as to why he snatched it too," Henry said as he searched through his bag.

It was then that Francine heard a flute and strings playing upstairs.

"I see our little friend has led us to your department," she smiled.

"Yes, he has. Well, since we're here, why don't I show you what I know about my art?" he looked at her confidently.

"Your art?" she questioned.

"Well, miss, while the whole purpose of visual art is to charm eyes. Music is meant to charm our feelings to think we are in some fantasy," he proclaimed.

"Wow, didn't know you could be poetic too," she teased.

"Shall we go, Miss Daye? Your musical tour is waiting," he said, speaking these words eloquently as he ascended the steps and held out his hand for her to join him.

She looked at him with a bashful look. She hesitated at first, but how could she refuse after seeing how chivalrous he acted? She took his hand and gave in.

"Isn't she a beauty?" Henry declared after entering his practice room, unraveling the covers that lay on the mahogany parlor piano. "Please, make yourself at home," he motioned. Francine entered and sat down on the bench in front of the piano as Henry closed the door shut. He peeked through the window just as a flash of lightning zipped through the sky.

"I hope you know, that playing for you means we are friends now," he said as he came over.

"Who said anything about you playing for me?" Francine countered.

In that moment, Francine began playing the piano in front of Henry's astonishment. With the stroke of her hands, she summoned up the melody and harmony of Chopin's *Nocturne op.9 no 2*. Amazed, he listened and watched her as she concentrated on playing it quite smoothly. He was impressed at her ability and marveled at how beautiful she looked from the reflection of the wood. Entranced until she ended on the last note, Henry clapped loudly, cheering her performance.

"Not bad, huh?" she smiled. "Now if you will, Mr. Concert Pianist." She stood up and gestured.

"Where did you learn that?" he asked.

"I took a few piano lessons when I was learning ballet and the waltz ages ago," Francine said, standing and waiting for him to take his seat.

"You don't say?" Henry smiled and sat down on the bench, "try this."

Immediately, the motion of his hands played a chord and two arpeggios. Then, the rhythm of a waltz began playing. It was a temptation that excited one's legs to dance, and at the same time, mystified the listener of a yearning somewhere throughout its melody.

As Francine listened, she closed her eyes and positioned herself, ready to move with the rhythm. And when the moment came, she joined in to the melody of Satie's *Je Te Veux*. And as she danced, Henry gazed upon how her legs carried her around and across the floor. With her arms stretched and her eyes half-closed, ever so hiding her enigmatic eyes among her graceful steps, Henry was deeply spellbound by her as she was to the music. By the time Henry ended the piece, Francine froze until there was absolutely no wave of sound coming from the piano. When she opened her eyes, she began clapping feverishly for Henry.

"Bravo, Bravo!" she cheered.

Henry, still sitting, gave a bow with the movement of his arms.

"And of course, to our dancer," he gestured to her. She gave a small curtsy and smiled.

"You know, you and I make a good team," he commented.

"We do," she concurred.

It was then that Henry had one more trick to get her to reveal something to him.

"Since you like my playing," Henry continued. "What do you think of my personal compositions?"

"It was," she paused before saying, "charming," she smiled.

"Then I take it you've heard it at my first concert performance?" he beamed.

There was a look of surprise on Francine's gray eyes.

"What? No! I...I've seen comments from reviews," she answered hesitantly.

"Really?" said Henry who was unsatisfied with that answer, "did the reviews find my performance compelling enough then?"

"Well, I suppose they did, didn't they?" Francine said, leaning her elbow on the piano

"Did *you* find me compelling that night?" Henry asked, looking at her eye-to-eye.
She flinched after that question.

"I, I…" she uttered softly before realizing she was being trapped again.

"You are impossible Mr. Leon. Impossible to encourage," she growled as he laughed out loud.

Suddenly, a loud thunder shook the building. The sound instantly provoked Francine to an induced reaction. She covered her ears and looked away. Alarmed, Henry looked at her, seeing how terrified she was from this reaction to the storm outside. He quickly went up to her.

"Francine, it's alright," assured Henry warmly.

Francine looked up after opening her eyes. She saw Henry up close to her, his arms wrapped around her shoulders. It was comforting as he held her. Francine stared enthrallingly at his assuring lips.

"It's just thunder, it's just noise," he whispered, "I'll make it all better."

He let go of her slowly and sat back down on the bench. And with the motion of his hands, he began the soothing sound of Chopin's *Nocturne op.32 no.2 in A flat major.* She listened and with the pressures alleviated, she found herself drawing closer to Henry as he continued playing. He was mesmerizing and so divine. And feeling the music within his interior, he felt the very essence of her soul within the notes he played. He then shut his eyes for a brief minute hoping her fear would subside by the time he finished the piece.

Suddenly, however, he found himself opening them after the touch of cold smooth lips laid upon his. Having leaned forward, Francine had kissed him in the middle of the piece. It was brief, and to her embarrassment she too suddenly opened her eyes to see what she had done.

"I'm sorry." she stumbled as she drew her head back.

It was then that Henry's hands stopped playing.

"That was rude of me," she tried to dismiss it, "please forgive me, I..."

Before she had a chance to excuse herself from him, Henry's eyes looked passionately at her until he stood up, and with his hands, reached for her face, pulling her closer to his mouth. Locked, he made sure he would not let her go this time. His arms grasped and held her tightly as he kissed her some more. While embraced, the taste of their lips could only muster a few more words after they separated for a moment of admiration.

"Am I compelling now?" Henry finally whispered.

She tilted his foggy glasses up to his forehead. And in doing so, Francine looked at him intensely, her flushed lips then replied,

"You've compelled me."

Part 2: Discord

-Chapter 1-

It is the beginning of summer in Liberty City. The goddess of discord had relished in the fact that Henry and Francine were now seeing each other more frequently. Now that Eris' plan had come to fruition of bringing them together, she had been obsessed with seeing them all the more. Watching the new couple crossing Empire State University's campus, something Henry and Francine had been doing every morning since they started seeing each other more, Eris noticed that they were so deeply in conversation that they hardly noticed a person a shoulder away from them. Eris had been stalking them from the start and end of each day in the past few days.

"I don't even have to shed my disguise to catch up to them. I must have shot my love arrow too deeply," Eris joked to herself as she passed them closely one day.

Henry and Francine had finally stopped by the art department courtyard for a more intimate conversation when Eris' focus was interrupted.

"Peeping on them instead of approaching them. How adorable!" a voice called out from behind her. Eris turned and saw no one except a figure of a man outside a café sitting there by himself. The man lowered his newspaper slightly before sipping his coffee. Eros smiled.

"Hey," remarked Eris surprised as she came over to him. "I've been looking for you since you went all bananas over Henry's triumph with Franny. Where have you been? You owe me a certain timepiece."

"Hold on my dear, let me first congratulate you on your successful match-making," he replied earnestly.

"Thank you," she said, trying hard to be humble as much as she could, "now I do believe the god of love, had said otherwise before."

Eros laughed and gestured to her to sit. "What would you like to drink?" he asked her as she sat down and refocused her attention on Henry and Francine.

"A coffee with extra sugar and cream," she said.

"Very well," said Eros as he called an attendant to take the order.

By the time the order came to Eris, she was smitten by disbelief of what Eros had suggested.

"Not fallen in love yet?" she cried, "have you been blind all this time?"

"Only when I want to," he replied nonchalantly.

"It's been a month since you saw them going googly eyes over each other thanks to my little Mayhem's help. How can they possibly not love each other by now? Look at them!" she pointed.

Both Eris and Eros saw that Henry and Francine were looking intimately at each other before her class.

"Calm down, my dear," Eros patted her hands, "if you don't believe me, take a look yourself."

Eros handed Eris the Ticking Heart. As she opened the case, the pulsing of the heart's body felt heavy on her cold hands. Its gears contracted with the veins and muscles as the pointer hands began to move slowly. She turned the watch to the direction of Henry and Francine and felt it beating faster. Its chronometer showed that the stage of "love" was not yet reached.

"What does it say?" Eros asked.

Eris shielded the chained pocket watch onto her breast out of embarrassment of her results.

Eros chuckled. "There is no need to feel discouraged, Discordia. It takes time. The bet is still on. You haven't failed yet," he smiled. "Why not…"

"Shush, they're about to leave," she interrupted.

Francine was about to turn and leave for her class when Henry stopped her.

"I trust that after this final exam you will let me be your first patron, missy?" Henry said as he leaned closer to Francine. Surprised by his silliness after a deep personal discussion on music and art history, she averted her eyes in the other direction, containing her affections.

"I think I spoil you too much," Francine combated as she gazed back with her doll eyes. "Now please, Henry, I do have an important *adult* exam to complete, run along," she joked.

"Very well, let me know the results as soon as you can," he commented before interrupting her final reply by saying "best of luck" and then quickly, he kissed her on the cheek before she had a chance to embrace him one last time. He quickly turned around and began leaving, right before Francine realized what had just happened to her. Francine smiled as he looked back for one last glance; her cheeks were warm, and her class seemed so far away now.

By the time Henry passed the café, he felt a hand locking his arm, he turned and saw Roxanne smiling at him.

"Roxanne! What a surprise," he said before he was rushed over to their table.

"Oh, Piano Boy, I should say the same about you," she said, "smooth moves leaving her wanting for more." She winked as she sat him down, sitting close to him.

"He learned that from me you know," Eros interrupted.

"Hello Mr. Romero, it's been a while," said Henry who noticed him.

"How are you Mr. Leon? Yes, it's been a long while hasn't it?" he replied. "I heard you and Miss Daye are going steady together, are you not?"

"Well, I don't know about together. We have been seeing each other more often, yes," flushed Henry. "I really want to thank both of you for helping me though."

"It's our pleasure, Henry," remarked Eris. "Tell us, how do you feel about her now?"

"Words cannot express it," Henry grinned. "Every time we're together I feel like a new man. She's wonderful. Everything I have ever dreamed of."

"How deliciously sweet," declared Eros, grinning with his brilliant white teeth.

"Yes…romantic," Eris repeated deviously, "your affections for her must show that you must truly Lo-v."

"Are you going to ask her to the ball?" Eros interrupted.

"That's right!" said Henry, astonished, "that's at the end of next month too. I had forgotten all about it."

As Henry began mumbling to himself about the urgency of the matter and that he had no idea how to dance and that many other young men were attracted to her too, Eris began assuring him that Francine would agree to it despite his assumptions that last time's speakeasy experience was a disaster and that it would dissuade her from even going.

"I don't even know how to dance," Henry broke down.

"It's not that hard, Piano Boy, just about following the beat and steps," assured Eris.

"Precisely, not hard at all," concurred Eros. "In fact, Roxanne is quite the dancer as I do recall."

"That's right! Roxanne, you and Jack were pretty good that night," Henry recalled.

"Well, I've had years of practice," she boasted.

"That's perfect, have Roxanne teach you how to dance," suggested Eros.

"What?" she replied, shocked that Eros had volunteered her.

"That's a terrific idea," Henry remarked, "with your skills I'm sure to impress her."

"But you already do, silly," retorted Eris, "plus, I've already let go of your hand on all courting matters since you began escorting her from her home and back."

Eris then began eyeing Eros with a look of resentment. Helping Henry would be no problem, but her ego of letting Eros control the whole situation was degrading for her to accept so willingly.

"Could you please?" Henry begged. "I know I'm awfully asking a lot after all you have done for me to get Francine, but I need you just this one more time, please Roxanne?"

"Oh, help the boy, Madame," Eros said, "after all, perhaps you'll get the *results* you both want."

"Damn you to Hades, Eros," thought Eris as she looked the other way, pondering the situation for a few seconds.

"Alright," she sighed finally.

"You will?" cried Henry, overjoyed.

"Yes, yes Hero Boy. Come to my building, street level at 12 sharp. There's a dance studio nearby."

"Thank you, thank you!" exclaimed Henry as he stood over to hug Eris.

Awkwardly, Henry let go after realizing what he had just done. Eris, flushed with surprise by his embrace, was still stunned after he had let go. He shook Eros' hand and then departed after saying how he was looking forward to tomorrow.

"Best of luck on asking her to the ball, my boy!" Eros called out to him.

"Well, aren't you pleased," said Eris. "I have to forgo more of my chaotic activities just to teach this tough nut to love."

"Come now my dear, this is a chance for you to finish the wager," he replied.

"I've already won, Eros," she protested, "your stupid device just hates me."

Eros chuckled as he waved for the check. "Very good, then why don't you keep it for now until the end results are in? I'm confident that lending it to you would prove your point if you win."

Eris looked at the watch and eyed its radiant machinery. Its organ-like texture felt like she had someone's heart in the palm of her hand.

"You sure?" she doubted, "you might not get it back, you know."

Eros grinned. "I don't see why not. I trust your ego will not let this wager go unfinished. And letting you borrow it may help me do my job if it could. I would like to see that. You are so close after all."

"Dancing? No problem," she declared at this challenge nonchalantly, "just one more lesson before this baby is officially mine."

****

The next day Henry met them at the dance studio near Eris' home. It was a place that Henry had not noticed until he stepped into an old two-story building that had been a small storage depot in its prior life. It was Eros, or the flamboyant Romero who had led him inside and up the stairs into a renovated loft that had a mirrored wall with just one window. It was not a gigantic room for dancing, but it had sufficient room for a small event, yet intimate enough for a few to dance. As they waited for Eris, Eros began entertaining him with his straightforward questions about Francine and Henry's feelings. Too shy to reply to most of them, Henry broke the inquisitions after eyeing the parlor piano that was in the corner.

While Henry was taking playing requests on the piano for Eros, who sat next to him quite closely, the door creaked open with a young flapper interrupting them. Surprised that it was not Eris, this attractive girl wore a leotard and stockings, and eyed Henry after he stopped playing.

"Hiya toots! Why'd you stop playing?" the flapper commented cheerfully.

"Pandora!" Eros called out as he jumped jubilantly out of his seat to hug her.

"Oh dear, so you've returned," Pandora commented dreadfully as she embraced him reluctantly.

"How have you been?" Eros asked as he kissed her plump cheeks.

"Great, ever since the last time you tried to match me up with that crazy merchant from Venice," she said sarcastically. It was then that Eris suddenly appeared from behind her.

"Some things don't ever change, do they," Eris commented.

Henry walked over to them while they were catching up.

"Pandora? Like Pandora's box?" he interrupted.

"Dora's the name, don't wear it out handsome," she introduced herself, "and no box; not about that anymore. Welcome to my studio, not bad for a potential dance school in the making, right?"

"That right? You're trying to become a dance instructor?" Henry replied.

"A pleasure," Pandora commented as she walked over to the wall to stretch. Pandora, although given immortality, was no goddess or special deity. She had opened a box that had unleashed the terrible evils into the world and had now been given a second chance to live in the mortal world as an ageless half-human.

"She's going to be your dance partner," said Eris who then whispered closely to him, "Francine agreed to go with you, yes?"

Surprised, Henry nodded and then appeared lost as Eris took Henry's hand to the dance floor. He knew Francine had not agreed to him yet but telling Roxanne now would ruin everything that he was planning for.

"Dora dear, didn't she tell you that he's learning the waltz today?" commented Eros, referring to Pandora's leotard.

"Oops, sorry," Pandora smiled as if she was in trouble.

"Some music, Mr. Romero," Eris commanded.

As Eros began the meter for a waltz, Eris had Henry face Pandora from the other side, who looked excited and vivacious.

"We will begin with the steps," instructed Eris.

"Don't worry about the hand positions just yet, Henry," she said to Henry after he held his hands up, waiting for Pandora to approach. Pandora giggled as Henry lowered his hands in embarrassment.

After Eris demonstrated the steps, Henry followed the music and mastered the steps quicker than Eris imagined, all in 20 minutes. However, when the time came for the two dancers to come closer, Eris saw a bit of hesitation as Henry's sweat and composure began to show while standing close to this charming looking girl. It was possible that Pandora looked like she could be Francine's age.

"Hold on," said Eris as she prevented his hand from touching Pandora's, "Let me demonstrate."

Eris took the gentleman's role and led Pandora.

"One, two, three," Eris counted, while Henry followed. He gazed at the two radiant flappers as they moved in circles.

Laughter from Pandora soon arose when the speed of the tempo changed according to the song and Eros' style change.

"It's now become jazz," appreciated Henry, remarking humorously and clapping to the beat.

"Okay, okay. Enough," Eris called out to Eros. "We'll save that portion for another lesson."

Out of breath after the music stopped, Eris led Henry back to the center and had placed his arm on Pandora's backside.

Henry's reaction was instant as his left hand barely touched Pandora's back.

"Hold her firmly but not too tight," Eris said. Pandora had a smile that was dangerous. The waltz played again.

"What's the matter? I'm not attractive enough for you?" Pandora commented as they went through the movements.

"Of course not!" Henry blurted nervously, "it's just I'm new to this." His voice went soft.

"Really Mr. Henry? Second base already though, huh?" Pandora commented after looking down casually.

Henry's eyes finally noticed his hand had reached her lower back.

"Sorry," Henry remarked, startled after placing his hand back under her arm.

Pandora giggled as she tried to calm him.

"How are you going to hold Franny if you're all flustered?" commented Eris on the side.

"Yeah," repeated Pandora, "why don't you hold me like you hold your girlfriend?" She winked, making him blush. As they continued, Henry's mood became more stoic and concentrated. His tension was clear by the sweat and rigidness of his steps.

During a short break, Eris went over to speak to Henry privately. He was sitting down leaning next to the wall while he was cleaning his glasses against his shirt.

"I'm sorry about that last comment," she told him.

Henry looked at her and smiled before replying, "It's quite alright. I needed it."

"But you are progressing quite fast, Henry," Eris continued. "By lesson five you'll be a pro."

"Really? Thanks," he replied warmly. "I don't know what it is, but I have this strange anxiety when I am in contact with most women."

Eris was not surprised and merely smiled at this truth.

"All except Francine," he continued, "but there were times her presence sometimes awed me to utter ice."

"Even now?" asked Eris curiously while Henry held up his glasses in the air to inspect them.

"Strangely enough, no. I always feel like someone's nearby telling me to make sure she's happy and enjoying my company. It derives from a compulsive state, pardon if I can't explain it."

"No, go on," she chimed in.

"It's almost like someone is watching me every time I'm with her. And I guess maybe it's all because of you," he said.

"Me?" choked Eris, contemplating how he was able to see past her cover and motives.

"Yeah, from all the lessons you've given me. The encouragements and the push to get out of my comfort zone," he continued.

Eris let out a breath of relief.

"I'm truly thankful. You're the first close female friend I've ever had who I can be myself with. Well, other than Francine of course."

Eris did not know how to reply to this compliment and looked at Henry as he took another wipe of his old weary glasses. He stroked his hair while contemplating this. There was a hint of sincerity in the words that came out of his tender lips. Eris noticed them and felt the gentle nature of her position.

"Let's continue," said Henry, interrupting the short silence.

While getting up, Eris quickly snatched his glasses out from his nose.

"Hey!" provoked Henry.

"Mr. Leon, this will not do. I can't have you adjusting and cleaning your glasses every other movement. We will have to take them off for now," declared Eris.

"But I need to see. I'm almost blind without those," he begged.

Gazing at his face, Eris noticed he looked different. This was the first time Eris was face to face with Henry without his glasses. His eyes were brown, and the elongated face captured a person so different from the first time they met.

"Alright, keep them on for now if you will. I believe Mr. Romero can find you better lenses, can't you sir?" she turned to him.

"Yes," Eros replied while approaching Henry's side, "I believe I can get you a pair you could even insert into your eyes."

"Well, that wouldn't make any sense. A glass inserted to my eye? I might as well get new eyes," laughed Henry after putting his pair back on.

"I'll see what Hephaestus can do," Eros whispered to Eris. She then nodded in reply.

Feeling appreciated, Eris continued to instruct. And this time, she could not take her eyes off his messy hair and long ears that seemed to be strangely familiar. His childlike smiles were even more peculiar while he rejoiced at the silliness of his turns and hand position mistakes. His state of mind was calmer and serene in the presence of Pandora. In fact, even Pandora noticed his change in attitude. It was even charming for Eris, who had caught sight of him gazing at her with a look much more striking than before.

For the next couple of lessons, Eris watched closely, seeing this side of Henry come out again. It was the very one that she remembered from that night he kissed Francine. She then remembered his and Francine's lips touching. It was a strange feeling, but she felt pleasant at the thought of it, recalling it every time she saw him happy.

-Chapter 2-

"No need for the frown, Franny baby, you'll do better next time. They just can't appreciate your style," declared Ruby, as she touched her friend on the shoulder after they exited their classroom.

Francine held her canvas up and looked at the score with disgust.

"A B+!" she said, "can you believe that? There's just no pleasing that, that…" she paused, "…that stubborn bloke!"

Ruby laughed at her comment. "Well, he isn't Mr. Assistant Art Director of Liberty Art Academy for nothing. But it was just an assignment anyways. It wasn't like he was criticizing any of your originals, just your Monet copycat skills."

"Ruby, you're not helping," Francine retorted.

"Sorry, my mouth is at it again," Ruby replied, "it's because I've been dry for weeks. All these exams have been preventing me from going out." She sighed. "Well come on dear, maybe time with your best friends at the new place on Crawford Street will cheer you up. Margret's waiting for us, right?"

Francine nodded after they exited the art department.

"Oh well, who needs him," Francine said, lamenting at the trivialness of her teacher.

"Atta girl," said Ruby, "that man is not worth your time one bit if he can't appreciate a genuine original if it bit him. And hey, speaking of men, heard you had a fella now."

Surprised at the change of the subject, Francine blushed.

"Hey, don't be silent, Franny baby," she continued, "Margret told me things about you and that piano major. What's his name again? Harry?"

"Henry," Francine replied softly.

"Oh, so it is true. Hey, you've been withholding information from me ever since you left me at the infirmary. Now spill."

Francine wore a look of confusion while Ruby interrogated her. She did not know what to say other than the feelings she was trying to contain. Francine did not know what had happened to Ruby that day and was puzzled at how she came to believe that it was her who took her to the infirmary. But then again, that evening was a blur. All she remembered was rain, music, and that crazy and impetuous act that she did, which overwhelmed every beat she took to touch and feel his warm face.

"I don't know what you are saying," she dismissed, "Henry's just been a gentleman lately."

"I don't think so," yelled a voice behind them.

Margret grasped their shoulders after leaning over on Francine from her comment.

"Margret, just in time," remarked Ruby contently.

"Franny's been with that romance pianist, Henry Leon, repeatedly," Margret teased, "I saw them."

"Margret not so loud!" Francine protested.

The two girls giggled uncontrollably at the truth.

"Well, you going to spill or not?" Ruby commanded, "you can't leave your best friends out."

"Yeah!" the other girl concurred.

"I've been seeing him, yes" Francine admitted shyly. Margret and Ruby squealed as they grasped Francine's arm.

"My Franny is all grown up," Ruby cheered.

"Did he ask you to the ball?" Margret asked with her gleam of satisfaction.

"He asked me recently," Francine uttered.

As the two burst out questions of their excitement for Francine's new relationship with Henry, they had obliviously walked through an event near them. This did not occur to them until Francine ignored their request for answers to physical intimacy when she saw a banner and musicians.

"Hey, there's a music competition today," she pointed, interrupting them.

Ruby and Margret's eyes suddenly turned and were bewildered by the sight of musicians practicing around them and the random notes playing all around.

"I wonder if any of them played in the club last night," Margret commented.

"I see a few," Ruby replied, "hey George!" she yelled.

While they were greeting the band members, Francine caught sight of a poster with a piano printed on it. She stepped to the side and looked at it closely. Seeing Henry's name on the roster for an upcoming recital, her face blossomed with glee. Unknowingly to her as she thought about him, she suddenly felt a hand on her shoulder.

"I see your boyfriend is going to play again," Margret teased her.

Francine flushed as she looked at her while Ruby
brought the boys over to crowd around the petite lady.

"Franny," called George, the trumpet player with the
strong jaw line. "You should come by more often with Ruby.
We need your lovely voice."

"Yeah, they could use a new singer. And how about
another pretty face alongside hers, George?" Ruby joked.

Unmoved but flattered by his charm, Francine simply
gestured politely to decline as they continued to flatter her. She
took a small step back as they all began to talk about their
performance in the recent competition. As she did, however,
the door behind her opened and surprised her as she turned
around to see a familiar face.

"Absolutely not! I will not have you skip more practices
until you're trained enough," burst Professor Valentini, the
recently promoted musical director of the department.

"Oh! I'm sorry dear, hey!" he gleamed, noticing a
familiar face.

"Professor!" reacted Francine, "It's been too long."

As soon as Valentini greeted her, a tall young man
followed from behind him and caught sight of her.

"Francine?" Henry interrupted.

Ruby and Margret's face gleamed with delight when
they saw it was Henry. However, this time he seemed different.
Other than a new suit he was wearing and his bare eyes, he was
a lot more pleasant to look at from that last awkward time they
met him.

"Why *hello*," they called out.

As her friends acknowledged and smothered over
Henry, Francine stood silent in front of the music director until
attention was brought upon her silence.

"Are you alright, my dear?" Valentini asked.

"Yes, I am, excuse me," Francine fretted, "how was the competition?"

"It's better you don't bring that up with him," Henry called out, "what brings you here?"

"We were just in the area," Francine confessed.

"Or by some chance, our Franny has led us to the romance pianist again," Margret whispered.

"It's a pleasure to see you again, Franny," said Valentini smiling. He whispered something to Henry and then quickly departed as George's band began greeting and talking to Henry.

"I would love to see you play some jazz at Crazy Cats sometime," George said lastly to Henry after telling him that he heard his performance last time. As the band concluded their praise for Henry, they departed, and Henry was left with the three flappers.

"Francine," Henry called out to her as she waited on the side, interrupting Ruby and Margret's questioning. "Could I walk you home?" he uttered.

The two girls giggled as soon as Francine nodded.

"Off you go, sweetie!" Margret said.

"Be in touch soon," Ruby concluded, winking before they walked off waving to them.

There was a break of silence after they left.

"I'm sorry about these days that I haven't seen you," Henry finally interrupted. "I was busy with this competition and a lot of other stuff."

Francine walked closely to him as she saw the face of the boy who had told her that he had once occupied the same seat on the balcony to see her come every week to the front counter at the library but was too shy to approach her.

"It's no problem. I understand," she assured, "how was the competition?"

"How were the results of your exam?" he said coincidently.

"Oh sorry," they both said again. "You first."

They both chuckled at this and resumed walking while revealing their day.

It was near dusk by the time their conversations ended upon a bridge at Park Central. And it was here that the young man and woman were not the only ones on this bridge together; at least, not below it. Eris stood below in the water listening attentively.

"It's not that bad. I'll try again. There are other competitions and plenty of chances for talent scouts to recruit," Henry said. "Come on Francine, tell me what is it that really bothers you?"

Francine noticed the patient and deep reflective eyes of his, trying to search for what it is that compels her to feel the way she does now. She threw some more bread crumbs to the pond in her silence. The fishes and ducks gathered closer to the shadows coming from up above.

"I'm just," she said. "It's not that I was disappointed about what my professor said. I'm just really overwhelmed with despair that both you and I don't seem to be going anywhere with our dreams. You are so brilliant. I was hoping you would bring me good news."

Henry turned around and suddenly chuckled after hearing this.

"What's so funny?" she inquired. "I mean I'm not expecting you to win for me or anything if that's what you're thinking, Mr. Leon."

"It's not that," Henry said. "I'm just so amazed that you have so much confidence in me and that it will make you sadder if things were not well with me. To be honest, your sadness over a B+ was already amusing."

"That wasn't funny," she insisted, "I do have confidence in you and a B+ is arbitrary. I'm just sad our mentors don't appreciate our hard work."

"I appreciate your work," he blurted, "although I still haven't seen your work, I know you're a brilliant artist."

Henry suddenly came closer to her. She held her gaze on him, staring into that silly face of his.

His arms held her, and she took refuge on his chest. It had only been less than three months since they had officially known each other, yet her arms that ravished his broad heavy shoulders held all the comfort and joy that she felt being with him. Everything about him seemed perfect yet flawed because of something only she felt she knew that would prevent her from being consumed with this god-envied affection.

"It's not just because I was the first fella that played for you during a storm, is it? Or was I one of the better-looking pianists you've kissed?" Henry joked again.

"Oh shush, you may be brilliant, but you are not the best-looking chap around. I'll make sure of that," she remarked playfully. This was not completely true, as Francine remembered how exquisite Henry had looked when he was performing in concert.

"Oh okay," he said disappointedly, failing to grasp her meaning.

As he looked the other way for that instant, she felt the warmness of his cheek as her hand caressed him gently. He looked back, and he soon understood it as she smiled at him.

She gazed at him until they fell deeply into each other, until they could see nothing but the touch of their voices slowly silenced by the vacuum of their lips.

Eris noticed the silence and peaked up from below after splashing some of the birds away from the bridge. Up close, Eris noticed that love like this may seem familiar to her. So familiar, yet strangely cheating in a way she felt in this reality. It is thus she was repulsed by her discomfort. Looking at the Ticking Heart, the needle hand swung closer to "love" but it would not budge any more toward the marker.

Eris reacted harshly to it. "Why isn't it working?" she grunted loudly, "I'm so sick of these love games. Hurry up and get a room or something."

"Did you say something?" Henry whispered.

"What?" Francine replied, "I didn't say anything. Did you hear something?"

At this discovery, Eris silenced herself.

"Never mind," he continued, "Francine, I know it's rude for me to ask you, but have you picked out your gown yet?"

"No. Are you excited about the ball?" she asked.

"Yes, I am," he continued, "I was just thinking about it. I wanted to ask you about it again."

With the mentioning of the ball, Eris suddenly felt a jitter.

"Wait, before you do," Francine interrupted, "I also have something I want to get off my chest."

"What is it?"

"I've decided not to go," she said.

The shock was felt.

"Why? You don't want to go with me?" Henry muttered.

"No! It's not you, Henry. I…" she continued, "I just don't want to go at all."

"Wait, I don't understand," he said as he let go of her to grasp what she meant.

"But you like to dance," he continued, "I assumed you would have wanted to go."

"I do enjoy dancing but I'm not fond of formal events like these," she breathed. "Please understand, I didn't mean to get your hopes up earlier. I'm sorry."

Henry looked at her with a face wondering what an enigma she was.

"It's alright," he finally spoke, "I was just going to follow up and say that I would be playing in the orchestra for that night."

"Oh? Henry that's wonderful!" she smiled, "I may not go but I'll go see your rehearsals before then."

Henry mustered a smile and embraced her again.

In his embrace, Francine could only think about how hard it would be to go. No matter how guilty she felt, she was afraid, afraid of her past coming to haunt and ruin her future with him. One day she would tell Henry about *him*, she thought. One day.

-Chapter 3-

Jazz music played merrily while Pandora and Eros danced together in the studio, just before they were interrupted by the door slamming shut.

Silence filled the room as they gazed upon the exasperated face of Eris.

"Uh oh, are we in trouble or something?" Pandora whispered to Eros.

Eris passed them and threw her things down on the floor as she went to pour herself a glass of contraband scotch from underneath the cabinet.

Eros gave a look of concern as he turned his head back to Pandora.

"Dora dear, take five. I'll check on our goddess," he said.

Eris sat down on the chair as she looked up at the ceiling, controlling her resentment. When Eros approached her, Eris steamed like a kettle.

"She said no! Can you believe that? All the things I've done for him and that boy lied to me about it."

Her volume shocked Eros as he was quickly drawn in to her continued ranting.

"What a little liar," she continued after a minute, "all these lovey emotions, and for what? I'm so sick of it!"

When Eros had heard enough, he tried to calm her down. "Please dear, let's talk about this more clearly. What has Henry lied about and what's this 'no'?"

"Franny never agreed to go with him to the ball," she exclaimed after standing up and gulping down her drink.

"Oh? Is that all?" Eros said with a relief. "Well, that's a shame."

"I'll go with him," interrupted Pandora. "I was his partner from the very start."

"Why that's a great idea!" Eros declared, then suddenly carrying her for the second round in the dance.

"Over my dead immortal body," Eris dismissed, ignoring their antics as she looked out the window in dismay.

"Come on Discordia, I'm sure Dora could be the *other woman*," Eros joked.

"Yeah! I'm sure I'll make her jealous," Pandora let out a sharp giggle before panting from her second twirl.

Considering this proposal by the two of them, Eris thought to herself intensely before seeing Henry in the window coming from a block away.

"He's coming," she said anxiously.

Eris hurried to her stuff and headed for the exit.

"You're going already?" Pandora called out after stopping.

"Whatever are we going to say to the boy?" Eros said.

"Just tell him it's cancelled and that I wasn't feeling so well," she said lastly before scurrying out the door.

By the time Henry arrived, he was met by the prying delights of Eros and Pandora inquiring about what had been going on between him and Francine and her rejection to the dance. Despite only telling them that Francine would not be going and ending with her own personal preference, Henry found it hard to escape their clutches. When Mr. Romero finally had answered Henry's demand that revealed Eris' condition, Henry immediately escaped from Pandora's grasps, whom had been pleading for him to take her instead. After slipping out of the studio, he went straight to Madame Roxanne's home.

Eris was lounging in lethargic pity after kicking her dance shoes on her floor. She looked out from her window and saw two arguments unfolding between a police officer and his superior.

"Chaos, how I miss bringing you everywhere I go," she said to herself. It was then that Mayhem came scurrying to her.

"Here, you can have this, buddy," she said, handing the Ticking Heart to him as he licked her foot for attention. He sniffed it and then took it. As she watched him tinker around with it, she sighed, wondering what had become of her identity in the months of this wager.

"Love is overrated," she said before hearing a knock on the door.

"Roxanne? Hey, it's me," Henry called out.

"Go away," she said before covering herself with a pillow.

Henry knocked again. "Roxanne, please let me in. I just want to check on you. Mr. Romero said you weren't feeling so well."

"I'm fine Piano Boy. Just leave me alone."

"You sure? You sound more agitated than sick."

It was then that Eris removed the pillow from her face and came slowly to the door, sitting herself down on the floor.

"Hello?" Henry said again.

"Why didn't you tell me she hadn't agreed?" she said sternly.

"Oh, how did you find out so quickly?"

"Never mind that. I just wished you would have told me the complete truth before committing to our dance lessons."

Henry chuckled after hearing why she was being this way. Eris did not respond openly to his lack of seriousness.

"So the secret's out," Henry sighed finally. "To be honest, I never thought she would disagree. It came as a shock to me as well. But if you wanted to know why I didn't tell you that in the first place, it was because I was sort of hesitant."

"Hesitant of what?" Eris finally replied.

"Hesitant because you'd stop helping me if you found out she hadn't agreed to go with me."

"I would have still helped you, Henry."

"I mean with the dancing lessons that is. I wanted to learn regardless of whether she would agree to it or not. I wanted to impress her with some moves the next time we go out. Something I should have done that night we went to that carnival. Do you remember?"

"Yes, I do. You failed miserably that night," she said before giggling.

Henry laughed. "I believe I can avenge myself."

"Really? Prove it, Piano Boy."

"I know a place my friend George is playing at tonight. I was going to ask Francine, but after today, I don't think my heart could handle two rejections. So? How about it?"

Eris opened her door and saw Henry's innocent yet silly face looking back.

"Only if you're buying and driving," she said with a smirk.

****

When they arrived at Crazy Cats, a nothing-out-of-the-ordinary French café by day and an alcoholic club by night, Henry and Eris were escorted by the tenant after a long password given at the entrance that unlocked a tightly soundproof hallway. It was not until they crossed the corner that Henry heard music downstairs in the cellar. They were led downstairs and seated at a table near a bunch of young people drinking away as they listened to the jazz band play the greatest hits of their time. Henry took notice of the trumpet player and waved to George Stanford. He replied with an eye gesture just before Henry got the chair for Eris. The whole atmosphere was dark yet vibrant with life. If people were not drinking, they were listening attentively or talking amongst their groups all in the ambiance of the smooth relaxing impromptus.

Eris looked down at her red dress as she sat down, making sure the ruffles did not wrinkle. She smiled at Henry as he came to his seat. This spontaneous event had made her jittered with excitement while she voraciously applied her remaining makeup.

"What would you like to start off with?" Henry said loudly over the music.

"You choose," she said, "I trust you."

"Really? Less than an hour ago you were implying that I was a liar. Should you trust a liar?"

"I trust your judgment of taste. Obviously, not your integrity, however," she chimed.

Henry chuckled at that statement and then went to the bar tender to order. He returned with a bottle of gin.

"He gave you the whole bottle?" remarked Eris.

"Yeah," concurred Henry, "I had thought he expected me to pour my own glasses but insisted I take the whole bottle."

"Compliments from the house," said a voice behind him.

Henry felt an arm on his shoulder and turned to see George Stanford extending his hand.

"Why hello, George," Henry said as he took his hand, "you're on break already?"

"Not quite," George replied with a cool grin, "just dropping by to say hello, and who's this beauty?"

Eris gave a smile as he took her hand to kiss.

"Miss Roxanne Smith," Henry proudly presented, "Roxanne, George Stanford."

"Ah, so you're *the* Roxanne," George remarked. "I've heard about your reputation in these parts."

"Oh?" reacted Henry, surprised.

"Thank you for the house warming gift, Mr. Stanford. Might I commend you on your last performances at *York* and *New Bells*. And what reputation?" denied Eris.

"You watch out, Henry," George teased, "I heard this dame go through glasses of gin fast and could break a man's heart as easily as his wallet."

"But not here. I've never been here," Eris replied humbly.

They all laughed and chatted about the band's performance for a bit until George left them. Eris listened attentively to Henry as he began talking about issues non-

Francine related for once. It was here that Eris felt the nervous tension go away as they chatted about mundane life and silly drunken people in the club. Eris looked about and felt a rebirth of the sensations she received from an act of discord or chaos. It was exciting talking to this mortal. They joked around until the music energized and propelled many of the people to the dance floor.

By this time, Henry, Eris and a few other people had just finished a drinking game.

"Hey, well what do you know," Henry declared, "here's my chance to show you something I've been working on, on my own." He got up from his seat and rushed over to Eris, pulling her hand toward the stage.

"Hero Boy, hold on, I haven't even cleaned up the spill yet," she said, laughing.

She looked at him as he shook his legs and arms with the rhythm. She followed his lead and to her surprise, the boy had gradually dragged to her a whirlwind of new freedom. He was a natural.

As she tried to contain her enjoyment, his dancing and funny faces only made her laugh more until they got closer to each other. By the time the music ended on a transition, Eris had found herself collapsing on his shoulders with ceaseless emotional inertia. Catching her, he held her and escorted her to her seat. Breathing heavily, Henry mustered, "water?"

Eris nodded and tried to relax her strangely tired body while he came back with water. It was then that Eris noticed the band had stopped playing and the chatter of the crowd began to fill the room again.

After drinking some water, Henry wiped his face with his handkerchief and smiled.

"How about that?"

Eris laughed madly and gave him a friendly tap on his hand.

"I'm impressed. Looks like these dance lessons have been paying off, haven't they? I guess your lie amounted to something after all."

"Thank you, then shall we toast to your accomplishment, Madame Matchmaker?" he said, pouring them glasses.

"A toast to your accomplishment," she smiled.

"Cheers," they said before George interrupted and called Henry to his side.

"Henry, how's your improv ability? My pianist bailed on his shift. Would you be willing to fill in?" He had a look of urgency as he looked at Henry.

"Uhmm, sure," Henry said nervously, "I'm not sure if it's good material though."

"He can do it," Eris interrupted. "When he's not a classical pianist, he's also a fantastic jazz composer."

Henry looked at Eris with a surprised yet flattered look.

"Wonderful," George declared, pulling him, "Come with me."

Eris gave Henry a wink as he looked back before following George toward the stage. She watched closely as George instructed Henry on the cues and what the band was after.

After a quick moment, Henry's composure had relaxed and the reflection of his radiant face shone on the keyboard surface. And in 1, 2, 3, his hands began an attention-grabbing solo. Eris looked on as he played, ever so entranced by his skill. By the time the band followed, Eris felt a familiar feeling she had not felt since her first encounter with Henry's first performance. Only this time, it was not unnatural from what she had felt before. She scurried over the table for more alcohol, presuming the feeling needed her to drink more and be drunken with mindless elation. She continued to drink and listen until the end of his performance. When applauses were given, Eris cheered wildly as George shifted the praise from the band to Henry.

After finishing their night at the club, Henry took Eris home. When the apartment door opened, Eris almost fell when she entered her gilded home. Luckily, Henry caught her while she was talking aimlessly about how Henry stole the show.

"Be careful Roxanne," he scolded, "this is the third time, you're not watching where you're going."

"I am!" she dismissed, "well, not earlier. My car door was mainly my car's fault."

Henry gave a look of amusement as he closed the door behind them. Eris went into the bathroom before Henry placed the car keys on her kitchen top and began searching for the light switch.

After switching the lights on, Henry gathered his belongings from the table and was about to get ready to leave when Eris returned.

"What a night wasn't it?" Henry said.

"It sure was, Piano Boy," Eris said. Her face was wet, and her mascara began to fade, prompting Henry to laugh.

"What's so funny?" she said.

He pointed to her cheeks.

"Oops! Silly me," she said nervously and went quickly back to wipe it off.

"It's very late. I better be going," he said as he reappeared in her mirror.

"Wait! Not yet," she demanded.

"Why not?"

"I…" she stuttered, thinking about what she could possibly say to make him stay longer.

"I want to talk to you about Francine," she said quickly.

"Some last-minute secrets about her?" he surmised, amused.

"Sure," she agreed with his answer. "Also, there's something I want to show you."

Eris had soon led Henry to the rooftop of her building after strongly grabbing his hand, dragging him up the steps. While going up, she made excuses for Henry to come up with her because of needing fresh air from all the alcohol she consumed.

"You could just be out on your balcony," he teased.

"It's not the same," Eris beamed, "and here we are."

She opened the penthouse door and they entered the rooftop. Eris pranced to the brick railing and waved to him to come closer.

"Beautiful, isn't it? We can see your whole university from here. Look," she pointed.

Henry went next to her and his eyes were mystified by the lights shining from the light posts from afar on his university across from the harbor that separated the city. Eris kept turning back to him while looking for a reaction from his face as she looked out. She did not want this trip to her roof to be for nothing. But his face was blank and emotionless. It was his silence that made her heart beat faster.

"I've never seen the university this high before," he finally said, "especially not from this distance." His tone was sincere and there was a bit of awe for what he may be feeling. He kept his eyes out in the distance.

"Are you alright, Henry?" Eris inquired.

"Yes," he spoke, "I was just admiring the beauty." He then smiled.

Eris breathed a sigh of relief.

"Francine would really enjoy this view," he continued.

"You miss her, don't you, Piano Boy?" Eris said.

"I miss her immensely," Henry said.

"Too bad she stood you up," Eris defended, "I can't believe she would do…"

"She has reasons," Henry interrupted, "I just don't want to lose her."

It was here that Eris remembered the Ticking Heart that Eros had lent her, and of all times, she was not wearing it tonight.

"Do you love her?" she interjected.

Henry turned to Eris, seeing if she was serious as he looked at her straight in the eye before speaking. Eris felt that Henry might have finally reached that stage while feeling her body grow warmer, despite the cool wind blowing on them.

"I'm not sure. I've never loved before. Unless you count the love for my mother and sister," he remarked jokingly.

Eris's violet eyes wavered in disappointment. Yet, internally to her, it was a bitter-sweet disappointment as she felt the gradual embrace of Henry's hands on her shoulders.

"Burrrr," it's pretty cold up here," Henry said genially, "we should get going."

Eris dismissed it. "Be serious, Piano Boy. Really, do you love her?"

Henry let go of her and stepped back as he sat behind the edge.

"Roxanne, how do you know when you are in love with someone?" he asked.

This had taken Eris by surprise. She looked at him with puzzlement.

"Every day," Henry began, "I think of her, I think about how great she is and how much I care about her. How great of a life we could have. I would play for a famous symphony in Europe, while she would paint every capital we tour through. That would be great, wouldn't it?"

Eris smiled at this answer. Yet, her hesitation and puzzlement only continued.

"If that is love; a vision, a feeling to be the light in her window and for her to be the light in mine, then it is a feeling I have never felt before with anyone," he continued.

"You must love her," Eris declared, "I have never heard these words from you ever, Henry."

Henry looked at her with embarrassment and then laughed.

"I guess maybe I do. But I was never the expressive type to begin with. What about you?"

"Expressive? Me? Of course not," Eris said, taken aback by his question, but stood proudly above him on it.

"Have you ever loved someone that you can barely describe it?" Henry asked.

Eris was puzzled. How would she respond to this, she thought? She suddenly smirked, "Never, men have always loved me more."

"Really?" he said, "I guess you and Francine are fortunate to be in that position. I feel I care about her more than she does for me."

"Love is a nasty game of chance and circumstances," Eris declared. "Always make sure the person you love loves you more."

"You sound like you had some bad experiences with love," Henry said curiously.

It was then that Eris glowed red and grew stiffer in her movements.

"It's not that I've had bad experiences, I just don't like the whole concept of love."

"How can that be?" Henry argued, "you're supposed to be an expert on love. You got me where I am now because of it."

"Well of course I'm an expert on love," Eris continued, "I'm just saying that I don't like it, that's all. You can still be good at your job and not like it, right?"

"I guess that's true," Henry said, "but how do you not like love?"

"I just don't," replied Eris.

"I don't know how any human being would dislike this feeling," he commented.

"Well, I guess I'm not human then," she snarled.

There was a short silence until Eris felt the texture and warmth of wool on her bare shoulders. It was Henry's jacket.

"I don't want you to catch a cold. Time to get back inside," Henry insisted.

She nodded and followed him. When they got back, Eris felt something she had not felt since the day she first met Henry on that back street where he saved her from the mugger.

It was a familiar feeling, but she could not grasp how to approach Henry after he went to the bathroom. She just stood there, at her entry way, wondering how she was at a loss for words.

Henry returned and took the jacket back from the sofa where Eris had placed it.

"Thank you for coming with me tonight," Henry said as he started for the door, "And thanks for showing me your rooftop."

"It was a pleasure," Eris quickly grinned, "I enjoyed myself. Did you?"

"Of course, I did," he said confidently. "I also relish the fact that my dance lessons didn't go to waste."

Eris walked him over to the elevator immediately after.

"Will you see Francine anytime soon?"
Henry opened the elevator door before turning toward her, "Absolutely. I'm not giving up on her," he assured.

Eris nodded in agreement and said goodbye. All the while Henry did not return one. Instead, Henry opened his arms and hugged her warmly. It caught her by surprise. She stood there stiff and oblivious to return his embrace. Yet, her arms lightly touched his body, feeling his warmth.

"Good night, Roxanne," Henry whispered lastly before he went down.

Roxanne faintly smiled and waited until the light of the elevator shined no more. When Eris returned to her room, she heard a muffed sound on the ground. It was a vibration. She checked the floor and found the Ticking Heart. Opening the hatch, a bell sound played louder, and the blood flew through its tube faster than ever before. The word, "love" began to appear on the center of the dial. The lips of the goddess smiled in victory. Roxanne Smith had finally achieved her "love" at last.

-Chapter 4-

Eris began slipping out of her garments as her tub filled with hot water. It was already midday and she had just awoken a few minute ago from a dream she had last night. Waiting for the water, she felt a chill go through her spine as she arched over to pick up the soap mixture for her bubble bath. She leaned over to pour the mixture in. While doing so, she noticed her reflection on the porcelain tub. She noticed how bare and dainty she had become as she touched her face. Being Roxanne was stressful. Her skin glowed pinkish as she wrapped herself with her arms. When the tub was finally ready, she climbed in and sank under the water. Slowly, her feet emerged out of the water and her long smooth legs stretched out. Eris's long lush hair splashed the tile as her head raised in silent tranquility. Her arms began feeling her ocean blue skin. Suddenly, she began humming a familiar tune as she scrubbed herself. She thought about last night. About how much fun she had. How good of a dancer Henry had become as he carried her in all the numbers they did. More importantly, she pondered how his touch felt enticing. She surmised that it was his talent. She assured herself that she must be very proud to have brought this out of him.

As Eris continued to caress her nakedness, she bit her lips after each tune she remembered. Evermore so, it was the image of Henry on the piano that brought back that dream she

Of Love and Discord

had; a dream that they were on a rooftop talking the night away. She fooled herself, because then she remembered that it was not a dream at all. And so instead, she realized it was the thoughts of Henry's provoking questions about love that had penetrated her emotional experiences in the darkness of the rooftop last night.

Meanwhile, Mayhem had found a guest as he came about the balcony. He barked at a familiar face that was looking through the screen doors of Eris' bathroom. This had frightened the fellow as he turned around trying to calm the dog down. But it was too late. Eris quickly jumped out and covered herself with her robes in time to catch the perpetrator in the act.

"You!" she yelled furiously, "didn't even care to knock, did you?"

Eros looked back as Mayhem began barking even louder.

"Sorry, I didn't want to interrupt," he smiled, embarrassed, "my dear, I was waiting for you."

What seemed to be fear suddenly took hold of Eros for just a second as Eris came closer and closer, pushing him down onto the sofa.

"You have a lot of nerve, Eros!" she finally said, "watching a lady bathe."

Eros began muttering excuses and asking for forgiveness in his usual tone as Eris began gripping him about the neck with her look of an inscrutable nature.

"Lucky for you, I'm in a better mood today because someone just won the jackpot," Eris declared joyfully. She then dangled the Ticking Heart with last night's results in front of him.

"So you have," Eros said with a tone of surprising relief.

"Yes, I have. Now I believe this is all mine now," she said. "I do believe you also owe me an apology for breaking into my house uninvited and for doubting me on this wager."

Eros chuckled before scrutinizing the watch. He was then silent for a moment as Eris looked at him proudly.

"What's the matter?" she said, "surprised it happened so quickly?"

"Discordia," he finally spoke, "a fine job for whatever you did yesterday. But I do believe here that we agreed that you'd get both to fall in love."

"What?" she gasped, "how can that be? I was there myself, the boy is in love. What makes you think Francine doesn't feel the same way?"

"Well, isn't her rejection to his request to the ball a sufficient answer?" Eros refuted as he stood up and calmly sat Eris down as he showed her the watch closely.

"I'm not lying. The watch shows me only one person fell in love. Perhaps this is a way for you to find out why Miss Daye refused," he continued.

"Excellent idea," Eris cried as she stood back up, "I'll show that little buttercup that my Henry loves her. Just you wait. I'll get her love even if I make her go myself. You'll see!"

Eros smiled as she dashed to her room to get dressed. As soon as she returned, she snatched the Ticking Heart from Eros' hands and went out the door.

"Well, my friend," Eros said to the dog, "It appears it's just you and me waiting for our ravishing goddess to make more miracles happen again."

He was going to pet him when the dog snarled at him with disdain.

"What? I was honestly waiting for her," Eros concluded while the dog turned away.

****

Francine gathered what was left of her art supplies into a trunk as she cleaned out her locker. She quickly went out of the building, carefully lifting it as she approached a man aboard a truck waiting for her to receive it.

"I got it," the man said as he rushed down to her.

"Thank you," she said.

"You're very welcome missy, is that all of it?" he said.

"Yes, that's all of it. Sorry for the wait."

"Not a problem," he said as he gave her his hand to climb aboard, "ready?"

Before Francine had a chance to say, she was interrupted by multiple loud taps on the vehicle.

"Hello!" a boy's voice cried out from below, "room for one more?"

"Sorry mac, this shuttle is already booked," the attendant said.

It was then that Francine noticed that it was Maxwell, Henry's orchestra friend.

"Hello, Maxwell," she called out.

"Franny! What a surprise," he said, smiling.

"Could you put in a stop for him?" she asked the attendant.

He nodded and then helped Maxwell and his cello case aboard.

"Where you off to?" the attendant asked as Maxwell sat down across from Francine.

"To the Metro Art Museum," he said.

"Do you have a date with Mary Ann today?" Francine asked.

"Heavens no, she doesn't care for fine art," he said, "but I see you're taking much of your art to some gallery as well.

"No, much of this is going back to the collection in London," Francine said.

"You're leaving us already? You're not leaving before saying goodbye, are you?"

"I'm not leaving," she quickly replied, "I promised my art professor to transfer it to a dealer at a seaport."

"Thank heavens. I was afraid of being the one to break it to Henry that his girl is leaving him before the ball next week," he joked.

A deep shower of guilt sank through Francine's body as she knew she was not going and had left Henry to go all by himself. But reliving a ball had struck fear in her more than letting the boy she had feelings for down. She was silent until Maxwell looked at her with puzzlement and interrupted her with another question. "Is everything alright with you and Henry?"

Francine suddenly paused her self-loathing as she smiled, "yes, everything is fine. I'm just worried about him, that's all."

"Oh? Worried that he still doesn't stand a chance to a musician like me?" he joked.

Francine chuckled, "he wishes he can be like you. I heard you were made an offer by the Boston Orchestra, is that correct? That must be marvelous."

"I actually turned them down," he dismissed. "I actually want to explore the jazz world and head down to New Orleans after graduation."

"Wow," she said. "Have you ever played with Henry on the side?"

"I don't think I could stand a chance with that jazz hound. He's going places with his original works. I heard George was so impressed at the club he played at last night."

"He was playing last night?" she commented.

"Yeah, he didn't tell you?" he said as he took out a cigarette and lit it.

"No, he did not. If I knew, I would have surprised him," she said sadly.

"Yup, I'm no match for *your fella*," he said smiling.

Upon hearing this, Francine blushed at how Henry was now considered to be her man.

"So if you're not going to meet Mary Ann, why are you heading to the museum?"

"To see your artwork, of course dear," he teased.

"I wish," she dismissed jokingly.

"I'm actually going to play for a small event there. You know, you should stop by. A few famous artists from Paris are exhibiting their works. Maybe I can introduce you to them."

"I'm honored," she said, concealing her interest, "but I better get going on my delivery."

"Of course, Franny."

The vehicle stopped in front of the museum seconds after. The attendant helped Maxwell down as Francine looked on to him heading to the event.

She sighed. She missed Henry very much. She should see him after. Yet in the back of her mind, she wanted to meet these artists. Lost in her own dream of brushes and colors, she wanted to be just an artist as Henry was to her. After Maxwell waved goodbye and the vehicle began again, she called for the attendant to stop. She then stepped out, the deliveries were to go out without her.

Eris had driven around campus in search of Francine or information on her whereabouts. By the time she got a lead that she was heading to a seaport, she quickly rushed there. However, the attendant that was with her had told Eris that she had made a stop at the art museum and said that they were instructed to make the delivery without her. This came off as fishy to Eris as Francine was a girl that never strayed from her tasks. She was a diligent student and was faithful to her lady-like conduct.

Upon arriving outside the museum, Eris was about to head up the steps when she saw Francine in front of some men on the balcony of the museum. Unwilling to reveal herself just yet, she found a little café on the portico where she could spy from afar until she could meet her. It was here that she saw how entranced and interested Francine was by the men talking. One quite close to her was Maxwell Stevens. She remembered him from the party way back. As she waited, she thought about how she could get Francine to change her refusal to go to the ball with Henry so that she would confess her love. It did not make any sense to Eris that Francine refused. Did it have something to do with some other man?

"Is she afraid of getting too close?" she suggested to herself as she looked at the Ticking Heart. There was a sense of nervousness as she thought about how Francine may be in the process of having second thoughts with Henry.

"Why, look who's up there," a female voice said.

Eris turned and saw two flappers looking in Francine's direction as they sat down gossiping and enjoying themselves.

"I'm not surprised. She's been quite flirtatious lately ever since she's been seeing that pianist."

"You mean Henry Leon? Is she really seeing him? Or is he just another passing fancy?"

"You tell me. You know all about Miss London. Hey, is it true she has a fortune back there?"

"Fortune Smorchen, she's from old money. It's her classy lady gimmick that's getting all the boys."

"Are you telling me she's one of those duchesses or something?"

"Shush...you didn't hear it from me. I hear every rich boy in the city is trying to capture her heart to grab British nobility."

"So that's why all the fellas are courting her. That's not fair," the girl puffed. They then saw Francine departing from the gentleman, excusing herself.

"See, it's her sweetness and mannerisms that get them. I tell you, I bet she's seeing at least a dozen boys every month and have settled for two or three in the meantime."

"Scandalous, some girls just have all the fun," the girl giggled.

It was then that Eris could not listen any longer, she immediately rushed into the entrance of the museum. A rage of discontent went over her as she thought about how Francine was just playing "lover" to Henry. "How could she?" she thought. "All this time I had thought she was a sweet innocent girl, but she's really diabolical."

With a greater regret for setting up Henry with Francine, Eris thought Francine did not deserve Henry's love. If anything, she herself deserved Henry's attention, not some rich girl. It was here that Eris had conceived an alternative. If Francine was not going to go with Henry, Eris would. She would be the girl that Henry's affection would turn to.

"Miss Roxanne, it's been too long," called out Francine as she came down the hallway.

"What are you doing here?" she continued, smiling, "there's so much I want to tell you."

"And there's so much I want to tell you, Franny," Eris said sternly.

"Is everything alright?" said Francine, taken aback.

With a smirk of confidence, Roxanne replied with a brilliant lie. "Yes, you need to realize that Henry will be going with me to the ball. He may not be good enough for you, but you have no idea how great he is."

"What?" puzzled Francine, "no, that's not the case at all."

Before Francine could protest, Eris turned away and immediately began to storm off.

"Wait, please," Francine called as she followed her out.

"Roxanne, please listen to me," she said again, now following closer to Eris as she descended the steps toward the street in the direction of where her vehicle was parked.

"What's there to listen about? Obviously, you think you're too high of a girl to be with Henry," Eris finally responded.

"No, I would never think that," Francine protested, "I, I…"

"I what?" said Eris as she was about to enter her car. Francine had a look of discomfort and nervousness. She was trapped and could only mutter the extent of her truth.

"I just don't feel comfortable going. And it's not because of Henry. Please, you just have to trust me that I'm not going with him because I just don't want to go at all."

As capricious as it sounded to Eris and with regard to the relationship between Francine and Henry, Eris calmed down and looked at her with a deep stare. And Francine, looking as if she had been accused of murder, stood there waiting for forgiveness.

"Okay," Eris said.

"Please understand," Francine continued, "I have general distastes of these formal events because I don't have pleasant memories of them. There, I've confessed. Please don't get angry with me. Henry has no blame in this. He is still very much a part of my life and I truly want him in it in the future after this event and even after he graduates."

Francine blushed red as she looked distraught and almost naked before her. There was a short silence as Eris patiently waited for those three words from her, "I love him." Yet, Francine did not say any more.

After hearing everything she said, even without those three words, Eris did not feel compassion or sympathy. Instead, she felt bent on accepting this reality for the better.

"Miss Roxanne?" Francine inquired, "May we talk about this more in detail together? Perhaps in a more intimate setting?"

Eris looked at her with disgust.

"There's nothing more to discuss. He's already decided to go with me," Roxanne proclaimed. "Farewell, my lady," the goddess barked.

She then drove off.

-Chapter 5-

Pandora began helping Roxanne with her makeup after she had finished hers in a hurry. Eros lamented about how hurt he was when Eris and Pandora were invited by Henry to the ball as his guests, while he was not invited to go.

"Sorry, Eros," Pandora had said, "maybe you're just not as pretty as you think you are."

The flappers giggled loudly as Eros laid on the sofa quoting Shakespearean quotes in his dismay.

Eris smiled as she looked at herself in the mirror, gazing at her powdered face and her hair for this occasion. She was used to preparing her face by herself, but such a formal occasion called for more attention that Pandora, the most active youth among them, helped her on. Happily, they chatted about how long it had been since they had been last cordially invited to such grand events.

"Tell me about it. I always have to invite myself," said Eris, "it's never a dull day that invitations never get sent to me, making me use my apple of discord when prompted."

"At least you can do something about it," Pandora commented, "no one ever wants me at their parties and I can't do much about it."

"Isn't it obvious why they don't invite you? Because you're an intrusive party pooper. Always asking questions, always opening things and pushing buttons you're not allowed to," Eros scoffed.

Pandora gave him a death stare as she went on to finish the finishing touches on Eris' brow.

"Ha-ha really funny, shut up, lover boy," defended Eris.

"And you goddess, don't get me started with your party crashing ways."

Before Eros could go on, Pandora helped Eris into her long blue silky dress.

"Such a beautiful dress, everyone at the ball is going to be looking at us thinking about who these two maidens are with Henry," she said excitedly.

"Yes," agreed Eris reluctantly. She thought about how unfortunate it was that she had to share that stage with Pandora, however.

When Henry returned the other day after Eris' encounter with Francine, he was requested immediately to the dance studio for a renewal of dance lessons. Nervous as Eris was to suggest that he should go with her, she took the chance and confronted him when he arrived. But not before some perfect news for her that he had to tell her first. Henry shared with Roxanne that Francine had recently behaved strangely around him. Her often bubbly and affectionate behavior had now been uncordial and unresponsive to his affections. After consoling him, Eris had convinced him that Francine was now perhaps uninterested in him.

"But how can that be?" Henry said sadly, "I thought she loved me."

"One can fall out of interest with anything, can't they? So can love," Eris explained. "Girls are quite fickle at times."

In his distress, Eris proposed that he let it be for the time being, and instead he should enjoy himself at the ball. When Henry protested that going now was pointless, Eris reminded him that he had already agreed to Professor Valentini's request to be a backup pianist there. Regretfully, he remembered. It was then that Eris was able to propose herself to be his date. When he agreed on the proposal, Eris' heart fluttered with elation before it was partly dismantled by his suggestion that she should also invite Pandora. Grudgingly, she concurred to this suggestion as his face was evidence enough to see that he treated her proposal as a mere kind repaying gesture for their dance lessons together, more than it being out of a possible affectionate bond. Because she respected him, she would share Henry's arm on their way to the ball.

Empire State University's End of the Year Ball was a hundred-year-old tradition that started at the University's founding. Held inside their gothic-style cathedral, the ball drew in the many scholars of the university—freshman, seniors, and faculty alike. And as a treat this year for all, a red carpet lay at the entrance.

Eris had stepped out onto the red carpet as she exited a horse-drawn carriage that she rode with Henry and Pandora, along with a few other attendees.

"This is so exciting," commented Pandora. "We're like motion picture stars!"

"Well, we are in the company of Maestro Henry Leon," Eris said.

"Nonsense, you ladies are the real stars. Come on," Henry said proudly, as he led them inside.

The party had already started as people filled a nave crowded with beautiful flowing dresses of all colors among the handsome tuxedos. Music played soothingly as Henry bashfully escorted them to a couple of friends he saw nearby.

"Henry! Well, aren't you a sight for sore eyes? One, two dates on each arm," George pointed.

The group met and joked while Eris smiled radiantly, meeting each new person. While Pandora flirted with the crowd, a waltz began playing. Eris' focus was then pulled to some gentlemen offering his hand to each lady. She then turned to Henry, who was busy laughing at a comment Pandora made.

As Eris waited patiently, Henry finally took notice of her and was about to ask for her hand before his action was interrupted.

"Let's show them what you learned, Henry," Pandora said, excitedly grabbing his arm.

"Oh alright," Henry agreed, smiling to Eris before he was pulled into this position. Eris only smiled back in disappointment as she began to wait impatiently for it to be over.

While Henry led Pandora in the waltz, Eris looked over to the band playing and found Professor Valentini in the background. He was talking to a few orchestra members and it was then that she noticed how radiant the other girls looked. Every one of them looked so youthful, and so full of energy in their gowns. No matter how divine and forever young her appearance was, it was times like these that Eris realized how old she was compared to the blissful crowd all around her. A bit of resentment came over her as she looked at Pandora's joyful face as she danced with him. Pandora even whispered to him and laughed as they turned. Worst of all was that he smiled back at her playfully.

When the first waltz was over, Eris immediately went over to Henry and Pandora.

"You are so much better now," Pandora complimented, before Henry was swooped away from her.

"Come on, Henry," Roxanne said, pulling him, "your warmup is over."

The second dance then began and Henry found himself continuing without a moment's notice. As they danced, Eris looked at Henry and saw how his face seemed so melancholic in his silence.

"Are you having fun, Piano Boy?" she asked.

"Yeah of course," he said tiredly but assuring.

Eris nodded with approval, trying to cherish every moment she could.

"By the way, you look lovely tonight, Roxanne," he said lastly as he held her closer.

"Thank you," Eris said, containing her blush.

Like the speed of a bolt of lightning, their dance had soon concluded.

Henry bowed to her and immediately she followed with a curtsey. Soon after, Henry was approached by Valentini.

Henry had to fill in for the next song while the previous pianist took a break. As Eris and Pandora mingled with Henry's friends and other compatriots of the ball, there was a deep longing for the same feeling Eris felt on the night of their outing together. With every glance, Eris noticed how empty Henry was as he played. Although he seemed joyous of having come tonight, there was no denying that he was incomplete. At least incomplete until the moment he saw the answer to relieve his soulless playing.

Henry was too focused, rushing to finish the music to even take notice of a girl slowly stepping through the crowd in her pink gown. But for Eris, it did not take long for her to gasp at the sight of the sunshine girl with flaxen hair emerging from the meadow of flowers. There Francine was, looking on to the dance floor, nervous, yet eyes filled with zeal to find what she had come here for. And as Henry played, his head flowed to the motion of his arms. His eyes half-closed until they fully opened to see that his desire was before him, like a beacon sent from the mirrors of God shining upon her glittering dress. And at that, the music that he was playing ended and another began. Abandoning his post after the transition, he went to her.

Francine felt the anxiety pressing down on her bare shoulders as she waited, searching for either Henry or a way out. All that she could think about was the fear of the past creeping up on her at any point as long as she was here. And as she walked in her heels, she froze after spotting Henry approaching her. And for that second, her mind cleared as she thought about the music, the rain, and him, when he played for her that night.

"You're here," Henry said.

"I am," she said shyly.

"May I?" he held out his hand.

Francine took his hand and then nodded. As the music played another waltz, Henry led her to the dance floor. They continued their gaze at one another as their feet swiftly stepped back, around, and forward, moving with the rhythm. And as they came closer, Henry held her with no hesitation, and with all the care in the world. And as she felt his touch, Francine's worries were no longer plaguing her for that moment. Indeed, in that moment, Francine felt that coming here was what she should have done all along. Her eyes rendered motionless as she twirled.

While the music continued, Eris stood there watching them. It was what Henry wanted, she thought. It was the main purpose of these dance lessons. And she had successfully accomplished uniting them together again. And this time, effortlessly. Yet, why was she feeling so empty herself? When the song began to come to its conclusion, she saw that Francine's hands were on top of Henry's shoulders, shifting slowly, wrapping around his neck as she rested her head on his torso. There was applause by the end of the dance.

"What is she doing here?" Pandora said, interrupting Eris' focus.

"I don't know," Eris said, "I need some air." Quickly, she barged out of the church.

When Eris exited the red carpet, she went to a nearby garden and thought about how much she resented helping Henry. She walked up to a fountain that had a statue of a baby version of the god of love pouring water from his vase. Looking at the curly haired, winged naked boy, she gave a smirk and blackened the water when she touched the water with the tip of her finger.

"I've made them fall in love, Eros," she grunted.

It was then that she heard footsteps running in her direction. When she turned, she saw it was Francine coming her way. Not noticing Roxanne, Francine made her way through the garden. Quickly Eris disguised herself as a tree before Francine stepped through the little gate into the fountain area.

Francine covered her face with frustration as she sat down near Eris.

"Why is she upset?" Eris thought.

"No, no," she cried, "It wasn't my fault. I loved him."

The mentioning of love quickly puzzled Eris.

Francine felt like a maniac at a time when the ending of the dance seemed to console her. But it did not. As soon as there was applause at the end of their dance, people had come to compliment them on their dancing. It was then that she knew she had to get out of there. She began recalling that night when they all judged her and surrounded her.

"Francine!" Henry called out as he was about to pass the garden.

Francine tried to regain her composure as she wiped off her tears before standing up. She was about to leave before she tripped on a tree root. When she fell, she let out a noise that alerted Henry to her.

"Now let's see whether you love him or not," Eris muttered under her breath.

"Francine," Henry said as he helped her up. "What's the matter? Have I done something to offend you?"

Francine shook her head and tried to smile.

"I'm sorry, Henry," she said, "I didn't mean to abandon the ball yet again. I just felt trapped and I saw so many eyes on me."

"You feel trapped? Is it with me?" worried Henry.

"No! That's not what I meant. I meant the environment."

Both Henry and Eris had a tough time believing that Francine could possibly be affected and thrown off balance by large gatherings and parties. Obviously, they had all been to a speakeasy before, after all. Because of this, Henry felt saddened and dismissed her reason.

"Francine," he spoke, "if it is because you don't want to be seen in public with me anymore, I understand. I know I'm no one special."

"That's not true. That's not what I am saying, Henry," said Francine, "I never thought that. And you are special, special to me."

"Then what is the real reason why you avoided me and ran away?"

Francine had a look of embarrassment after she realized how much of a coward she was, and for the way she acted toward Henry.

"I'm sorry. I should have told you that ceremonies and formal events like these have always repelled me because they remind me of *him*."

"Him?" emphasized Henry.

"A man I loved before," she said, "someone who cared for me deeply and I loved so much. He was taken away from me in a ball during my 16th birthday."

"And it reminded you of him?" he said grimly.

"Yes," she said, "I'm sorry. I didn't want to relive the pain and guilt. I did not want the past to come back to me, and for you to be burdened by it. Please understand, I truly want to be with you. But I was scared to go and face some specter in my life. I don't want you to be associated with my past. I..."

Before Francine could continue, Henry pulled her to him and his lips silenced her. She embraced him as he held her by the waist. She was no longer stiff and troubled.

"Francine," he whispered, "I have something to tell you."

"What is it?" she said calmly.

"Whatever happened in the past does not burden me. Whether you still love that person or regret what had happened back then, it will never stop me from loving you."

And at that, Francine's eyes opened at the mention of those words.

"Oh Henry," Francine exclaimed, "you're too good for me."

As they embraced, the music creeped closer into the garden. Henry asked if she wanted to continue dancing. Together, they slow danced to the beat.

In the scene that lay before her, Eris began to shrink her branches as she transformed slowly into a snake. Slithering away from them, the young man and woman looked oddly as they noticed the garden had become more spacious than before.

Eris returned home alone. And as Roxanne sat on her sofa with her gown in silence, she covered her face. She was regretful that the wager had made her soft about everything. As she kept thinking about tonight, she destroyed the flowers that Henry had given her before they arrived at the ball. Then, in a rage of anger, she began to wreak havoc in her apartment, destroying the wonderful decorations and furniture she had bought that created Madame Roxanne, the Matchmaker. Taking the Ticking Heart from her clutch, she held it in front of her as she studied it. It was hers now to do what she wanted with it. And in that minute, blackness devoured the timepiece's exterior.

"No one loves forever," she said, "now I'll show Eros. I'll show them all, the power of chaos." In a demonic manner, she laughed, and with that, the goddess of discord was her old self again.

-Chapter 6-

The warm breeze blew Eros' curls as he waited for Pandora to change into her bathing suit. They had just driven from the city to an oasis-like beach town for a pool party at Hermes', the messenger god, summer home.

"Stop peeking!" Pandora cried.

"I'm not!" he called back to her as he leaned on the stall next to hers. "Please darling, love's aphrodisiac is no peeping tom," he declared as he tipped his sunglasses jokingly.

"Whatever," Pandora said as she finished and barged out.

"Finally, I was wondering whether Hermes would have to personally come to us to deliver a message that the party was over already," he teased.

"Stop embarrassing yourself," she said. "Gosh golly, I don't know how the goddess of chaos and strife could keep you around so long." She then began to head up the hill toward the beach house by herself.

"Because I tutor her on the ways of love-making," he called out gleefully, following her swiftly.

When they knocked on the grand door, it opened as if they were the gates to Olympus. Many demi-gods, goddesses, nymphs, and lesser gods were present around the pool area. The whole area was already festive after the two entered the party. As jazz music played in the background, Eros saw the sight of Hermes lounging alongside a couple of nymphs.

"Last one to the pool is a rotten mortal," blurted Pandora.

"Go on ahead kiddo," he said, "I want to say hello first."

"Why hello ladies," Eros greeted Hermes' nymph circle.

"Hellooo Eros," the nymphs greeted back gleefully.

"Oh, it's you," Hermes grunted, showing him no attention.

"Hermes! What a party we have here. How are you my good man?"

Eros sat close to his circle as he began to wrap himself around the nymphs. He began to sweet talk them as Hermes looked uninterested under his shades. Hermes lounged with pride. As an Olympian god, he was tanning his bronzed skin and lean body. With such a perceived demeanor, even Eros' boyish charms annoyed him.

While the nymphs giggled at how poorly constructed Eros' jokes were, Hermes finally reacted and gave in to his pathetic ploy for attention.

"What do you want, Eros?" he said.

There was a pause in the punchline.

"Why, to tell you some interesting news that all the gods should know about," Eros cheered.

"What is it?" the nymphs all said curiously.

"Now, now ladies, give me some space next to Hermes and I'll tell you," he said. As he scooted up to the lounge chair next to Hermes, Hermes sat up and looked at him with disgust under his sunglasses.

"Now that's better," Eros said, "you can't believe that my work has been quite interesting these days."

"Yes, I heard you got a certain goddess of chaos to help you with your work," said Hermes.

"So you've heard, how excellent," he smiled. "Yes amazingly, she had no idea what she got herself into."

As Eros laughed, Hermes looked puzzled.

"What's so funny?" he asked.

"Oh nothing," Eros continued, "you just have to be there to see how desperately she was trying to prove to me that love is some trivial matter. If love wasn't hard for her to understand in the first place," he giggled.

"Tell us," the nymphs cheered.

"But I heard she was able to get two mortals to fall in love and that you wagered your timepiece for it," Hermes said.

"I suppose she did. And miraculously she proved to me that she could get them to fall in love, after all."

The nymphs began muttering in disbelief.

"Then why are you so elated that you lost, silly?" a nymph commented.

"Because beautiful, my loss unraveled itself to be an interesting turn of events."

"And what was that?" Hermes inquired.

"You see, my cunning Olympian, she believes her wager is a win, but she has no idea that just because the device showed her that they were in love, it did not mean the cycle of love was over. In fact, I was surprised in the beginning. Even proud that she could achieve such a feat. But after I officially relinquished my Ticking Heart, she challenged me on that notion and that she could destroy the love she created in one instant with her deviousness. And as you know, being me, I could not resist. I had to see what she would do next."

"Poor couple," a nymph said.

Eros laughed, "more like poor goddess. You all have no idea how futile her attempts were after she wagered with me again."

"Seems she's going to take your job," Hermes interjected.

"That's exactly what she wants. But I shall tell you this, she is wagering her apple of discord for it," he continued.

"That gold pendant of hers?" another nymph said, "did you agree to it?"

"The very one," Eros replied sharply, "and yes, I did."

"That's foolish," Hermes said, "she already has your timepiece, and now you're wagering your job. And let's not forget, breaking these two mortals apart may be her specialty."

"I wouldn't worry," Eros continued, "chaos and strife might be her strengths, but so far, her tricks and her devious child's play have been complete embarrassments. I was there to see all of them fail. One instance, for example, she tried to ruin their picnic at the park with a bee's nest!"

"Do tell," Hermes inquired.

"My pleasure," he continued, "when Henry was looking for their kite that was stuck up a tree, Discordia had purposely forced the kite near a bee's nest. As soon as he began climbing, his determination to retrieve the kite made him oblivious to the nest nearby. But as soon as he found the kite, he realized that retrieving the kite would mean being stung if he was not careful. With the calls and concerns of Francine below him, he knew he could not return empty-handed, so he went ahead, carefully, reaching for the kite."

"Was her intention to injure the boy?" a nymph asked.

"Gods no, that would be too easy for the goddess. Her intention was more diabolical. She had intended for Henry to retrieve the kite harmless, but not without him being responsible for an unfortunate accident. You see, as soon as he told Francine that he had retrieved the kite and was coming down, the goddess sought to unleash her plan. Shaking the tree softly, she had intended for Henry to hold on to the tree while she cut the bees nest, letting it fall on top of Francine."

"That's so mean," they gasped.

"Indeed. Her intention was for Henry to come down perfectly safe, but see Francine run in panic and pain. If Henry were to see a disfigured Francine, she assumed that Henry would lose taste in Francine's pretty face. Even more so, she had hoped that Francine's anger and frustration that she suffered in this accident would propel her to associate Henry with her misfortune and then cause discord to unveil."

After Eros grabbed a martini from a server, he took a sip, then smiled at how much attention he was bringing.

"Well?" some of them inquired in suspense.

Eros continued, "of course that did not happen. Miraculously, his hold on the tree was not impaired and he was able to see the bees' nest slowly tipping. He dropped from the tree and quickly pushed Francine away right before the nest fell alongside of him."

"What a hero," they all praised.

"Yes, but poor boy, although his fall was minor with cuts and bruises, he was stung by a few of the bees and Francine had to treat his bloated face on a park bench nearby. Luckily, she had a small first aid kit with her."

"What a courageous act," one nymph commented.

"That was so romantic! He saved her, and she nursed his wounds after," another cheered.

As Eros basked in the glory of telling the triumph of love over Eris' masterminded plans, Hermes had a look that Eros noticed was not pleased. Instead, he had a look that was in disbelief at what had happened.

"It sounds like Henry had a guardian angel," Hermes finally said.

"Perhaps he does," Eros said, "because everything that demented goddess does only results in her making them love each other more."

"You're exaggerating. Just because you're the guardian of love does not mean you can fool everyone here that the couple is impervious to chaos. And that the goddess can't cause discord among them," Hermes suddenly erupted.

"I don't imply that at all. But I do mean that everything she did, whether discord or some misfortune happening, it only made their love stronger. Here, if you don't believe me, look at this list of all the things she has done."

Eros took out a roll of paper from his pocket and rolled it open for all to see. Almost everybody there then began to crowd around it.

"Where did you get this?" one demi-god commented.

"She left it on her countertop," Eros answered, "believe me, I was there to see her carry out these plans one by one."

They all began to read it out loudly:

Plan	Goal	Action	Result
A	Displease Henry and Francine's attraction to each other	Disfigure Francine's face w/bee stings and blame Henry.	Failure: Henry saves the day.
B	Cause discord among the two	Pose as Museum guide on their museum date; Challenge Francine's art knowledge and give false information to Henry.	Failure: Argument did occur, but both got over it and made up after spending more time with each other during a painting activity.
C	Show how much a coward Henry is	Use Mayhem (my dog) to scare Henry in front of Francine.	Failure: Francine played with Mayhem and saved the day.
D	Test Francine's loyalty	Spread rumors of Henry's past and then try to seduce Francine disguised as another attractive man.	Failure: Francine trusts Henry too much and was not attracted to other males of similar qualities.
E	Seduce Henry with another female	Have Pandora seduce and take advantage of Henry just before Francine arrives on date.	Almost success: Francine got all rallied up, causing jealousy; However, a failure because Pandora apologized to Francine (after feeling guilty) and told the truth about the incident to her; Francine forgave Henry after a week of silence.

Hermes was the only one not amused by the laughter each immortal made when they realized the lengths Eris went to break them up in such elaborate schemes and failing each time. He had a stern look as he watched Eros finish his stick of olives from his drink. With every incident mentioned, Eros smiled and took a bite in enjoyment.

"Wow," someone commented, "this Francine must be someone special."

"Absolutely," Eros interrupted, "there are many things that make this girl more than meets the eye. Such secrets the goddess of discord can never understand."

"You chose well, god of love," someone said to Eros.

Eros laughed as he denied the choosing them to fall in love. "They chose each other," he declared.

It was here that Hermes, silent and stern looking, got up from his seat and approached Eros.

"Here Hermes, have a look yourself," Eros said proudly.

As soon as Eros spoke those words, he was immediately grasped by the neck by the hands of Hermes' strong choke. As the crowd watched in surprise, Eros gasped for air and could only muster a few words from his impaired throat.

"Was it...something, I said?"

Hermes' body began to soften and reformed itself into no other than the goddess of chaos.

As soon as she appeared before everyone, the masses dispersed quickly, like thieves caught in the act.

"Why are you all leaving the party so soon?" Eris called out loudly, "come hear how our guest-of-honor tells the rest of the story!" She continued to choke him.

"Discordia," Eros said desperately, "sorry..."

"It's you," Pandora called out after she woke from her pool nap, "what did Eros do now? Where's Hermes?"

"Oh, he's a little occupied. And Eros is just about to get his head ripped out from his pretty body."

"You like talking ill of me in front of everyone?" Eris taunted, "I bet you thought you were really smart taking my list, huh? I bet you foiled all my plans!"

Eros was turning red as he desperately pleaded for mercy.

"I think he learned his lesson," Pandora called out as she came over.

"Oh no," Eris said, suppressing her anger, "lover boy here is going to suffer my wrath for his big mouth until he spills what I need to know."

Pandora shook her head in shame.

"Why can't I break them up?" Eris screamed for an answer.

Eris shook Eros some more, "and what's this secret about Francine that you've been keeping from me?"

"Let go...of me...first, I'll tell...you," Eros uttered in her grasp.

Eris then finally released him.

After gasping for air dramatically on the ground, Eros was stared down by the tall goddess above him. She demanded an answer.

"Well?" Eris scolded, "what's so special about Francine?"

"She's pleasant, unlike you," he muttered under his breath.

"What did you say?!" Eris sparked.

"I said she's not a peasant like you discovered," he corrected in fear.

It was then that Eris remembered her recent discovery of Francine's reputation and her special status.

"So, what if she's a countess?" Eris said, "there's no secret to that if I know it."

"But does Henry know?" Eros said.

"Does he know that Francine is from old English money?" Eris asked Pandora.

"I don't think so," she replied, "the boy is really clueless of the reputation they've acquired as well."

"Eureka," Eris said, "how could I miss that? Now I know what I must do."

"And what is that?" Eros asked.

"To break them up, of course," Eris said excitedly, "let's go Pandora, I might need your help to dig up some dirt on a lady, an English lady. Prepare for Plan F."

"A Plan F?" Pandora hesitated to say, "I have a feeling it's getting personal now."

Pandora followed Eris out as she wondered to herself what the goddess was recruiting her for.

-Chapter 7-

On the boardwalk which stood next to the scattered remains of the carnival tent that had hosted the Zimmerman Circus speakeasy, Henry and Francine walked amongst the lighted carnival rides and stands, not empty as it was before. And this time, there were no parties or alcohol, only innocence. Innocence that brought young love here. And among the beach shore, young love finds itself vulnerable to intimacy and dubious dreams.

"Step right up! Give it a go, sunny boy. Come one, come all, witness this young man win a prize for his lady," called out the game stand man as Henry prepared his aim.

Francine watched closely as Henry prepared himself to knock all milk bottles off the target. Although she had refused for them to play again after they both failed the first few times, Henry was adamant to win a prize for her.

"I'm going to win you one," he assured, "it's not a date without winning a prize."

"But you've already taken me to so many. That's already a prize," she said, "all the time together is enough." Henry, like most young men, set out to surpass the sentimental, even often neglecting it.

With the last ball in his hand, Henry threw the ball, hitting all the bottles off.

"A win!" cried the game stand man.

"What would you like?" Henry asked her.

Francine looked up and saw a penguin with a bow tie. It had reminded her of that concert where she had first saw Henry perform.

"That one," she pointed.

The two walked distantly apart as they began to exit the boardwalk onto the beach. Francine was quiet after the last game. She held the penguin in her arms as she contemplated her feelings. In the darkness of the shore, she felt the cool ocean breeze and the calming sand between her sandals.

"Are you still upset with me?" Henry finally said.

"What?" surprised Francine, "why would I be upset at you? You just won me something."

She smiled back, confused, as Henry chuckled at his silly inquiry.

"You're just a bit quiet. I thought you hadn't gotten over that incident with Dora," he continued.

"Oh that. You're pardoned from it," she teased.

"Then may I ask, my darling Francine, what is on your mind?"

"I was just thinking about the last few months together," she said, "reflecting on all that has happened."

"You haven't lost interest in me, have you?" he interjected.

"No! Of course not, silly," she replied with haste, "I'm just thinking about how selfish I was to have been the center of your focus. You've already graduated, and yet, you haven't found yourself a position yet."

"Don't ever feel guilty for being the center of my focus," he said as he stopped her. He stood over her and brought her close.

"What about the orchestra? Why don't you go back to Professor Valentini? I'm sure he can..."

"I can't," Henry interrupted, "I've already turned my back from those aristocratic fancy wigs. I won't be a playing monkey for orchestras."

"I understand, but Henry, I worry about you. You were great at it. And I'm sure over time you will get your turn to play your personal work again."

"Francine, you were not there the day after my concert. Valentini, along with his board of critics, said my material disrupted the symphony. They told me that next time I would need it to be reviewed before I could even consider playing them or anything new again."

"I didn't know that. I can't believe it, I thought it was sublime," she smiled lightly.

Henry let go of her and walked toward the waters, shrugging off the compliment. For some reason, Francine saw that he was beginning to doubt his own ability. Her words seemed more like pity than praise.

"I'm sorry if I'm getting too personal," Francine said.

"It's fine," he looked back, "sometimes I'm as lost as the sea."

Francine came over to him as he sat on the sand. Her arms grasped his neck as she held him dear.

"What about you?" he asked, "you know, all the times we've been together, you haven't really talked about your future, nor your family for that matter."

"Henry," she began.

"Well?" he continued.

"My parents have been dead for a long time now," she said calmly.

Stunned, Henry suddenly felt the guilt of asking.

"I'm sorry," he said, "I know your past is not something I should ask about."

"No," she said, "you have a right to know by now. It's true I don't talk much about my family back home in London. It's because there isn't much to talk about. I came to America to live a new life."

"You came all by yourself..." he acknowledged.

Francine nodded as she smiled warmly.

"Just to become an artist?"

"Life is an art," she replied, "I wanted to leave my old life in London. I always knew I wanted to travel. Then I said, 'why not'? If the Puritans did it for religious freedom, I will do it for an artist's freedom."

"That..." Henry said, "is such a beautiful thought."

"It's not beautiful," she said remorsefully, "there is no future for an empty canvas. Henry, my work isn't good." Francine then began to wail immediately.

"That's not true," Henry said confidently as he held her close while she sobbed.

"You're a talented artist. Everyone we know has told me what a great painter and student you are."

"But you haven't seen them," she said, "I've never showed them to you."

"You have nothing to be shy about," he said, "I will see them one day when the galleries are filled with them."

Francine stopped sobbing as she contemplated her wants and dreams. She remembered the offer that day when she had met the famous curators in the event Maxwell had invited her too. She had a chance to display and promote her original work after they considered viewing it. Francine's realization made her feel better after his assurance.

"I want to paint freely," Francine said.

"Paint freely?" Henry remarked.

"You asked what I planned for my future," she smiled, "I want to find a secluded place in the countryside and just paint. And when I'm not painting or reading, I would have famous guests over at my country home. I would learn from the best."

Henry smiled warmly as he relished in her dream.

"It'll happen. Probably sooner than my dream of being the next Gershwin," he chuckled.

Henry suddenly stood up and began to take off his shoes.

"How about a swim?" he said, smiling.

"Right now?" Francine said doubtfully, "it's too cold."

Henry began to take off his shirt as Francine looked away with a pinkish glow in her cheeks.

"Please, Henry," she murmured, "someone could see, it wouldn't be appropriate. We are not even dressed for it."

"Come on! Summer is about over, and this is the first time we have had a chance to touch the water."

Henry came closer to the water and looked at Francine with a mischievous look.

"Hey," Francine reacted, after Henry splashed her with some water.

"Come on in. The water is not as cold as you think," he cried back as he shivered a little.

"You silly boy!" Francine cried back. "Come back here. You deserve a splash back."

Francine came closer to the tides and laughed as she began to splash him back.

As they conducted their splash quarrel, Henry suddenly felt an instant fallback as his foot tripped on a rock in the sand. Immediately, he fell into the water.

"Henry!" Francine cried in the darkness. "Where are you?"

Her worry intensified as she looked all around the tide, her dress and hair now all wet. In desperation, she searched deeper for him, braving the cold.

"Henry!"

Suddenly, her cries were silenced as Henry emerged from the water behind her. In a rush of anger, she began hitting him frantically.

"I'm alright, I'm alright," Henry tried to say as he calmed her.

"But I'm not," she said, frustrated, "I thought you drowned."

They held each other. "I'm sorry," Henry said, "I only wanted to lighten the mood."

As they dried themselves on the bench nearby, Francine had noticed that Henry was looking at her with curiosity as she began to dry off her hair and clothes. It was then that she realized what she was doing in front of him. She immediately stopped and covered herself before Henry turned the other way in embarrassment.

"I'm dreadfully sorry," he said. "I didn't see anything, I promise."

Pink as she could be, Francine was silent. Before she had a chance to react, however, she felt the hands of Henry draping her with his coat.

"I only noticed your damp hair," he said.

Francine looked at him with intensity as she too noticed how Henry enchanted her, by the wetness of his hair and the dimmed light that captured the dark and grayness of his skin. His touch came closer, helping her shed any bashfulness that they may have had. Then there was nothing but freedom in the intimacy they shared for the rest of the night as they lay on the shore. The song of the ocean continued to play as the darkness of the night breathed heavily and sharply amongst the motions of the living sand.

****

The beginning of the school year saw fruition for Francine's artwork. The Metro Art Museum was exhibiting new artwork, and Francine was selected by her professor to be the one and only guest artist from her university for Modern Youth Art week. She was invited to meet new patrons and traveling artists from around the world. With bourgeoning excitement, the museum crowd gathered around the exhibition as Francine stood proudly next to her professor, listening and talking to a few illustrious patrons.

"Keep it up, young lady," one patron said to them, "there is certainly great potential for you yet."

"Thank you, Mr. Weber, I really appreciate it," Francine said.

"A pleasure," he said as they shook hands.

"You see, a lot of the extra critiques paid off, didn't they?" said her professor.

Francine smiled in honesty and embarrassment.

The professor pulled up two chairs for them to sit.

"So, are you tired from the fame yet?" he asked.

"It's only been a couple of hours," she said, "and the people here don't just come to see me."

The professor laughed, "wait till you get a whole exhibition to yourself. Trust me, that's when it gets overwhelming. Not to mention, incredibly hard to differentiate between flattery and honesty. So where is your pianist? Is he coming to see your work today?"

Before Francine had a chance to reply, she continued smiling at the viewers around her exhibit. She then turned back to the professor with a blank look. It was her way of concealing her grasp of the right words to describe her emotional mixture.

"He's off with a few of his band members touring New Orleans. He's looking for inspiration for his next work," she said.

"Crowds are already calling for his next piece? Marvelous. I suppose there's always demand for jazz pianists nowadays. You know, you should join him next time. There is a lot of inspiration in New Orleans. Certainly, this city is too dry and dirty for anyone."

"I wanted to," Francine said, "but I've been too sick to go. I didn't want to be a burden."

"It is a shame he can't be here. But then again, the musician's life is always on the move. Where do you plan to go after you graduate, Franny?" he changed the subject.

"I'm not sure," she said.

"Will you move with him? Live the life of an artist?" he chuckled.

"Perhaps," she smiled at the thought.

"An artist's life and his work are not everlasting unless you have patrons. I hope your fella knows that too. Even if he gets paid a lot from parties, it is after all, show business."

Francine knew better that Henry was worth way more than an entertaining performer. He was a composer and artist that deserved better. However, she respected her professor too much to say anything. She was silent for a solid minute before the professor stood up to comment one more time before leaving her side.

"Remember Franny, even a lady as talented as you needs a stable household. You can still continue to paint, but let's be real, a bohemian lifestyle is an illusion to escape reality for the young and poor."

Francine sat there thinking about what her professor had said. It was not the first time she was told this. In fact, she had personally learned this herself. She knew that an artistic life requires more than just freedom. And even more so, money was not the end of it. The echoes from her past reminded her how far she had come in thanks to security and stability from the man she had lived with. A thought suddenly appeared in her head, "what will the future be like if Henry and herself were chasing their artistic dreams forever and together?" Romantically, it sounded so pure and pleasing, but it revealed that she would be betraying her wants for nurturing family and duties she had refused to acknowledge, even now.

"Francine," her professor called, "there's someone I want you to meet.

Francine went over to him and saw a tall lady dressed in black and partly veiled.

"Hello, welcome," she smiled.

"She'll give you her insights from her work personally," her professor commented. The lady turned her head and Francine saw a face she had not seen for a while.

"Miss Roxanne!" she exclaimed.

"Hello, Franny," Roxanne grinned.

"Oh good, you two already know each other. Miss Smith here is impressed by your painting. Maybe if you can sweet talk her, she'll be your most important patron. Good luck," he said before leaving them as they began to catch up with this chance encounter.

"It's beautiful," Roxanne commented as she viewed one of Francine's paintings that depicted the boardwalk from the shore, "I just love the deep rich colors in the background and the lighting."

"I try my best to capture that mood of that evening sundown," Francine said, "it took me a while until I could put that image of that night on the canvas."

As Francine was about to ask her where she had been over the summer since she last saw her, Eris immediately interrupted her question. "I'm sorry about that day I lashed out at you about not going to the dance with Henry, my dear. Please understand, there were so many mixed signals that I found unfair and unjust for him. I was just trying to prevent him from getting his heart hurt."

Francine was taken by surprise at this apology. Moreover, the reason behind it.

"You were concerned for Henry? Is that why you two went together?" Francine said.

"Yes dear," she continued, "I don't know if you know this, Henry came to me for help to woo you."

Hearing this, Francine blushed with embarrassment.

"He really did that?" Francine replied with disbelief.

"Come on, let's have a little girl talk," Roxanne said, "why don't you give me a short tour of the galleries?"

Eris followed as Francine led her through the hallway.

"I'm sure you two are quite steady now, correct?" Roxanne asked.

"Yes, we are. Please tell me more, were you responsible for all his actions before?"

"Oh no, your fella is a lot more charming than one can expect. I merely invited you two together to the Carnival and told him to be on his best behavior. Other than that, Henry and I have been close like this ever since," Roxanne crossed her fingers.

"I had no idea you two were that close," Francine commented.

That comment had sparked Eris with a hint of offense.

"Well now you see how concerned I was when you didn't want to go with him. But you've surprised me, Franny, you showed up and ever since your dance together, Henry has not shut up about you. I just wanted to say that I am happy for how things have turned out."

"Thank you, Miss Roxanne," Francine finally said, "I actually hadn't made up my mind until you showed up that time when you did. If anything, I should give you my gratitude."

"There's no need, dear. And stop with the formalities already. Just call me Roxanne."

Francine nodded.

"Has Henry seen your work yet?"

"No, not yet. He is touring with his friends in New Orleans."

"Oh, that's right."

Francine's mood had suddenly begun to fade.

"What's the matter?" sensed Roxanne.

"I'm just a little concerned about the future of our dreams now that I am going to graduate this semester. Henry keeps putting off the thought of what's to come after winter. I've mentioned the subject briefly to him, but all he told me was that it'll be alright."

"No heart-to-heart conversation about it together?" Roxanne asked.

"I don't want to burden him and his music," she said.

"Well that's something to think about," Roxanne interjected.

"What do you mean?"

"Where both you and Henry's future desires lay. And whether you both want the same thing."

"We both have artistic dreams. And I do feel we have similar wants," Francine uttered.

Francine thought about the times where they had disagreements and incidents that had occurred, but it made her cherish their time together. She was silent as she waited for Roxanne to reply.

"Don't feel too stressed about it, dearie. How do you say it in England, 'keep your pecker up'?"

Francine smiled at her use of that expression.

"I was just there a few days ago, you know. I've had quite a discovery."

"You were in London?" said Francine, surprised.

"Yes, traveling around, I thought I might visit the places where my Franny grew up," Roxanne grinned, as if she had an evil thought.

Suddenly, Francine found a bit of discomfort at how she phrased that. It was as if Roxanne knew something about her more than a simple leisure trip would yield.

"Did you enjoy your stay?" Francine asked, trying to change the meaning of what Roxanne meant by that.

"My dear, I enjoyed every moment learning where you grew up. And what's more delightful, I found the people to be quite helpful."

Roxanne had a look that was piercing through Francine's exterior. There was something more.

"Did you just stay in the city?" Francine tried to say as she moved around the gallery room, distracting herself as she looked at the paintings on the walls.

"Mostly," she continued, "but I was invited personally to the country at an estate that wanted to know more about you than I of them."

"You mentioned me?" said Francine nervously.

"Yes, of course," Roxanne said, "and you can't believe what I found out."

"I think it's best that I introduce to you the rest of the presenters that are in today," Francine dismissed.

As Francine tried to lead Roxanne back to her gallery and then say her farewell, she was suddenly cornered when Roxanne went ahead of her and touched her to slow down. Francine backed away a little and stood behind a wall.

"What's the hurry, Franny?" Roxanne said contemptuously, "there's still so much to talk about."

"Please," Francine pleated, "I suddenly don't feel well. May we continue the tour another time?"

"You think I'm a fool?" Roxanne demanded, "I know why you're here, Countess."

Francine's eyes widened with distress as she looked straight into her violet pupils.

"You see, I know there are some people back in England who are expecting you to come home after your little excursion in America. I also know that there's another man. And you're here for your own personal gain," Roxanne pressed.

Francine was silent as she looked down in disgrace. Enormous guilt then began to redden her complexion.

"But that's not really a discovery because everyone at your university already knows this. Maybe except for Henry. Does he know?"

Francine shook her head and suddenly she began to feel her eyes dampen.

"I knew it. I knew some rich perfect girl wasn't going to consider a poor pianist seriously. No, you've been playing with his feelings this whole time. All he was to you was some amusing musician you would fancy for a little bit, and then when the spark is gone, you'll go back to your prince."

Roxanne was about to leave her side after saying this before Francine's sobbing was suppressed and she refuted. "You're wrong!" Francine cried back to her, "I do love Henry. And I was never playing with him. My feelings for him were always true."

As Francine stood her ground, Roxanne turned around before glaring at her.

"Stay away from Henry if you know what's best for him," Roxanne said.

Hearing this, Francine was surprised the second time. Only now she felt something else about Roxanne. She was no longer the same person she once knew. In her heart, Francine did not feel a bitter resentment at what she said. Instead, she began feeling pity for Roxanne. There were feelings there. Somewhere beneath her protection of Henry.

"I will never hurt Henry," Francine finally said.

Roxanne gave a blank stare after turning back once more.

"They're coming for you. You might have to sooner or later," she told her.

-Chapter 8-

Eris froze with shock after Henry had returned from his trip and brought her the news. He stood before her with an elated face and clear words that she only wished she had heard wrong.

"Come again?" she asked, denying it.

"I'm going to ask Francine to marry me," he repeated.

Eris was silent, barely uttering a word.

"That's wonderful, my boy!" said a voice from the other room. In came Eros.

"Mr. Romero? What are you doing here?" Henry asked.

Eros went straight to congratulate the boy after surprising them with his visit.

"Yes, why is he here all the time," Eris grunted.

"When are you going to do it, lad? Let me tell you the best way to do it. First, you have to bring her to somewhere romantic and then…"

"Hey! Why don't you let the boy explain himself before you give him any wild ideas," Eris reprimanded.

"Right, right, then tell us Henry. What made you come to this decision?" he asked.

"I know it's kind of early," Henry said.

"Never early," continued Eros, "every couple has their own time for matrimony."

"Like you said, Mr. Romero, it's love. I've discovered that she and I are meant to complete our artistic dreams together. I love her, and she loves me. There's no perfect time. We talked about going to Paris one day to follow our dreams. She also wants to go paint there. If I don't do it now, we may never get that chance to be and create together."

"What does he know of love?" Eris thought, "I was the one who supplied you with it."

"That," Eros spoke, "is the cutest and most romantic gesture for marriage I have ever heard!" Immediately, he took Henry's hands in admiration and shook them.

"My boy, you have my blessing," he continued.

"Thank you, sir," Henry replied bashfully.

Eris felt a black hole inside her heart. It sucked any joy she had and even any anger she might have had hearing it. Simply, she looked at Henry with a blank face. If he was going to ask her for her blessing, she would then not know how to respond. If it were Madame Roxanne, she would say "certainly." But now Eris' intentions were not to see them marry each other. Quite the contrary, she wanted to prevent this before it could have the slightest chance of even happening.

"Roxanne?" he asked, "could I trouble you to ask for one more favor?"

She breathed a sigh as she thought about what to say to him.

"What is it?" she finally asked.

"In private?" he looked at Eros.

"By all means, Henry," Eros said, smiling as he covered his ears and went out to the balcony.

Henry led Eris to her kitchen and showed her something from his pocket. He took out a box.

"I got Francine a ring," he said, showing it to her gleefully, "and I was hoping you would be willing to help me surprise Francine with it. You were always her confidant in the beginning. Maybe you could hint to her that I may not be sticking around with her. Then, when she's contemplating it, I'll come in and sweep her off her feet and relieve all her doubts. That way, she'll definitely agree to marry me."

Eris looked at the diamond ring. It looked expensive, and someone with his salary must have saved for months to get it. She thought about all the clubs he played at to earn it. But, she knew that this ring would be pointless. Francine would not marry him. He ought to know what has been going on since they met each other.

"Well? What do you think?" he inquired eagerly.

"Henry, you have an awful way of pulling strings to get what you want," joked Eris earnestly.

"So, you'll help me?"

"Henry, you need to know something," she tried to say as she got serious.

"What is it?"

"There's no easy way to say this, but… Francine is not going to marry you."

"What? How can you say that for sure? Did you talk to her?"

"I've discovered an awful truth while you were gone. Francine has another lover back in England," Eris said.

"Yes, but he's gone from her life," Henry refuted, "it's only she and I now."

"You've heard it already? Well then you should know that she's promised to him and she'll go back to him once she finishes her studies."

"No, she's staying with me," Henry said, flustered. His tone was getting more frustrated and irritable as Roxanne tried to persuade him out of it. She continued to tell him what she had discovered in her trip.

"You must have heard the rumors by now. She's a countess, nobility, for pity's sake. She has more money than you can ever imagine. And she's expected to marry her own kind after her studies are completed. I'm sorry dear, she's only fancying you until she has to leave," Eris concluded.

Eris waited for Henry after his silence and his frowning complexion. She felt an uneasy feeling for bursting his excitement earlier, and now she had no idea of how to comfort him. Immediately, Henry went over to the counter and took his belongings.

"Where are you going?" Eris asked, "please Henry, it's hard to take in but you needed to know the truth."

As Henry opened her door, he looked at her with a powerful gaze.

"I need to know for sure," Henry said, frustrated.

When the door slammed shut, Eros returned and saw Eris in thought. Eris, although pleased with what was to come in the end, sighed again as Eros came to ask her, "Well, that was quite heartbreaking news. Did you make all that up or did you do something?"

"Eros, I wish I could claim that to be my doing. But that's the truth. We did not know Francine Daye. The girl is betrothed to her English relative. When her graduation comes, she's sailing back whether he loves her or not."

"Did you meet them when you were digging up her secrets?" he asked.

"Meet them? I contacted them myself when I found out who she was," she tried to smile.

"My, it seems like you might actually succeed in breaking them up after all," Eros commented sternly as he looked over through the window.

"Follow him, god of love," Eris said solemnly, "Give him some comfort as he learns the truth and mends his broken heart."

"You will not go to see it?" he asked as he prepared to leave.

"I've caused all the discord required. Go, I'll be here if he needs me."

Even though Eris was minutes from victory, she had a bit of hesitation in her voice.

As Eros looked over to her one more time, he saw how Eris reacted. Her face looked like she had just committed murder and was figuring out how to move on with her next plans. When he stepped out, Eros heard one more thing that Eris said as he exited.

"Countess Francine Diana Young, of Kent," she muttered, "you can't marry him. You don't love him. You can't love him. That's the end of it."

****

Francine was painting with her art class at Park Central when Henry had begun his search for her. She had begun painting the landscape of the pond and the bridge, which was surprisingly busy today because of an event nearby, and all of it had yielded frustration for her as she tried to calm her mind from what Roxanne had said to her last week. She felt conflicted when Roxanne had found her out. Despite being already promised to someone else, everything was different now. It had changed for the better.

Francine knew in her heart that she had no intention of going back to London. She had decided this when she first arrived in America. All her efforts were to escape the life she once had there and to escape "them." But why was she feeling guilty? Roxanne's words echoed a commitment she had made there. Yet it was a commitment that was forced upon her. If Count Thomas Young had never died her destiny would have been different. Yet, her gratefulness to him had made her realize that his family, and if she could call them her family, back in London, made her feel compelled to honor their agreement.

But now, Francine thought about Henry as she added a few brush strokes on her water. Deep within the battle that was going on in her mind between which path to choose, she knew that Henry had drastically influenced her more to stay here and leave all obligations behind her. However, the only problem with that was what sort of life she would live without the financial connections back home. Despite her aspirations to paint and travel, deep within she had wanted a stable life. A real family to call her own. But would all of that even matter for long as she loved Henry? She felt trapped, uncertain of what the near future held. All she could do now was look at what she painted and see that it was not the pretty landscape her classmates were painting. It looked more like a river of chaotic colors blending into a whirlpool that portrayed the eruption of her self-direction, drowning.

When Francine began to look at the landscape once more, her instructor came to console her. And while this was happening, Francine noticed a person rushing through the park making his way through the crowd, desperately. By the time the person had crossed the bridge, she plainly saw that it was Henry.

"Francine!" he called out. The students turned their heads as they watched him come up.

"Henry," Francine said shyly, "is everything alright?"

Henry had a frustrated and tired look as he held her hands.

"May I talk to you in private, please?" he said flustered, "I'm sorry everyone, please go back to your work."

"Young man," interrupted the instructor, "we are in the middle of a class. Can't you come back later?"

Francine quickly turned to her instructor and asked politely to be excused for a break. He reluctantly agreed after a few pleas.

"Is something bothering you?" Francine asked him after he took her to the side.

"Francine, I need to know. Is there another man in your life besides me?" Henry said sternly.

Surprised by his question, Francine knew that she could no longer hide anymore. Whether this was the right time or not, the man she loved was in front of her asking her about not just her past, but her future as well. Her emotions could no longer hold it in any longer. She began feeling warmer as her skin reddened, feeling exposed.

"So, there is someone back home, isn't there?" Henry said as he looked at her with patience.

"Yes, there was someone I was promised to," she said, "but I never loved him the way I love you. And I will never go back to him or London."

Henry was silent as he looked baffled by what she said.

"Henry," she sobbed, "this is the truth. I have never spoken to him or any contacts in London since I've arrived here. Please don't leave me. I'm sorry, I'm so sorry. I should have told you before."

Henry tried to comfort and cover Francine's tears as he thought about what Roxanne had told him. She had hidden this from him. It was true. Yet during Francine's testimony of her love, he felt there was no betrayal in his heart as he thought he might have felt since leaving Roxanne's home. Instead, he felt the contrary. He had the answer he wanted all along.

"If you want time to rethink about us," Francine said disappointingly, "I'll understand."

Henry let go of her and took a step back. He did not take his eyes from her as his hand reached inside his breast pocket.

"Henry," Francine said, getting ready to accept the inevitable end of their relationship in the middle of her speculating class.

"Marry me," Henry told her as he showed her the ring he bought.

Utterly surprised by this, Francine was speechless and looked at him with awe.

"What? Are you being serious?" she uttered in disbelief.

"I am," he continued, "I love you, Francine Daye. That's the end of it."

"Then I'll marry you," Francine cried as she embraced him.

In the backdrop, the speculating class started clapping as they watched them. Henry and Francine looked back at them and smiled in embarrassment. He held her hand, proud of what they had done. While they cheered, the god of love stood not far from them as he watched with pleasure.

"All it takes is a shot of love to make a couple drop everything and be with each other. Atta boy, Henry. Discordia is not going to like this one bit though," Eros concluded before clapping for Henry's accomplishment.

-Chapter 9-

When the news of Francine's acceptance to Henry's proposal reached Eris by Eros, it did not come with excitement, as one would expect. Not only was Eris in a rage and resenting the miscalculated error, she became severely depressed that Henry and Francine would be together at last and for good. Eros, who had wished upon the success of Henry and Francine's relationship, agreed that Eris' ways of bringing them together to gain the Ticking Heart yielded a great win for Eris and that her ill-will of upscaling the wager of destroying the relationship on her part, was nonetheless foolhardy and superfluous.

It was Pandora who was the only one who understood Eris more and more. She knew that it was not just a gamble of Eris' pride. A wager between gods may be a rivalry, but one thing that did not make any sense was whether Eros was the true rival. And as Pandora pondered this, she realized that Francine was the true culprit that thwarted her plans. Not Eros, who merely spectated, fooling her to believe that he was involved with them in the first place. She knew it was not her affair to interpret their wager, but she always had suspicions while supporting the goddess in her quest to sabotage the love. She had a feeling that Eris developed a fondness for the mortal

Henry as well. A dangerous fondness that meant more than just her wager.

While Pandora was in the process of returning to her dance studio from Eris' home after seeing her in a devastated state of depression, the image of Eris in tears was hard to take in. Pandora had learned from her that Henry and Francine had planned for a very small wedding but wanted to wait until after Francine's graduation after December. And that was not far. Strolling along the boulevard toward her dance studio, a yellow car revved its engine and passed her quickly as it headed in the same direction.

"What's his hurry?" Pandora commented, irritated by it.

When Pandora reached her dance studio, the same car from earlier was parked in front. She saw a person outside her studio looking for any signs of life in the window.

"Hey, no classes on Mondays," she told him loudly.

The boy turned around and she saw a boy near Henry's age in an oversized driver's uniform looking back at her, startled.

"Sorry, miss," he replied quickly, taking off his hat. She noticed he had an unusual accent.

"Can I help you?" Pandora asked, questioning his intention to be here for anything but dance lessons.

"Yes, I'm actually searching for a Miss Roxanne Smith. Does she live here by any chance?"

Pandora noticed that the car parked was still running and there was smoke coming out from the rear passenger window.

"Who's it to you?" she said, staring down the innocent looking boy.

"My lord requests an audience with Madame Roxanne. He understands this is her address," the boy articulated, but it came out butchered in his accent.

Pandora thought about this surprise for Eris for a second. Who in the world was looking for her?

"Do you know her?" the boy asked.

Before Pandora had a chance to reply, they were interrupted.

"Pip!" grumbled a voice from the car. A well-dressed man came out of the car. He had just finished his cigar and was brushing one of his hairs from his neatly combed head.

"Have you driven us to the correct address or not? It's getting bloody freezing and my leg's cramped from waiting here," the man insisted.

Looking at the man up close, Pandora immediately recognized him. It was the Lord she and Eris visited when they went to England.

When Pandora accompanied Eris to Britain, she had been hesitant to dig deeper into Francine's life. Ever since Pandora apologized to Francine for trying to seduce Henry one time, she and Francine have become promising friends. But when Eris and Pandora were there, the search had yielded almost nothing about Francine until they gained some insights from multiple sources. They learned that she was the heiress of the departed Viscount Young of Kent. But, it was much more complicated than it seemed. Rumors from the common people had revealed that he was killed one night at a ball. It was also coincidental that Francine was the last person to be with him before his death. Further rumors had also stated that Francine was never the daughter, but an adopted orphan the Viscount admired, ultimately becoming part of his household.

The search concluded when Eris and Pandora found themselves in the estate of the former Viscount Thomas Young, now managed by his younger brother, Edward Young. When they were granted permission to enter the residence after telling the butler that they knew Francine, they met Lord Young briefly with a few questions he demanded answered first. Eris, being cautious, did not reveal where Francine was exactly.

Upon their exit from the estate, Pandora had complained how bad of a host the lord was and how little he had told them of Francine. In fact, they only learned of Francine's past betrothal from anonymous sources there. As for Eris, she had concluded that the family did not know much of Francine's life in America and only knew she was in America studying. Their encounter had shown to her that Francine was not missed but sought after when the count began to ask them about her. Francine was exclusive to her family. It was only hours later that Pandora realized they were being followed, soon after leaving the estate that time. Despite Eris not believing her, she was right.

"Sorry, my Lord," the boy replied, "I will try to contact the listings again for her."

"Hold on," Lord Young commented as she looked at Pandora, "you look familiar. Wait, I think I remember you. You accompanied Madame Roxanne that time, didn't you?"

"Yeah," Pandora replied, "what do you want her for?"

"My dear girl," he continued, "it's about Franny. She needs to come home."

The image of Francine's smiling face as she listened to her friends appeared on the glass inside the Ticking Heart. There was something about that radiant face of hers that everyone liked. It was a contagious smile, almost like an angel who knew just what you were thinking as she listened to you. Everything about Francine only made Eris grumble as she held this delicate girl's live image in the palm of her immortal hands. Francine had everything, and now she will have Henry for good.

"Look at how fake she looks with that smile of hers!" Eris cried, "it's so toxic. Only I know what a witch she is under that little ball of hay hair."

As Eris lamented and grunted on top of her balcony, Eros only smiled as he lounged on a chair reading a magazine. Eris continued viewing the Ticking Heart, seeing what Francine was doing now, talking to her friends about her new engagement at a café.

"Have you given up already?" Eros asked. "All you've been doing this week is moping around gazing at her. Goodness, congratulate her or something. After all, chaos is sweet when you pretend to practice civility in the beginning, isn't it?"

"Oh, what's the point? I've tried everything and going to her now would only raise her suspicion even more after what I said to her," Eris said before closing the Ticking Heart.

"What did you say to her?" he asked.

"Basically, stay away from Henry you harlot, or I'll tell your family," Eris said nonchalantly.

"Oh my, I see your point," Eros said, surprised.

"By the gods! How in the world did my female intuition turn upside down? How have I known that she would deceive

Henry again by twisting her words and saying that she had passed up on her betrothal from England?"

Eris sat down on the ground as she patted Mayhem in misery.

"Even now, you cannot admit that Francine truly loves Henry," Eros commented.

"Because she doesn't deserve to love Henry," Eris wanted to say but stood silent as she looked at Eros begrudgingly. She knew in her heart that Francine loved him. But she couldn't allow her to. Henry, as Eris thought about him, could do better and only she could be the one to provide that to him somehow.

Looking at the Ticking Heart again, Eris teared a little. She knew she was too late to stop their marriage. And with frustration built up inside her, she concluded that Francine must be removed from the picture for good. But how? The wager, she thought, was not worth her apple. She will need it to end Francine's life, she thought with contempt.

"My dear, be prepared to answer the door. I believe we will be having a few guests," said Eros.

Eris gave a puzzled look before looking out the balcony to see a group of people entering her building with another person that looked like Pandora. Leaving the Heart on the table near Eros, Eris stood up and walked away.

"What's with you, goddess?" he retorted, "why are you giving up on your crush on Henry?"

"What?" said Eris, caught off guard.

"Admit it, you love him," Eros declared.

Hearing these words, Eris was stunned. She could not believe it. Eros, the fun-loving god has insisted that she was crushing on a mortal, and with a tone that was deadly honest and uncanny.

"I..." she began, "I may have developed a kinship with him perhaps, but 'love' is a bit too rash to say, isn't it?"

"Whatever you say," Eros said before laughing. His laughs were beginning to give her chills as she walked away to get the door that rung.

"Before you open that door and greet Pandora," Eros called out.

Eris stopped.

"Do give love a chance. Because it's not over yet," he continued.

"What do you mean by that?" she asked curiously.

"I'll tell you later," he said before walking toward her balcony railing. "Go welcome our guests first," he then gestured.

When Eris opened the door, Pandora suddenly barged in without hesitation.

"You're back," Eris remarked.

"Roxanne!" she cried, "they're here! I can't believe it."

"Who's here?"

"Franny's rich folks, they're downstairs waiting for you," Pandora continued as she patrolled all around her living room.

"How did they find us here?" Eris commented.

"Beats me. Are you going to see them?"

Eris looked over at Eros, but he was nowhere to be found. Whatever it was that Eros was trying to say, she had a feeling that he was up to something. In this unexpected occurrence, Francine's family visit had comforted her, giving her hope again. Now was the time to strike. It was not for a silly trinket or being right anymore. Her feelings now had revealed to Roxanne that she would steal Henry from Francine with whatever it took.

In Eris' apartment sat the Viscount, Lady Daisy Stone, and her son Daniel. As Eris spoke to them about Francine and what had brought them here, there was something that felt strangely unfamiliar to Pandora. She tried to shut up her curiosity as she looked onto Daniel Young, the supposed heir to the late Viscount Thomas Young. There was something quite spoiled about him as he looked bored while the Viscount and Lady Stone talked. Although he was well-groomed, his attitude was revealing of his unpleasant character. He grumbled to his mother about wanting to go visit a clothing store nearby, just before saying that he wanted to go to a speakeasy tonight too. And there was the Viscount, his gargoyle face looked onto them as if he was up to something more than just finding Francine. The only person that looked quite composed was the skinny pale woman, Lady Stone, who was the widow of the late Viscount. She sat there looking unbothered and professional, supporting the Viscount's request to see Francine immediately and their plans to go back.

"Franny must be going back before her 22nd birthday. Her agreement was that she would marry Danny after studying in America for a short while," said Lord Young before sipping some coffee.

"I see. Franny will not inherit her status if she fails to marry," Eris commented.

"My late husband's will would serve as the binding contract. Francine has given us her word that Danny would be her husband by the time she returns from America," answered

Lady Stone, "Eddie, why don't you show her the paper she signed that we all agreed on for allowing her to go to America in the first place."

Lord Young dug into his front pocket and handed it to Eris and Pandora to see.

Looking at it, Eris saw that Francine had signed this attachment to the will with red. Pandora looked amazed and wondered how Francine would do such a thing. To surrender her life just so that she would follow some will and go to America.

"What if she marries someone else?" Pandora asked.

"Impossible," Lord Young commented, "Thomas, my brother, had specified that the title and wealth shall remain in the family. Marrying someone else would only divide our estates. Believe us, there were many noble and affluent suitors that asked for her by the time she was 16. We've considered it, but we think it is in the best interests for us to follow his will."

"But is she not the daughter of the late Viscount?" Eris asked.

"No, she is not my niece nor is she the daughter of my brother. She was a distant cousin that my brother had been the godfather of and adopted. Thus, Danny is not directly blood related." Lord Young's voice rasped as he declared this.

There was something puzzling about Francine's family that Pandora had thought did not make a whole lot of sense. They came all the way here to force her to marry her son, and now fiancé, and not the lover from London they thought she had all this time. She looked at Eris as she wondered what she was going to do. Eris had a look that was neither mystified nor unsurprised. Indeed, Eris had a poker face as she began to tell them something that would shock them.

"You must know then, my lord, that Franny is about to get married to someone," she said, "here."

"What?" they both said as they looked astonished, "to whom?"

"To a jazz musician. They are planning it right after Francine's graduation."

"That's absurd!" Lord Young cried, "there's no way that will happen."

Lady Stone was silent after hearing this. She had a fierce look as Eris looked at her, enjoying this moment of reality.

"Then you must take us to her immediately," Lord Young insisted, "we need to have a word with her."

A miracle had occurred for Eris. She now had reinforcements to bury Francine's love for Henry for good.

"I know where we could find her," Eris declared.

"Danny," Lady Stone said to him, "Tell Pip to prepare the car."

"Mother, don't tell me I still have to stick around for this," Daniel protested, "just have her brought back to England when I get back later. I really have to be going."

"It would only be for today, dear. Franny needs to see that you came all the way here for her," she replied, "now come along."

Daniel opened the door and found Pip in front of them, startled like before.

"Let's go, you idiot. Go start the engine," Daniel demanded.

When they were about to head out the door, Eris excused herself for a second to shut her balcony door. It was then that Pandora went up to her out of concern.

"Are you really going to take them to Francine?" she asked.

"Of course," Eris replied without hesitation, "our search in England finally paid off, didn't it? Dora, you've made me quite a happy goddess today."

"Yeah, I suppose it did. I just hope they don't hurt Henry and Francine too badly," she replied. Pandora knew that this was probably not possible. But she tried not to think about it as she followed the Viscount and the family out. Eris was about to leave when she noticed something on the table where Eros was seated earlier. It was at the spot where she had left the Ticking Heart, only this time it was not there. Instead, Eros left a note:

I shall borrow the Heart a little bit until you finish your wager. True love has yet to come…

Eros' earlier accusation kept wandering in her head while she talked to Francine's so-called family. Do I love Henry? Is this why I am trying to get rid of her? The goddess only knew that this spark of jealousy and desire was alien to her. But having the Ticking Heart did not matter anymore, now that she believed that a device could never truly reveal the emotion of love. Instead, what Henry asked before—*How do you know when you are in love with someone?*—seemed to reveal more of what she was now after.

-Chapter 10-

Francine's friends had just dropped her off at her home from a day of being the center of attention during their outing together. After congratulating her again and reminding her of scheduling a time to pick out dresses together, they waved goodbye and then drove off. By the time Francine reached the staircase to her door, however, she heard an engine behind her as it approached the street of her house. Wondering whether it was her friends again returning for more reminders and encouragement for her to go out with them again tonight, she turned to smile, hoping to bashfully decline as she just wanted to read. Of course, her smile was met with shock when she saw who it was stepping out.

"It's you," Francine said, startled and speechless. "How…how did you find me?"

"What? No warm welcome for the brother of the man who saved you from that dreadful orphanage?" said Lord Young as he approached her, smiling.

Lady Stone had also gotten out of the car from behind him. Francine's terrified eyes remembered her very well. Daisy Stone had the same look on her face that she had given her since forever. Those cold, unapologetic eyes of hers that peered deep into her. Of all the people in the world, Francine had dreaded seeing her the most.

"There's much to discuss about Franny," Lady Stone said, "let's talk about it inside your 'little home' that you made yourself here in America." There was a hint of resentment in her voice.

The Viscount led the way before he turned back to the car. "Danny!" the Viscount yelled, "get out of the car."

Seeing Danny step out hit Franny with her inevitable reality. The last time she saw him, he was barely a man. Now, exactly her age, he was a ripe young chap ready to become the future lord.

"Well, it seems little Franny has grown up, hasn't she?" he said as he followed them, pleased.

Eris and Pandora were still in the car when the Viscount and Lady Stone got out to meet Francine. The Viscount had requested that they give them a moment with her alone, with Eris having politely agreed. Daniel got out of the car and signaled for Pip to drive them off somewhere for a free meal in the meantime. The car stood motionless, parked a block from Francine's home.

"Where do you wish to go, Ma'am?" Pip said as he looked ahead at the home where Francine lived. Pandora looked worried as she looked at Eris for answers.

And like Pip, who was busy looking in Francine's direction, Eris wondered what they could be talking about.

"Roxanne," Pandora commented, "what now?"

"Pip," Eris called out loud.

"Yes, ma'am?" Pip said, turning around from his concentrated look at Francine's home.

"I just remembered my physician lives near here, I think I shall go visit him," she said.

"Where does he live? I'll drop you off there," Pip replied.

"There's no need, flyboy. I'll just walk over. It's only less than a block away. Why don't you take Dora to somewhere downtown for coffee? I'll be here waiting for Lord Young as soon as they finish."

Pip had a look of uncertainty after hearing the request, just as Pandora gave a look to Eris assuming Eris was going to spy on Francine's family.

"Keep him busy and find out more about the Viscount if you can," Eris whispered to Pandora. Quickly, Eris opened the car door and stepped out.

"Wait, Ma'am," Pip called, "I'm not sure whether my lord will allow me to let you go unescorted."

"It'll be fine, I'll be here waiting for you as soon as you come back at 6. And look at you, now you have this beautiful woman to yourself," she winked.

Pandora played along and began to assure him as Eris waved goodbye and walked in the direction of Francine's home. As the car drove away, Roxanne disguised herself again and went up to Francine's door. Listening in, she heard the ultimatum given to Francine.

Francine could barely hold herself together as the Viscount and Lady Stone began to formally sit themselves on her furniture, waiting for her to brew the tea. As the clock ticked above her kitchen wall, her heartbeat skipped a second faster as she prepared herself for what she was about to tell them. As she prepared the tea in the kitchen, the shine of the diamond on the ring on her finger distracted her as she waited for the hot water. Looking at it, she wondered whether she should take it off, so as not to surprise them right away of what plans she had before they came. But the thought of Henry's face kept reminding her that she must face them with the intent that she would no longer go back to England and marry Daniel.

Daniel waited patiently as he stood a few paces away from her looking at her artwork with a smirk. The painting that was still out on her easel was the landscape she did when Henry came to propose to her. And although it was not Franny's best work of Park Central, it was her window to her emotions of that day. Quickly, Francine went over to it and covered the picture.

"I'm sorry, my house is a mess and my mediocre work is all over the place," she protested as Daniel looked at her with interest.

"You haven't changed. Belittling one's work as always, Franny," Daniel said. "Relax, I'm here to observe and stand in for whatever the two have in mind. I don't want to be here anymore than you do."

Francine knew this obviously. Daniel was always the one to be silent and unmoved by what was going on. And although he was never as shrewd and overcritical as his mother, he always seemed to be her shadow, never prying but lurking beneath the power between his mother and his uncle.

"You shouldn't have come," Francine replied half-heartedly. She had reddened a little as he looked down on her with his inquisitive eyes.

"Who's that?" he asked as he pointed to what looked like a portrait in her room.

The portrait was something Francine had painted when she thought about that day she shared her first kiss with Henry on that rainy night.

"Oh him, he's famous around these parts. I've been really interested in jazz, and I chose him as a subject."

"It's him, isn't it?" Daniel surmised, "you've found someone here. I'm not surprise."

Francine looked at him with a saddened heart, even though Daniel was her fiancé from the promise she'd made to Lord Edward Young and to his mother, she knew that he had once had feelings for her when they were much younger. And although one might say it was a childish crush, he had always resented that she never saw him as anything more than something like a brother. From then on, he never looked at her the same way again.

Despite having no feelings for him from the very beginning, Daniel had somehow matured to inherit his father's charming and warm face. Something about that made her feel uneasy, talking to him again. It was like seeing the late Viscount again.

"How are you, Daniel?" she asked, trying to smile amid her finished brewed tea.

"Been better. I think you'd better hurry with the tea, you know how impatient my mother gets. It'll save you a lecture from her."

Despite how spoiled and childish Daniel was, his soft spot for her came out now and then.

The Viscount wasted no time in scolding Francine about not keeping in contact with them after that year she had left England. It was not because he cared about her safety or was concerned. They had wanted to keep an eye on where Francine was and what she was doing by the time she promised she would come back to England. Before coming to Empire State University, she had previously been at another university and was only there briefly before skipping out and changing her address on short notice. For the last four years, she had been living by herself, having made strides in severing the ties to home. She had been successful, until now.

"You will come back to England with us next week," Lord Young declared.

"But there's only about a month left until my graduation," Francine protested, "I can't leave, and I don't want to leave."

"Insolence!" Lord Young grumbled, "how dare you talk back to me at a time like this. If my brother was still alive and knew you'd spent five years on your American escapades without fulfilling your duty for the whole reason we adopted you for, he—"

"You never adopted me," Francine interrupted.

"Oh, you thought it was my goody brother who adopted you from the love in his heart? Rubbish, he adopted you because he felt sorry for you. Without him, you would have been stuck in that orphanage."

"Be grateful that my departed husband, the son of a Viscount, even considered adopting," Lady Stone added.

Francine tried to hold back her tears as she looked at them. In a way, they were right about that part of her past. She was no noble like they were. She had nothing before Thomas Young came into her life and adopted her. He could have adopted someone else. Her life had been a fortunate chance into nobility. And now the life she had pursued for her dreams and passions were ending.

"Why must you do this to me?" Francine uttered. "I have a choice to do what I want with my life and to marry who

I please. And even with Thomas gone, he would have wanted me to do it too."

Lord Young began chuckling. "Wanted you to? You don't know who my brother was. He was a drunk who only cared about what people thought of him. That's why he donated to charity. That's why he's been so gentle and kind to everyone. God rest his soul for all the waste of compassion that killed him."

"You're wrong," Francine snapped, "if you were only half the man he was!"

Everyone was surprised when Francine said that.

Immediately, with a swish of her hand, Lady Stone struck Francine's face.

Silence filled the room as Francine looked away, wounded.

"Don't you forget what we did for you," Lady Stone asserted, "you would have been imprisoned or back on the streets if it weren't for us vouching for your innocence. So don't you dare speak ill of us in any way. You were the only one with him in his room during your ball when he passed."

"Mother! That's enough," Daniel said as he held her back and relaxed her.

Francine dropped to the ground as everything came back to her with traumatic grief. That night, on her 16th birthday, Francine was the first to witness the murder scene of her benefactor and the closest thing to a father. Screaming when the blood of her father that had spilled on her dress, she rushed out into the ballroom, interrupting her ball. All eyes were upon her as she cried in fear and pleaded for help. The blood trail had put her not only as a witness, but as a possible suspect in the late Viscount's murder. She was the last person with him in his study a few minutes before he was murdered. And because of that, no one vouched for her except Lady Stone and the Viscount's brother. The debt she owed to the Young family was for more than just her adoption. Indeed, she owed them her life. And at any time, their power and money could be easily taken back upon their will.

"Franny, please," Lord Young pleaded, "we know that you are currently engaged to someone else. You must tell him that you're already engaged and thus his engagement is now voided. Do you understand?"

"But I love him," Francine uttered as she tried to stop her tears, "doesn't that mean anything?"

"Love?" Lady Stone commented, "what do the young know of love? Don't be confused with romantic dreams and thoughts of eloping, because that's all love is—childish escapes. This jazz musician of yours, regardless of whether he is talented or not, is not suitable for a lady nor worth anything in a marriage. Listen to me, if you married him you would not live a life of a countess nor live a stable life with children, a house, and all that you desire."

"I will be free," Francine interjected.

"Free of what? Free from obligations? Free to love? Don't let romance novels fool you. We're not free no matter what. Order and affluence keep us above these simpleminded follies."

After saying this, Lady Stone came to Francine slowly and stood at her level. She saw the ring on Francine's finger. A mix of feelings overwhelmed Francine as she looked at her.

"A trinket of a ring," Lady Stone commented as she held her hands, "this is all the love he can buy?"

Francine could no longer look at them anymore. In that second, she succumbed and fell, collapsing onto the floor. Quickly, Daniel rushed to her and held her as he looked at her pale porcelain face.

"Is she alright?" Lord Young asked.

"She'll be okay," Daniel said, "she just passed out. Probably from the shock."

"Let's take her back to the hotel. Get her up will you dear?" commanded Lady Stone.

Eris and Pandora were escorted home after Pip dropped the family off. Eris was silent on the ride back despite Pandora and Pip asking her if she had seen or heard anything. Her answer was that she did not hear much other than that Francine was shocked when the Viscount and Lady Stone told her that she had to return home immediately.

"To marry Daniel, right?" Pandora pressed on.

"Yeah, just like what they told us," Eris said.

"Is that all?" Pip inquired, "come on, Miss Smith, tell us more."

"Is it your place to learn so much about your lord's affairs?" Eris reacted.

"Relax dear, Philip was an orphan too, with Francine from the same orphanage," Pandora defended, "he's only curious and concerned about her."

"Really? Well what do you know about Franny? Will she do it? Marry him?" interjected Eris.

"I'm not sure," he replied hesitantly, "Franny has always been the head strong type. But then, she's the most pleasant girl I know. She got me my job, you know. There's been no one kinder or good-hearted as her in my life."

Eris contemplated whether Francine would fight to stay and be with Henry or follow the Viscount back to England.

"Do you happen to know why the late Viscount adopted her?" Eris asked.

"From what I remember, it was because she was quite smart and charming. She looked after us orphans despite being the same age. One day, this gentleman, the late Viscount, showed up and went over to talk to her while she was reading some Dickens book. After that, the late Viscount kept visiting, and gave her new books, even supplied the orphanage with new canvases and painting supplies so that she could do art."

"Did he adopt her after?" Pandora asked.

"Not for some time. He took his bloody time, that's for sure. By then, I was already adopted when I heard the late Viscount came to get her. Didn't make any sense for a rich bloke like him. Here you are, ladies. This is the correct address, right?"

"Yes, thank you," Eris said right before stepping out, "maybe you'll get your answers when you see them soon."

"Yes, I am dreading that," Pip said as they got out.

"See you soon, Philip!" Pandora cheered, "thanks again for supper."

When Pip departed, Eris turned to Pandora with a stern look.

"Dora, never mention this to Eros, and definitely not Henry," she said.

"What's the matter?"

"I just want to make sure that Francine is out of the picture for good."

Pandora had a look of concern as she heard this. "You really want to win this wager, huh?"

"It's not about winning anymore. It's about…" Eris paused before finishing her sentence. Pandora waited for her answer as Eris turned in the direction of her home.

"Henry," Pandora uttered softly, for her.

Eris merely ignored what she said. She kept walking until she was all alone.

Pandora thought about it some more as she walked throughout the city. More and more, she realized that now her role in this wager was turning more unpleasant than she would have wanted. However, it did make her rethink love. Somewhere beneath it, she realized that she had lost touch of what it is to love and what it was like to be mortal. But she knew she had to see how everything turned out for Henry and Francine.

In the next few days, Pandora followed Eris, hoping to discover what love was and what it was like to love.

-Chapter 11-

Pandora followed Eris from afar while the goddess tracked Francine to her meeting with Henry at Park Central. While Francine sat there on the front seat by herself, Eris sat behind her, invisible, in her immortal form. Dressed warmly for the winter, Francine looked out the window of the trolley as she thought about that day that she, by chance, saw Henry riding on the same route with her. She remembered how they barely knew each other, yet from afar, she had always sensed that when they did see each other, no one in the world existed but them alone. When she had departed from the trolley that rainy day with a bit of disappointment that they never got a chance to talk, Henry had shown up when she had least expected it. Since then, she knew that her life was changing for the better. There were more reasons for her to stay in America and make a new life for herself. She had thought that she could have painted away her loneliness or traveled excessively in the states to find herself. But it was nothing compared to the time she spent with him. With Henry, she felt there was hope.

Looking at Francine's face in the reflection from the window, Eris thought about how troubled Francine was. But curiously, she had a feeling that Francine's facial expression revealed that she was ready for what she was about to do than any signs of true sorrow for her predicament. Francine's face was like a doll, painted with a face neither joyful nor sorrowful, enigmatic at least. Yet, looking at Francine and remembering how she tried to stand up for herself to her family, Eris could see why Henry fell for her. It was not because of her beauty alone, she had this courageous charm and wit that a man would be a fool to give up. Because of that, she was dangerous. Because of that, Francine would always be better than her if Henry had to choose between them. With her gone, Eris would finally have the chance to be with him at last.

When Francine arrived and stood on the same bridge at Park Central, the same one she had painted of the time Henry had proposed to her, she began anticipating for his arrival. Resuming her role as the black swan of this third act, Eris swam in the lake, gazing at Francine's melancholy, while she stared aimlessly at the freezing water. Francine suddenly turned and looked at Eris with an expression that scared the goddess. It was an expression that almost seemed like she knew who the swan was.

"Where are your friends, beautiful swan?" Francine finally commented, "you better fly south soon. Home will always be here for you when you return in the Spring."

Francine then gave Eris a genuine smile that seemed forlorn.

"And I will always be here with you when we get married," Henry interrupted as he appeared behind her, smiling.

"Hello, my love," Henry said as Francine turned to him, "I'm sorry I'm a little late. What's on your mind?"

Francine went forward and embraced him as he held her tightly.

"I missed you so much," Francine said.

Henry looked surprised as he held Francine's embrace.

"It's as if you haven't seen me for a decade," Henry laughed, "is everything alright?"

Francine was silent as she felt him. She remembered what she was going to say to him, but the words could not come out. All she wanted was to enjoy the moment longer with him.

"Francine?" Henry asked as he continued to hold her, worried and mystified.

Eris waited patiently for Francine to answer as she stared enviously at their long embrace.

"Come on rich girl, do it already. I don't have all day. Make your choice and be done with it."

Eris turned her attention away for a second and noticed the Viscount's car pulling up near the park entrance. She now felt reassured that things would go her way this time for sure.

When Francine finally let go of Henry, she continued to look at him passionately with her sincere eyes. She knew that she could not stall it any longer.

"I," she began, "I can't."

"What is it, darling?" he replied.

"I can't marry you."

Hearing this, Henry doubted what was said.

"What are you talking about?" he asked, surprised.

Francine's hand slowly pulled the ring from her finger before turning away from him in disgrace.

When she turned back with the ring in her hands, Henry now knew that she was serious.

"What have I done?" he said in disbelief, "are you not ready? Oh please, just tell me that's your only reason. I promise I'll wait. I promise I'll be better."

Francine's eyes grew redder as she uncontrollably felt the weight on Henry's heart. Henry then came over to her, trying to assure her that he could wait for her, holding her hands.

Francine loved the comfort of his hands but knew that the longer she prolonged this the harder it would be. She released her hands from his with the ring handed back to him.

"We, we can't be together," Francine tried to say.

"Tell me why," Henry demanded, frustrated, "do you not love me anymore? Why suddenly have you changed your mind?"

Francine owed him the truth despite not wanting to hurt him.

"I'm returning to England. I'm sorry, I am to be married there," she said quickly.

"Who's making you return to England? You told me you were not going to marry him. You can't still have feelings for him, do you?"

"I do not love him, but I must do what I must do," she sobbed.

"So you're forced into this," Henry concluded. "Francine, tell me, do you love me? That's all that matters, please. We can work this out together."

Though she was sure she loved him, being with Henry and sharing a life together was a mere romantic dream, just as Lady Stone told her. She knew she was guilty of thinking this, but it was that thought in her head that had long festered and was now released to her reasoning. Henry's vagabond dream of traveling the world in pursuit of artistic dreams was not real. She had to go back. Back to reality.

"I'm sorry, I can't," she cried. Immediately, she turned away from him and rushed toward the direction of the Viscount's car. Henry watched in desperation and despair before going after her.

"No, Piano Boy, don't go after her," thought Eris. Immediately, she too followed him, this time transformed back to Roxanne.

Francine rushed to the entrance of the park and cried her eyes out before a honk of the Viscount's horn signaled where they were. As she entered the car, she looked back with only a glance as Henry called out to her. When Henry came to the car, the window rolled down.

Hoping to see Francine so that he could tell her to wait for him, the Viscount peered out.

"It's over, chap," Lord Young commanded, "Franny must marry her own kind. You got nothing that she needs in her life."

"I'm what she needs," Henry asserted before yelling louder for her, "Francine!"

Henry desperately banged on the car as he watched it go, but it was hopeless as the Viscount commanded Pip to drive off quickly. Soon, Henry stood there alone on the edge of the sidewalk. There was nothing left to do but walk back with his heart slowly burning into ashes.

Eris waited for Henry to return to the park after seeing what had happened. With her fortuitous victory, Francine was finally gone and now the goddess had a chance to be with Henry at last. But looking at Henry as he walked back, she never realized how devastated he looked.

"Henry," she called out to him, "I saw what happened."

Henry sighed, "she's going back to England to marry another."

Eris went over to him and prepared to embrace him as he stood silent in despair.

"I'm sorry, who could have known that she would go back on her word when you proposed to her. There, there my dear, now you know the truth."

Henry backed away from her and looked at Eris with eyes that seemed like he knew more than just what Francine told him. Eris felt the cold tension of him looking back at her. Had he known that she was partly responsible for this?

"It's because I'm not rich," he lamented, "it's because I am not worthy of her."

Immediately, he rushed away from Eris, brushing her offer of affection.

Eris watched him as the shadow of his former self, the shy pianist that Eris knew so well, gave her a cold shoulder, escaping her once again.

Roxanne staggered forth to a bench after this moment and felt the responsibility weighing on her, pushing her down. From then on, she knew she loved him for sure. She felt his pain, Francine's dire words, and abandonment from loving someone who did not love you back. His sadness was the guilt in her heart. She thought of the despair in Henry's face, the heartache of losing all that they struggled for. Suddenly, she realized her face was wet. Her hand felt the warm droplets that had undone her makeup. She could only fathom that this was the product of her regret and mutual anguish. Who could have known that a goddess like herself could cry like a mortal?

And somewhere not far from it all, Pandora also lamented. Now she had seen and even tasted the pain brought forth from not just Henry and Francine, but also from her and Eris' actions. It was later then, that Pandora gradually stopped seeing Eris and Henry completely. She had not felt this way in a while, not since that time she opened the box that brought all the evils into the world.

Part 3: Concord

-Chapter 1-

Roxanne hurried through the hallways as she made her way backstage.

"Haven't you found him yet?" she commanded her stage assistant.

"We've looked everywhere backstage, ma'am," she replied. "He's been in his room the whole time until now."

"Well, look again!" Eris commanded, just as two other people returned from their search without results.

"Gods," Roxanne muttered as she snuck a view of the full house that had attended tonight. She was losing her nerves as she wiped the sweat from her hair. The symphony orchestra continued playing the *Waltz of Flowers* and was anticipating the next piece to start at any moment without Henry.

"Don't just look backstage. I want…" Roxanne said before her concentration was interrupted as she spotted a figure that looked like Henry peeking from one exit that led to the balcony foyer.

"Yes, ma'am?" the assistant inquired, "what is it that you wanted?"

"Never mind on that search," she replied, "I think I found the maestro."

By the time Eris arrived on the foyer to get Henry, Henry had just finished a conversation with the bar host as he lounged on the sofa with a brandy in his hand.

"Well, let's hope Roosevelt has more to offer us, just like this good brandy," Henry toasted.

The bar host chuckled as he looked at his watch, wondering when the star of the show was finished with his break.

"There you are, Piano Boy!" Eris called out, relieved.

"Ah Roxanne! Have you met John the bar wizard? John, Roxanne, my manager," Henry cheered.

"Just great maestro, right before your final performance too. Get back in there or I'll drag you back," she said sternly.

Henry tried to rise from his seat as he laughed. "Don't worry, I have it all down."

Suddenly, Henry fell back down.

"Come on, come on," Eris said as she helped him up, "how many has he had?"

"This is his second," the bar host said, suppressing his smile, giving her a glass of water for Henry.

Eris forced Henry to drink it as she hurried him backstage.

Applause filled the room as the orchestra finished. While Henry began sobering up with a wet towel given to him by the assistant, Eris scolded him throughout until the master of ceremony interrupted her.

"Ah Mr. Leon, nice of you to get back on time," he told him. "You're up."

"Don't screw up," Eris teased as she hurried him.

"Watch the master at work," Henry replied proudly.

Eris watched him as he got back on stage with the applause filling the room again for his return to the piano. In all his charm, she saw him play with focus and ease, with no worry and without any side effects from his maniacal irresponsible drinking during the second act.

"This is the fourth time he's been in-and-out of his performances lately," the company director commented as he stood next to Roxanne.

"You know great musicians and artists," she replied, "you just can't control them."

"Well, let's just hope his personal manager does or we'll lose what's left of his wealthy patronage. It's a tough economy now for classical. Even the rich are scaling back on their entertainment."

"Henry's more than just a classical pianist," Eris refuted, "he's something everyone would pay to see." Eris looked on and saw that Henry was looking back at them as he played. He smiled at her.

The afterparty of Henry's 10th successful concert marked a joyous time for Henry's career. Not only was he offered to play live on the radio by various music companies, many new symphony hall directors that were present in his performance offered new contracts for him to play on their stages. Eris, now handling all his business affairs, filled their hearts with consideration as she drank with them. Everyone was present, even Henry's best friend Maxwell Stevens congratulated Henry's success. Merrily, Henry entertained them before excusing himself to get some air on the balcony.

Henry watched silently as he viewed the city streets from above. Watching the world go by, he reflected upon how life had treated him these past few years. Seven years had passed since his graduation and all the underground jazz gigs he had done with George's band. He could have stayed on that route, but his part ended when his heart was broken by Francine. His jazz career began to crumble when George was lynched one evening after a show on his way home as he walked alone. It was a horrible revelation to see that such a great man like him had died because of the color of his skin. Since then, his old aspirations had come to a closed. It was not until Roxanne's efforts to rekindled his love for original composition that re-ignited his success.

"You alright, Maestro?" said Roxanne who appeared before him as she entered. "The party is about over. You should go say goodbye to them."

"I'll see them again at next week's concert," dismissed Henry.

"What's on your mind?" she asked, "exhausted by your popularity already?"

Henry laughed a little. "Yeah, I need a break from seeing how spectacular I am."

"Oh my, I created a monster," she joked back, "glad life is treating you well."

"It is. All thanks to you, Madame Roxanne Smith, matchmaker and music manager."

"That didn't sound enthusiastic," she commented, "bad news?"

"Jack is dead."

"Jack Walden?"

"Yeah, Maxwell found out that he took his life after suffering years of money troubles since the downturn. I thought he would have been alright after selling his bookstore. I guess not."

"I'm sorry," Eris replied, "he was a good man." She thought back to those memorable times at the bookstore, and Walden being her date to their first speakeasy fair together. It all started at Walden's.

Henry was silent as he recalled a sudden thought in his head. It was not just sadness of his former boss passing, but a sadness that a memory shared in his bookstore was now growing fainter. And because of that, he recalled the image of Francine briefly—that time when Walden was talking to her, while he himself was too shy to approach her.

"I'll find out where he's buried and send our condolences to his widow," said Eris.

Henry kept thinking about the fading image of Francine as Eris waited for an answer.

"Henry?"

Henry turned and nodded. "Yes, please send our condolences."

Eris could see the forlornness in his eyes as he looked out. When they were not silly and awkward, they were so focused and mysterious.

"How about we get out of here?" she told him, "there's a surprise I want to show you at my place. Maybe it'll cheer you up."

"A surprise?" Henry said, "not another view from your apartment, is it?"

Roxanne laughed, blushing a little. "Oh it's something much more entertaining and brand new."

When they arrived, Henry was surprised by a limited edition Bösendorfer baby grand piano inside her home.

"Isn't she a beauty?" Eris declared, "had it shipped straight from the workshop in Austria."

"These go for thousands of dollars," Henry uttered in disbelief, "don't tell me you spent your last cut on this."

"Well, you know… I've been spoiled by lessons given by the Maestro himself, and so I thought, why not?"

Eris looked at how intrigued and serene Henry was as he looked inside it. She was happy it was making an impact on him.

"Now you have a better piano to serenade Charlotte with," she commented.

Henry chuckled, "we're not together anymore."

Eris gasped, "What? You've only been together for a couple of months and you already decided?"

Henry looked unbothered, merely concentrating on the new piano.

"To be fair, she was only interested in me because of my musical career," he continued.

His hands felt the ivory keys as he heard the tones.

"Sorry, may I?" he asked.

"Of course, I would feel ashamed if you had not wanted to try it out," Eris said as he sat next to her on the bench.

Henry began playing some tunes and scales as he tried the piano out.

"Well, to be honest, I didn't like her in the first place," Roxanne continued.

Henry smiled at that comment. "I figured. How about you, *Madame Roxanne*? Now that you don't do your matchmaking business anymore, has there been a match for yourself to settle down with?"

Roxanne blushed a little at his rebuke.

"No, I'm too ancient for marriage or love."

"What are you talking about?" Henry insisted, "you haven't aged one bit since the first time we met."

"You're just flattering me," she replied.

"No, I'm not," Henry said. "All the girls that I came across always said that you were beautiful."

"Beautiful is a cheap word, Henry. That's not enough to impress any girl nowadays," she teased.

Although at hearing those words, Eris felt joyous inside. It was not what she expected him to say to her. But it was probably the best compliment she had received from him since she mentored him on the ways of love. Yet, she did not believe it was the sincere truth.

Suddenly, Henry thought back on a comment he had heard from someone. "Well, someone said that you could pass for a goddess or an angel, I think…it was Francine."

The mentioning of her name immediately caused silence in the room. Henry looked surprised that he mentioned her after all these years.

"You still miss her, don't you?" Eris asked frankly.

As Eris waited for an answer from him, Henry closed his eyes and breathed.

"No," he dismissed, "she's no longer a concern in my life. A fading memory."

"There's nothing wrong about it. You must still have some feelings for her," she commented.

Henry looked at her with a look of resentment. Henry remembered how Francine never looked back on her decision. Therefore, his heart felt it should do the same. Francine was not worth mentioning anymore. She was with her own kind and he could never forgive her for backing out from their love.

Eris wanted to tell him about that day Francine's family came to her but hesitated to tell him out of fear. Instead, she tried to suppress it again while Henry began the transition for Tchaikovsky's *June.* Hearing him play, she felt a deep sensation rising through her as she felt the warmth of his body near her as he sat close. At first, it seemed like any time he played. It was delightful and stimulating. But, this time, the theme of this piece was so sorrowful and mysterious that she felt an underlying presence through his playing. It was a girl that appeared beside them, draped in a loose long cloak that covered the paleness of her face. The specter of Francine lurked in every other note.

As she kept on listening, Roxanne felt sadness in her heart. She knew that Francine was not really gone from his life. And evidently, she knew Eris could not contain her love for him either. She had purchased this piano for him. And as grateful and sincere as Henry was to her, Henry could never be hers. Eris merely closed her eyes, trying to enjoy the moment that she had with him, at the very least.

"Roxanne," a voice called to her.

Eris slowly opened her eyes and saw Henry's soul piercing eyes toward her.

"Are you listening at all?" he continued.

"I have been," Eris said gleefully.

"Then please continue, the second measure," Henry said smiling back.

Eris noticed that she had lost concentration from her lesson and felt embarrassed, hesitantly continuing the song she was supposed to play.

"Good, good, not that fast," Henry instructed, "now crescendo."

Eris was elated when she ended.

"How was that?" she said proudly after finishing.

"Not bad," he teased, "seems there is something of a pianist in those hands."

"Well, they aren't just to look at," she giggled.

Eris placed her palms on top of Henry's hands to compare them.

"Nothing like your machinery."

Slowly, before Eris retracted her hands, Henry's hands turned, and his palms grabbed hers.

Surprised, Eris immediately searched Henry's face for what he was doing.

"They are a beauty," he commented, "why haven't I noticed how small your hands are?"

Roxanne blushed as she pulled her hands back.

"Thank you, you flatter me," was all she could reply with.

"Let's try the next song now," he said casually.

Eris tried to keep her composure after nodding. She began the next piece but could not shake the feeling of Henry watching her in a different light. It bothered her until she pressed a few wrong keys and got off tempo. Anticipating Henry's pestering her playing, she heard silence until her hands suddenly felt the warmth of his hands again.

"More like this," Henry instructed.

When Eris turned her head to look at him, she felt his face upon hers. Their lips suddenly touching. Kissing him, her heart pounded with excitement as she gasped for breath before locking again.

She tried to hold back, "Henry, please, we shouldn't get carried away."

They then fell to the floor, expressing the desire in their hearts as they felt each other.

Although she enjoyed this, she felt embarrassed. She felt conflicted with how fast they were moving. Yet, the wetness of his lips only intensified the sensation as he began kissing her neck. Eris could not hold back, the turmoil of this thirst forcing her to feel him more and to unbutton his shirt, ravishing his mortal chest.

His hands then ran down her shoulder, slowly sliding her dress straps down.

Henry's hands reached further down her chest, and Eris felt him caress the Apple of Discord that she wore.

"A golden apple," he commented, "is this the key to your heart and desires?"

Eris looked at him blankly and noticed something strange about that comment.

Ignoring her, Henry began reaching down even more when suddenly Eris realized that this was all wrong.

"Stop it," she insisted.

"What's wrong?" he replied, "didn't you want this?"

"This isn't real!" she shrieked.

Suddenly, the world around her shattered like glass. Henry looked at her once more before his face and body hardened into clay. When Eris stood up, Henry's body fell apart. All that remained was a pile of dirt.

Eris awoke to find a blanket on her after putting her head down on the piano to rest during his playing. She looked around and found that Henry had departed last night after playing for her. The lucid dream struck her with confusion as she felt the dizziness in her head. Suddenly, she heard footsteps and stomps in her kitchen. She thought it was Mayhem on her countertop pillaging through her stuff until she heard a familiar voice.

"Had a pleasant dream, sleeping beauty?"

Eris came out and saw Eros sitting in her dining room, having made breakfast for himself. He waited for her to come in before he began eating it. Years had passed since she last saw him. The sight of him suddenly evoked her to confront him with caution.

"You!" she uttered, surprised.

"Miss me?" Eros said before laughing.

"It was you, all of it," she continued in disbelief, "not even my dreams are safe."

"Sorry, thought I'd surprise you with a gift since I didn't get any souvenirs," Eros smiled.

"Is this how you greet me after being gone for years?" she raised her voice. Although Eris tried to hold her disgust and irritation at Eros' trick, she knew that she had to be careful around him now since he knew of her love for Henry. He knew things and could do things that even she could not foresee.

"You have a lot of nerve for doing that," she raged with anger.

"By the gods, all I did was make you feel loved in your dreams. Relax Discordia, I can't see your dreams, only that I had a feeling it was pleasantly romantic."

"It wasn't," she uttered disapprovingly, "why are you back?"

"I was sick of my holiday around the world and thought I'd come back, now that the world needs more love in these times," he said, eating his toast in a dignified manner. "I see things are good with Henry."

Eris sighed before sitting herself across from him. "Is it? I've followed him for seven years and I was there to help him launch his career."

"Yes," he concurred, "his name is mentioned quite frequently in my travels of late. I'm elated that it was you that made him what he is today."

"No, I did not make him, he could always do it. All I did was love him and support him."

Eros smiled greatly after hearing that statement.

"I can't believe I'm saying this, but this time it's real. And I'm not just saying it because I am in despair like before when we used to talk about him. Love astounds me," she admitted.

Eros nodded his head as he finished his milk.

"And what have you discovered?"

"I have discovered Henry and Francine were a golden match just as you had intended," she said, reluctantly.

Eros looked at her questioningly.

"I believe the time has come for you to know the truth, Discordia," he declared.

"What is it?" she said, getting up to get a glass of water.

"Do you remember that time when we were at the park and you tried to steal my envelope?"

"Yes, of course, that was the beginning of all of this," she called back.

"The truth is," Eros said hesitantly, containing signs of his guilt, "that card was not meant to have Henry's name on it. He was not the person I had intended to strike with love."

"Then I assume it was meant for Francine." Eris looked at him in a solemn manner.

"No," he said.

Falling from her hands, shocked by her sudden revelation, the glass cup shattered. And in that instant, Eris heard the cruel twist of fate that was revealed to her by the god of love.

-Chapter 2-

After discovering that she had been manipulated and played by the god of love, Eris cried heavily with hate and disgust as she pressed on her pillow and lay on her bed. For the second time in her life, she felt powerless.

"I hate you Eros, I hate you, you despicable scoundrel," she yelled, "may Zeus damn you to the darkest depths of Hades!"

Eros stood near her as he looked over her with remorse.

"Why did you do this to me?" she demanded, "tell me why!"

"If you could please hear me out, you need to know that it was beyond my control."

"Beyond your control?" she looked at him angrily, "you're the god of love."

"I am, but I could not bring myself to shoot you that night," he protested.

"Then who shot your arrow of poison? Your mother? That wretched witch!" she cried.

"No!" he said, holding her hands down, "there was no interference from any god."

"Lies," she barked, "now I see what a horrible fate I have found myself in thanks to you. Not only have I neglected my duties as the bringer of destruction, I have fallen for a mortal and stolen his one true love from him."

After a moment, Eros suddenly laughed after she said this.

"What's so funny?" she retorted, looking back at him with disgust.

"My dear goddess, all along you have never neglected your duties. Did you not forget? Our wager was that you make them fall in love. And you did. And as I recall, you wanted to prove that love could bend to chaos. You did just that. Henry and Francine were separated by a cruel fate of discord and chaos."

Eris looked up and suddenly found truth in his statement. With everything that had happened, despite being the target of Eros' love list, Eris did not neglect her duties as a goddess. She had proved that chaos and discord could challenge and even end love.

"Only irony is, he still loves her," she whimpered.

"What is this?" Eros remarked, astounded, "after all these years he is still in love with her?"

"You shouldn't have disappeared so early," Eris retorted, "you've missed out. Henry never found a girl like her ever again."

Eros scratched his head as he sat down, intrigued by how dedicated Henry was.

"Does he not know that Franny has married now and is in England?" he asked.

"That's what happened," Eris said, "she went back, and I received a telegram from her relatives telling me that she had been married at Saint Paul's."

"There's more to that," Eros said, "many things have happened in these seven years."

"Oh?" Eris looked intrigued, "what became of the little countess?"

"My dear," Eros leaned toward her as she sat up, "I think it's best that our dear adventurous Pandora tell you this. I had only heard it from her. She has all the details."

"What? She has returned too?"

"Yes, she's back to visit old friends. I bet you didn't know that she's seeing a British navy chap."

"No way," Eris gasped. "Where is she staying now?"

"I'll write you the address. I saw her yesterday briefly. She's expecting to see you soon."

After Eris received the contact information for Pandora's current residence, she contacted the place and arranged a meeting to see her.

While Eris readied herself to leave for this tea invitation, Eros looked at Eris with curiosity. "I'm curious my dear, are you still convinced that I had a part in making you love Henry?"

Eris was silent until her eyes turned to him.

"Eros," she said in a calm manner, "whether or not you had something to do with making me fall in love with Henry, it was you who intended that I be the target for your little love experiment. Did I fell in love with him when he first played in that concert? I don't know. I only know that my feelings for him came from my heart when he and I began chasing after his girl. I am the goddess of *chaos* and *discord*. Love had always come from those two things until now. This is not about a wager anymore. This is for the reconciliation of love and discord. I am going to make things right again."

Eris got her things and went out the door soon after. After she had left, Eros went out to her balcony and waited for her to exit the building. When he had seen her down below, Eros said to himself, "who could have known that she would have taught me so much about love after all? Leave it up to the fates that had me miss my shot that night." He then giggled.

****

Pandora was staying with a friend outside the city. After arriving at the front of the gates, Eris was led in by an attendant into the house where Pandora stayed. She had to wait for her as the attendant mentioned that a Mrs. Davis was busy on the telephone talking to someone important on the line. While Eris waited, she thought about how Pandora suddenly stopped joining on them and disappeared after Francine left the picture. Since then, the last time she heard she had gone off to Europe in search of answers to her personal immortality.

"Well if it isn't the goddess of chaos herself?" called out Pandora sweetly, appearing before her from the stairway.

"Darling!" Eris greeted with a friendly embrace. They kissed cheeks and Pandora held her hands as she began to talk about all the adventures she had had since they departed from each other.

"You've changed," Eris commented after they had sat down for tea.

"Not too much, I hope," Pandora replied, "I'm still a crazy dancer."

They both chuckled.

"Darling, looking at how much you have matured, I see myself a thousand years older," Eris continued.

"Oh, stop it Discordia," she playfully declined, "we all know that I can't hope to inherit your godlike agelessness. I may have opened that box, cursed the world, and given myself everlasting youth, but I can't hope to look any year older than 16. But I now see what it is to live a mortal life again."

"What do you mean by that, Dora?" Eris asked.

"It's Mrs. Philip Dora Davis now," she gleefully corrected.

"By the gods!" gasped Eris, "you've married a mortal?"

Pandora nodded her head as she poured some more tea for the goddess.

"Well don't just leave me hanging, dear!" Eris demanded cheerfully. "Who is the lucky gentleman? And when did this happen?"

Embarrassed, Pandora tried to keep her composure as she softly responded to Eris.

"Nine months ago. I'm surprised that you weren't going to criticize me."

"Criticize you?" Eris said, "I mean, I'm astonished that you did such a thing. You're obviously not the same Pandora I knew seven years ago. Even that, by golly, I knew you for centuries to never settle for any fella."

"I know," Pandora protested, "but I can't help but fall under the influence of Eros and see what love can be."

Unfortunately, that makes the two of us, Eris thought regretfully. "But you never fancied anyone that was worth loving," Eris said.

"Yes," she replied, "at least it was until I met Pip again."

"Pip?"

Pandora nodded her head and looked at the goddess as if she knew who she was referring to.

"No, you didn't," Eris replied, flabbergasted, "the driver? How in the world…"

"Pip is a navy officer now. We met when I decided to move out of this city in search of myself. I just so happened to be near the White cliffs of Dover picking up shells near the beach when I found myself seeing a familiar face in a crowd of sailors running by. After being reacquainted with him, one thing led to another."

"That's what everyone ends it with," Eris declared.

"You seem disappointed. I thought you were happy for me?" Pandora teased.

"I am, dear," Eris said, "love stories are more than relevant to me now."

Pandora looked at Eris with intensity as she tried to figure out her secrets.

"How is Henry?" she began.

"He is well. But the person I came here to talk to you about is…"

Pandora interrupted, "there is much to tell you about Francine."

Surprised by Pandora reading her mind, Eris began to listen to what Pandora had planned to tell her. Pandora told Eris everything she knew about what had happened after her departure. Having married Philip, she had corresponded with the Youngs briefly every now and then. When Francine returned to England with her so-called relatives, she married Daniel a month soon after. Accepting her fate, the two began a relationship which Pandora described to Eris as a relationship lacking in sparks for each other. How she knew this was because of the way they treated each other in a matter that was amicable but rigid. This was evident in the strict schedules they kept when they saw each other, and when they engaged in other matters. When they do get a chance to see each other, their conversations were usually bleak and about gossips from London. Other than that, talking about routines warmed up their respect for each other over time.

Hearing about the married life of Francine Young had made Eris wonder whether she still thought about Henry. It was obvious from Pandora's description of her home and country villas that she was living a life fit for any affluent heiress. Yet Pandora had described her conversations with Francine to be deceivably white rather than chromatic as she was perceived to have and had wanted.

"I know how you feel about Francine," Pandora said, "but please know that Francine's life was never what we imagined it to be. Other than a quiet life in her home, Franny would often suffer verbal abuse from her mother-in-law. It only got better when 'he' was out of the picture."

"He? The brother?" Eris guessed.

"Yes, Edward Young lost almost everything in the market," Pandora said, "the shock came to him and in one year, he had silenced his own life."

"I guess Francine must have been relieved now that Daniel's mother had no back-up."

"Unfortunately, the Viscount had neglected his finances during that time and Daniel was forced to take over a family coffer that was quickly depreciating. Poor Danny, he had to sell a lot of their belongings to keep their manor and a couple of servants."

"How unfortunate," Eris concluded, "I never imagined Francine's luck to be quite the opposite of what she had hoped for after her marriage."

It was then that Pandora looked at Eris with a displeased and serious gaze. Eris was confused at the sudden shift of reaction to her comment. Was there something wrong in what she said?

"Is everything alright?" Eris asked.

Pandora sighed and continued to look grudgingly before she spoke again.

"Discordia, I'm afraid the Francine you thought you knew was never the one we had planned to sabotage."

"There's more?" Eris wondered.

And it was then that Pandora told Eris the story of an orphan named Franny who was blamed for the murder of her adopted father and blackmailed by his wife and brother to share the inheritance money by the only means of marriage. How she knew this was from Pip himself, who had witnessed it all happen that night at Francine's first ball. Viscount Thomas Young was murdered, and Francine had become a suspect in the case that shook London. With no reasonable evidence to convict anyone, the case was dismissed but the anguish between Francine and her estranged family had begun to suffocate her. In her love of academics and art, she left to study abroad in America with promises to return home and to honor an arranged marriage her so-called family had guilted her in to. But it was Francine's hope to move on from her old life in England. And she did. She recreated herself and slowly severed ties from her benefactor's family.

Telling her this, Pandora realized that Eris' conscience had finally begun to kindle when she asked if she could go with Pandora back to England to see Francine again.

"What is it that you want from her now?" Pandora asked her.

Having heard all that had happened to Francine, Eris was silent and could hardly fathom the connection her role in Francine's life was. Looking at Pandora now, Eris saw that her pointless jealousy of Francine was the source of not just her misery, but also Henry's. There was only one thing left for her to do.

"Dora, please let me come back with you on your return voyage to Britain."

"Will you not cease your destruction on that poor girl?" Pandora replied.

"No, that's not why I'm going," Eris declared. "Henry must be with her again."

"Does he still feel for her?" Pandora looked surprised.

"He does, he always did," Eris said.

Pandora noticed a bit of uneasiness in her voice.

"And does Francine still feel for Henry?" Eris demanded.

"The last time I spoke to Francine was two months ago. And during that time, I could feel that Henry was still in her mind. She had asked me before I left if there was a chance to see him again, I would pass that invitation to him to come see her in England."

"Then it's settled, I must reunite them again," Eris declared.

With the show of frankness, Pandora was a bit hesitant in her decision.

"That doesn't sound like you. I surmised that you were probably at peace with her, but this is quite the surprise."

"I know, Dora," Eris said as she began gathering her things.

"Going so soon?"

"I must, I'm sorry dear. There is a lot for me to think over. Let's just say that I owe that girl a third chance at life."

"And Henry?" Pandora interjected.

"His happiness and his love," Eris said as she slowly stood up to embrace her.

"How soon can he go?"

"I shall talk to him immediately," Eris replied.

Pandora remembered the resentment Henry had felt when Francine left. It was no surprise when Eris said this that she knew Henry's feelings had continued to linger on for all this time.

"There is one more thing you need to know about Francine before you leave," she said before Eris turned.

Hearing of what had happened from Pandora about Francine, Eris gasped and realized that the chaos she brought years ago had not ended. Now without a doubt, she knew that love was Francine's last hope.

-Chapter 3-

Eris had not informed Henry of Francine's status until a week of searching for him. Indeed, for the past week, she had tried his house and had even visited, but there was no answer nor was there any sign of him. She tried his contacts and his family, but none had seen him recently. After contacting a couple of friends, she remembered that Maxwell Stevens might know where Henry Leon may be.

After reaching his house, Maxwell had a look of surprise when Roxanne revealed that the Maestro was missing.

"I am terribly worried that he might have left the state. What's even more excruciating is that I found out he missed one of his concerts and cancelled two for next week without letting me know," she told Maxwell.

"That serious? He did all that in the past week?" remarked Maxwell, taken aback as he tried hard not to smile.

"It's not funny, Mr. Stevens," replied Eris.

"I'm sorry," Maxwell tried to say as he chuckled a little, "I'm just surprised he didn't tell you what's he's been up to."

"Oh?" she gave a stern stare, "what has he been up to?"

"See for yourself," he said as he pointed behind her outside the window. It was then that a loud engine noise began to erupt and surround the house.

Seeing a new yellow roadster pull up to the driveway, Henry honked its horn as the passengers cheered.

"What an amazing ride!" yelled a girl who was riding with Henry at the wheel.

Another girl was on Henry's other side giggling as he took off his fogged goggles.

"Maxwell!" Henry called out, "up for another ride? We have more company this time."

Maxwell came outside his stairway, trying to keep a straight face as he called out to him amid the roaring engine.

It was then that Eris followed him out of the house and caught Henry's sight with her uncontrollable, disgusted stare.

"Sure, company," Eris mocked after Henry shut off his engine.

"Roxanne," Henry said cheerfully without a concern in the world as he jumped off.

"Look at what I got," he said as he gestured to his car and the girls.

"You didn't get any of us yet," one girl teased.

Eris continued to look at them with revulsion as Henry began to introduce the girls to them.

"You wouldn't believe how fast this machine goes," Henry commented, "money well-spent."

Maxwell congratulated him as he began to show them around his automobile. While the girls began to reapply their makeup on the side, Eris tried her best to be on her good behavior as she repeatedly gestured to Henry that she wanted to talk to him privately.

"In a minute, Roxanne," Henry kept replying as he continued to spill knowledge of the vehicle to Maxwell, who was in a difficult spot while listening to his car lecture.

"See, that's how they were able to get put more horsepower in this baby," Henry continued.

"Superb," Maxwell commented, trying to look interested as he looked at Eris.

"Henry, please," she continued, "I have to talk to you privately. It's about you cancelling your future concerts without letting us know, and not showing up for the last one."

Henry turned to her briefly. "Oh, it's nothing. My fans can wait." He then turned back to the attention of his car. Eris could not believe what she was hearing.

"Henry, it's more than just about your fans," she said, "you owe it to your career."

Henry ignored her.

"What would Francine have thought?" she told him before touching him.

There was a sudden silence as Maxwell heard that clearly.

This time Henry looked back and muttered, "Francine? Why would she care?"

As this was happening, Eris' immortal crystal-clear ears overheard one of the girls whispering about how excited they were that Henry was going to lavish them with an expensive meal at some fancy restaurant tonight. They were even dreading that Eris might come along and crowd the seats in the car.

"I bet her long legs would be sticking out," one girl gossiped as she laughed.

Disturbed and even more disgusted, Eris made sure Henry was not going anywhere tonight. With a swish of her hand, the engine suddenly grumbled. The girls moved away, alarmed, but were not far away enough for the engine exhaust to burst out and dirty their dresses.

"Gahh!!!" they screamed, "Henry, your blasted tin junk is spitting out smoke!"

Henry rushed to the engine, but it had already dissipated by the time he found anything.

"Are you alright?" Maxwell said.

"Do we look alright?" one girl barked.

They stormed off as Henry called out to them, turning back to the car soon after.

"I don't understand," Henry said, "this must be a defunct model."

"I'll search the listings and find you a repairman," Eris told him as he closed the hood.

"Yes, please do," he said, flustered, "I just can't believe it."

"I have to go, maestro," Maxwell concluded, "take care of yourself."

"Alright, goodbye," Henry said, distressed.

As Henry tried to clean himself off, Eris looked at him with seriousness.

"What do you want?" Henry finally asked sternly.

"Please, Hero Boy," Eris began, "I'll get your car fixed but we need to talk soon."

"Alright," Henry huffed, "come to my residence later and we'll talk, seeing as I won't be going out anytime soon."

That night, Eris inquired as to why Henry had been acting so rashly lately and neglecting his professionalism in his musical career.

"Because I have money and status now," Henry declared irritably, "I'm someone now. People don't care how good I play, they only care about how un-ignorant they look when they listen to me."

"What about your work?" Eris argued, "you're a great composer, yet you refuse to play your work during your concerts. Why?"

"Because my work is not worth playing for those rich fat aristocrats. But it wouldn't even matter anyways, even if they do like it, they don't care. They just want to hear this famous monkey play for them."

Henry kicked a piano stool as he looked away from Eris.

Scared and frozen with awe at how Henry was behaving, Eris wondered whether he should even meet Francine again. But in her heart, she knew she had to tell him.

"Henry," Eris said, "what about Francine?"

Hearing her name again, Henry looked at Roxanne with agitation.

"What about her?" he grumbled, "I don't know why you keep bringing her up again. She's gone from my life."

"Because," she tried to say, "she wants to see you again."

Suddenly upon hearing this, Henry stared at her, wondering if she was serious or not. The thought of Francine suddenly brought the painful memories of her leaving him. Protecting his pride, Henry began to trickle a laugh. "Stop making this up, Francine doesn't want anything to do with me anymore."

"That's not true," Eris protested, "Dora just came back from England and told me so herself. You don't know this, but Dora has been in contact with her since after the marriage."

A stake in the heart was felt as Henry heard that word, "marriage." It was a betrayal, marriage with the rich count were remnants of the past, burned and destroyed.

"Even if this was true, I don't want to see her," Henry declared. He could not forget the decision she made to not choose him because he had nothing.

"What?" Eris said, surprised, "why not? Don't you still love her?"

"I once did," he continued, "but I don't feel anything for her anymore. She and I are from different worlds, and there's no point seeing the wife of a count. She's with money now."

"But don't you see? You have money now," Eris cried, "you are worthy, if not always worthy."

Although Eris made a point, Henry's pride could not leave him. He had loved Francine, but he could not compel himself to forgive her and let the past go. But there was some desire to see how she was doing. Despite it, he concluded in his mind that it was not worth the effort of opening his wound again to see her.

"I don't know," Henry concluded, "the journey would be too far even if she came here."

Seeing that Henry was beginning to compromise, Eris remembered that reuniting them was the underlying motive, but she could not keep one more piece of information that Pandora had told her that could force him to reconsider.

"Remember," Pandora had said, "Pip had written to me specifically to not mention her sickness to him."

Remembering it, Eris went to Henry and tried to comfort him by assuring that meeting her again would not be painful.

"No," Henry interrupted her, "let's just forget it. I have a lot to compose anyways."

Seeing that she was losing him again, Eris stopped him just before he was about to change the subject.

"Henry, Francine has taken ill. There may not be much time," she interrupted.

Immediately, it was then that Henry stopped resisting. He turned back to Roxanne and asked her what had happened to Francine. He was then told about her life that he had not known, and the guilt brought upon her by her adopted family. And the next few days, Henry and Eris agreed to put off his future concerts and purchased the earliest ship tickets to Great Britain with Pandora to see Francine. Eris assumed that Henry had finally overcome his grudge with Francine. Yet, it was not the absolute truth. Henry loved her, and all he wanted was a reason to see her again, despite his pride.

****

When Eris returned home the night she spoke with Henry about Francine, she finally succumbed to the lethargy that had plagued her all day. She collapsed on top of her sofa and tried to relax as her body ached with tiredness and minor aches.

"What's going on?" she said out loud, "I've never experienced such fatigue before. It is as if I just ran a marathon uphill with a boulder attached to me."

She tried to sleep, but soon realized that her head was now ringing with pain and dizziness. She soon began to breath loudly as she felt the air from the room being sucked out.

"It must be this mortal body," she thought, "I'm just not used to being in mortal form for so long. I'll just change back."

As Eris' body prepared itself to shapeshift back to her radiant self, the pigment of her skin and her limbs dispersed. However, instead of fully changing back, her powers began to retract, and her mortal self ultimately took over.

"What's happening?" she thought, "why can't I change back?"

She tried again, but the same thing happened, until a point where she tired herself out.

As she gasped for air, she looked up to her ceiling and tried to remain in control. She tried moving her body, but it was also no use. As her eyes tried to look outside, toward the lights on her balcony, she began to see all the colors move in all directions. Gradually, her vision blackened.

-Chapter 4-

Huge puffs of smoke blew out of the ship's exhaust pipe as it set sail for the British Isles. After crowds waved farewell and the horn called out to the high seas, the chilly wind blew Henry's coat as he stood on deck watching as they left port. Eris and Pandora were on the second deck watching him as he warmed himself while they conversed about the letter Pip had sent her.

"How long does she have?" Eris asked.

"They don't know," Pandora replied, "the doctor said she's already in the middle stage of her heart condition. Pip is by her side almost every day."

"And Daniel? Has he broken his gambling habits yet?"

"Pip said he has. But he has been drinking a lot more. I don't know if he's there for her every day. Pip says he goes out to the pub some nights to escape it all. And the mother still hasn't left the institution."

"Just horrible," Eris commented. "First the father, then the brother, and now the son. Poor Franny. Dora, there must be a way to cure this girl."

"They are trying, but as far as medicinal aid, they have reached mortal limitations."

It was then that Eris brought up something that was worth mentioning.

"What about us? Are we not immortals? Can't we do something?"

"Perhaps you can, my goddess," Pandora replied.

Eris' face gestured hopelessness as she realized that her powers of chaos could never hope to cure a mortal being. She looked at Pandora for an answer as she thought about it. As she looked over the railing, she suddenly began to feel dizzy again and wobbled when she stepped backward.

"Are you alright?" Pandora cried as she held her.

"Yes," she replied, "just lightheaded."

"Seasick?"

"Yes, perhaps."

Pandora soon realized the futility of this. Gods do not feel such things.

"Roxanne?" Henry interrupted.

They turned to him after seeing him coming up toward them, with his handkerchief covering his nose.

"Are you alright?" he said as he helped her.

"Yes, I'm fine, Piano Boy, just a little seasick."

"Please, let me help her, Dora," Henry offered.

They pulled her to a seat and gave her some water.

"Henry? How are you feeling? Maybe it's best that you rest down below," Eris said.

"It's just the common cold," he said. He turned to Pandora, "Dora?"

"Yes, Maestro?" Pandora said as her concerned look turned to a smile.

"Sorry, may I please speak to Roxanne alone about something?"

"Sure, of course," she replied. She then stood up and left them.

"After these many years, Dora still has a crush on you," Roxanne commented, trying to lighten the mood.

Henry laughed, "well I honestly hope not. I do not want to have to deal with her husband too when we get there. Are you feeling better now?"

"Yes, I am. I don't know what it is, but the sea always seems to shake me up a bit."

"Yes, it was like that for me before too when I was a child," Henry said, "try tilting your head a bit back on the backrest and relax your shoulders."

Eris followed his advice and breathed as she looked at him with curiosity.

"So, Piano Boy," she began, "what did you want to talk to me about?"

"Roxanne," he spoke softly.

Hearing her name spoken so warmly brought joy to Eris in the ever-so-close friendship they shared.

"I want to be honest with you," he continued, "I've thought about this a lot the past few days. I have been so frustrated with how powerless I was, not knowing what Francine had gone through. There is guilt and regret for everything that I had done and have not done for her."

Eris felt the uneasiness as she listened to him speak of guilt. Henry had no part in this. Everything that had happened was because of her, not him.

"If I had only known earlier, if I could have known more about her past, just maybe I could have convinced her otherwise," his voice sulked.

"You're too hard on yourself," she replied, "everything that happened was between her and uncontrollable forces. There is no way that you could have prevented it."

Henry stood up irritably. "You don't know that. I was going to be her fiancé. Part of my job was to be there for her and listen to everything, including her family's past. I was just not curious enough to ask her because I thought it would be too intrusive. I should have fought harder when she left me at the park."

"That comes with time," Eris countered, "and you did run after her."

Silence filled the deck as they thought back to that day. Eris, feeling that Henry should know one more piece of information for him to feel more at ease with his guilt, had hesitated to tell him before. She should have told him that she had met and knew that the relatives were coming for her. Now if any time was the time to tell him of this awful burden, she had carried all these years, this was it.

"Henry, you need to know," she began.

"Know what?" he replied, still distracted by his thoughts.

"The day her relatives arrived," she continued, "I met them."

Suddenly Henry's face looked surprised as he heard this.

"What? Why didn't you tell me about them before? You could have prevented it all?" he demanded.

Eris' eyes hesitated as she continued slowly.

"I… I did not trust Francine."

Like a dark cloud with winds of fury, Henry's reaction to this penetrated through Eris' subconscious. All the guilt she had felt was now exposed, and what it really meant to feel terrible for the actions she had done.

"I'm sorry," she said, now regretting that she had told him.

Henry continued to look at her with disappointment and betrayal as he thought about what to say to this. With no words in his mouth, except his eyes, he stood up and turned.

"Henry?" Eris touched him, "please, listen to me. I wanted to save you that time."

"Save me from what?" he mustered the words to say as he looked at her one more time.

"Save you from her…" Eris continued but stopped as she realized that her secret was coming out.

"Yes? That's it?"

Eris stumbled as her voice began to creak with despair,

"and save you for me."

With no words to answer this, Henry merely looked at her with remorsefulness and inconceivable doubt.

"Henry?" Eris called, "please speak to me."

Henry inhaled and exhaled before he could muster any sympathy for her.

"I need to be alone," was all he mumbled before he walked away.

"Henry!" Eris called desperately as she followed him. But as she did, her dizziness suddenly came back, forcing her to stumble onto one knee by the time he had gone below deck. Her head was aching again.

"Gods!" she cried, "why now, of all times."

Fortunately for her, however, the aching and dizziness only lasted for a few seconds more until she found rails to lean on as she recovered. As the pain subsided, she thought about what she had just done. She had regretted breaking Francine and Henry apart, but now she regretted even more, after telling him that she was responsible for it.

"There you go, you scared him off," whispered a voice.

Eris looked around her and could not see anyone but passengers walking along.

"Over here," Eros called again from above.

Eris looked up and saw Eros flying with his wings above her.

"What are you doing here?" she said.

Eros made a descent onto the deck and landed near her while his wings began to retract.

"Sorry, dear," he said as he dusted himself off, "I missed boarding by half an hour, so I had to fly here. Dora invited me to England to see Miss Daye, oh, I mean Countess Young."

"I can't ever be rid of you, can I?" she commented.

"Oh, cheer up, darling," he said, "I'm sure you would want me around." He smiled. "I promise I'll just be nearby when you need me. I won't accompany your visit or anything sentimental, of course.

The goddess fixed her hair as she tried to relax from what had happened to her.

"I see that you are exhibiting signs," he said.

"It's nothing, Eros," she said, "I've just been human so long that my form is getting heavier for me. Naturally, I would be a little weak."

"Is that so?" he replied, "careful, my goddess, signs of your condition seem dire for your power."

"How do you know that?" Eris asked, surprised, "has that happened to you?"

"What? Being mortal for a while?" Eros replied, "I don't often indulge in mortal forms for too long. But I know that it is dangerous for us gods to take mortal forms for too long without changing back."

"How so?" she asked.

"Much like how mortals cannot breathe the airs we breathe in the heavens of Mount Olympus, nor dive to the depths of Poseidon, gods are weakened by the life forces that make mortals so weak when we transform our shape into them. We never notice this when we take a mortal form because our powers are greater. But, never returning to eat and live in our immortal selves, we exhibit the poisons of man."

"Poisons?" she gasped.

"There is not much to say about man. We become what we created," Eros continued, "that is, man's flaws and their short mortal lives."

Thinking about what he had just said, Eris felt compelled to disbelieve it. In her mortal form all these years was never that bad. But why now? Why was she losing her powers to change back?

"Anyhow, Discordia," Eros said, "be sure to be your lovely goddess self again or else…"

Eris felt worried as she looked away distressed again. The fact was before her, she was losing her god powers and transforming back would be getting harder and harder if she continued to assume this persona for who knows how much longer.

"But I see now you can put Roxanne on hold, now that Henry won't be talking to you," he teased.

Eris hissed at him, "I told the truth. Don't put salt in my wounds."

"I see, now he knows you had a little crush on him," Eros smiled, while pinching her cheek slightly.

Eris brushed his hands away and grunted in inner misery.

"Even if he doesn't want to talk to me anymore," she declared, "I'll still be there for him."

"That is the sweetest thing I've heard from your mouth, my dear, I am so proud of you," he giggled.

Eris looked once more to the bottom of the sea as she thought about Francine's condition.

"She'll be fine," she thought, "I'll make sure she'll recover, and that Henry will be with her again. Even without my powers."

Looking at her reflection in the water, she did not see the goddess of chaos. More and more, Eris knew that her own immortality was weathering away, and the image of Francine peered back at her. What was even more surreal was that Francine had the look of an imperishable maiden. It was as if she and Francine were one and the same.

****

It was the beginning of fall when Eris and Henry arrived in Britain. By the time the ship docked, among passengers quickly disembarking from the coming cold, Pandora received a telegram from port informing her that Pip was not able to receive them as he had promised in Pandora's letter. Instead, the telegram requested her to call him from the dockmaster's telephone. After speaking with him, she was instructed to go alone to Lord Young's manor, out of the central city. Hearing that Roxanne and Henry were not invited to come right away, Pandora had to lie for her husband in order not to raise alarm that Francine's husband had still not returned from his business trip in the city, and that the manor was left with only two servants and Pip to take care of Francine and the debt collectors that kept appearing every day since Daniel's disappearance.

"It won't be long," Pandora concluded as they exited the dockmaster's office, "Pip just wants to see me about something first. We'll send for you as soon as possible. Please, make yourself comfortable at the inn I arranged. Let them know Dora sent you. They'll take good care of you, Maestro."

Henry looked at her with disappointment as he grunted on the steps, huffing his breath.

"Ridiculous," he grumbled just before walking away from them. Henry felt estranged by everything around him in this foreign country that Francine had only described to him briefly when they were together. Not only was he still upset by Roxanne letting him down, he suddenly felt uneasy about seeing Francine again now that he was so close to seeing her. A mix of emotions had rendered his nerves fearful and spiteful of the unknown. The only thing he could make sense of was that Dora saw meeting her husband again as the main priority.

"It'll be alright," Eris said to Pandora, "I'll make sure we'll get there. Do what you need to do."

"Thank you," Pandora replied, "but it's not really about Pip and me. Nor Francine's condition yet. Danny is still missing."

"What? That unreliable brat still hasn't returned?" Eris scowled, "let me help you."

"Don't worry about it," Pandora calmed her, "just make sure Henry prepares for the worst if it ever comes down to it. I'll send for you two soon."

"Are you two done yet?" Henry called out to them.

"Coming!" Eris called out to him.

"He's definitely not the same shy pianist that barely held my arm in our dancing days, is he?" Pandora commented irritably, "all that fame has made him full of himself."

Eris sighed. "Henry's been astray from himself lately. Being with him for years, I know that he puts on the worst of himself to cover his good intentions. He has a good heart. Trust me, he is still that boy inside."

"It seems you know his heart as well as you know yourself," Pandora replied.

Eris reddened at this comment, "Henry is just like any musician or artist. Always lost in his emotions."

"I hope so," Pandora concluded.

After parting from Pandora, Roxanne and Henry continued together into the city by taxi. Having passed the Palace of Westminster, and having been dropped off near a section of the River Thames, they continued their walk to the inn that Pandora had arranged for them. Henry looked over on the other side and noticed an old building a block down that was marked for demolition.

"The inn should be just a little bit further down," Eris called back to Henry.

Henry stood still as he looked onto the demolition site. He observed and realized that the building must have been a school at some point.

"What do you see?" said Eris as she stood behind him.

He pointed in the direction of the building and then continued ahead of her.

As Eris observed the old building, she saw a plaque that read:

Meriwether Orphanage Home

Francine was all they thought about soon after.

After settling into their inn, Roxanne insisted that she follow Henry to the pub the next door over. Still upset at Roxanne, Henry tried to keep his distance as he stood over the bar.

"Come on, Piano Boy," Eris spoke to him, "what will it take to give your manager a decent conversation, with answers other than a 'yes,' and a 'no'?"

Henry barely looked at her as he continued to drink and contemplate.

"Nothing?" Eris said while positioning her face at every direction Henry looked. It was then that someone recognized Henry and came over to him.

"Henry Leon?" said the gentleman, "can it be? The maestro himself, a patron of this pub?"

"Hello," Henry said, suddenly smiling.

"My goodness it is you," he continued, "I'm a big fan."

Right away, the fan began commenting on Henry's work and performances. Soon after, a small crowd of fans appeared.

"What are you doing in London?" they asked, "are you playing for any symphonies here in London?"

Henry looked embarrassed as he tried his best to answer their questions and signed a few autographs. Eris looked on and smiled. The thought of Henry's fame reaching out of America, and especially here in London, had her thinking that even Francine must have heard of Henry's success over the years. After the fandom began to fade, Henry took another drink and relaxed himself as he sat down on the chair. Having taken his attention away from Francine's condition, and Roxanne and Dora's excuses, Henry breathed a little easier. When Eris came back to him, his agitation had even calmed down a bit.

"Well aren't you the latest sensation in all of British society," Eris beamed, "didn't know you were famous here too, did you?"

"I presumed I would be known in some circles," Henry replied.

Eris snorted, "that's a good thing. Means that Francine must have known what you've been up to in the last few years."

This baffled Henry. It was true, he thought.

"I suppose," he said, "though that doesn't change anything. Doesn't change the past."

"Come on, that makes a difference," Eris declared, "it means she must have thought of you if she's reaching out to you again."

"But in what aspect?" he growled, "only because I am a world-renowned concert pianist now? Or simply because she is ill?"

"Henry!" Eris retaliated with shock, "it doesn't matter why she reached out to you but that you came."

Henry thought about this as he took the last of his Scotch down his throat.

"Don't you remember what I've told you?" Eris continued, "she was forced to marry. If she had a choice, she would have picked you. And somewhere in that proud head of yours you think she chose the other because she wanted the life of a countess and that you were a nobody back then. But that wasn't true. You were someone great in her life. And for whatever reason, she had to take the other route. Not because she did not love you, but only because she loved you too much to have you be a part of her excruciating circumstances."

There was silence as the pub began to see the serious conversation that was going on between Roxanne and Henry. As Henry awakened from his drunken delusions of why he was seeing Francine again, he suddenly looked up and saw how embarrassed he was in a pub with Roxanne telling everyone out loud the ultimate reality, unintentionally.

Looking into Henry's eyes, Eris could see the old Henry again inside.

"I'm sorry," he said, "you are right, Roxanne. I just miss her too much."

Before Roxanne replied, a loud thump shook the pub. Everyone turned and saw one of the new patrons enter and fall to the ground.

"Another drunk dead bastard," the pub owner said as he came over to the man.

Roxanne and Henry saw that this drunken man was in a deplorable shape: completely unshaven, wearing clothes he probably had not changed for days, and a face that had aged in years.

But there was something unique about that man that Roxanne noticed. Despite the condition that he was in, he still had something about him or what he wore that was really dignified.

"Where are you going?" Henry asked, surprised as she went over to the drunken man.

"Just curious," she called back.

The man tried his best to get up as the pub owner began to shoo him out of his establishment.

"Come on, off with you," he demanded as he tried to grasp him, taking him out of his door, "good god man, you stink, best you sleep elsewhere."

The drunken man grunted as he tried to demand water and for him to let go.

"Wait," Eris tapped the pub owner, "let me do it. He looks familiar to me."

"Suit yourself," he replied.

"Hey," Henry said as he came beside them, "be careful."

Eris looked at the drunken man and lifted him up. The man's grizzly face covered his appearance, but Eris could make out a somewhat familiar face. The stench quickly repulsed Henry as he took a step back from helping her.

"Daniel?" Eris spoke to him.

The man's eyes barely opened as he mumbled something.

"Daniel Young?" Eris asked again.

"Who wants to bloody know?" the man finally answered.

"Hey, take him away from here," the pub owner called out.

Henry assisted Eris in taking Daniel to the side as they prepared to question him.

"Get some water," Eris instructed. They splashed some water on his face.

"Is it really him?" Henry asked, baffled.

Eris dug into the man's wallet and found an identification.

"Yup, that's him alright. The Viscount of Kent."

The next day, Eris and Henry were notified by the innkeeper that a telephone was waiting for them. Pandora told them that they were now able to come. Hearing this, Eris also informed her that they had found Daniel.

"Wonderful!" Pandora said on the telephone, "I can't believe you managed to find him. I'll send a ride for you all immediately."

When a car was sent for them, Eris and Henry dragged Daniel inside. This time he was more sober, and Eris made it her effort to clean him up a bit. But even then, he was still a mess. Henry had last night tried to bathe him because his stench was beginning to consume their room. As Daniel slept through the ride, Henry and Eris sat silently as they gazed at how stricken Francine's family had become.

"Francine deserved better. I don't understand how she would still stay with him," Henry commented.

"It wasn't always like this," Eris replied, "he was a decent man before. Before the market crash, before his uncle's death.

"And you said his mother has been institutionalized?"

"Yes, I'm afraid so."

"A pity," Henry concluded.

They arrived at Yale Manor at Kent in the late afternoon. It was the last country home the Viscount still possessed. That, and their primary residence in London, which the family had left behind to lease as they went south to get far away from the Viscount's debt collectors, among other troubles.

Upon arriving, Winston, the butler, welcomed them inside.

"My lord," Winston said as he saw Daniel with them, "I'm so glad you're finally back."

"Too soon of a return, Winston," Daniel tried to say as he tried to snap out of his migraine.

Eris and Henry glared at him with contempt.

"At last," Pandora said as she entered from the study. She went to embrace them.

"What are you doing here?" he grunted.

"Taking care of all your business and Franny as I have for months now," Pip scolded as he entered from the stairway.

Pip was not the boy that Eris had remembered from the time he drove them from Francine's home. He had grown much more mature and leaner over the years and had shed all aspects of his youth ever since he joined the Royal Navy. Daniel immediately shut up as he walked away from them without disgrace.

"Hello, Miss Smith, it's been too long," Pip said to her.

"And you must be The Maestro I've heard all about," he said as he shook Henry's hand.

"I am," Henry said.

"I'm sorry about not seeing you two together yesterday," Pip continued, "you must understand that we had a lot of people here demanding their affairs be handled. I'm not a businessman by trade, so I had to consult a lot of people to help Franny out."

"I understand," Henry said, "and, how is she now?"

Suddenly they heard the stairway quake as small footsteps descended below them.

"Thomas," Pandora uttered, "you didn't wake your mother, did you?"

"Mummy's already awake," said a small skinny boy, "she told me that daddy's home."

Henry was at a loss for words as soon as the boy showed up. All he could do was look at him with an intense curiosity. Eris, too, was surprised that Pandora did not mention Francine having a son all this time.

"Daddy's here," called out Daniel as he slowly came out again, still mildly drunk. Immediately, the boy rushed to him and embraced him.

"There's my boy," Daniel said as he returned the same embrace.

Eris and Henry looked at them in disbelief. Somewhere deep in that drunken and diluted brain of Daniel's was still the husband of Francine, and father to her child. At this time, Pandora gave a look of guilt as she saw their reactions. She had never wanted to mention this to them in fear of Henry not coming.

"Now that Francine's awake," Pip continued, "shall we go see her?"

Henry followed him as he walked up the steps, followed by Eris and Pandora. All the while Eris had noticed that Henry could not take his eyes off Thomas. He was still flabbergasted. All the emotions that he had before did not prepare him for this confrontation with the women he had first loved. Now it was clear that Francine, despite calling him here, had moved on. Her child was evidence of that.

Pip knocked on the door to Francine's room. Hearing a faint sound that sounded like Francine was far away, Henry's heart pumped with uncontrollable fear. He knew he still cared for her, even after seeing her son, but his regret of not sharing a future with her had now begun to make him feel like he was meeting her for the first time again. Could it be that this Francine was not the one he had once known and loved? A mix of emotions ran through his blood as Pip opened the door.

Inside Francine's room, Henry's eyes saw a faintly familiar person. Francine lay resting on her laced bed. Her now long flaxen hair and sunflower-like cheeks were unmistakable as she turned to them. Her eyes focused and gazed on Henry for the first time in forever, and a twinkle of hope and sadness appeared.

"Hello, Henry," she said with that same bright voice.

It was then that every hesitation and emotional discord that Henry had subsided. All he could do was return a smile back to the girl he realized now he'd never fallen out of love with.

-Chapter 5-

Eris and the others left Henry alone with Francine. Back downstairs, Pip began talking about Francine's condition and what the doctor had been doing to help her. Eris had learned that Francine was suffering more from her heart condition, and that it was making it harder for her to breathe and move.

"Her appetite hasn't been well either," Pip told her, "the doctor said her organs were also failing, especially her lungs."

"That's terrible," Eris said gravely. She suddenly thought about what Henry might be feeling seeing Francine in this terrible state. She too was fearful of the worst that may happen to her. Not only was she concerned for Henry, but she also felt a certain regret for not being a better friend to Francine. It was her envy that resulted in their separation.

"Where has Daniel gone?" Pip asked Winston. They came to the study and noticed that even Thomas had disappeared.

"His lordship has taken Master Thomas out to the back for some archery lessons," Winston answered.

"Well, at least he's a good father," Eris remarked.

"Good father?" challenged Pandora irritably, "I doubt a good father would leave for over a month without any word, especially when his wife is dreadfully sick."

"Now Dora, dear," Pip said as he held her hand to calm her.

"Please, Miss Smith, make yourself at home. It might not be my house, but I grew up partly here, did you know that?" Pip tried to utter in a happier tone.

"Pip grew up with Franny and Daniel here," said Pandora, "he was adopted by the late Count's gardener and worked here almost all through his life."

"Is that so?" Eris remarked, "I must say Pip, you've gone far. You're not the same boy I remembered seven years ago."

"I'm still the same," he replied shyly, "but perhaps the navy has changed me."

"Changed him?" interrupted Pandora, "they're promoting him to be a noncommissioned officer and given him six months leave."

"Oh my," gasped Eris, "now I can see why Franny left you with so much trust in these estates."

Trying to contain these flatteries, Pip tried to change the subject and asked Winston if he could bring the tea.

"Why do you not get it yourself?" Winston replied nonchalantly. Eris was immediately taken by the butler's response.

"Don't mind him," Pip said, embarrassed, "I'm still that young gardening boy to him. I'll be right back."

Eris and Pandora conversed about London life as they tried to make the best of an unpleasant situation. But it was hard as Eris sighed and thought back to Henry and Francine upstairs.

"Don't worry," Pandora tried to calm her, "I'm sure they're enjoying their time together."

It was then that Eris suddenly began to cry.

"What's the matter, dear?" Pandora said as she rushed to her side.

"I just feel so helpless. How could this ever have happened?" Eris cried.

"There, there. Franny was happy to see you when you saw her, wasn't she?" Pandora assured.

"Yes, but it's still my fault," Eris said.

"Your fault?" Pip said as he reentered the room with the tray, surprised by her tears. "Heavens, what are you talking about, Miss Smith?"

"It's nothing, dear," Pandora said, "she's just emotional about what's happening to Franny."

As they continued their conversations and tried their best to console Eris, another regretful conversation was being discussed upstairs.

After a brief cheerful but faint welcome by Francine to Eris and Henry, it was Eris who decided that the two should be left alone despite the protests of Francine and Henry. Of course, Eris had known that it was only their polite nature to decline. But as soon as the three left them, Henry came closer to Francine's side and held her hand, looking at her with the same gaze he had given her when he was too shy to approach her years ago. As Francine grasped his warm hand, her lips, ever so much the same tender and warm joy that had stunned him, smiled again. They remained silent after Eris and the

others departed from them. This silence made them even more
nervous to speak to each other. While Henry tried to think
about something to say to her, Francine examined him with
curiosity. Henry was still that boy she remembered but had
features that were now so manly. He was not as skinny as he
was before and now had light facial hair that made her giggle a
little.

"What's so funny?" Henry asked her as he smiled,
embarrassed by her stare.

"Nothing, Henry," she replied, "I'm just looking at how
much more handsome and charming you've become. I bet the
girls are all over you."

Henry chuckled, "Yes and no. I'm still the bumbling
idiot who's still oblivious to their feelings."

"Nonsense," she said sweetly, "you always seemed to
be there when I needed it."

Henry caressed her hands more as she said that. "I'm
sorry about everything," Henry tried to say, as sincerely as he
could. Seeing her made him feel guilty for not having been
there when she was sick.

"Sorry?" remarked Francine, "sickness is inevitable, Mr.
Leon. There is nothing to be sorry about."

"That may be true, Francine," he said, "but…"

Francine's eyes widened after he said her name. For
years she had not heard his dear voice say it so affectionately.

"But I'm sorry for not seeing you earlier. If I had
known, I would have been there. I would have come to visit
you often or even prevented this from happening in the first
place," he continued.

"Don't be sorry, silly," she assured, "whatever happened to me before does not matter anymore. If anything, I should be sorry. Sorry for having broken your heart that day."

Francine suddenly began to tear up a little after saying this. She meant it. Not a day had gone by when Francine had not thought about what she had left behind. It was not so much regret as longing for things to have been better. Even for her circumstances to have been different.

"You did what you had to do," Henry said, trying to comfort her tears with his hands, "I know all about it. About your relatives, Daniel, and even the late Viscount."

Francine held his hands to her cheeks as he finished wiping her tears. Holding his pianist hands, she thought about the concerts he had played with them. They must have been lovely.

"The late Viscount raised me as his own, Henry," she said, "I loved him like a father."

"I know, dear," Henry said sincerely, "I understand now."

"Henry?" she said to him passionately as she let go of his hands and placed her hand to his face.

She gently touched him, making sure it was really him.

"Yes, Francine?" he replied affectionately again.

"I missed you."

Hearing these words, Henry's heart began to melt. And with the tears that were beginning to come from his eyes, he wept with bitter happiness.

"I missed you," he tried to say as his watery eyes stared into hers.

Her face was so angelic to him as he gazed at her. Not much had changed about her radiant appearance other than becoming thinner from her condition. She was undoubtedly womanlier, with her choice of clothes and her natural motherly maturity. Yet, it was the same girl that he had wished he was with in all those missed years. Henry had wished he was with her all those times, seeing her gradually blossom into who she was now. To grow older together, to live every day with your love, and be forever young and forever older. Henry was like any person who had ever loved, wondering what a life they and their past lovers would have had if they had stayed together. But in their time together, regrets meant nothing. Only what is left to mend.

"I've seen your name in the papers," Francine said, "Maestro Henry Leon. Oh Henry, I'm so proud of you."

Henry blushed, "I never could have done it if it wasn't for you."

"Me?" she said, "you deserve all the credit. You were always brilliant. Somehow, the first time I saw you perform live was the first time I saw the making of a great musician."

"You spoil me. You always have," Henry remarked bashfully.

"Well it's because you always spoiled me," Francine replied gleefully.

"And you've never really admitted that you saw me that time at my first concert performance."

Francine laughed. "Because I was too shy to admit it that time. A girl can't show her fella that much enthusiasm."

"My dear, enough about me," Henry declared, "I've seen that you have a lovely boy now."

"My Thomas," she answered, "have you met him yet?"

"I've seen him," Henry said, embarrassed, "but I wasn't officially introduced."

"I'll introduce you to him tonight at dinner," she said, "he's a sweet boy. I believe he wanted to go see his father about archery. That boy, he's so active yet innocent. Kind of like you, Henry."

"Me?" Henry looked surprised, "I was never active in sports."

"No, but you were so active in your books and your music," she argued, "speaking of which, I hope to hear it one day again."

"You will," he replied confidently, "and I hope to see your artwork as well. Seeing how you've had so much time as a countess, you must have had plenty of time to paint."

Francine laughed with her sweet laugh of hers. It was like their school days.

That night, Henry and Francine dined together with Thomas, Roxanne, Pandora, and Pip. Daniel was out again in a nearby town. News of this had disappointed Francine and concerned the others. For Henry, however, he was relieved. Although he did not despise Daniel, being in the presence of the man who stole and married his dear love was truly an awkward affair if not disdainful. Nevertheless, Francine's condition seemed to be better from the look of her heading downstairs by herself with minor assistance instead of being carried. The disease had weakened her muscles. Every time she stood up on her legs, she would feel them cramping. But tonight, they behaved themselves and her pain was minor enough for her to walk slowly. With Henry assisting her, she felt evermore stronger.

After dinner, Henry played for them on the grand piano in the parlor. After playing a few of his composed works and improvisations, he decided to dedicate one performance personally for Francine. Only he did not tell them it was for her. Instead, he began playing her favorite composer, Frederic Chopin. And what Henry selected was an unusual lyrical version of the piece, *Etude op. 10-13 'Chanson de l'adieu'*, sung and arranged by himself. And he began, voicing his emotions to each melody line as he played:

> *Hello, my sweet dear, I dream of you*
> *And I do miss, all the times we spent*
> *I won't forget, that day we met, and the happy days, too long ago*

> *Hello, my sweet dear, I promise you*
> *That someday soon, we will grow old together*
> *Your hand and mine*
> *And even if discord falls upon us, with our hands torn apart, life*
> *empty and unkind, please hold on*
> > *Because I know*
> > *That I will miss you go*
> > *Always loving you so*

While Henry sang, all that was happening and had happened in Francine's life suddenly paused for her, in her mind and weakened heart, Francine felt and remembered all the times they spent together. Everything they said to each other. She held her tears as she continued to listen. And as Henry continued playing, he listened very carefully to all the words that he was singing. Every emotion that they felt, he felt the universe connected them, that he and Francine were singing it together like that night they danced and played together before their first kiss. When the music ended, silence filled the room until they began clapping. Everyone praised his talent except Francine. She was silent still. But it did not matter, all Henry ever wanted was for her to listen to him play for her again.

After the performance, they decided to play a round of cards until Thomas fell asleep on Francine's lap an hour after. Pandora insisted on taking her child to his bedroom, but Francine declined politely. Although she felt weak and tired, Francine wanted to continue showing that she was getting better. Of course, carrying her five-year-old boy proved difficult in her condition and Pip managed to do it for her.

"You must be tired too, Franny, why don't you let Henry help you up to your bedroom?" Roxanne commented afterward. She winked at him.

Both Henry and Francine smiled at each other. She did not have to even suggest it.

After Henry helped Francine into her bed, he kissed her on the forehead.

"Today was wonderful," he said.

"And the next days to come will continue to be so," she replied sweetly.

"It will, *my lady*," Henry said sweetly.

"Do stay longer here in England," she said.

"As long as I am needed," he said as he began to leave her, "goodnight, Francine."

"Chanson de l'adieu," she said.

"Sorry, come again?" he remarked.

"The name of the piece you played, 'Song of Farewell.'"

"You guessed it," he smiled, "I hope you forgive my horrible lyrical rendition of the piece."

"No, I love this version," she said affectionately.

She yawned as her eyes began desperately trying to stay awake, "it beats saying sad goodbyes any day."

As Henry stepped back toward the door, still looking at her angelic body lying there barely awake as she gazed at him still, he felt so happy that they were together again.

"Tomorrow, my love, there will be more and more," he whispered lastly.

-Chapter 6-

Unfortunately, the next few days were not blessed with more encore performances or whole-hearted conversations like the first. Francine passed out after breakfast and was carried back upstairs with Henry's help. The alarm was frightening for everyone and worsened after when Francine began to breathe rapidly, barely uttering a sound. They sent for the doctor immediately while Henry tried to calm her. However, this proved difficult as Henry became agitated at how helpless he was in this situation.

"Get that damn doctor over here now!" he yelled across the hall as he held her hand.

When the doctor finally arrived hours later, Henry was ushered out by Pip after the doctor demanded that he stay calm.

"Please, you must save her!" he told Pip, grabbing his arm. Eris also tried to calm Henry as she looked hopelessly behind the closed doors before them. Everyone in the house looked hopeless that day. But none more than Henry and Eris as they waited together impatiently for Francine's condition. Pandora busily escorted Thomas outside and told him that everything would be alright. She sent for the maid to come immediately to watch over him.

The doctor stayed in there for about an hour before coming out. He assured them that she would be alright for now and would need to rest more but looked grimly at them as he prepared to tell them more.

"Her condition is getting worse, I'm afraid," he began, "I have never seen anything like it. Her heart is beginning to fail, and the disease has already affected her lungs. She needs to be hospitalized as soon as possible. There is no way to put it better, but this is the only thing I can recommend for her now."

This had affected everyone, shocking them with grief.

"No," Henry refused to believe, "it can't be. She was getting better yesterday."

"Is there anything, anything that can be done if she was hospitalized?" Pip asked.

"Let me use your telephone," the doctor said, "I need to consult with some colleagues. But as of now, I can't say for sure."

"Yes, please, doctor," Pip said as he began leading him downstairs.

Henry, with his hands in his face in anguish, felt hopeless as Eris and Pandora tried to comfort him with their mutual sorrow.

It was then that they heard Pip yelling in anger from the stairway.

"Where were you?" he scolded Daniel, who had just returned from last night.

Daniel was informed by Winston of what happened, and he then immediately rushed upstairs.

"I'm sorry," Daniel said, passing him as he shifted his attention to the doctor.

"Please, doctor, tell me, will Franny be alright?" he asked, worried.

The doctor refused to say any more after giving the bad news and had merely directed his answer upstairs for everyone else to answer him.

"I'll deal with you after," Pip said sternly as he escorted the doctor down the hall.

When Daniel walked up and began asking them what the condition was, Henry looked at him with a hateful glare that Eris had never seen in him before.

"Out with it, will she be alright?" he asked again.

No one answered him until Pandora shook her head.

"I have to see her," Daniel insisted as he headed for Franny's door. Quickly, Henry grabbed his shoulder and pulled him away from the door.

"Let go of me!"

"Why should I?" Henry snarled back, "you've been gone the whole night and the last month without seeing her even once. And only now you care to see her?"

Henry looked furious as Daniel shook his arm off and stood his ground.

"That's my business, and she is my wife. I have every right to see her any time I like. Now get out of my way," he demanded. It was then that he reached for the doorknob once more.

Suddenly, Henry surprised everyone. He clutched his fist and struck Daniel in the face, pushing him down to the floor, then hitting him repeatedly. This prompted Pandora and Eris to stop the fight as they tried desperately to pull Henry off. It was difficult as Henry continued to beat him. Fortunately,

Pip had heard everything and got back just in time to break Henry away from the beating he was giving Daniel.

With intense ferocity, Henry withdrew, but not before ridiculing him, "I'm not going to let your sorry excuse of a man be alone with her ever again!"

"Out!" Daniel mumbled with his bruised mouth, "out of my house!"

Pandora led Daniel to get medical attention downstairs as Pip tried to calm Henry. Eris looked onto Francine's room and saw her asleep still. "Fortunately, she did not have to see this," she thought.

Later in the day, Eris kept watch over Francine while Pip and Henry tried to settle everything that had happened with Daniel in his guest room. As Eris looked at the small frail girl beside her, she kept thinking about how Henry reacted to her condition and the fight with Daniel.

"Is this what true love does to a person?" Eris spoke softly to herself as she wondered. Suddenly, Eris felt a small touch from her hands. Francine's eyes began to twitch as she tried to speak softly.

"How are you feeling, sweetheart?" Roxanne asked her.

Francine's gray eyes looked up and saw Roxanne in front of her.

"Better," she said softly, "what happened outside?"

Eris knew she should not tell her for Henry's sake, she assured her that Henry was just really worried about her and was just pacing around the hallway loudly, demanding answers.

Of course, Francine knew better. Despite being passed out, she was awakened by the sounds of grunts and yelling from Henry and Daniel's voices. But instead of shining the truth light on Roxanne, she simply nodded.

"Has the doctor left yet?" Francine asked, "has he told you about my condition?"

"No, the doctor is still here," she replied, "and not yet, he's still unsure of your condition. He's talking to his colleagues at the hospital now."

"Alright," Francine concluded, "Roxanne?"

"Yes, dear?"

"Thank you for taking care of Henry all these years. You always knew him better than I did."

Eris smiled, surprised that she would say that.

"I don't know him that well," Roxanne replied, "if you count babysitting him and promoting his concerts as taking care of him, then darling, consider yourself lucky."

Francine wanted to laugh but only merely smiled as she lacked the energy to.

"Franny," Eris continued, "I'm sorry about the past and how I accused you of using Henry that day at your art event."

Francine was reminded of that time. And although she felt hurt from her words, she knew it was not out of hatred but something that she felt for Henry genuinely.

Before Francine had a chance to reply, the door opened with Henry and Pandora along with Thomas in her arms entering.

"Mummy!" Thomas said as he rushed to her. Francine tried to embrace her son as he stood over her.

"How are you feeling, Franny?" Pandora asked as she tried to pull Thomas down from the bed.

"A little better, thank you for watching him, Dora," Francine said. She looked at Henry and saw that his face looked like he had seen a ghost. As he came over to Francine, he was still silent, yet attentive.

"I'm so sorry we couldn't do more after breakfast, Henry," she told him.

"No, think nothing of it," he replied.

"We'll leave you two alone," Pandora said contently. "Come on, Thomas."

"But I want to be with mummy," he puffed.

"It's alright, let him stay," Francine gestured, "he has his toys in here anyways."

"Okay, stay away from mommy and Uncle Henry now, play over there," Pandora gestured to the toys in the room.

As Thomas played with his toys, Henry held her hand again. Francine noticed the bruises on his knuckles. Before Henry had a chance to cover them, Francine looked at him with a concerned face.

"Henry, please forgive Daniel. He's not himself these days because of everything that has happened."

"How can I after he left you here alone with no one except Pip and your butler?" Henry protested, "he's your husband, he should have been here."

Francine nodded. "It doesn't matter anymore. All those days waiting for him has made me accustomed to it." She then took Henry's hands and led them to her cheek, "Though I have not been accustomed to your absence."

Henry held her close to him as he wrapped his arms around her. Despite what awaited with her condition, Henry wanted to cherish what time he had left with her. He had dodged a bullet. But the bullet was close, and it grazed his fatal point. He knew that the next hit would be not so fortunate.

That evening, Henry was summoned to come outside on the patio by Winston. The doctor met everyone there except Francine and Thomas. After speaking with his colleagues, they had decided that hospitalization with intensive care would be the best option for now. However, it was not guaranteed that Francine's illness would be cured.

"During this time," the doctor told them, "they will provide as much care for her as possible and monitor her condition. I'm sorry to say, however, that after discussing the symptoms and sharing the medical history with my fellow doctors, there is no cure."

Henry's heart dropped after hearing this.

"But, there is one risky procedure that may work."

"What is it?" they all demanded.

"It will involve surgery," he said, "a transplant of new organs with new medical machines that will keep her alive for it to be successful. One colleague mentioned to me, however, I must warn you. This has never been attempted successfully before. I cannot guarantee that she will survive the process."

Immediately, they all looked dumbfounded.

"Let's try it, doctor," Daniel finally said, "we don't have another choice."

"I hate to say it too," Pip said, "but what else have we got?"

"No," Henry interrupted them, "I won't let Francine die in pain."

"It's not your choice," Daniel retorted, still spiteful of Henry.

"Well it sure isn't going to be your drunk self to make that choice," Henry refuted back.

Daniel quickly pushed him, and they were ready to go at each other again if it were not for Pip holding Henry back.

"Enough!" the doctor raised his voice, "I'm sick of this bickering. Now your lordship, you need to know one thing. As much as I would like the medical practice to be a universal right, this procedure would be gravely costly."

"How much would it cost?" Eris asked.

The doctor took a piece of paper out and showed a rough estimate of the cost. Suddenly, Daniel was stunned. Pip could see it in him. He knew he did not have the money. Being his substitute assistant, he was fully aware of the debts and the money he had left. He would never be able to even secure a loan.

"Then it's over," Daniel concluded in grief, "bloody over."

Soon enough, he turned his back and went back inside, ever more the same destroyed Viscount.

"I'll talk to Francine about it," Pip assured, "I believe she has a choice in the matter."

When the doctor took his leave, Henry escorted him to the front door and thanked him. After he did so, the doctor told him some information about Francine that he did not want to share with Daniel. Hearing this, Henry was saddened to find out that Francine may only have half a year left to live at most.

In the remainder of the night, after everyone had gone to bed after talking about it once more, Henry went to the study to clear his mind. As he sat on the chair, he wondered what the best option was for Francine. With much anxiety and worry, Henry looked around in agony. What could he do? It was then that Henry discovered a part of the wall near the corner of the room that had a crevice. At first, he thought the paint had cracked and formed these lines, but looking again, he discovered that there was a small hole that a key could go through inside the wall. Light was shining faintly through it. It was then that he realized that there was a skeleton key on the table near him.

Although at first, he thought it improper to snoop, his curiosity wanted to know. He took the key and opened the walled door. After opening it, he saw a small window with the moonlight shining through. And what he saw around him was a room filled with paints and art supplies. At last, Henry saw Francine's artwork in all its beauty. His heart fluttered with enchantment as he admired them one after the other.

There was one bold painting that drew him closer. Under the faint light, he could make out that there was a young man playing the keyboard in it. He smiled.

"Mr. Leon," a voice called out.

Henry turned and saw Roxanne looking back at him.

"Thank goodness it's only you," he said, surprised.

"I see you can't sleep, Piano Boy," Eris said, "but hey, at least you found something that Francine would be too sick to mind."

"I just stumbled in," he said, embarrassed, "I've been thinking about the doctor's advice."

"It was hard to hear," she concluded, "but now, Pip has let Francine know about her condition and the choices she has."

"He did?" Henry's face flushed, "how did she take it?"

"There's not much she can do about it, either," Eris said sadly, "but she said she wanted to be hospitalized if it meant less of a burden for everyone."

Looking at Francine's paintings once more, Henry began tearing up a little as he thought about Francine's soul into her lifelong works. Roxanne looked at the painting and touched him to comfort him. She too felt his anguish while she looked at the portrait of Henry.

"We'll think of something to make it better for her soon," she finally said.

Suddenly, Henry had a bold idea after seeing the painting once more.

"Roxanne, I need your help," he told her.

"What is it?" she said, startled.

"I need you to contact every symphony and concert hall and tell them that I am going on my global tour."

Eris was in utter disbelief. "You're going to leave Francine?"

"No, I am going to save her," he declared, "I want you to make them all pay a hefty amount for my concerts." It was then that Eris realized what Henry was going to do.

"But Henry, that's impossible, no concert hall would ever pay that much. You would have to play hundreds of concerts to even get close to that amount. And even if you do, would there be enough time to save Francine by then?"

"The doctor told me six months at best," Henry sighed, "during which I'll just have to secure an upfront payment and a loan if I need it."

"No institution would loan you that much," Roxanne interrupted.

"Then my music will have to be greater, and concerts more prolific than ever before."

Roxanne looked at him as he went over to the parlor piano outside the room. He looked at the keys as he began thinking. She knew he was already starting to compose for his next concert. And there was no way to talk him out of it.

-Chapter 7-

Over the next few days, Eris was already at work contacting numerous cities to tell them that Henry Leon will be performing a grand tour. She negotiated contracts and corresponded with contacts between countries. And as for Henry, when he was not in the company of Francine in her room looking after her, he was downstairs in the parlor composing and playing. It got to a point that Francine requested that she wanted to sleep downstairs so that she could be with him as he played. Daniel, of course, rejected this at first, but was convinced by Pip that having her there would be better for her health as she did not have to go upstairs, and it would aid in her transition to a foreign hospital bed.

Henry cherished every moment with Francine. Although majority of the time, she slept, he thought his work was aiding in her recovery. On the night before he was about to depart for his first concert in London, Henry suddenly stopped playing when he heard a whimpering in the kitchen. He turned and looked at Francine on his shoulder, sleeping after listening to him attentively earlier. Before he went to investigate it, he carried her to the makeshift bed and tucked her in. Checking the kitchen area, he noticed the basement door was opened and a light was shining below from where the sound originated. Going downstairs into the wine room, he saw Daniel with his hands covering his face, weeping. He had just finished another bottle of wine and did not notice Henry until he came closer.

"Daniel," Henry called him.

Daniel looked up with his tearing eyes and suddenly covered them in shame.

"Get out of here," he bawled, "you've already taken my house and my wife, leave me here to grieve."

"I haven't taken anything from you," Henry said calmly, "please, let's forget any misgivings between us. We all just want Francine to get better."

At first, convincing Daniel to come upstairs ran into resistance as he wailed to stay in his misery. Henry, with his pity and guilt from having taken Francine's attention away from him, helped carry him back upstairs and into his room where Henry tried to assure him that all he wanted was to care for Francine one last time. He also wanted to make sure her worries were resolved. With no reply from Daniel, Henry was about to exit the room before he began uttering something back to him.

"I'm sorry," Daniel said, "I was never a good husband. My uncle and my mother should have never forced Francine to marry me. If it weren't for my weakness, knowing what I know now, I would have refused, and she would have been with you."

Henry turned back at him and sighed. "It doesn't matter anymore, Daniel, just look after her and your son now. And stop drinking, I'll make sure your financial situation will recover after all of this."

"How is that possible?" he inquired.

Henry did not say. He closed the door behind him and walked back downstairs back to the parlor. Unnoticed, Eris had been there watching. She had seen everything. Following him from the darkness when he went back to Francine's side, she saw that he continued composing as he looked at Francine. His tired eyes never strayed from his mission.

When dawn approached, Henry made sure he had his suitcase all packed and the papers that he had composed with him while he waited for Roxanne to come downstairs. Roxanne had reluctantly agreed to Henry's request that they would leave without giving a formal goodbye to everyone, especially Francine. Henry had wanted things to be inconspicuous as he knew that saying goodbyes would be too hard for Francine and himself to fathom. When Roxanne had come downstairs at last, Henry helped her with the suitcases while Winston hurried outside to greet the driver, who was waiting. It was silent and cold out. Not even the birds were up to sing.

"Are you sure you want to do this, Henry?" Roxanne asked after returning from hauling all her suitcases outside for Winston and the driver.

"I'm not," he commented sadly, "but for Francine's sake, I want the best for her."

"She will be devastated that you left without a goodbye," she reminded him.

"She already knows I'll be in London," he said, "regardless, she expressed to me that she wanted me to continue my concerts."

"Yes, but she doesn't know you'll be gone for a longer time than anticipated. What would happen when she discovers that you won't return by the time her condition worsens?"

"I know," Henry said earnestly, "I'll write and even phone her that the concerts have forced me to delay my return for the time being, but that I will be there when she gets her operation done. You've already let the doctors know that I will be paying for everything, right?"

"Yes, Hero Boy," Roxanne said disappointedly, "it just doesn't seem right to leave her when she wants you close to her the most now. It'll be almost like what Daniel has done to her."

"No," he refuted, "he'll be there to take care of her. I've talked to him."

"But it's not Daniel she wants with her. It's you she loves. It's you who should have been her true husband." Before Eris could say anymore, she caught herself mumbling too much of the truth and of her own guilt in this matter.

Expecting Henry to react with rage, Eris was suddenly surprised that this did not bother him. Instead, Henry merely nodded and went back to the parlor where Francine was sleeping.

The look of Francine sleeping was a peaceful sight. Her physical features did not show that she was ill. Instead, she looked so blissful in her sleeping gown and her freed hair laying on the makeshift bed as if it was a green hill filled with flowers somewhere in Switzerland. Henry went over to her and felt her face, then her hair lightly. He then kissed her cheek and was taken aback at her sudden head and eye movement. Fearful that she was about to wake up and find out that he was leaving, he started caressing her arm and whispered in her ear, "there, there my love, it is only I."

With her eyes still closed, she spoke before yawning, "I know my love, can't sleep again?"

"No, darling," he continued, "I just wanted to tell you that I've been so happy to be with you these past weeks."

Francine held his hand. Still barely awake, she said faintly, "I'm happy that I've met you entirely."

Hearing those words, Henry's heart melted. He did not want to be torn away from her hands now. He held them a little bit more until Winston came and gestured to him from afar that the driver was waiting. Henry nodded and waited for Francine to fall back to her deep sleep.

Finally letting go, Henry kissed her forehead one more time. As he stood up and began walking back out, he took one last look at Francine. He mustered all his strength to not weep anymore. He knew that this may be the last time he may see her ever again. Thinking about every regretful decision he had made in his life, he forced himself to turn away and proceeded out towards the main entrance where Roxanne waited for him. He thanked Winston for waiting and for not letting Pip or the Viscount know of their early departure, then he left him an envelope enclosed with his thanks and apologies for his short stay. He knew that Francine, despite not saying goodbye to her, would understand what he was doing. That it was not because he was selfish, but because he was desperately finding a means to the cure for her—through music.

-Chapter 8-

With the drive to raise the money for Francine's operation, Henry's creative energies poured into his playing and catapulted his performances through endless concerts and recitals in every major city in Europe. Every day, he sat at the keyboard practicing and composing. And in addition to his performances at night, and on occasions during the day, he maximized all the time he could for selling his work. So much so that Roxanne had difficulty keeping up on the promotion of his new work as she sent every piece of music to publishers who sought to be the first to publish his work. Concert after concert, the people loved him. Concerts were often sold out and there was so much demand for him to perform that many concert halls immediately booked him for his second tour, paying him in advance. Of course, much of this prolific success was partly possible because of a goddess. Eris had used what powers she had left to be in multiple places at once to seal contracts.

Amid these concerts, however, Eris was always concerned for Henry's mortal limits. Henry would work through many nights neglecting rest and would only eat a few bites to keep his stomach from growling. It got to a point where he only drank water and coffee. But no matter what Eris did to pressure him to rest and eat a little bit more, Henry would only press her to work harder for new performances and contracts. There were times that Roxanne would refuse and play mother, pestering him to take care of himself or else she would stop helping him. However, this proved difficult as Henry would ignore it and try to do all the contacting himself. This pressured Roxanne to help him even more because she cared for him too much for him to work any harder than he already was. And so, his concerts continued, always thinking about the day that Francine's operation would bring his efforts into fruition.

Applause filled the air when Henry's performance in Paris, France came to an intermission. As soon as the curtain closed and people began talking amongst themselves while exiting to the foyer, Henry immediately rushed away from his piano, through some of the orchestra members, shoving some of them away in desperation. All the way, he tried holding his cough and wiping off the sweat from his head with his handkerchief. He coughed and coughed after making his way to the restroom. He went up to the sink and splashed water on his face as he tried to sooth his dried red eyes. The stage's lights were an annoyance to the restless eyes that filled his rugged worn-out face. As he tried to breath after all the coughing, he noticed that his abdomen felt like it wanted to burst. As his head pounded from the headache he had for the past several days, he drank some water from the faucet to calm his nerves.

"Come on, hold it together," he told himself, "just one more hour of this."

"Henry?" Roxanne called out from the door, "are you alright?"

She knew he was sick. Yet, despite her advice for him to see a doctor, he insisted it was just a cold and that it would pass. He had been saying this for the past month.

"Yes," he called back, "I'm just freshening up."

Henry quickly fixed himself. Yet it was pointless as his face looked so pale, thin, and ghoul-like.

When he stepped back out, Roxanne felt his head.

"Henry, you have a fever," she said, alarmed.

Henry only looked at her with a serious face and simply turned away as he began his approach back to the stage. Eris wanted to cut the concert short, but she knew Henry would be furious if she made this decision. And there was no stopping him as he conversed with the conductor of the next act, then proceeded to sit back down on his bench.

Henry played with the same ferocity after intermission. And as he played, he thought about Francine and all the times that they shared together. And what life could have been if they had been married. They would have come to Paris and lived out their bohemian lifestyle together, traveled, and might have even had a family of their own. He knew that it was impossible now. Francine's life was hanging by a thread. And that thread may be cut at any time now that her operation was scheduled for tomorrow. As far as its costs, he was told last they only yielded three quarters of it. Barely enough to even get the family out of their debts if Francine did survive. And if the operation was not successful, he will have failed her. And her son would be forced to live the life she had lived in the orphanage. Constantly these thoughts consumed him. He knew he could not live with himself if that were to happen. The banging of keys continued as he let out all frustrations into his playing. His music was his tormented soul being let out.

After nearing the end, Eris watched him. All she could think of was his undying goal to save Francine. Sacrificing endless months of his time, he was coming closer to his goal. Eris knew that she must intervene to get him the money even if his pride was bent on saving Francine himself. And as he played, she felt his pain, and felt the same love he felt for Francine.

Henry's eyes began to irritate him more until it provoked him to close them. Blinded, he heard his heartbeat pounding faster than the notes played in a second. He felt the dampness of the keys after noticing his face was dripping with sweat. Every second was unbearable for him as he kept playing, dry coughing while he made his way to the second-to-last part of his piece. Trying to not rush through it, Henry thought about Francine's pain, and how he must suffer just a little bit more until the crowds begin to cheer when he played his last note. And it happened, with a standing ovation at its end.

Henry stood up to take a few bows as they lavished him with praise. Immediately after, he rushed away from stage, covering his face as he went backstage toward his room.

"Henry, Henry!" Eris called to him as she rushed to him. She knew that he was succumbing now.

Henry turned and could not take it anymore. He coughed again on his handkerchief. Immediately, he fell in her arms when she came to him, passing out as his fractured body barely held the sleepless nights and hunger strikes that he had inflected on himself. Eris held him while urgent care was sent for. And when help finally arrived, Henry was lifted away on a stretcher. And not a minute after, Eris discovered blood on that handkerchief.

Waiting for news of Henry's condition, Eris paced around the hallway in the hospital in desperation as she kept blaming herself for letting him get back on stage for the last few days.

"I should have been more forceful," she grunted as she waved her hands from side to side.

It was then that Eros made his way down the hall and spotted her.

"My dear, how is he now?" said Eros.

"I'm not sure," she said, "I only heard that he needed critical care. They told me to wait here as they monitor his condition. I'm so worried, Eros, you should have seen him when he was on stage; he looked half-dead."

Eros nodded. "Why don't we go in and look at how they are doing?"

The thought of transforming back to her invisible goddess self suddenly embarrassed Eris. She tried but it yielded no results as her form refused to turn back.

"I've tried," she hesitated to say, "would you please go in?"

"Oh my goodness, Discordia," Eros remarked as he realized what was happening, "you can't change back, can you? By the gods, you've stayed mortal too long."

Biting her lip in disgrace, Eris quickly tried to change back. However, to her dismay, her body remained Roxanne.

"It doesn't matter now," she told him, "please, just go in discreetly and see how he's doing."

Eros looked at her with worry before nodding, then entered through the walls.

Henry lay there motionless as the nurse cooled his fever down with a towel.

"He's hanging in there," the doctor commented in French as he looked at Henry's readings.

"Shall we begin moving him out of urgent care?" the nurse replied.

"Give him a few more hours here, I am not sure what his state would be with the shape he is in."

"Very well, doctor."

Eros returned to Eris who was sitting down with her face down on her palms.

"How is he?" Eris spoke after looking up.

"He's resting. The doctor commented that he was in a terrible state."

Eros sat beside her as she breathed heavily.

"What do I do, Eros?" she said, "what if Henry doesn't make it? I can't imagine a life now without him."

Eros tried to calm her while he was obviously taken aback by her affectionate words.

"Must I accompany him to the River Styx?" she continued, with her eyes red and her face puffed with despair.

As Eros sat there with her bellowing on his shoulder, he began to contemplate in silence.

"Eros?" Eris mumbled as she waited for an answer.

It was then that Eros turned to her and was about to say something but stopped.

"Eros?" she continued, "what were you about to say? Is there something we could do to help him?"

"My dear," he finally began, "there is a way, but I am uncertain of whether it's worth it. I have heard from Hermes himself that Hades would be willing to grant new life again for a mortal if a plea for a life is made."

"That's it!" Eris remarked, "we'll just go down to the underworld and see Uncle Hades about it. Why didn't I think of that?"

"Hold on, goddess," Eros exclaimed, "don't think he'll easily grant us this request."

"He has to," she retorted, "we'll make a good offer for him."

"And what will you offer him?"

Suddenly Eris realized that now that her powers were less of her former self, she had no way of leveraging a comprise or service that Hades may want. But then, as she thought about it, she realized that she still had her Apple of Discord.

"There is something," she said finally, before taking it out from her purse.

"Heavens no!" Eros remarked, "you will give away your powers?"

Eris had a bit of regret as she looked at her apple. But for the sake of Henry, she would do it. This was the only leverage she had that Hades could possibly accept.

Suddenly, the doors to Henry's room opened and the doctor came out. He went over to Eris. What Eris heard was no surprise from what she'd surmised about Henry's condition. She had learned that Henry's life was now hanging by a thread. Whether he would recover was dependent on his body and his will. They could not help anymore.

Being let inside, Eris immediately went to Henry's side and whispered to him that he had to get better.

"We can only give our best care and hope that he gets better," the nurse said solemnly before she left them.

As Eris held Henry's hand, she sobbed immensely at the frail, pale body of Henry.

"Discordia," Eros finally spoke, "he has not yet passed. Hades will not help us if Henry has not yet passed into the underworld."

Eris wiped her tears before turning to him. "That is why he must not just live. He must live forever."

"What are you saying?"

It was then that Eris took the Apple of Discord from her hand. She handed it to Eros as he looked at how intense her emotions were for Henry. Holding it in his hand, Eros could see what she was implying. Would she surrender the powers of chaos and discord in exchange for his immortality?

"No Discordia," Eros gasped, "your apple for the Apple of Everlasting Life? I cannot do this."

"You must, Eros," she cried, "you will go down to Hades and tell him that I will give my powers up for the power of immortal life for a mortal soul."

"I can't," Eros remarked, shaken.

"I would go if I could," she continued, "but I must be here."

Eros looked at Henry, whose breath barely expelled through his dried lips as he lay dying beside the goddess, who seven years before had only wanted to play tricks and mischief upon him. But now, she stood beside him pleading for his life.

"It will be done," Eros concluded, "I will go."

Throughout the night, Eris stayed by Henry's side. It was not until the next morning that Henry began to awaken.

"Henry," she called to him as his eyes began to open.

When they did, Roxanne quickly embraced his hands with salvation.

"Oh, Henry," she said, "I was so worried."

"Do we have enough?" Henry uttered.

"Enough?" Roxanne said, surprised.

"The money," he weakly replied.

Hearing this, Eris was not surprised that Henry would disregard his own condition.

"Yes, Henry," she said to him.

Henry tried to breathe as he looked around him, still dazed.

"Henry, please don't worry about that. I'll take care of that."

She then began to wipe his face with a cloth.

"How was the operation?" he continued, "did she survive?"

Forgetting to check up on the status of Francine, Eris suddenly realized that she had completely neglected that the operation was performed yesterday.

"I haven't heard from them," she told him.

Henry then had a look of sadness.

Eris knew that Francine stood on the balance of life and death for Henry.

"Hold on, Hero Boy," she exclaimed, "I'll find out. Please, just hold on."

Immediately, Roxanne rushed out of Henry's room to the front desk.

"Please," she told the desk clerk in French, "I need to send a telegram to London."

When the telegram was sent, Eris began pacing back and forth from Henry's room and the hallway again as she waited impatiently for the reply. It was then that she sat down beside Henry and looked at his silenced face as he laid sleeping again. The sacrifice of his health for Francine's had destroyed him. The warm smile, the childish look of his, all dilapidated, saddened Eris. When she began to give up hope again, she saw Eros return in the form of Mr. Romero.

"How did it go?" she asked impatiently, "has he accepted the apple?"

"He has," he replied in a grave manner, "but there is a condition."

"What is it? I'll do whatever it takes."

Eros handed her back the Apple of Discord, but now it had a distinctive look to it. He gave a look that was uncertain and cautious before he proceeded inside to see Henry. Eris could see that Hades had altered the apple. It was redder and there was something dark about it.

"Henry will have to take a bite of the apple for eternal life." He turned back to her.

"And then he will live?"

"He must agree willingly that he will live forever without the feeling of loving Francine."

Stunned by such a condition, Eris said, "that's next to impossible! Why would Hades make such a condition?"

"He knows of your doing, Discordia. He grows envious of seeing them in love."

"And what of Francine? We don't even know what her condition is yet," she argued.

"Actually," Eros interrupted, "Hades himself assured me that Francine has lived through her ordeal."

Coincidently, a knock on the door interrupted their conversation. Eris went to open it and saw that it was the nurse from the front desk.

"*Excusez-moi, votre télégramme,*" the nurse told her as she handed it to her.

After thanking her, Eris read the message. It was from Pandora.

"Well?" Eros inquired.

"Franny is in stable condition after the operation. But no sign of improvements so far. We will wait until doctors give updates about her heart," Eris read.

"You see, she has not crossed over the River Styx just yet," Eros assured.

Although relieved that Francine was alright, Eris' concern now was how Henry would respond to this news. Certainly, this would offer hope and encourage him to get better. But would he ever stop loving Francine so that he could accept the apple? And even if he recovered on his own, could she even accept the fact that he may die someday? Thoughts of Henry dying scared her. Henry was everything to her now. And although he did not love her as she had so wanted, she could not imagine a life without him. She knew she had to try.

The doctor soon came in to check on Henry. Roxanne let him know that Henry had awoken an hour ago briefly and could even talk.

"*Très bien*," the doctor commented. "I will see how his heart is and take another blood sample."

After he did so, Eris looked out the window and thought to herself as she wondered when he would wake up and accept the apple. It came to fruition as Eros came by and touched her on the shoulder.

"What will it be?" he asked, pointing to Henry's head slowly moving.

"Henry?" she said as she rushed back to him. "Henry dear, I have received word of Francine. She's in stable condition."

Henry's eyes finally began to open after hearing this. His eyes were red and looked at her as if he did not know who she was.

"Henry?" Roxanne and Mr. Romero pleaded.

Slowly Henry's lips began to move, "take good care of her," he muttered slowly.

"Yes, we will definitely," Roxanne said quickly, "and you will too as soon as you get better."

Henry took a deep breath, but it was interrupted by his erupting coughs.

Roxanne quickly grabbed a glass of water from the table and pushed the straw to his mouth.

Drinking a little, Henry then began to speak more clearly, "will I die?"

"Of course not," Roxanne assured, "the doctor had been surprised by how you responded to me earlier. After all this, Henry, you will see Francine again and everything will be okay."

"Monsieur Leon," called the doctor, who showed up at the door again, "glad to see you're awake." He went over with his nurse and began applying a syringe to his arm. After finishing, he gestured to Eris.

"Madame Roxanne? May we talk?"

"I'll be right back, Henry," she assured him, "Mr. Romero's here to make sure you'll be better soon too."

As Eros went beside Henry and assured him that Francine and himself would be alright, Roxanne followed the doctor to the hallway to discuss an important matter. It was then that her new-found hope had almost completely disappeared as the doctor informed her that the blood sample had showed that he had contracted a disease that has affected him severely.

"Is it treatable?" Roxanne pleaded.

"Possibly," he replied, "there is this new medicine that I have applied. But Monsieur Leon has waited too long to treat it. I did not want to tell you this before because I was not sure what his condition was after many tests. But now we must wait for the medicine to take effect."

"*Merci*," Eris said after.

Seeing Eros speak to Henry closely and intimately, Eris knew that she had to intervene to save his life. The medicine, although giving him a half-chance to live, looked bleak as she gazed upon his pale, malnourished face. She went to him again and held his hand.

"Henry," she began lying sincerely, "the doctor says you'll make it."

Although good news to hear, Henry's face seemed to not believe in it.

"And I have something for you to eat and get better," she continued, taking the new Apple that Hades had manipulated. "You need all the strength you can get to recover."

"Yes, Henry, take a bite and regain your energy. There's not much to worry about, now that Francine is alright," Eros said, knowing what she was about to do.

Eris mildly grinned after noticing Eros' help in consoling Henry. Eros then began whispering to Eris on what Hades commanded her to say to Henry to agree on for it to work.

Henry tried to open his mouth as Eris helped him sit up.

After taking a small bite, Henry thought about his life. In the condition he was in, he had doubts that he would live another day to see Francine well again. The thought of Francine surviving her operation, however, relieved him of his worries for her. Yet, despite everything, the future seemed bleak.

"Henry," Roxanne asked, "you have already done all you can for Francine. Now it's time for you to focus on getting better. There is no sense in sacrificing your life now. Would you not like to live longer and if it was possible, live forever in happiness than die loving her in the state you are in now?"

Hearing this, Henry considered his life and Francine's. Francine, despite stable in her condition, was not guaranteed to survive from what the doctor had told him that night when Francine was resting from her critical syncope. All the money and arduous work he had accomplished would have been for nothing. The family would still be in debt and Henry would have to see his beloved die without him in her arms. And if she had survived, Francine could truly live again. And possibly, their life together could pick up from where they had left off years ago. Even if they could not eliminate the debt, it would be worth it. To even hold her hand, walking side by side in Park Central again, that would be his only desire now.

Suddenly, before Henry could respond to Eris, he began coughing heavily. Then, all that he could remember before passing out was Roxanne calling for the doctor, after he had coughed up more blood and fallen back on his bed with the feeling of his chest on fire.

"Henry?" a voice that sounded like Roxanne called to him, "Please, you must fight on."

Henry wandered through a dark forest as he tried to follow her voice.

"Where are you?" Henry called out,

"Roxanne!" The voice then went silent.

After hearing silence for a moment, he suddenly heard crying in the near distance. It was then that toward the end of this forest, he saw a light in a building. Henry ran toward this building. Going up the stairs and through a colonnade, Henry saw a candle flame inside a room. He opened the door and found the source of the crying. It was Francine, only much younger, sitting on a piano bench sobbing, not noticing that Henry was in front of her.

"Francine!" Henry called out to her as he came closer.

Francine looked up with her gray eyes staring back at him in sadness.

"Francine, I'm here now," he said as he tried to reach for her.

Suddenly, Francine stood away from him, still silent.

"What's wrong?" he said, surprised.

"Stay away from me," she finally said.

Hearing this, Henry was stunned and replied with regret, "my love, what have I done for you to say these cruel words to me?"

"You only cared about yourself," she said, "because of you, I am dead."

"No!" Henry cried back, "I've been playing and composing for you all this time. You will live. I'm sure of it."

It was then that Francine ran away from him, and at that moment as Henry tried to follow her, to tell her how sorry he was, the light extinguished.

Henry woke up to the cries of Roxanne as he regained consciousness.

"Henry," Mr. Romero reacted, "I'll go get the doctor," he told her.

It was already night by the time Henry discovered that his condition had gotten worse.

"Henry," Roxanne embraced him lovingly.

"Roxanne," Henry began, "Francine is dead."

"What?" Eris reacted, surprised, "impossible, I contacted London again and Dora assured me that Francine was still stable."

Henry calmed down a little before tearing.

"It was because of me that Francine is dying," Henry declared, "it was all because of me not being there for her."

"What? No!" Roxanne refuted, "you were saving her life all this time."

"Take care of her," he continued, "tell her I still and will forever love her."

"Henry, you will take care of her. Stay alive, no love full of regrets is worth dying for. Give up the thought of dying even if it means a life without her. Tell me that you will continue to live, even live forever if given the chance, if she passes."

Henry reacted by shaking his head and spoke softly, "Roxanne, thank you for everything that you have done for me. And the life you suggest, to live forever, must be a curse if it means living without the one you love."

"What?" Eris cried heavily, "no please, you must accept life. Live forever with me and your music. You will love again. Francine loves you and would want you to live longer, even without her."

When Eros came back with the doctor and nurses, they quickly checked Henry's pulse and monitored him.

"How is he, doctor?" Eros asked.

By the looks of Henry's ghastly face and blackened lips, the doctor realized he had no answer for them.

"Doctor?" everyone cried.

Eris turned her attention back to Henry, seeing that his eyes were drawing heavier and heavier.

"Don't go, the world would lose a great musician," Eris snuffed.

"Please, Maestro," Mr. Romero pleaded, "you must not die, listen to Roxanne. Tell us that you still want to live and accept that you may even live an eternity more. You can still see Francine very soon. She is alive, my boy."

Henry simply shook his head, denying it all while lying there, exhausted and drained from his suffering. He could not live longer as much as they wanted him to live forever. A life without Francine was unbearable. There was no more will to fight, he felt he had done his part. He thought about the last song he had dedicated to Francine, *Chanson de l'adieu* by Chopin. Thinking back to the lyrics that he wrote for Francine, he began hearing them in his head.

And then there he was, playing the piece on the piano with Francine next to him this time.

The lyrics were not what they were before. He was not saying "hello" to Francine anymore as his previous lyric began. Instead it ended differently...

"Farewell, my love..." He had sung when his song began to end,

"Farewell, my love."

"Farewell, my love."

"It's all my fault!" Roxanne cried, "I broke you two up. Please, don't say goodbye to us," she tried to persuade him.

No matter how much Roxanne cried and told him of her guilt, Henry barely listened. It was not because he lacked pity for her, nor did he resent all those years of not being with Francine. He had no energy to regret anymore. All he wanted was to save Francine, whether she would live or not, he was content to have tried. His suffering was short while Francine's had been long. He hoped that she could live a better life now on the chance that she did survive. He would accept this sacrifice without regrets.

Henry looked at Roxanne once more. His eyes looked relieved and thankful.

"Give love a second chance," Henry muttered to her. He had remembered that night at her rooftop, where she had confessed to him that she had disliked the concept of love.

Hearing his words, Roxanne looked deep within herself. Henry was the whole reason she gave it a chance in the first place.

"Oh Henry, before you, there was only chaos. What you and Francine had, that was my first true love," she told him with all the joy and sorrow in her heart. Eris was not sure if Henry had heard that, for soon after, Henry took his last breath and the music he had heard slowly stopped playing, fading into silence, and then nothingness.

-Chapter 9-

Soon after Henry's death, Eris' mourning and plans for his burial were put on hold as she gathered what strength she had to cross the English Channel alone. She was not going to look back at the body of the man she loved behind her. Despite resenting and regretting all that she had done to Henry's life, Francine was now the only person left that Eris cared deeply for, who had been in a coma ever since her operation half a month ago. Upon arrival, she was met with Pandora's arms as the two grieved together on the fates of these two mortals. Although Francine was in stable condition, they were not sure whether she would wake up again. It appeared to them that her disease had affected her brain earlier, even possibly affecting her ability to be fully conscious. This did not sit well with the already broken-hearted and broke Viscount. Despite Francine's survival, Pandora had recalled that Daniel remarked that his wife, and mother of his son, was now living in a vegetative state, but at least "she did not have to see their great descent to the poor house."

By the time Eris arrived at the hospital, she greeted Pip again with a miserable looking Daniel waiting outside Francine's room.

"I'm sorry about the Maestro," Pip said wholeheartedly as he embraced her, "we grieved and mourned the past week when we heard. Please, tell me, had he received the news that Francine lived because of him?"

"I tried telling him," Roxanne said, trying to contain the feelings that she had felt that time. She held her tears this time. "But Henry was unsure whether she had a chance or not. And even if he believed it, it was already too late for him."

Pip gave a look of grief before looking down, trying to contain it all.

"But he fought to save Francine," she continued, "Henry always performed, doing all the concerts he could to get the money."

"We were aware," Pandora responded, "every newspaper and radio broadcast talked about his concerts. I'm still amazed at how much he accomplished in the past months."

"And was it a success?" Pip asked, looking at Daniel, who had his head on the table nearby, fast asleep from his misery.

Eris took an envelope from her bag and handed it to Pip. "Take these documents to a bank. All the money we raised will be transferred to pay for the rest of Francine's operation, as well as any remaining debts."

Total shock came to the faces of Pip and Pandora as they reacted to the contents on the envelope. "You two have done it," they said.

"No," Roxanne dismissed, "it was all Henry. Even when I told him that we had enough to pay, Henry was not sure if it was enough entirely. He wanted to raise more."

"Roxanne," Pip reacted, "there is more than enough remaining to pay for her son's schooling for the next 20 years and even purchase two acres of land. Daniel will be overjoyed once he hears this."

"I'm glad. Now, may I see Francine?" she asked.

"Of course," Pip said before he opened the door to the room for her.

When Eris entered the room, she gazed upon the muse who had so enchanted Henry. Despite struggling through her illness and her death-defying operation, she had changed little in appearance. Like the image of a sleeping princess, Francine lay there breathing softly, oblivious to all that had happened in her stage of limbo.

"Franny, dear," Pandora spoke sincerely to her, "Miss Roxanne is here to see you."

She had hoped that perhaps telling her everything that was happening in the moment would give some miracle for Francine to wake up. Eris could see it in Pandora's eyes. Somewhere deep inside, she too, after all these years, regarded Francine like a sister and cared for her deeply.

"I'll let you two be alone with her," Pip said before stepping out.

Eris held Francine's hand as she sat next to her. Curiously, Pandora looked at them with some hope.

"Have you spoken to Eros about a feasible way of saving her?" she asked her.

"Yes, I have," Eris said without turning back, "immortals or gods cannot interfere with the process of mortal lives. Life or death, that much cannot be changed."

Pandora gave a look of discouragement, but then realized that this could not be final.

"But what about Henry?" Pandora asserted, "you told me before that he had a chance to live after you made a compromise with Hades to have him live forever if he wanted to. Does that offer not still hold?"

"It does still hold," Eris replied, "but it's not that simple."

"Can you not go back to Hades again and request that we accept eternal life for her?"

"Yes, Eros has assured me that this is possible due to her given state."

"Then it must be done," Pandora concluded, "if not, who knows what the fates have in store for her. She can't live like this, Discordia. She might as well be dead."

Suddenly Eris turned to Pandora and gave her a look that stunned her.

"I'm sorry," Pandora said shamefully. There was a silence soon after.

Although it was reasonably true that being alive without truly living was not death, it was not much better. But Henry had fought so hard for her, all those efforts had yielded some merit in her being alive.

"Dora," Eris finally spoke, "you need to know that Eros has told me that accepting eternal life or even just to live again is not as easy as it sounds. Like Henry, she would have to surrender her love and even memories of Henry. She would never remember all his love. She would surrender her free will to us. She will no longer be the Francine we once knew after it."

"Oh," Pandora acknowledged with disappointment.

"That is why I'm here debating whether it is worth it," Eris concluded, "would it be what Henry would have wanted?"

There befell on them a moment of sorrow. It was now evident to both that a mortal life truly mattered, more than some trick or wager the gods had played on mortals for eons. For once, Eris realized that mortals were now the ones controlling her decisions, not the other way around.

"Henry gave his life and his love for Francine to live again," Pandora finally answered her, "I would think he would have chosen this decision for her to live if he had to. At least, that's what I believe now."

Eris believed that this may have been what Henry wanted. His sacrifice, and even her memories of loving and remembering him meant little compared to the restoration of her life. Yet, those words that Henry said to her were forever engraved in her head: "To live forever must be a curse, if it means living without the one you love." And even then, this condition was worse. If she continued to live, she would not remember Henry ever again even if she tried.

That was the difficulty of these choices. To be immortal could mean a never-ending life of new loves. Yet the latter meant dying with the belief in your love of a single person, essentially becoming a martyr.

Eris took the apple from her bag and held it. A piece had been bitten off by Henry that night when he died. He did not live because he refused the choice of immortality. If Francine were conscious, would she have done the same? It now became clearer to Eris—it was Francine's choice, not hers nor anyone else's. The choice must come from her.

"So it is true," Pandora commented, "Hades transformed your Apple of Discord into the Apple of Everlasting Life in exchange for your powers."

There was silence as Eris recalled what Eros had told her a few days ago. It was the last encounter with Eros before she left Paris to see Francine. Eros had tried comforting her as she mourned for Henry in a nearby Parisian park. That day, he had brought news that Hades had made another offer for the goddess if she wanted Francine to live again.

"No," Eris gasped after hearing what Eros had told her, "she would die after all Henry had done for her?"

Eros nodded. "I'm afraid so. Francine's soul will not stay forever in the condition she is in. Very soon, Hades will come for her. That is why I must tell you that your only option is to offer the Apple of Everlasting Life to her."

"But, how can I?" Eris rebuked, "life but no memories or any emotion for the man who had given his life to save her? And let's say even if I did, how can I possibly get her to agree and eat the apple, Eros? Move her mouth to agree and then spoon feed it to her?"

Eros nodded his head despite how silly it sounded. "That is why Hades informed me that he has alter his powers with the given situation. He is going to let you make that decision for her. You will have to implant the Apple and make the choice."

"What? Like apple sauce? Ridiculous," cried Eris, frustrated, "whether she lives or dies, she is doomed to a fate I could not imagine for her. She deserves better."

With those words from the goddess' lips, Eros seemed surprised.

"Discordia," he said, "it is almost as if you now really cared for the poor girl."

Eris reacted to his statement with no hesitation. With all the pain she had felt losing Henry, she now saw that love meant more than just romantic love.

"I do, Eros," she said, "despite all the discord I've caused, despite my jealousy, Francine was a part of Henry's life, as she was mine. It's true, these mortals were all but pawns in the wager we had. But this day, I realize that they mean more to me than my place in this universe."

"But," Eros protested, "do you not realize that your feelings for them have suspended your powers and have weakened you? You are no more the Goddess of Chaos as you are Roxanne. You can't even change back to yourself."

Eris looked at herself, realizing that all the changes that had happened were because of her role in this constant pursuit of Henry and Francine's relationship. And as she began feeling her mortal flesh, she believed that Eros' accusations were true to some degree. But Eris, in her stubborn ways, refused to lament that her powers were gone. She knew she could still do something without it.

"I am still the Goddess of Chaos and Discord," she declared confidently, "with my apple or not, I swear Francine will stand up and live her life again. I may have lost Henry, but I will not lose her."

It was then that Eros smiled and touched her shoulder. He then took something from his coat pocket and handed her a wrapped box. "Don't open it yet," he said, "once you make your decision for Francine. Send my regards to her whether she lives or dies. You'll know what to do with it later."

With barely any words to say to Pandora, Eris stepped away from Francine's bed. With the apple in her hand, Eris walked away from them toward the door just as Pip and Daniel reentered to check on them. She made her decision, and as Pandora stood there motionless in despair, she realized that Francine had stopped breathing.

After calling for help, doctors and nurses rushed in as quickly as they could to revive the countess. But it was pointless. Pandora knew that Eris had chosen death for her.

She watched idly and teared amongst the rush of cries and medical pleas from everyone in the room.

Eris stepped out of the room after Francine took her last breaths. Tearing without hesitation, her grief began to take hold of her, shoving her down to her knees.

"Please," she cried, "don't let her die, have mercy on her and take me instead! Let me die a thousand years if she could live decades more. Let her love be not forsaken."

Bawling for a less unfortunate fate, Eris discovered how much she hated herself. And in her moment of sorrow, she felt a movement vibrating in her bag. Reaching into her bag again, she realized it was coming from the wrapped box that Eros had given to her. Unwrapping everything, she discovered that the Ticking Heart had been reacquainted with her again. It ticked louder this time, to a point where she could feel the watch's vibration.

Looking at its gears and hands, the meter pointed to *True Love.*

"What's good about knowing that you have true love, when love cannot bring the dead back to life?" she wailed. The Ticking Heart had become nothing but a remorseful object. An annoyance more than something she had so previously coveted before.

Suddenly, she felt a surge of rage. Taking the apple, she grasped it tightly, only to then smash it into the Ticking Heart with all the strength she had. In seconds, the device began to break apart just as the apple weathered away in indentations, juices gushing out. She kept doing this until the apple became mush. The device soon began to reveal its face and inner gears. Soon the ticking faded away, as the sound subsided into silence.

Suddenly, Eris felt something after her hits stopped. She brought it to her ears and heard it. The Heart had a pulse. She discovered that what she had uncovered soon after was more than just the Ticking Heart when it transformed itself. It was no longer a mechanical device enchanted by Eros' powers, but a second organic heart that pumped, not blood, but from the juices of Eris' destroyed apple. The same one that was transformed by Hades to be an eternal pass from the underworld for whoever takes a bite from it.

Eris felt the heart's powers regenerating her as she stood back griping it. Shedding Roxanne from her body, Eris was her immortal body again. And as she glanced below at her old self, she now knew how to save Francine. Looking at the heart once more, she saw the second chance for life.

Having given up on Francine, the doctors and nurses offered their condolences to the family before they exited. And as Daniel wept for his wife to return, Pandora and Pip grieved in silence. Eris entered the room unnoticed with the Heart in both hands. Its steady pulsing had alerted Pandora after she glanced from Pip's embrace to see with her very eyes, the tall, pale blue-skinned goddess before them, walking to the lifeless Francine with a Heart enchanted by what could be help from the divine.

Eris looked at Pandora before she took the heart in her hands and held it above Francine's chest.

"Her time has not come yet," Eris told her.

Speechless, Pandora watched her place the heart onto Francine. And with that action, the heart was absorbed into her. And in that moment soon after, Francine Daye breathed once again.

****

Pandora was the last person to see Roxanne after Francine's miracle. On that day when Francine woke up to her family, Roxanne was not present. And despite Pip searching for her later, the search was called off by Pandora who knew that Eris had wanted to be alone after seeing Francine live again. The goddess had, however, visited one last time when she came to see Francine's discharge a week after. Of course, the goddess had no more intention to be Roxanne anymore. She wanted to relay a final word for Pandora, and that was for her to watch over Francine and her family. When Pandora asked Eris where she was going, she did not receive a clear answer other than a possibility that she may take a similar retreat that Pandora had taken before she met Pip.

"Farewell, darling," Eris told her, "perhaps my chaotic path will again cross yours or even Francine's one day."

"Let's hope not," Pandora teased.

And that was the last time she spoke with the goddess. Pandora remembered that Eris was not satisfied with one other thing that had changed Francine's new life. Perhaps, she was searching to resolve this. Nonetheless, Pandora now had a mortal life to live as she watched Francine live hers.

-Chapter 10-

It was nearing the end of spring when the Viscount leased a new vacation home in the countryside, not too far from Paris. His new-found investments had yielded good returns amidst the recovery of the economy. Indeed, in a short year, he was able to absolve all his debts and could finally invest what money he had left to save the Young family. And it was during this time that Daniel was given a new chance at life to reestablish himself in civil society, and with his family. After the purchase was made, Daniel took his countess and his son there, swearing that they would spend every summer there. This was good news for Francine as she finally had a chance to paint the French countryside and receive notable artists. Quickly, they settled in and found their new house near flowery hills to be as majestic as they imagined it.

Francine was busy on her canvas as Thomas played with the neighborhood kids in the fields below her. Among sunflowers, Francine only thought about how wonderful it was to finally be here. As the wind blew softly, she took a step back from her canvas to view her work.

"*Magnifique,*" she praised herself in French. It was then that she heard a horn from behind her.

A car approached from the road away from them and Francine smiled before waving back. When the car stopped

near the bottom of the hill, Thomas came by and waited for his
father to step out. And when Daniel did step out, he
immediately embraced his child, lifting him up in the air with a
warm heart. He asked where his mother was and pointed in her
direction above him.

"How is my sweet Van Gogh today?" he called up to
her.

"Hot and messy," Francine called back sweetly, "I'll be
right down soon."

When they returned home, Francine went to put her art
supplies away in her makeshift studio near the parlor room that
had been filled with many items since their move. It was then
that she noticed something that was not there earlier. Going
down she noticed a covered grand piano.

"Darling?" she called out.

"What is it?" Daniel called back faintly.

"Was there always a piano in this room?"

"A what?"

"A piano."

Daniel entered and saw her lifting the covers off the
piano.

"Oh," he remarked, "I hadn't noticed it until now,
either. That's funny, could have sworn that there was just old
furniture covered here. I guess now you can entertain your
many esteemed guests," he laughed before stepping out toward
the stairway.

Francine closed the door to the room and sat herself
down as she began playing a few melodies. All the while she
thought it was peculiar that she had not noticed this piano's
presence when they first moved in. Soon after, she remembered

that she had brought something from her collection over to show to her Parisian guests. She got up and went to her small studio to retrieve it. When she found what she was looking for from her collection, she brought it over to the piano and took a small stand out, placing it on top of the piano. The artwork she had placed on the piano was the one piece in her established portfolio that she cherished most. It was the portrait of an unnamed musician that she only vaguely remembered meeting from her past when she was studying in America. It was something about him that made her cherish this portrait so much. She knew she must have admired him so. But since her operation, all she remembered was that he was famous and had passed away before her recovery. Looking at his face, she sensed there was something about him that she wished she could remember. She could not even remember his name, no matter how many times Dora talked to her about him.

Before setting herself to try out the piano again, Francine noticed that she still had her apron on from before. Immediately, she went back to her studio to store it. It was then that something began to happen as she slowly took her apron off from her summer dress. Suddenly, she heard music. It was the piano being played from the room. "Is it Daniel?" she thought. But he had not touched an instrument since primary school and was hardly ever musical. The only person left that could play was Thomas. But he could never play like this, despite his age. Francine felt an eerie feeling as she went back to investigate.

When Francine walked out to see the source of the music, her eyes gazed upon the man from her painting, now playing the piano before her. It was then that Francine gasped when she saw him play so calmly, eyes closed, with no knowledge that she was there until she realized who it really was.

Tears flowed as she whispered his name.

"Henry," she uttered it again slowly with the full emotion of her heavy heart. And as he played until the ending note, Henry slowly opened his eyes and smiled as she approached him.

About the Author:

Weidan Sima was born and raised in Honolulu, Hawaii. After spending five years writing his debut novel, amongst college exams, heartaches, and the demands of emerging adulthood, he can proudly say that it was all worth it. *Of Love and Discord* was finished thanks to partly finally saying farewell to his island home of twenty some years and moving to California with nothing but two suitcases and a dream. He lived that dream and is now home to take care of his aging parents and planning his next vacation abroad.

You are more than welcome to contact him for inquiries or comments relating to his book:

Email him at weidansima@gmail.com